Merryn Allingham was born into an army family and spent her childhood moving around the UK and abroad. Unsurprisingly it gave her itchy feet, and in her twenties she escaped an unloved secretarial career to work as cabin crew and see the world. The arrival of marriage, children and cats meant a more settled life in the south of England, where she's lived ever since. It also gave her the opportunity to go back to 'school' and eventually teach at university.

Merryn has always loved books that bring the past to life, so when she began writing herself the novels had to be historical. She finds the nineteenth and early twentieth centuries fascinating to research and has written extensively on these periods in the Daisy's War trilogy and the Summerhayes novels. She has also written two timeslip/parallel narratives which move between the modern day and the mid-Victorian era, *House of Lies* and its companion volume, *House of Glass.*

For more information on Merryn and her books visit http://www.merrynallingham.com/
You'll find regular news and updates on Merryn's Facebook page:
https://www.facebook.com/MerrynWrites
and you can keep in touch with her on Twitter
@MerrynWrites

Other Books in this Series

CARIBBEAN EVIL

Merryn Allingham

CARIBBEAN EVIL

This novel is entirely a work of fiction. The names, characters and incidents portrayed in it are the work of the author's imagination. Any resemblance to actual persons, living or dead, events or localities is entirely coincidental.

First published in Great Britain 2020 by The Verrall Press

Cover art: Berni Stevens Book Cover Design

ISBN 978-1-9997824-8-1

Chapter One

The island of Malfuego, August 1955

Nancy heard the clamour before their vehicle rounded the corner: a heavy tramp of feet, the banging of small drums, yelling voices that cracked with strain. Their chauffeur swung the saloon out of the side street and onto the main road, peering out of his window at the mass of people gathered there. 'Not good,' he said.

Nancy followed his gaze: a large, white building, flags flying from its roof, stood proud against a cloudy sky. A huge crowd had formed at the bottom of the steps that climbed to an impressive pillared entrance.

'What is this place?' Archie Jago, sitting next to the driver, craned his neck to look past the man. It was the first time he had spoken since they'd left the airport.

'It is State Assembly,' the driver answered.

'Can't we go another way? Things could get ugly here.'

'Not possible.' The man was curt, concentrating on nosing his sleek black vehicle through the knot of stragglers wandering across the road. 'We go slow.'

That was a statement of the obvious, Nancy thought, since there was little chance of going at any other speed. Sharing the back seat with her husband, she felt Leo fumble for her hand and pull her close. She looked past him at the sea of placards and the line of navy uniformed police.

'Why are they protesting?' she asked, squinting to read the banners being waved aloft.

'The same reason as always, I imagine,' Leo said. 'Unhappy people making their views known.'

'Many people.' The chauffeur nodded towards his fellow islanders. 'Not good life in Malfuego.'

'And the people in that building can make it better?'

The driver made a clicking sound with his tongue. 'For themselves, mebbe.'

'So what's new?' Archie's barb was characteristic. For Leo's assistant, the world was divided into us and them.

By now the car had come to a complete stop and Leo shifted impatiently in his seat. 'Can't you keep going?' he asked sharply. 'We're already very late. The handlers took forever to unload our luggage.'

The driver shook his head. 'Not possible,' he said again.

The police were holding the line well, wicked-looking wooden sticks in their hands. But now the crowd was turning away from the police ranks and facing towards the Assembly building itself. Halfway up its white stone steps, a slim figure waved his arms, bidding for their attention.

When the young man began to speak, the crowd's uproar gradually died. People listened intently, standing motionless, the placards they carried drooping and forgotten. The man's speech barely carried as far as the car, but Nancy managed to pick out several words through the open window—democracy, assets, injustice—enough to understand the gist. He was evidently a skilful orator.

'It looks as though they have a leader,' Leo remarked.

The chauffeur nodded again. 'Gabriel Sekela. A good man.'

The good man was now well into his stride and even the police had relaxed their vigilance and were listening to him. Then just as the last stragglers had crossed the road and bunched themselves onto the opposite pavement, there was a sudden commotion. Men—three of them—had circled around the police ranks and arrived at one side of the crowd. Balaclavas masked their faces and they wielded staves that made the police batons look little more than matchsticks. With a loud whoop they ploughed their way into the gathering, chopping a pathway through the defenceless people until they reached the bottom of the steps.

The road ahead of their car was clearer now, but the driver, his mouth half open, appeared mesmerised. Gabriel Sekela had stopped speaking and was looking bemused. But not for long. All three black-masked men lunged forward and began beating him with their weapons until he fell to the ground and rolled down the steps to land at the feet of the horrified crowd. A pool of blood gushed from his mouth.

The senior police officer, paralysed until now, ran forward and shouted an order at his men. But if it was to arrest the perpetrators, he was too late. They had disappeared into the mass of people as though they had never existed.

'That poor young man,' Nancy said, her breath coming fast. 'But who were those men?'

'Let's get moving, driver.' Leo was peremptory. 'The way is clear now and we need to be gone.'

'But who were they?' she asked again.

'Hired thugs by the look of it,' Archie said.

'Bad men,' the driver concluded. 'This is Malfuego.'

Nancy leaned back into the leather seat, appalled. This was her introduction to the Caribbean. She hadn't wanted to come but Leo had been adamant he wanted her with him.

He'd eulogised over the benefits of a complete change: how good it would be for her to rest after so many days of sickness. How good to enjoy several weeks of sunshine.

But it was with reluctance that she had packed her suitcase. The morning sickness had just begun to abate and she was keen to throw herself into work again. She had been only a few months in a job that had taken her an age to find; a job she loved. But Leo had been insistent she must be with him and, because her sense of gratitude to him ran deep, she had agreed.

For his sake, she must try to enjoy this trip. And it was true that when they'd flown over the island a few hours ago, she'd started to feel a good deal more cheerful. As the light aircraft circled to land, Malfuego had looked beautiful. The outline of a misshapen peak had come into view, pearl-grey at first, then violet, and finally green-ridged as it emerged through a confusion of soft white clouds. Then out of nowhere a wide sweeping bay, its sand white-gold, and a red fishing boat, sail inflated, skimming across its waters. Leo was probably right. A short holiday would do her good. But the scene they had just witnessed, a scene of utter brutality—the crowd cringing in terror, the red blood spilling across white steps—had made her want to turn the car and head back to the airport.

Her husband bent forward, his expression concerned, and spoke in the chauffeur's ear. 'Is the villa far? I thought Mr Garcia mentioned the house was in town.'

'Yes, in town,' the man said.

Leo spread his hands in bafflement. But the driver's words proved true since the town, it seemed, consisted of little more than several dusty thoroughfares strung along the coast, lined by a profusion of small wooden buildings. Dressed in a rainbow of colour—pink, lilac, violet—their mellow tints were countered every so often by the garish yellow or red of stalls selling cooked food. As they drove on, the houses, some no more than broken-down shacks, became sparser. And between them, almost cheek by jowl, she noticed the wrought-iron gates and paved driveways of a number of grand mansions. The island appeared an uncomfortable mix of extreme wealth and soul-sapping poverty.

A few minutes later they were turning through another pair of wrought-iron gates. The sign read *Belvoir*, picked out in gold leaf. Beautiful view. It suggested the island's mix of languages—French as well as English, and no doubt several African tongues, too. Ahead of them lay a large square building, washed a brilliant white, its high jalousie windows propped open. The walls looked to be at least three feet thick—to keep the house cool, perhaps—and a carved wooden veranda ran along three sides of the building. Wild hollyhocks grew either side of a solid oak front door. As the tyres crunched to a halt, a young woman, dressed in maid's uniform, appeared on the front steps.

Gesturing to them to follow her inside, she led the way to the first floor, opening a door at the top of the stairs. 'This will be your room, madam, and the professor's.'

Nancy hesitated on the threshold and felt, more than saw, Archie brush past her and stride towards a room at the far end of the landing. He'd made it very clear that he no more wished to be here than she. Not that he had anything against the island, as far as she knew—it was sharing this villa with her that he'd hate. In London it had been possible for them to keep their distance from each other and, on the ship to Venezuela, Archie's cabin had been several decks below theirs. But here they would be forced to live at close quarters.

Nancy was ushered into a large, airy space with windows looking out over the sea. She hadn't realised the house was so close to the shore and immediately crossed to the French doors and walked out onto the balcony. A greyish blue sea stretched towards an infinite horizon while, above, mounting grey clouds blocked the light. But then, as she watched, the clouds cleared quite suddenly, liberating the sun to bathe the world in its warmth and turn grey to silver.

'Bathroom is next door. Towels and soap there for you,' the young woman said, appearing at Nancy's shoulder.

'Thank you… I'm sorry, I don't know your name.'

'I am Zamira King. I look after you and the professor and Mr Jago. I can unpack your case?'

Nancy stepped back into the room. The chauffeur had unloaded their luggage, and her case and Leo's had been placed on a long wooden chest that stood by the doorway. The chest was the only article in the room that wasn't white. Billowing nets, a dazzling white counterpane on the large bed, and several chairs, limed and bleached, with wide arms shaped like a crab's claws. Mirrors on every surface reflected back the room's lustre.

'No, thank you, Zamira,' she said firmly, not wishing to be completely idle. 'We can unpack for ourselves.'

'Then I must ask what you wish for breakfast?'

'I really don't know.' Nancy was surprised. Shouldn't they be talking about dinner first? 'Fruit, bread?'

The girl gave a small bow in acknowledgement. She was beautiful, Nancy thought. Glinting black hair, gleaming skin, eyes a sparkling brown. A shining girl. But there was something behind the shine. A tension, a sense of emotions being contained. It sounded in the young woman's voice, it showed in her stiff gait. Was it sadness? Or anger even?

Before Nancy could say more, her husband had pushed through the doorway carrying a bag in each hand and Zamira had slipped away. 'I can't imagine how much you've packed,' he said teasingly.

'I wasn't sure of the climate. One article I read said it would be hot in August, another said it would be raining.'

'It's more than likely to be hot *and* raining.'

He dumped the holdalls on the white tiled floor and came over to her, wrapping his arms around her slight figure and kissing the top of her head. 'You look unhappy, Nancy. Don't be—you're going to love it here.'

'I'm sure you're right,' she said dutifully, though she had no idea how she was to amuse herself while Leo was busy; the idea of lazing in the sun had never appealed and she would find it hard work. Trying to shake off her low mood, she said brightly, 'The maid—Zamira—didn't seem too concerned with organising dinner.'

'Eating for two already?' he teased again.

He seemed to take a delight in reminding her of her 'delicate condition', and she hated it. Not that she was completely opposed to motherhood—she had slowly begun to accept the idea—but it was Leo who had been ecstatic when she had first broken the news.

'Not really,' she answered him as equably as she could. 'But I thought you might be hungry. And Archie certainly will be.' Though more likely thirsty, she thought. Whatever the island's speciality drink, her husband's assistant would find it soon enough. But if it kept him occupied, Nancy was grateful.

She seemed to spend a lot of time feeling grateful. Mostly to Leo. She could never forget that in marrying her, he'd saved her from Philip March—a man unable to accept their engagement was over. March had turned into a dangerous stalker, intent on hurting her and hurting her badly. For months she had lived in fear of his attacks as they had grown steadily more frightening, until Leo had ridden to the rescue, not exactly on a white charger, though it had felt that way.

She was forever in her husband's debt—an obligation she could never fully repay—and now, since their honeymoon in Venice a year ago, her guilt had multiplied. She was not the wife Leo had expected, that was clear, but there was worse—she was hiding secrets from him. Her secrets and Archie's. It was no wonder she was always trying to atone.

'Well, none of us need go hungry.' Leo clicked open the catches on his case and began to unpack a pile of neatly ironed shirts. 'We're eating at Jackson Garcia's. He was kind enough to invite us to dinner on our first evening. The car won't be here to collect us until seven, so you've a few hours in which to rest.'

Rest sounded good. It had been a long journey, nearly two weeks by sea to Venezuela and, from there, a flight on a worryingly small plane. Now they'd finally arrived, Nancy would have much preferred to spend this evening at the villa.

'I wish I'd known we were to go out again,' she said a trifle sharply.

Leo looked up from his unpacking. 'Don't be a grump, darling. You'll like Jackson and I understand his wife is charming.' When Nancy continued to look unimpressed, he walked over and took her hands in his. 'I need to get to know the people I'll be working with. Dinner tonight is a good opportunity.'

She frowned. 'How many will be there?'

'All of them, I hope. But I'll be working closely with two in particular. One chap is travelling from Trinidad. He's advising on African art, and he should certainly be there—he's coming by local ferry. Another fellow is flying in from Bombay. I'm not sure when he'll turn up. It will be a team effort, and naturally I have to meet the team.'

Last year Leo had returned from an exhibition of native art, excited to have met Jackson Garcia. Jackson, apparently, had been so taken with what he saw at the exhibition that he'd decided there and then to fund a gallery on his home island. It would display the art of the different ethnic groups on Malfuego. Within two months, he'd sent Leo a contract and engaged some very expensive architects to prepare detailed drawings.

'But what will you be doing?' Nancy asked. 'Building work hasn't started yet, has it?'

'That's the clever bit. We're here to make suggestions before the builders actually begin. As a first step, I want to recce the site Jackson is proposing. At the way the light falls, for instance, the difficulty of maintaining a consistent temperature, that kind of thing. And access, too, though I imagine Jackson must have that very much in mind. The gallery is going to be a big draw for the tourists he wants to bring to the island.'

'And this will take two whole weeks?'

'At least. I have to liaise with everyone who's involved. We'll need to arrive at some kind of consensus on the shape and division of the building.'

Leo stowed his now empty suitcase beneath the bed. 'Do you want a hand?' He gestured to her bags, as yet untouched. She shook her head, attempting a smile. 'No. I'm fine. But thank you.' She opened the case and began to pull out several frocks, spreading them across the cotton counterpane.

Leo stood watching her for a moment. 'It will be good for you to meet my colleagues, Nancy.'

'Yes, of course it will.' She was desperately trying to recover her spirits, but the thought of spending days alone in Malfuego was increasingly unwelcome. And the scene they had witnessed on their way to the villa had unsettled her badly. She couldn't dismiss it from her mind. 'I wonder if any of Mr Garcia's other guests saw the violence this afternoon?'

'No idea, but you should forget it,' Leo said cheerfully. 'There's always some upheaval or other in these islands. Nationalist movements and so on. Not our business. I'll order some tea, then I'm off for a shower. When you've unpacked, make sure you take a nap.'

Chapter Two

Nancy was glad she had packed the red dress. Initially, she'd decided against taking it, but then at the last moment had slipped it into the open suitcase. It was bright and flattering and, when she looked at herself in one of the long bedroom mirrors, it showed her still slender figure to advantage. She ran a hand across her stomach—no sign yet of a bump, though everyone she met seemed to know of her pregnancy. It was hardly surprising since Leo had been intent on spreading the news that he was to be a father. Endearing, she supposed, but she would have preferred to have kept it to themselves for a few months at least. There was always the possibility of something going wrong.

'I love that dress!' Leo had come out of the bathroom and was gazing at her in appreciation. 'I saw it when you came back from shopping a while ago. Why have you never worn it?'

'We've had a poor summer and the dress hasn't been warm enough—it's too flimsy to wear at home.'

'You were brave to buy it!'

'With my first pay packet,' she replied. 'And it's as well I did—it should do just fine tonight.' There was an element of challenge in her tone.

He gave a little shrug and went over to the dressing table,

picking up the two brushes he'd laid out, and set about vigorously taming his greying hair.

He was a distinguished-looking man, Nancy thought, and a stubborn one. The job she'd found after many months of searching had proved contentious. Leo had not wanted her to look for work. He was quite capable of keeping her in considerable comfort, he'd said, so why would she want to start on the lowest rung of a new profession? She'd tried telling him that her need to work wasn't all about money. She wanted a job for her own self-respect, needed it to feel connected to the world. There was no possibility of working again at Abingers or any other auction house. Leo, as a visiting art expert, had connections to them all. She had been forced to look elsewhere, and it had been a wearisome search until the day she had seen the advertisement for an apprentice restorer.

She still felt passionate about art. Not her own daubings— they had gone by the wayside—but to be so fortunate as to handle some of the best artwork in the world. To be part of a team focussed intently on a single masterpiece, their only purpose to make the painting live again. A lowly apprentice she might be, but Nancy had been accepted there as an equal. She'd found none of the hierarchy she'd fought against at Abingers. No sense of women being in some way inferior— indeed, their delicate touch was an advantage. And she was learning. In three months she had learnt so much and loved every minute.

When the doctor had told her she was pregnant, she'd refused at first to believe him. She had been married a year and, as the months had passed, had begun to hope there would be no baby. It wasn't the 'right' frame of mind for a censorious world, she knew, not the way a woman should feel, but she couldn't be otherwise. And instead of joy, the doctor's words had left her feeling desperate—all the hard work in finding a job she loved was going to be for nothing.

Leo adjusted his tie. Dark suit, white shirt, polished leather on his feet. He always knew just how to dress, and she liked that in him.

'You look smart,' she said, smiling.

'Come here.' And when she did, he enfolded her in his arms. 'You look more than smart. You'll wow them.'

She wasn't inured to the flattery, but had no real desire to wow anyone. The best she could hope was to survive the evening without saying or doing the wrong thing among such a mix of strangers.

'You'd better stop hugging me quite so close or my hair will fall down.'

'I like the hairstyle, too!'

She had tried hard to pin the curls into some kind of order and had wondered if she might ask Zamira for help. But after clearing the tea things, the maid had disappeared to her own quarters—she had a small room in the basement—and Nancy had seen nothing of her since.

Leo looked at his watch. 'The car will be here in a second. We'd better collect Archie.'

But when they reached the hall, it was clear that Archie intended to go nowhere. He was still wearing the clothes he'd travelled in and his dark, uncombed hair stood up in tufts.

Leo gestured to the creased shirt and trousers. 'What's this?'

Archie's expression was bland. 'I don't think I'll come, boss, if it's all right with you. I'm tired—I'll be fine staying back.'

It wasn't unusual for Leo's assistant to be unsociable. And Jackson Garcia was apparently a very rich man—the chip on Archie's shoulder was sharp enough to find that irritating. Was that it? Nancy wondered. Or was it part of a deliberate intent to keep his distance from her wherever possible?

'No, it's not all right,' Leo said unexpectedly. 'I want you there. You're going to be working alongside these people as much as I am, Archie, and I need you to meet them.'

His assistant looked mutinous.

'Come on, man. You can't be tired. You're an ex-soldier and here's Nancy, coming on for three months pregnant and raring to go.'

'I'm not dressed for it,' Archie pointed out.

'How long is it going to take to have a quick wash and put on a change of clothes? A few minutes, no more. If the car arrives, I'll tell the driver to wait.'

Archie paused, seeming to weigh up the situation, then gave a little shrug and made for the stairs.

'I don't know what's got into him,' Leo said.

Nancy, perhaps, could have enlightened her husband. Archie had successfully stayed out of her way for almost a year, travelling to Cornwall to see his sick mother as soon as they'd arrived home from Venice, then making sure that the day they left for Cornwall, he was back in London. And so it had gone on for months. If she stayed in the house, Archie found errands in the city. If she and Leo were invited to an event—an exhibition, a show, a talk, a party even— Archie chose to stay at home. But the trip to Malfuego was something neither of them had been able to avoid. They were being thrown together again whether they liked it or not.

Malfuego. She'd known the name as soon as Leo had mentioned that work was taking him there, and she'd feared the worst. In her mind Malfuego was inextricably linked to Venice and Venice to the perils that, along with Archie, she'd faced there.

*

It was still light when they left for Jackson Garcia's, though dusk was falling swiftly. Nancy was surprised to find they turned inland almost immediately. Somehow, she'd imagined Garcia would have built his villa on the coast, but she was glad of the chance to see a new landscape. For a while they travelled along a flat plain, the only life, it seemed, tall regiments of sugar cane and sheep that were thin and brown. Occasionally a rusting, abandoned car came into view, ivy wandering its broken body and knitting it to the earth.

Soon, though, they began to climb. The hill was steep, with scraggy woodland on one side of the road and a huddle of flat roofs on the other. She craned her neck to peer through greenery at the haphazard scattering of timber cabins, wisps of smoke billowing from their doors. Through the open car window, she could smell the burning charcoal.

As they climbed, the patches of vegetation—sage and blackthorn, she was sure—grew less frequent, their green turning to an inky blue in the darkening air. Ahead, a distant mountain, veiled in grey mist, and a sky turning the palest lemon as the sun melted behind its sharp peak. Mr Garcia's home must certainly have a view.

His house was almost as she'd imagined, white with green shutters and doors, and elegantly symmetrical. It stood at the end of a long, winding drive, lined by palm trees and surrounded by manicured lawns and bougainvillea in abundance. The property spread itself wide: outhouses, stables, and a set of office buildings, were clustered at an angle to the house. A circle of gravel led to its imposing front door. Nancy blinked. A portico sheltered the door and of all things, a small cannon and several cannon balls sat to one side of a welcome mat.

She was still trying to absorb this image when their

driver—a different man from this afternoon, with a different saloon car, but both Garcia's she assumed—swung the vehicle around the circle and stopped immediately in front of a uniformed man, standing rigidly to attention. She glanced through the car window, wondering if there were any more oddities to be seen. A veranda ran around the first floor of the building and, when they were ushered inside, she could see why. The living quarters were upstairs, the bedrooms down.

'French plantation-style,' Leo murmured to her, as they walked up the carpeted stairway to be met by their host.

The house may have been centuries old, but Jackson Garcia was nothing less than shiningly modern. Leo had dressed smartly for the evening, but his host wore an open-necked shirt and casual trousers. Nancy glanced down and saw a pair of leather sandals, handmade no doubt, but still sandals. She caught a glimpse of the woman standing in his shadow and felt a wave of relief that she wasn't alone in having made an effort. His wife looked suitably chic in a cocktail dress of midnight blue.

'My dear friend,' Jackson greeted Leo effusively. 'And Mrs Tremayne. How wonderful to have you both under my roof.'

'My roof, too, Jackson.' The woman glided forward and held out her hand. 'Isabella Garcia,' she introduced herself, and smiled winningly. Nancy liked her.

'Come and meet everyone.' Jackson steered them towards an open doorway.

The drawing room had the magnificent view Nancy had predicted, the dark ridges of the mountain top just visible against a stunning sunset. Its furnishings, too, were as opulent as she'd expected: long curtains of red patterned silk hung at a wall of windows that filled one entire side of the room, and an array of dark furniture sported matching red silk cushions. Not to be outdone in colour, a large bejewelled statue of a peacock stood in one corner. The whole was a display of considerable wealth, prompting the question in Nancy of how Jackson Garcia had amassed such a fortune.

Jackson ushered them towards a slim middle-aged man hovering uncertainly by the window with a glass of juice in his hand. 'Cy Devaux, meet the Tremaynes,' Jackson said with a flourish. 'Cy arrived this afternoon—like you—though he hasn't had so far to travel.'

'Trinidad?' Leo asked.

The man gave a small smile. 'Indeed. I am looking forward to working with you, Professor Tremayne.'

'Leo, please. And this is my wife, Nancy.'

Cy Deveaux had a firm handshake and Nancy liked him immediately. 'And…' Leo looked around. 'My assistant, Archie Jago.' Archie materialised beside them.

'Mr Jago,' Cy said. 'We have spoken on the telephone, I believe.'

Archie nodded and offered his hand, but said nothing. And in seconds their host had bustled them away for more introductions. Nancy soon lost count, but one man stuck in her mind. Ambrose Martin was the owner of the best hotel on the island apparently—a large man dressed flamboyantly in white linen suit and patterned shirt, but with a quiet voice. She thought his eyes looked gentle.

'How good to meet you,' he said. 'Come and say hello to my daughter, Anya.'

He spoke with a Caribbean twang and the pride in his voice was evident. The young girl was certainly someone of whom to be proud. Dressed in a fitted frock of patterned silk, she was a vision of slender beauty.

The girl nodded shyly, her long dark hair curtaining her face, but she'd barely had time to shake their hands before a young man stepped forward, almost pushing in front of her.

'Luke Rossiter,' he said, his voice a decidedly English one. Home counties, Nancy thought. A privileged background. But trying a little too hard?

'Ah yes,' Ambrose seemed to remember, 'my assistant.'

'Personal assistant,' Luke said, a determined smile on his face.

Leo was soon plunged into an animated conversation with his colleagues, leaving Nancy trying desperately to think of something interesting to say. Isabella and Anya were pleasant women, but Nancy was tired and her feet had begun to hurt. Archie, meanwhile, glass in hand, stood silently to one side. It was going to be a long evening.

Just when she thought her legs would buckle, Jackson called over their heads, 'Dinner's up. This way, folks,' and busied himself gathering his guests together to follow Isabella into the dining room.

Nancy noticed that Luke Rossiter had laid his hand on Anya's arm, seeming to take charge of her. The girl looked as though she would shake him off, but then walked quietly beside him into the dining room.

Chapter Three

Name cards had been placed around the table and Nancy found herself between Cy Devaux, her husband's colleague, and Ambrose Martin, the hotel owner.

Once the starter of crab soufflé had been served, Ambrose turned to speak to her. 'I hope I might soon welcome you to the Serafina, Mrs Tremayne. I'd very much like to show you around our hotel. I believe we are the most luxurious retreat in the Caribbean.'

'Thank you. I'd love to visit. I'm sure the hotel is very successful—I imagine it has a long history.'

She was expecting another colonial plantation house, but Ambrose disconcerted her. 'Five years old tomorrow! You look surprised.'

'I imagined that it was a heritage building.'

'It should be—the site it occupies certainly is. A mill that belonged to my family was originally there, but when the sugar business deteriorated so badly, something had to be done. A new hotel was my answer.'

'And you used the same site?'

'Razed the mill to the ground,' he said delightedly. 'And replaced it with the most beautiful building you'll find in the whole of the region. Except—I intend to make it even more beautiful.'

'Are you talking shop?' Jackson interrupted.

'I'm flaunting the Serafina.'

'You have a right to flaunt, Ambrose,' Isabella put in. 'And when Jackson's gallery is finished and folks begin to flock to the island, more people than ever will see what a miracle you've built. You must definitely visit, Nancy.'

Ambrose nodded energetically. 'And Anya will look after you when you do.'

Anya, a spoonful of crab soufflé halfway to her mouth, smiled awkwardly behind the curtain of dark hair.

'Anya works with her father,' Jackson said. 'She is learning the ropes—isn't that the phrase?'

'And I'm the one teaching her,' Luke put in, his voice even more carefully modulated. Nancy thought his glance possessive.

'And Virginie. She's teaching me, too,' Anya said in a quiet voice.

'We must definitely *not* forget Virginie,' Ambrose said. 'She is my housekeeper. Nothing gets past that woman. Every surface glows, every sheet is starched, nothing is wasted, nothing stolen. She's a treasure.'

Luke's mouth tightened into a thin line. 'Luke, too, of course,' Ambrose added quickly. 'I plucked him from a London hotel and he's done me proud. Smart, efficient. Has all the energy I had as a young man. I'm truly blessed.'

The maids had cleared their dishes and were now making their way along either side of the table, serving a braised chicken stew with an accompaniment of rice. Nancy hoped it wouldn't prove too highly spiced. Her stomach had only just begun to feel her own again.

'Did you have a good journey from Trinidad, Mr Devaux?' she ventured to ask her other neighbour.

'Yes, thank you. For once, the ferry was on time, though

my taxi was held up in the town.'

'The demonstration, you mean? Do *you* know what the people were protesting about?'

'I believe there is a dispute in the island over land.'

'What kind of dispute?'

Cy Devaux took a while to answer. 'I believe a law has been proposed that limits the amount of common land available, which means, of course, that people lose the space to grow their own crops.'

Nancy's eyebrows rose. 'Then I'm not surprised they are angry.'

'Their upset is understandable, I agree. Malfuego, you know, is not a prosperous island and people scrape a living as it is.'

'But why propose such a law?'

Cy cast a surreptitious look towards his host. 'I think members of the State Assembly are keen to develop the island—and that needs land.'

Jackson Garcia had overheard and weighed in. 'We are. It's the only way to make the place prosperous, Cy, you know that. Development is the key. We need to build the kind of cultural attractions that bring in visitors—the hotel, the gallery, any number of future projects, will attract well-heeled tourists, which in turn means money and jobs for the islanders. People will benefit in the long run, but they're stubborn. They can't see further than their noses.'

'That is certainly one way of looking at it,' Cy Devaux said.

'It's the only way, old chap,' Jackson boomed. 'These people—they're peasants mostly, with little education and absolutely no understanding of commerce.'

'Do any of them sit in the State Assembly?' Nancy asked.

A silence fell around the table. She noticed Leo stare hard

at her. She had asked the wrong question, it seemed, but she waited for an answer still.

Her host gave it to her. 'The Assembly represents the cream of Malfuego society, Nancy. People who have knowledge, money, special skills—people who have travelled and know the world.'

'It's possible, isn't it, Jackson, that the peasants you speak of know their own world? Know what suits them?' Cy Devaux spoke in a soft voice but Nancy could see that, quiet man though he was, he would not be browbeaten. And neither would she.

'The ordinary people of the island aren't part of the Assembly then? Is there no chance for them to vote?' she asked.

'We're a democracy and we vote, though naturally not everyone has that opportunity. But the island is politically stable now and it needs to stay that way.' Jackson was beginning to sound defensive and she saw Leo's frown deepen. Archie, she noticed, was smiling broadly, his deep blue eyes alight with mischief.

'But surely that's the whole point of democracy.'

'You don't understand how things work here, Nancy,' her husband said.

'I'm trying to. That protest meeting this afternoon—it's evident that people have a real grievance. And the violence. Did you see the violence, Mr Devaux?'

He shook his head. 'I'm glad to say that I didn't.'

'We did, and it was quite terrible. The poor young man who was speaking was clubbed to the ground.'

'That's regrettable,' Jackson said, 'and exactly why demonstrations are a bad idea. They can get out of hand. They should be banned—for people's safety.'

'It wasn't out of hand,' Nancy countered. 'Not at all. It

22

was peaceful until three masked men appeared and started attacking people. For all I know, they may have killed that young man.'

'Let us hope not.' Isabella had entered the fray. 'Now, who can manage dessert?'

*

The Garcias' guests drifted back to the drawing room for coffee, but Nancy didn't follow. She felt stifled and, murmuring to Leo that she needed some fresh air, made her excuses to Isabella. She found Archie at the top of the drive, slowly enjoying a cigarette.

Meditatively, he flicked ash from his cigarette. 'You won't change their mindset,' he said, without turning his head. They were the first words he'd addressed directly to her in days. 'And you've pissed Leo off.'

'That's too bad. I had to say something. Why didn't you?'

'I'm the hired help, remember. I know my place.'

'Oh, do stop it, Archie. I thought we'd finished with that.'

'Now why would you think so?' The moon had risen high in a clear sky and, beneath its white stare, she saw a mocking smile pull at his mouth.

'Possibly because we both nearly died in Venice,' she said. 'After that, it seems petty, ungracious of you to nurse a chip when you're talking to me.'

He smiled slightly, but the mocking look had gone. 'The social graces aren't my strong point. I thought you knew that.'

'Archie—' She reached out and touched his arm. 'Can we—?' He didn't flinch at her touch, but he wasn't going to help her either.

'Can we?' he repeated.

She had been going to ask him if, somehow, they could

23

recover the friendship they'd forged when, side by side, they'd faced extreme peril. But before she could, the headlights of an approaching vehicle shone through the trees and flooded the driveway in an arc so bright it challenged the moon.

Within seconds, the car had drawn up beside them, the chauffeur smiling and tipping his cap. He was the same driver who had brought them to the Garcias'.

Archie ground his cigarette butt into the gravel. 'I better tell Leo our carriage has arrived.'

'I'll go. I need to thank the Garcias for their hospitality and say goodbye.'

Nancy felt frustrated that she'd been unable to put into words feelings that had been building for a very long time. She and Archie had left Venice as friends—at least, she'd thought so. At times it had felt they were more than that, but that was something she hadn't allowed herself to dwell on. Then, in London, the friendship had faded, mutated into what she could only call deliberate indifference. She'd felt irritation at first, then sadness, then anger. And lately—was it since Leo had announced her pregnancy with such great fanfare?—Archie had been almost hostile. Did he fear his job was at risk? A small baby was hardly a threat. Leo would go on working, go on needing an assistant. It was her life, not Archie's, that would be disrupted.

*

Leo barely said a word to her after they'd made their farewells, standing back for her to scramble into the car and then silently climbing in beside her. The silence continued as they drove back down the mountain, the driver negotiating the hairpin bends and overhanging vegetation with skill, and depositing them at the villa's front door within the half hour.

'Will you be driving me tomorrow?' Leo asked the

chauffeur.

The man beamed. 'Roland, sir. I will. What time?'

'Around eight thirty, I think.'

'We go to Mr Garcia's office?'

'Yes—no, I want to go somewhere else first. Wait a moment, and I'll get the address. Unless you know the site where Mr Garcia is planning to build?'

'No, sir. I'll wait.'

Her husband got out of the car and strode indoors without a backward glance, leaving Nancy to make her own way to the front door. The chauffeur was turning the car while he waited for Leo, and she was about to walk into the house, when a figure darted from the shadows and tugged at her arm. She recoiled in fear, but then sensed Archie right behind her.

He grabbed the marauding hand and tore it free. 'Who the hell are you?' he demanded.

'You remember me?' It was a voice she knew but couldn't place. 'You must remember me,' the voice said. 'Renzo. Renzo Hastings.'

She felt her heart sink. When Leo had first pronounced the word 'Malfuego', she'd thought of this boy but then brushed aside her fears, imagining he was no longer on the island or, if he were, that she was most unlikely ever to meet him again.

'Well, I'll be damned.' Archie laughed, and for the first time in an age he sounded like himself. 'What are the chances?'

Chapter Four

'I heard you were in Malfuego — it's worse here than Venice for gossip,' Renzo said. 'So I came.'

'How very nice of you to pay a visit.' Archie's tone was dry. 'Though perhaps not an entirely welcome one.'

'That's what I thought. It's why I hid over there.' The boy pointed to the clump of hollyhocks. 'But you helped me before, and I reckon you can help me now. You're the only people I can ask.'

'How are you, Renzo?' Nancy took a step back. 'Certainly looking a good deal better than when we last saw you.' The boy was still thin and gangling, but his face in the moonlight was no longer skeletal.

Renzo gave a sheepish smile. 'Kicked the meths for good — and the brandy.'

'And you're living with your father now?'

'Yeah. In a pretty fancy house the other side of the harbour. *Le Citronnier.*' He pulled a face at the name.

'And how is it working out?'

'It's okay, I guess. Dad's put me back on the right road at least.'

The boy's manner seemed awkward and, to Nancy's ear, he sounded less than enthusiastic. But at least if he'd stopped drinking and was being well fed, it had been worth risking

Leo's wrath to rescue him.

'Concetta still writes to me, you know,' Nancy said. 'She told me she'd seen you off from Venice, but didn't know where you were. You never let her know you'd arrived here.'

'Yeah, well, the journey was worse than I expected. The boat ticket my father sent got me as far as the States, but then I had to work my way down here and it wasn't easy.' Renzo's accent had become more strongly American as he pondered the difficulties he'd faced.

'Do you think we might cut the socialising?' Archie broke in. 'Mrs Tremayne may have helped you last year, but that was the end of it.'

Nancy ignored her companion's truculence. 'How do you think I can help?'

'I'm not asking for me. I'm asking for my friend, Riel. Gabriel. He's the best friend I've ever had and he's in real danger. I've no-one else to turn to.'

'Gabriel?' She frowned. The name was familiar. Only this afternoon… 'Not Gabriel Sekela?'

'You know him?' Renzo asked eagerly.

'Let's say I've heard of him.'

'He's a great guy. Really caring. I've learned about the island from him. He's trying to do his best for the people here, but there are forces at work who want to destroy him.'

Archie's lips clamped together, as though he were trying not to laugh. 'That sounds to me like the plot of a very bad novel.'

Renzo stared at him. 'It might do, but it's true. Riel is in hospital right now, covered in bruises and with stitches in his head and three broken ribs. The doctors are checking for internal injuries. I've just got back from seeing him and he looks in a real bad way.'

'I'm sorry to hear it,' Nancy said. 'We saw the attack when

27

we were driving through the town this afternoon. But—'

'Then you'll know the kind of threats he's facing,' Renzo interrupted. 'They're after his life. Those guys—the thugs in masks who went for him—they're just the latest. A month ago, he had his motorcycle tampered with—the tyres were slashed. And one night last week, he was attacked in the street. The police said it was muggers, but it wasn't. Then today—well, you saw what happened.'

'We did, and as I said, I'm very sorry, but I can't see how we can possibly help him.'

'*We* can't,' Archie put in harshly. 'And before you collect any more trouble, Mr Hastings, you better scarper.'

'But you *can* help,' Renzo insisted, reaching out with a skinny hand as though to stop them leaving. 'You can find the people who are threatening him.'

'That's a job for the police,' Archie said.

Renzo shook his head. 'They won't do it. Half of them are corrupt—they're in the pocket of politicians. And the other half are too scared to do anything.'

'If the police have no authority, who would act on the information, even if we discovered who was behind the violence?'

Nancy's brain was ticking and she could feel herself wanting to find out. Wanting to help. It was clear the crowd this afternoon was right behind this young man, and Renzo's words had painted a picture of someone who loved his island and wanted to do his best for it.

'There are one or two decent cops on Malfuego,' Renzo said. 'If I had real evidence to offer, I could find one.'

'Then find one. And find the evidence—yourself.' Archie was uncompromising.

'I can't. If my father knew what I was doing, he'd throw me out. He's insisted I stay clear of Riel.'

Nancy's curiosity increased a few more notches. 'Why doesn't he want you to be friends?'

'I'm not sure. He said Riel was a troublemaker and to keep away from him, but—'

'But?' she prompted.

'I think it's more than that.' Renzo stubbed at the gravel with one foot. 'Dad does business with some of the people in the State Assembly, and Gabriel is determined to reform it.'

'And you think your father is worried that his business will suffer if you're seen to side with Gabriel?'

'Something like that. I know I daren't ask him for help—I'm kinda on probation still. Though I'm finished with the drinking,' he said hastily. 'But even if I risked it, there's no way I can find out who's responsible. I've no contacts, no clout. But you have. I heard Professor Tremayne was invited here by Jackson Garcia and he's the fattest cat in the whole Assembly.'

'My problem, Renzo, is that Professor Tremayne wouldn't wish me to get involved,' Nancy said gently.

'But you *must* get involved. It's a matter of life and death. Can't you see that? They'll murder Riel if he doesn't stop his campaign. And he won't. You found out stuff in Venice, didn't you? Not just me and the forgeries—but the old lady who was killed at the theatre. You found out who did that. I'm right, aren't I? Please—at least go and talk to Riel,' he finished desperately. Beneath the porch's dim light, Nancy thought he looked far older than his eighteen years.

'That was last year,' she said. 'Things are different now.'

She wasn't entirely sure why they were, but she knew she would be foolish to become entangled. Yet the boy sounded so wretched and looked so utterly desperate that she found herself wavering, despite knowing that she should not.

'If I can, I'll try,' she said suddenly.

'Nancy? What's keeping you?'

Leo's voice acted like a starting gun on Renzo. In an instant, he had backed into the bushes and, with a rustle of leaves, had disappeared into the darkness of the garden. She was left looking at Archie who shook his head at her very slowly.

'Nancy?' Leo had arrived in the doorway, the address for the waiting chauffeur in his hand. 'What's going on out here?'

'Nothing very much. Archie was telling me what he knew about wild hollyhocks, that's all. Remember, his mother is an amateur botanist.'

Archie's face was a study of outrage and she took pleasure in it.

'Archie? Hollyhocks?' Her husband's tone verged on the exasperated. 'It's bedtime—I've an early call in the morning. You, too, Archie.'

'Sure thing, boss,' his assistant said, and walked past them and up the stairs to his room.

*

When Nancy came out of the bathroom, Leo was sitting on the bed, looking gloomily into the distance. He jumped up as soon as she appeared. 'Are you feeling all right, darling?' He sounded solicitous, but she knew it concealed a fear that she had once more become unpredictable.

'I'm tired, but otherwise absolutely fine. Are you thinking of the hollyhocks? That was just something silly—his mother, Morwenna, must have written recently and it prompted Archie's memory. He knows far more about plants than you'd ever guess.' She spoke as airily as she could.

'I wasn't thinking of the plants. It was Garcia that was in my mind. He and his wife were kind enough to invite us to dinner on our first night here, but you seemed to go out of

30

your way to antagonise him.'

'I don't think I did.' She pulled back the covers on the bed and slipped between cool linen sheets.

'So, what was it? Why bring up the demonstration at the dinner table?'

She yawned. 'Someone had to say something.'

'That's where we disagree, Nancy. I don't think it was at all necessary. And it worries me that you seem to want to get involved in something that isn't your business. I don't know what went on in Venice—no, don't turn away—I know something did. I'm not completely stupid. But I thought you'd forgotten whatever nonsense you were engaged in. All those wild stories you wanted me to believe.'

'Wild stories that happened to be true.'

'Okay, I accept that in that case I was wrong. But I'd hoped we'd left that behind—your desire to poke around in things that don't concern you. I thought you were settled. Particularly now we've a baby on the way.'

She turned to face him, pulling the sheet up to her chin. 'I'm not poking around, Leo. I simply mentioned the unjustifiable violence towards that young man. And far from condemning it, Mr Garcia's solution was to ban all demonstrations. I suppose that would suit him. He seems to run the island as his own fiefdom.'

'You know nothing about the island or how it's run.'

'Not much, I agree, but I'm beginning to get the picture.'

Leo padded over to the bed and jumped in beside her, then grabbed her arm none too gently. 'You must stop this. Whatever the politics of this place, they don't concern us. Garcia does. He's the one paying me a very sizeable fee, plus all our expenses here.'

She shook herself free of his hold and sat up, her slight form stiffening. 'I keep hearing about Jackson Garcia's money. How very wealthy he is. But do you know how he made his fortune?'

'A freight business, I believe. He may very well still run it. Why?'

'Freight sounds a bit vague. What goods does his firm carry and where?'

'Does it matter?'

'I think it matters that you know what kind of man you're working with, and that includes where he gets his money from. Can freight really be that lucrative?'

'What do you want me to say? I'm not a businessman. I've no idea what his empire covers. All I know is that he's a rich man keen to build a fabulous art gallery, and I'm here to be part of it. And enjoy a small break, too. Apart from a week in Cornwall, I've not had a day free since our honeymoon. I thought this trip to Malfuego would be relaxing, as well as providing me with a project I can get my teeth into. As my wife, I'd hope you'd be supportive.'

'Of course, I will. But perhaps you should—'

'And perhaps *you* should realise that it's Garcia's money, and money like his, that helps to pay for the house in Cavendish Street,' Leo said sharply.

And for me to idle my life away beneath its roof, if I choose. A dependent woman, she thought. A grateful woman. By marrying her, Leo had rescued her from a terror that was destroying her life. Her embittered fiancé would no longer pursue her if she was someone else's wife, that's how Leo had reasoned, and certainly this last year he'd been proved right. She'd had a few wobbly moments in Venice when she'd imagined that Philip March might still be hunting her, but that *had* been imagination, and since their return to London there had been no sign of him. She'd gradually begun to relax, to walk down the street without constantly turning to check.

Or turn a corner without dread in her heart. Relax sufficiently to begin to kick against always having to feel grateful. Always having to follow Leo's lead.

Like this evening at the Garcias'. Nancy had taken to Isabella but not to her husband. She'd been far more doubtful about him. Leo should have been, too; he should have enquired into the man more deeply before beginning this project. He'd misjudged people before, and badly—it could be that he'd also misjudged Garcia. But it was pointless to warn Leo. He'd made up his mind and she was expected to follow, or at least not to rock the boat.

She lay down again and turned back on her side, then felt her husband's fingers stroking the nape of her neck and his lips kissing her ear.

'I know you're tired from the journey,' he said. 'And maybe I shouldn't have asked you to come, but you're here now and for the next few weeks you can simply laze in the sun. Isabella was telling me she'd be delighted to take you to her country club whenever you'd like to swim. The Serafina has a pool, but the club will be more private. What do you say?'

'I'd like it,' she murmured.

'That's a blessing at least.'

He leaned over to turn out the light, then cuddled up to her, spoonlike, and was soon breathing deeply. But Nancy, fatigued though she was, could not stop her mind humming. Renzo Hastings. When Leo had first spoken of Malfuego, she'd had a sinking feeling that the events of Venice might resurface, but comforted herself with the thought that it was unlikely she would meet Renzo again, even if he'd made it to the island. Yet here he was and looking a good deal better than when she and Archie had found him living hand-to-mouth on the Giudecca, using his only skill to forge paintings.

They had helped him escape from certain death—his young body was close to being wrecked by meths and brandy—and escape, too, from criminal charges.

But what exactly had he escaped to? He seemed uncertain about his father and desperately worried for his friend. And Nancy could see he had ample reason. Gabriel Sekela hadn't died this afternoon, but he'd been hurt badly enough to be hospitalised. Apparently for speaking out on behalf of a people who had nothing. This was a man who deserved help, but how could she aid him without getting mixed up in a way that would infuriate Leo? Tonight she'd promised Renzo she would try. But had that been foolish; her heart ruling her head?

Chapter Five

Despite her best intentions, Nancy overslept and, when she tumbled downstairs, it was to see the car had already arrived and Leo was greeting their driver. Archie was in the hall, checking through the small case he carried.

'Are these all the plans, Leo?' he called through the open doorway, waving two slim rolls of parchment in the air.

Leo turned back to him. 'That's all I've been sent. I'm hoping Garcia will have something more substantial to show us at his office, but they'll have to do for now. They should give us some idea of how the gallery fits into the site.'

Her husband walked back to the car and climbed into the front seat, and Archie prepared to follow.

'Archie,' Nancy said urgently.

He spun round, evidently surprised to see her.

'If you can, will you go to the hospital?'

'What?'

'Gabriel Sekela. Will you visit him today and hear his story?'

'No, I won't. I've no intention of getting involved in Renzo's shenanigans and neither should you.'

Nancy clutched her flimsy wrap more tightly around her. The morning air was surprisingly chilly, and she was acutely aware of Archie's gaze. 'I promised him that I'd visit Gabriel.'

'Then you shouldn't have.'

'I know,' she said miserably. 'It's kept me awake. But I did make a promise and I can't see how to keep it. But you could. When you and Leo get back after the site visit and everyone meets up in Mr Garcia's office, there may be a chance for you to slip away. You could ask Roland to drive you to the hospital.'

'And lose my job? No thanks. Just for once, take my advice and forget you ever met the Hastings boy again.'

With lowering spirits, she watched him climb into the back of the car. She shouldn't have made even a half promise to Renzo, but now that she had... And she wanted to help Gabriel Sekela. He'd looked a proud man, a man whom people trusted. It was wrong that he was being threatened, if what Renzo claimed was true. And it had to be true. The evidence of her own eyes told her that.

She closed the front door and wandered down to the kitchen. She had no real wish to eat, but she imagined Zamira would have made breakfast and it would be rude to refuse it. The maid gave a little bob of her head as Nancy walked through the door.

'Your breakfast is on the veranda, madam. You will like the sun.'

'How kind of you. I think I would. We've had precious little sunshine in London this year.'

She was halfway up the stairs again when Zamira called after her, 'Madam.' The girl cleared her throat. 'This afternoon—I can be free? I will be back to make dinner.' Zamira's body was rigid, her soft curves stiff and awkward. It seemed a very important request.

'Of course, you can,' Nancy responded warmly. 'You will have plenty of free time while we're here and you must take it. My husband and Mr Jago will be out most of every day and I require very little.'

The maid gave another small bob of her head. 'Thank you, madam.'

It made Nancy uncomfortable to play the grand lady. In London, Mrs Brindley, Leo's housekeeper, was a law unto herself and would never think to consult her supposed mistress on anything to do with the household. And when they'd honeymooned in Venice, it was Concetta who'd looked after them—she'd been a friend, though, not a servant. Had become a friend, Nancy corrected herself. Somehow, she couldn't see that happening with Zamira. Concetta was a mature woman, confident in herself and her place in her city, but this girl was tense, uneasy, altogether too contained.

Nancy dressed quickly and in a matter of minutes was sitting on the veranda that wrapped around the entire ground floor of the building and was wide enough to house a good-sized table and four wicker chairs. Zamira had set a place so that Nancy could look out at the sea without being directly in the sun. She hadn't expected such thoughtfulness. She drank a tall glass of orange juice, then took a spoon to a bowl of chopped mango. She would at least go home healthy.

The sun glinted gold across the ocean, a shimmering pathway trembling with the movement of the sea—forming, dissolving, then re-forming once more. Below she could hear the ceaseless whispering of the surf, embracing the skeleton of rocks that strung out below the cliff. She peered over the wooden railing. A large bird, grey against the deep blue of the sky, perched on the largest rock. Its wings were horizontal, feathered tips reaching out into the windless sky. Then head down, it plunged into the sea, a slight ripple the only sign of motion, and in less than a second the bird had regained its place on the rock.

Contentedly, Nancy ate her way though the bowl of fruit and followed it with toast and coffee. Leaning back into the chair's deep cushions, she felt at peace. Could she stay here all day? It was tempting, but when the sun rose higher it could become oppressively hot. And really, what a waste of a day.

She carried her empty china down to the kitchen where Zamira was washing the floor. The girl started up when she saw Nancy, intending to retrieve the plates.

'No, don't get up. I'll leave them here.' Nancy indicated a small table just outside the kitchen door. 'Breakfast was delicious, thank you. I wanted to ask you about buses. Are there any that go into town from here? I thought I might do a little shopping this morning.'

'Yes, madam. One every hour. On the half past. The bus stops down the road.'

Nancy looked at her watch. 'Then I better make haste if I don't want to twiddle my thumbs for an hour.'

She'd picked out a sundress to wear that she'd bought in the Church Street market, a splashy affair covered in large pink flowers. It was far bolder than she would normally choose, but judging from the clothes she'd seen last night, it would do well enough for a saunter around the town.

With a quick wave to the maid, she grabbed her bag and sun hat from the sitting room and was out of the front door and speeding down the driveway. The stop was way down the road—Nancy could barely see it in the distance—but already she could hear the loud rumble of an engine, growing louder by the second. She started to run but it looked hopeless, and she was about to resign herself to a long walk or a long wait, when the bright yellow bus drew up alongside and the door opened.

The driver grinned at her from his cab. 'You want the town, missus?'

'Oh yes. Thank you.'

He ran off a ticket for her and Nancy fumbled in her purse, then realised she had only bank notes to offer. The small amount of local currency that Leo had left was still sitting on her dressing table. She offered a note to the driver without much hope and he duly shook his head.

She blushed bright pink and began a stuttering explanation, ready to get off the bus and start again, when a bright-eyed lady, her face and arms deeply tanned, intervened.

'Here. This should do it.' The woman handed several coins to the driver.

'Thank you so much,' Nancy said with real gratitude.

The bright-eyed lady gathered in the folds of her long turquoise dress and patted the seat beside her. Nancy happily accepted the invitation.

'You must be Mrs Tremayne,' the woman said.

Nancy blinked. It *was* like Venice, she thought. Worse than Venice. The news of their arrival had travelled around the island within twenty-four hours.

'Don't look so worried. We've been expecting you. I'm Virginie Lascelles, the housekeeper at the Serafina.'

'Oh, the hotel, Mr...'

'Martin. Ambrose Martin. You met him last night, the one in the white suit? Ambrose is a good sort. For an Englishman.' She gave a loud laugh and her dark eyes held a sly sparkle.

'You are... French?'

'Malfuegan, but yes, originally French. My family's been here for two hundred years—we were quite something in those days—but we've lost any importance we ever had. That's a theme you'll hear often.'

'The island does seem a mixed community.'

'A ragbag,' Virginie said, and laughed uproariously again. 'Now, where are you off to, Mrs Tremayne?'

'Nancy, please. I thought I'd take a look at the shops.'

'It's going to be a very small look then.' Virginie grinned. 'There aren't too many shops for tourists on the island. At least, not yet.'

'I wasn't thinking of a tourist shop exactly. More a place that sold craftwork. Something distinctly Malfuegan.'

The woman's eyebrows rose.

'I'm interested in different crafts. I'm training in one myself—as a picture restorer,' Nancy said in a rush. She wanted so much to believe that it was still true, that she could continue the apprenticeship when she returned to London.

Her companion put her head on one side. 'In that case, I think you may be in luck.'

'Really?'

'I've a friend who sells local handiwork. She fashions jewellery from shells but sells other people's pieces, too. There's a guy who's a woodworker and another who's a potter. Would you be interested?'

'I would, but I doubt I'd ever find the place.' She had a good idea where such a specialist shop might be—in the deepest corner of what passed for Malfuego's capital.

'I'll take you,' Virginie said, surprising Nancy. 'I don't need to be back at the hotel for a few hours.'

'I don't want to take up your free time.' Nancy was apologetic. 'You must have plenty of errands in town yourself.'

'Whatever they are, they can wait. If I take you to the shop, I'll get to see my friend, so I win as well.'

The bus had been following the coastline, slowly winding its way downhill, and stopping every few minutes to pick up more passengers. By the time they reached the ramshackle bus station, the vehicle was full to bursting and it took a while for the women to extricate themselves. As soon as they were free, Virginie led the way, setting a brisk pace down a narrow road that ran to one side of the terminus, then zigzagging a path through several back streets that were little more than tracks. She'd been right, Nancy thought. She would never have found this place on her own.

The shop, when they arrived, was what she'd hoped for and she spent a contented half hour browsing its wares. The pots were beautiful but too large to carry, and the various sculptures—strange, tortured figures—she dismissed as soon as she saw them. Leo would have thrown them out of their London home without a second thought. But the small wooden horse she found was beautifully carved and she chose it immediately. She was sure her baby would love it. The friend—Virginie had introduced her as Clara—watched patiently, and Nancy felt duty bound to praise the jewellery, though it was not her style. But maybe a bracelet? She could give it as a gift some time in the future.

When her purchases were finished and they'd said goodbye to Clara, Virginie surprised her again. 'Have you time for a drink?'

'If you have.'

'I've always time for a rum punch.'

'Rum? Perhaps not. I've been feeling a trifle queasy.' To put it mildly, she thought. Then in a rush of confidence, she said, 'I'm pregnant.'

'Wonderful! Congratulations! Then it's fruit punch for you. I guarantee you'll like it.'

They found seats at a café on the waterfront, probably the most picturesque part of the town. A flotilla of canoes bobbed on a sea that was glassily transparent—shallow at this point, but soon melding into the darkest blue as the waters deepened. Brightly coloured dinghies floated nearby, intermingled with several expensive yachts, majestically at anchor. Like children clinging to their mother's skirts, Nancy thought, and smiled at the image.

'This is heavenly,' she said, taking a long draught of the fruit punch.

Virginie nodded knowingly. 'The punch isn't as good as we make at the Serafina, but it's not bad. Still, you'll see for yourself. You're getting an invitation. A special tea for the Tremaynes!'

'I didn't know. But I expect Leo will tell me when he gets back.' She waved away several audacious sparrows that were scouring the tables, the boldest pulling packets from the sugar bowl and pecking them open.

'Have you worked at the Serafina long?'

'Since it opened, five years ago. I started as a chambermaid, but I've been housekeeper for three years now. It's a big job—some very demanding guests—but I'm thriving on it.'

'That's quite a promotion.' Nancy was curious. She couldn't imagine her companion working as a chambermaid, even as a starting point. 'What made you take the maid's job?' she asked, after a pause.

'There's not much work on the island. You'll hear *that* soon enough, too. I started off as a companion to an old lady up in the hills—when I left school. It was an in-between kind of job. I had my school certificates but there was nothing else going at the time. Anyway, I liked her and she liked me, but then she went and died, and I was without a job again. Her nephew took over the house and asked me to stay on. He was a bachelor and he'd always had help.'

Virginie pulled a face. 'You know the type—gets to middle age without learning to tie his shoelaces. I found I didn't much like working for him and, when I heard that Ambrose was going to pull down the old sugar mill and build a hotel there, I didn't hesitate. Needy bachelor out—chambermaid in.'

Several schoolgirls walked by and Nancy watched them

admiringly. Their short-sleeved cotton shirts were crisply white, their skirts grey pleated and their hair tidied back into tight knots.

'That was me once,' Virginie said, a laugh in her voice.

'They look as though they know exactly where they're going in life. You did, too, I bet. You've done so well, and very quickly.'

'Naturally.' She gave one of the roars that Nancy was growing familiar with. 'I'm a cute cookie. That's what the Americans say.'

'Mr Martin, Ambrose, mentioned the sugar mill last night. It didn't seem to worry him that he'd destroyed a piece of history. In fact, he seemed delighted.'

'I'm not surprised. Knocking that mill down was his little bid for freedom.' Virginie stretched her legs full length and waggled her toes.

'How do you mean?'

'The Martins—phew! Tight-arsed. That's also American. His parents were furious when he did it. The mill had been in their family for centuries, but they'd handed it over to him—all quite legal—and they couldn't stop him doing what he wanted. It was their biggest sugar mill but, in any case, they've kept hold of several more.'

'The family own other property?'

'Half the island, darling. They're an old settler family. Originally slavers. They still live in the old plantation house—Ambrose and his daughter, Anya, and his stuck-up mother and father.'

'You really don't like them, do you?'

'Ambrose doesn't either, so I'm excused.' Her smile was wide.

An open-air taxi, with gaily painted sides, stopped a few feet from them and a bare-chested man—a tourist Nancy presumed—his stomach the size of a giant's pie baked red by the sun, slid stickily off its leatherette seats and onto the road. They watched while he staggered to a nearby table.

'It will be ice cream,' Virginie whispered.

Nancy smiled back, but she was still thinking of the Martin family. 'Where is Ambrose Martin's wife?'

'Where indeed? Jacinta left the island nine years ago and hasn't been seen since. It wasn't a particularly happy marriage, by all accounts. I think she was his parents' choice, not his.'

'But to leave her daughter at such a young age…'

'Yes, poor darling. Anya was just ten when she lost her mother and then her aunt. It couldn't have been easy for her, but she seems to have come through.'

'Her aunt? Was that Ambrose's sister?'

'It was, but she drowned. A swimming accident just after Jacinta left. At the time, there were rumours—Charlotte Martin was a strong swimmer, she'd go into the sea in all weathers, and it shouldn't have happened. But then, there are always rumours. And Ambrose has turned out a good father.'

'What kind of rumours?' The Martins were beginning to sound decidedly murky.

'That his wife leaving and his sister's death weren't unconnected.' There was a long pause before Virginie said, 'The old slave families are a pretty closed bunch. They don't marry out. Keeping it in the family, if you know what I mean. And people talk.'

Nancy was silent, trying to understand what Virginie was saying. Then it dawned on her and she felt shocked to her depths. Brother and sister? Surely not. Yet it would explain his wife's sudden departure, leaving her young daughter behind. And perhaps Charlotte's accident. But it was rumour, as Virginie said, and rumours could distort horribly.

'I'm glad Anya has such a good father,' she said quietly.

'We met her last night. She is very beautiful.'

'Too beautiful,' her companion said cryptically.

Nancy had been about to ask what Virginie knew of Gabriel Sekela, and whether the hotel considered his political activities a risk to its business, but a second thought decided her to stay silent—at least for the moment.

'I'm afraid I'll have to get going,' Virginie said. 'I'll walk you back to the bus station. You might have to wait a while, but one will turn up sooner or later. Ask for *Belvoir*. The driver will drop you off at the gates.'

Obediently, Nancy got up from her chair but, as she did, felt a sharp pain deep in her stomach and a slight wetness that dribbled down her leg. Her heart gave a little jump. *Please don't let it be that.* She wanted to ignore the problem, but knew she mustn't. 'I need to go to the bathroom, Virginie. I won't be a minute.'

She was more than a minute. As she'd suspected, it was blood, not much more than a trickle, but blood nevertheless. She felt her stomach twist with fear, and it took a minute of deep breathing to calm her sufficiently to walk out of the toilet and back to Virginie.

'Are you all right? You're white. Whiter than you were, I mean.'

'A bit of a shock, that's all. A warning maybe. The baby—'

'Something's wrong?'

'I hope not, but there was a little blood.'

Virginie took her arm. 'Let's find a cab. We need to get you home. Lie down and rest until this evening. And don't worry—it happens sometimes. I've seen it with friends. If you rest, it will get better.'

'And if it doesn't?'

'Then that's the time to call the doctor, honey.'

Chapter Six

She took Virginie's advice and, as soon as the taxi had dropped her at the villa, climbed the stairs to her room and lay down on the bed, still fully dressed. She was grateful there was no sign of Zamira in the house. The girl carried a tension with her that was uncomfortable to be near, and Nancy hoped she would take as much time away from *Belvoir* as she wanted. It was soothing to be alone in the house.

The long windows were open and the soft murmur of the sea filled the room. She lay flat on her back, her limbs stretched, trying to ease the mild cramp that still bothered her. Gradually, she began to feel calmer. The very bad pain was over and it had only been a small trickle, she told herself. Now it seemed to have stopped altogether. Virginie must be right. It could happen around this time, nearly three months in. It didn't mean she was in trouble. But while they were here, she must make sure she led a quiet life. No more running for buses, for a start.

A light breeze cooling her cheeks and the shushing sound of the waters below had her drift into a doze, when a door banged. Zamira. Already? But they were not the maid's footsteps—far too heavy. They were Archie's. She knew them by heart. What was he doing back so soon? She glanced at her watch. Three o'clock. Perhaps they had finished at Garcia's office for the day, yet Leo seemed not to be with his assistant.

Better get up, look normal, or Archie might start asking questions, and she knew she would tell him what had happened at the café. The indifference she'd managed to sustain in London was already crumbling, and the urge to be close to him, to talk intimately, was very strong. She must fight it. It was living in this house, side by side on a small island, that was the culprit. There was nowhere to hide, nowhere that she and Archie could be unaware of each other.

'You're home early,' she called out. Archie was in the hall taking off his shoes as she walked down the stairs.

'Yeah. I dipped out. We spent the morning at the site, but after lunch it was back to Garcia's. They gassed on for an hour and then decided I wasn't needed, thank the Lord. It was a meeting with the architects—and so much hot air about "art" it's a wonder the office didn't float away.' He picked up his shoes and went to walk past her.

'What's the site like?'

He stopped and considered for a moment. 'Pretty impressive. Leo likes it, which is a plus. It means we might get off the island a bit quicker.'

'You don't like Malfuego?'

'Do you?'

'I'm warming to it.'

'You might not feel so warm when I tell you what I've just heard.'

'I want to know but I need to sit down. Come and tell me.'

She led the way into the sitting room and slumped onto the sofa. Archie stared hard at her but made no comment. He took the chair opposite, his shoes still in his hand.

'Well?' she asked.

'I went to the hospital as instructed.'

Nancy leaned forward. 'You did? You said you wouldn't.'

He gave a shrug. 'I had the time.'

'And you saw Gabriel Sekela?'

Archie nodded. 'I talked to him a fair while. He's a bright bloke and on the side of the righteous. But there are plenty here who aren't. They're trying to force through a law that gives the members of the State Assembly *carte blanche* to requisition land for so-called development. In other words, to make money for themselves. And the people who own the land or rent it get turfed off with minimal compensation, if any.'

He was talking to her as he used to. Sharing thoughts. Sharing opinions. That was something she'd missed. 'It's what Cy Devaux told me last night,' she said. 'At the Garcias' dinner. I thought he might have got it wrong.'

Archie put down his shoes and lay back in the chair, pushing his hair from his forehead. In recent weeks he'd abandoned his military cut and a frame of dark hair softened what could be a severe face.

'He didn't get it wrong, and this Sekela chap is fighting it tooth and nail. But he's got one helluva problem—he has no vote, and neither do any of the people affected. So how does he stop it?'

'He's evidently trying.'

Archie pulled a face. 'He's printing leaflets exposing the swindle and delivering them around the island. Holding rallies, too, like the one we saw. He's even been in touch with an American radio station. They're interviewing him—and that should spread the word beyond Malfuego. But it's an uphill struggle getting a rebellion started.'

'And a dangerous one, judging by what we witnessed. Does he think he'll succeed?'

'He's confident if he gets enough aggravation going, most of the Assembly members will think again. It's two or three of the biggest nobs that are pushing for it. But that's if Sekela gets the chance to create a sufficient storm. Our friend, Renzo, was right about the "accidents" his mate has suffered. And Sekela seems to be expecting more.'

'How awful.' She sat thinking for a moment. 'Renzo didn't know who was behind the threats, but does Gabriel? I guess it has to be one of the "big nobs".'

'He wasn't throwing out accusations, but I could see he thought Jackson Garcia the main suspect. It doesn't take much working out—and what we heard last night suggests it could be true.'

'And Ambrose Martin? The hotel owner? Did Gabriel mention him? He must be almost as important.' The Martin family was still very much in Nancy's mind.

'Sekela seems to have a soft spot for him. Probably because he's got a soft spot for his daughter.'

'Anya?'

'She's quite a looker. You can't blame him. But there's also the clown who was following her around last night. The one who speaks as though he's swallowed a plum.'

'Luke Rossiter?'

'Yeah, him. Any whiff of rebellion will be bad news for the hotel. Rossiter might see his job going if the tourists stay away. This Luke bloke could be just as keen as Garcia to have Sekela fail.'

'But Gabriel has no proof against any of them?'

Archie shook his head. 'All he knows is that he's under threat and, since the battering we saw could have killed him, not to mention the slashed tyres of his motorcycle, it's pretty clear that someone wants him off the island. Either that or they want him dead. Just as Renzo said.'

Nancy felt a wave of helplessness. Instinct was urging her to investigate—to pay visits to Jackson Garcia and Ambrose

Martin, to speak to Luke Rossiter and the people who worked for him, to wander around town and talk casually to whoever was willing. But she could do nothing. Despite Renzo's plea, she shouldn't even think of it. A few hours ago, she'd had a warning. But Archie...

'So what?' she began.

'Nothing. I'm doing nothing and neither are you. It's not our problem.'

'Like Marta Moretto wasn't our problem.'

'She wasn't, and look where that landed you. And me,' he added gloomily.

'But we helped. We helped give her justice.'

Archie leaned towards her and took her hand in his. It was the first time he'd touched her in months, and she felt a tumble of excitement and wished she didn't. 'Nancy, you're to let it go.' He sat holding her hand for what seemed like minutes, then disentangled himself. 'Come flying instead.'

'Flying? What are you talking about?'

He got up and flapped his arms in the air. 'You know, flying. I had a bit of luck at the hospital. When I got there, Sekela was having something or other done to him, and I couldn't see him immediately. But I got talking to a doctor — young chap, full of beans. He's learning to fly and he says it's the best feeling ever. I'll clear it with Leo, but I reckon he'll be happy enough, as long as I go in my spare time. And judging by today, there'll be plenty of that.'

'But you don't know how to fly.' She was bewildered.

'That's the point. I'm going to learn. I've always wanted to. I'm useless on a small boat, but in the air, I'll soar.'

'The airport we landed at — it was very small.'

He grinned. 'And so is the plane I'll fly.'

'But won't the lessons be expensive?'

'I've a plan. I'm going to ask Leo to pay.'

She gaped at him. 'Really?'

'It will help him. If—when—I get a licence, eventually, I'll be able to fly him wherever he wants. Well, within reason,' he amended.

Nancy was doubtful. If Archie was seasick, wouldn't he be airsick, too? But he'd appeared fine on their short flight from the mainland. Still, how useful would this new skill really be? Why would Leo pay for expensive lessons? Maybe to keep his assistant busy and away from the villa? Quickly, she quashed the suspicion. Her husband could have no idea of the feelings that she and Archie had buried without a word passing between them.

Archie got up and walked to the door, then turned and asked suddenly, 'Is Zamira in?'

'I don't think so. I haven't heard her. Why?'

'Something odd happened as I was leaving the hospital. I'd got to the reception desk and there was one massive racket going on. The security guards were trying to shuffle this woman out of the building. They were trying to do it gently, but she wasn't going anywhere. She kept shouting that she had to see Gabriel. The nurse behind the desk must have told her a dozen times that she couldn't. That Sekela didn't want to see her.'

'It was Zamira?'

'The same. She started beating her fists on the desk, saying she'd taken the afternoon off especially and she had to see him. It was very important, more important than they'd ever know. The nurse just went back to her paperwork, but the guards grabbed Zamira by the arms, then picked her up bodily and deposited her outside.'

'How extraordinary. She's seemed a little strange to me ever since we got here, but I thought that was simply the way she was.'

'It might be, but in between the tears she was shouting and cursing like a Cornish fishwife. And that's some cursing. Unless, that *is* the way she is.'

Nancy got up and joined him at the door. 'I ought to go down to the kitchen—see if she's back.'

'Nancy.' He was inches away and she felt the familiar tingle of warmth flood through her. 'Remember—don't get involved.'

'I'll try to comfort her, that's all.'

But when she walked into the kitchen and saw Zamira on her knees, her head bowed to the tiled floor, a keening sound coming from her lips, Nancy knew a gentle comfort would be wholly inadequate.

'Zamira,' she said hesitantly, and tried to help the girl to her feet.

'Sorry, missus. Sorry, madam.' The girl tried unsuccessfully to stem the tears.

'Please come and sit down.' Nancy led her over to one of the kitchen stools and drew up another beside her. 'Here, take this.'

Zamira blew half-heartedly into the proffered handkerchief, then dabbed it limply around her wet face.

'You don't have to tell me why you're so upset,' Nancy said, 'but sometimes it can help to share a problem.'

The maid shook her head.

'Mr Jago saw you at the hospital,' she mentioned, hoping the information might encourage the girl to talk.

Zamira stared, blinking back more tears. 'He did?'

'Yes. He told me you were very upset that you weren't able to see someone. A patient.'

'Riel.' The girl sniffed.

'Gabriel? Gabriel Sekela?'

The girl nodded unhappily.

'How do you know him?' Nancy didn't want to intrude too far, but it was a strange fact that so much on this island seemed to come back to this young man.

'He live next to my folks. I know him all my life. We at school together. Sweethearts.' Zamira blew her nose again, this time more forcefully.

'I see.' Nancy wasn't sure she did, but she would try. The maid twisted the handkerchief in her hands. 'He go to Florida for three years, but he say that when he come back, we be together.'

'And you aren't?' Nancy's voice was gentle.

'We were.' The girl became suddenly strident. 'We were 'til all this trouble.'

'You mean the politics? Gabriel's fight for a vote?'

Zamira look puzzled. 'No. Drugs,' she muttered.

Nancy's eyes were huge. 'Drugs? What has he to do with drugs?'

'It's the smuggling—from Venezuela. Coca.'

'And Gabriel is involved in the smuggling?' Nancy was truly shocked. The maid's words had shattered her image of the young man.

Zamira shook her head violently. 'No, no. He try to stop it.'

Another reason for the young man to be threatened. Nancy's head was spinning. Drugs were big business and the gangs behind them ruthless. Perhaps she had been too quick in assuming the threats to Gabriel were from the likes of Jackson.

'But I don't follow—how has it made things bad between you?'

'It get Gabriel to meet the white folks. He went to the big hotel. Plenty drugs sold there, and he meet this girl.'

Nancy suddenly understood. 'Another girl? I'm sorry.'

Zamira sat looking down at her lap. 'It's sad, I know,' Nancy said tentatively, 'but it happens to most people at some time in their lives, and they do get over it—eventually.'

'Not me.' The maid's voice was bitter. 'How you get over this?' And she pointed to a slightly swollen belly that Nancy had not noticed before.

'You're having a baby?' she gasped.

'And he Riel's, for certain. You tell me—how I get over that?'

Nancy was rendered speechless. Before she could think at all sensibly, Zamira jumped up from her stool and grabbed a teatowel. 'You can't tell me,' she said, looking over her shoulder at Nancy. 'No-one can. But Gabriel pay for what he done. I make sure of it.'

Chapter Seven

The sound of the front door slamming had Nancy jump to her feet. She was as bewildered as she was appalled. How could Gabriel Sekela have behaved so badly, abandoning Zamira when she needed him most? And what had the maid meant about his paying the price? Were the accidents he'd suffered something she knew about? Were they something— Nancy hardly dared think it—that the girl had arranged herself? Politics, drugs, and now abandonment, all reasons for Sekela to be targeted. Too many reasons, too many threats. Nancy felt her brain beginning to seize up.

'Nancy? Where are you hiding?' Leo sounded happy.

'I'm here,' she called out, arriving in the hall as her husband was halfway up the stairs to their bedroom. He retraced his steps when he saw her.

'I was in the kitchen talking to Zamira about dinner tonight.' She excused herself the lie.

'Good, good,' he said absently, and gave her a hug. 'Perhaps you can get her to bring us some tea. I'll be down in a minute, just as soon as I've had a shower.'

The last thing Nancy wanted was to go back into the kitchen but, when she walked through the door, the maid had disappeared, presumably to her own quarters. She quickly made a pot of tea and had loaded the tray with cups and saucers and a small tin of biscuits she'd found in one of the cupboards, when Zamira came back.

'I take the tray for you, madam,' the maid said formally. She had washed her face and combed her hair, and donned a starched pinafore fresh from the laundry. It was as though she had pushed the crying girl to the back of a cupboard and turned the key.

By the time Leo reappeared, Nancy had gathered her wits sufficiently to decide she wouldn't mention Zamira's plight to him, at least not at the moment. She wanted to make sure of the girl's story, since it seemed to contradict so badly the man she'd thought Sekela to be. Who was likely to know the truth? Renzo Hastings perhaps. If she felt well enough tomorrow, she could pay him a visit. She remembered the name of his house and, if she took a cab there and back, the journey would be effortless. In any case, this afternoon's rest had worked—her stomach still gave an occasional twinge, but that was only to be expected. It was nothing too serious.

'A good day?' she asked, as Leo walked into the sitting room, newly crisp in a short-sleeved shirt and casual trousers. She always enjoyed looking at him—he was a handsome man.

'Pretty good.' He sank down beside her on the sofa and let out a sigh of contentment. 'I've a fair idea now of the layout of the whole building and how each gallery section relates to the rest. But we can't do any detailed planning until Joshi arrives. He's stuck in Bombay at the moment with a sick wife—still, he's promised he'll be here as soon as he possibly can.'

Nancy poured two cups of tea and waved the biscuit tin at him.

'Mmm. Thanks. We had a good lunch but I'm still peckish. So, what did you do with *your* day?'

'Nothing much. Enjoyed the sun. Had a rest this afternoon.' It wasn't exactly a lie, but neither was it exactly the truth. It was best, though, not to alarm him. She crossed her fingers that when he met Virginie, the housekeeper would say nothing of Nancy's trip to town.

'Excellent. Just what the doctor ordered, or would if he were here. And tomorrow—more sun and more rest.'

'I suppose so.' Rest and sun were all there was. The visit to Renzo would be brief, and somehow she would have to fill the remainder of the day.

'You sound disappointed, but I've a treat in store. Tomorrow morning I'm meeting the construction team. Archie, too. There will be a few hours discussing materials, building methods, that kind of thing, but then we'll have to wait for Joshi to arrive before we can go much further. And…I had an idea. How about a picnic lunch?'

Nancy's smile was warm. It was Leo's thoughtfulness that endeared him to her. 'What a wonderful idea. I'd love to see more of the island.'

'That's what I thought. Roland is ours for the duration and, when I spoke to him about it on the way back, he knew the perfect spot. We'll get Zamira to pack a basket and as soon as I'm back from Garcia's, off we'll go.'

She cuddled up to him. 'You are a lovely man, Leo.'

'And you, my darling, are a lovely woman.' He kissed her full on the lips and twirled a curl of her hair around his finger. 'I'm glad our Indian expert is late. It means I get to spend more time with you. While we're picnicking, Archie can write the few letters I need to get off. Where is he by the way? Have you seen him?'

'Probably in his room. He came in an hour ago.'

Leo's expression was wry. 'He's been a grump ever since we landed. I guess there's not much here to keep him interested. The work hasn't really started yet and there's no nightlife to speak of.'

'I expect he'll find a bar in town.'

'Bound to. The rum is said to be excellent. He'll scoot after dinner, you'll see.'

But Archie eschewed dinner altogether, leaving the villa around six as they were having a drink on the veranda.

'Even better,' Leo said, as his assistant called out a goodbye. 'Dinner *à deux*.'

Archie wouldn't stop at a few drinks, Nancy was sure, but she hoped he would be circumspect. He'd seemed genuinely concerned at the threats against Gabriel Sekela, and the last thing she wanted was for him to say the wrong things to the wrong people. To get drunk perhaps and begin talking loosely, even throwing accusations around. She'd had no time to tell him of Gabriel's crusade against drugs. That was a dangerous business and would involve dangerous men, and she didn't want Archie stumbling into it, unaware. As for their pregnant maid, she would deal with that herself.

*

She was up bright and early and, once the men had left for Garcia's office, searched the sitting room for the list of telephone numbers she'd been told a helpful member of Jackson's staff had provided. It took only a few minutes—she found it filed carefully away in the single drawer of the small cane desk. The name of a taxi firm appeared halfway down the first page and she rang them straightaway. She would be glad to get out of the house this morning. Zamira had hardly spoken a word to her since their encounter yesterday and was now cleaning the bedrooms with an energy that verged on fury.

She called up to the maid to say goodbye as soon as she

saw the cab at the front door.

'*Le Citronnier,*' she told the driver. 'I believe it's on the other side of the harbour.'

The man nodded, needing no further description, and soon they were following yesterday's scenic route along the coast to the waterfront, but then continuing past the bus station until the line of small houses dwindled and, in their place, much grander plots appeared. The driver slowed before he swung the car through a pair of carved wrought-iron gates, guarded either side by two stone lions. Nancy was impressed. And surprised. She'd imagined that Renzo's father would be doing well enough on the island, but the house—a three-storey square building with an immense portico—looked as though he was doing more than well. She wondered if she'd meet Scott Hastings this morning.

Renzo himself was at the front of the house, bent double over one of the many flower beds, jabbing at the ground with a trowel and looking perplexed.

He jumped up when he heard her footsteps on the gravel. 'Mrs Tremayne! How did you find me?' He didn't sound too pleased.

'You're not difficult to find. I didn't expect you to be a gardener, Renzo.' She pointed at the flower bed, its earth slightly disordered.

'I'm not,' he said gloomily. 'I don't know what I'm doing. Dad employs a handyman who knows far more about plants than I do. But I need to contribute something for my keep.'

'No job then?' The night he'd come to the villa there had been little time to ask him if he'd found work.

'I've helped out at the hotel several times when they've been short staffed,' he said defensively. 'But it's impossible to find a proper job here.'

Nancy decided against mentioning his experience as an

artist. A former forger was unlikely to find work on Malfuego.

'I'm sorry for turning up like this, Renzo, but there's something I need to talk to you about. I hope your father won't mind I've come uninvited.'

'He's not here to mind.' Renzo sounded more cheerful. 'We had a break-in last night and he's gone to town to report it—at least, I think that's what he's doing.'

'How concerning for you. Was there much taken?'

'No, it was kinda weird. Dad collects old silver and some of it's pretty valuable, but he's not missing a thing. The guy who broke in must have thought the stuff would be difficult to sell. It was a pretty botched job—smashed window, Dad's desk broken into. I expect he was looking for ready cash, but my father doesn't keep it at home.' He straightened up and puffed out his cheeks. 'So, what was it you wanted?'

'I needed to speak to you—about your friend.'

'Riel? You've been to see him?' Renzo threw down his trowel. His eyes were bright.

'Archie, Mr Jago, went to the hospital,' she admitted. 'And you were right about the threats against him—the harm he's suffered.'

'Can you help?' he asked eagerly.

'At the moment I can't see how exactly.' The unhappiness in the boy's face prompted her to add, 'I haven't given up hope entirely. It was something different, though, I wanted to talk to you about. Can we sit down somewhere?'

She could feel her stomach cramping again, though she'd felt fine when she left home. It was standing around, she thought, that was the problem, pushing to the back of her mind the fact that yesterday when the trouble had started, she'd been sitting at a café table.

'Sure. There's a seat in the garden.' Her companion led

the way to the rear of the house. A large, closely-cut lawn greeted them, bordered by bougainvillea and bisected by a line of palm trees that led to an elegant summerhouse.

There were a number of benches dotted around the garden and Renzo gestured to the nearest. When they were both seated, Nancy said, 'We have a maid at the villa called Zamira King. Do you know her?'

Renzo nodded. 'She's a friend of Riel's. He lives next door to her family.'

'Is she more than a friend?' Nancy phrased her question carefully.

The boy waggled his thin shoulders. 'She was. Riel said they were at school together and then they dated for a while. But that's all finished.'

'So I believe. Do you know when their... their understanding ended?'

'I think it was when Riel went to the States. Not much point having a girlfriend miles away.'

'Why did he go to America?' It was a digression, but Nancy was curious.

'He went to college. Took a degree there.'

That gave Nancy pause. Mrs Sekela must be well-paid by Malfuegan standards to fund a boy through three or four years of university, yet if the Sekelas lived next door to Zamira, their home was likely to be modest. The paradox lodged itself somewhere in the back of her mind.

'I wasn't here when Riel left for Florida,' Renzo went on, 'and I've no idea what was going on between them. I've only known him this last year, but I do know Zamira's been a nuisance ever since he got back.'

'How do you mean?'

Renzo pursed his lips. 'Well, Riel's mother got sick. Very sick. That's why he came back to Malfuego, and Zamira helped him nurse her. I guess it seemed natural—she lived next door and had known Mrs Sekela all her life. Riel told me Zamira was thrilled when he came back and delighted when he got the job as a tour guide—she must have figured he'd be staying in Malfuego and that she and Riel would be like they were before. But he didn't want that. Anyway, when his mom died, Zamira got really pressing and he had to tell her he wasn't interested. But she didn't want to hear it and she still doesn't. She won't give up.'

'It seems a bit hard on her,' Nancy said cautiously. 'Gabriel must have been glad of her support while his mother was very ill. It seems reasonable for Zamira to expect their friendship, or whatever it was, to continue.'

'Riel was grateful all right and maybe he leaned on her too much, but afterwards he just wanted to be free. I know he tried to find a way of breaking up that wasn't too hurtful, but Zamira just wouldn't accept he wasn't up for marriage. Then he met someone else, and that was it.'

'Did you know that Zamira is pregnant?' Nancy blurted out, and then felt dreadful. She hadn't meant to break a confidence in speaking so frankly of the maid's plight.

But Renzo appeared unimpressed. 'No, I didn't,' he muttered, 'but I'm not surprised.'

Nancy frowned. 'Why do you say that?'

'Because when Riel told her very definitely to push off— in the end he had to be brutal—she went bananas. Drinking and flirting with guys around the port every night. With the way she was carrying on, I wouldn't be surprised if she was pregnant three times over.'

'You're saying the baby isn't Gabriel's?'

'Gabriel's? Of course, it isn't. He never, you know… He would have told me—we're buddies.'

'Zamira seems convinced it is his baby.'

'She might want it to be, but it isn't.'

Nancy got up. Her back had begun to ache, and she tried stretching to relieve it. If Renzo was right and this baby's father was a man Zamira had met on a drunken evening out, there wasn't much hope of any permanent match. She felt a growing concern for the young girl.

Renzo shot a look at her worried face. 'It's not a big deal,' he said, getting up and walking beside her to the front of the house. 'Plenty of kids here don't have fathers, and people don't seem to care.'

Nancy was going to say that Zamira cared, and that she cared, when loud voices interrupted their conversation. Rounding the corner of the house, she saw two men: one had to be Renzo's father, and the other definitely an islander, though he could easily have found work as a Hollywood extra. Tall and athletic, his dark brown skin glistened in the hot sun.

'Gibbon Bass,' Renzo said disparagingly.

'He looks… who is he?'

'He runs a boat between here and Venezuela.'

Nancy's mind began ticking furiously. Venezuela, boats, drugs. And Renzo's father who owned a palatial estate. No, she mustn't go there. She had a bad habit of putting things together that weren't always true. She could hear Archie's caustic voice saying it.

'He knows your father well, by the look of it.'

There was an argument going on and Bass, who was at least half a foot taller than his companion, was looming over Renzo's father, his finger pointing aggressively. Nancy couldn't hear what was being said and, as the men became aware they were no longer alone, their altercation stopped abruptly.

'Renzo!' The older man walked towards them, leaving

Gibbon Bass to turn and disappear without a word. 'You must introduce me.'

The boy looked uncomfortable. 'This is Mrs Tremayne, Dad. I knew her in Venice.'

'Ah, yes. My son's rescuer.' Scott Hastings smiled broadly and, for a moment, Nancy was mesmerised. His teeth—strong, square and startlingly white—seemed almost predatory. 'How strange you should end up in Malfuego, Mrs Tremayne. But good.' He spoke in a soft American drawl. 'It gives me the opportunity to thank you.'

'Really it was nothing. And it's good to see Renzo looking so well.'

Scott glanced at his son and gave a small grimace. 'Yes, I guess he does.'

Nancy was puzzled. This was the first time she had seen the two of them together, but she had little sense of their being father and son. They were more like acquaintances than family. Perhaps that was understandable, since for years they'd lived separate lives. Yet, even with that proviso, there was still something unnatural about the Hastings household. It was clear that Renzo had been unhappy to see her at *Le Citronnier*, had seemed glad that his father wasn't at home when she arrived, then tight-lipped over Gibbon Bass's presence.

'You must come over for tea some time. Nancy—isn't it? And I'm Scott.'

'Thank you, Scott. I'd love to.'

It would keep her in touch with Renzo and she was beginning to think that might be important.

'I'll walk you down the drive,' the boy said gruffly. 'I can see your taxi waiting in the shade.'

'What's your father's business?' she asked him, as they walked. 'Couldn't he find you a job in his firm?'

'He did, but I was pretty useless. I left after a couple of weeks.'

'And you wouldn't give it another go? It might work better next time.'

Renzo looked down at the ground. 'I don't want to. It wasn't right for me—it was a relief to leave.'

She gave him a swift glance. He looked quite sick at the thought of working for his father again and she wondered why. Was he unhappy about the way Scott Hastings made his living?

'It's freight,' Renzo said offhandedly. 'Organising transport for goods to go overseas. It was a yawn.' A coincidence, perhaps, that Garcia was also in the freight business.

The cab driver got out of his car to greet them and opened the car door for her.

'Then let's hope a permanent job comes up soon,' she said, climbing into the back of the taxi. 'At the Serafina perhaps.'

Renzo mopped his forehead with a dubious looking handkerchief. It was considerably hotter now than when she'd first arrived. 'Yeah, let's hope.' He dabbed again. 'Or hope I get off this island altogether. That would be good.'

Chapter Eight

Leo was as good as his word. He was home a little after twelve o'clock, having left Archie at Garcia's office, writing up the notes from that morning's meeting.

'Zamira has packed a basket for us,' Nancy told him, 'but she's also left sandwiches.'

'Let's forget the sandwiches and go. I can't wait to throw myself into that sea.'

Nancy had expected a fairly lengthy ride to find a beach that was accessible—the coastline seemed entirely rock-strewn—but in a surprisingly short time they were at the bay that their driver, Roland, had mentioned.

The chauffeur dropped them at the end of a rutted track and pointed to the narrow path ahead. 'Straight on through the trees—and have fun!'

'Give us till around four,' Leo told him, lugging the picnic basket out of the boot.

'Sure thing.' Roland waved them a cheery goodbye and began to reverse back along the track.

The narrow path forced them to walk in single file until the trees began to thin and a crescent-shaped bay of white sand appeared in the gap. The turquoise sea rippled gently in a breeze that whispered its way to land.

They stood side-by-side, quite still, amazed at the beauty

before them, and then with an uncharacteristic whoop, Leo ran onto the sand, basket swinging from his hand, and kicking off his shoes as he went.

Nancy was equally entranced but followed more slowly. When she reached him, he smiled broadly. 'What do you think?'

'What do you think I think? It's perfect.'

'Let's find a spot to make camp.'

Whatever early morning coolness there'd been had disappeared hours ago. Above them was a cloudless sky, deep blue, with the sun a glowing orb. It was the hottest time of the day and Nancy felt her skin scorch. Leo gestured to the trees behind them. 'Let's get into the shade.' He took the woven blanket she was carrying and spread it in the deepest shadow he could find, stowing the picnic basket alongside.

'A swim. We have to have a swim,' he said, pulling his shirt over his head.

Nancy undressed almost as quickly. She'd bought the emerald ruched bathing costume in a hurry and hoped it still looked good. It was only in these last few days that her figure had begun to change—fuller breasts, a slight swell of the stomach.

'You look wonderful.' Leo stood gazing at her, then reached for her hand and pulled her down the beach and into the water.

The sea was unexpectedly cold but, after the first stinging sensation, Nancy dived into the small waves and with firm strokes swam out to Leo who was already treading water. He wrapped his arms around her and held her tight.

'This is what we need more of,' he said, kissing her deeply. She tasted the salt on his lips.

'More Caribbean?'

'More time together. We don't get enough.'

'You have to work. I understand that.'

'But *you* don't, my darling. And now you'll be home so much more, it will make a difference to us. You'll see.'

It would, she knew. But it wasn't a difference she wanted. It was when Leo voiced such sentiments that she felt the distance grow between them, conscious of the gap she seemed unable to bridge. With a quick tug, she freed herself from his embrace and swam back towards the beach.

A few yards from the shore, she was surprised by the ocean's pull, strong enough to drag sand, pebbles, even bodies, beneath it. It had her stagger back and she was struggling to find her feet when, suddenly, there was sand again beneath her toes. Then just as rapidly the swell caught her again, the seabed disappeared, and she was treading water once more. Yet one more swoosh had the sea pick her up and deposit her on the beach itself. Waters that appeared placid could be dangerous—that was something she should remember.

After she'd towelled herself dry, she moved the blanket into the sun and lay stretched there, waiting for her husband to return. It had grown hotter even in the short time she had been in the water. Gradually, she felt herself meld into the white-gold sand, so silky to the touch. The sun's heat suffused every one of her muscles, and she closed her eyes against the bright light and listened. The rhythmic slap of waves came to her, the sweet call of a bird in the trees behind, then the scuttle of tiny lizards and the sound of a million insects.

'Great, wasn't it?' Leo had arrived and was spraying her with small droplets of water.

'Ugh! Go away. I'm busy baking myself.'

'Not for too long or you'll get sunstroke. We must move further back in a minute. There'll be more shade as the sun travels round. There's a veritable jungle behind us.'

She sat up and glanced over her shoulder. There were shades of green as far as she could see and textures ranging from the smooth to the spiky. In the distance, steep hills were similarly covered, though vegetation grew sparser towards each summit. And at their centre, an immense malformed peak, an enormous dark shape, rising up against the glittering sky.

Nancy pointed to it. 'Is that Monte Muerte?' She'd read the name back in London, having borrowed a guidebook from the Marylebone Library. Disappointingly, Malfuego had warranted only a paragraph.

'So I believe. It means deadly mountain, or something similar. It's an old volcano.'

Deadly mountain, and Malfuego—bad fire. Neither sounded too promising. She shaded her eyes, craning her neck to view the highest mountain on the island. As she did so, there was a dull rumble that seemed to come from its direction.

'What's that?' she asked, startled.

Leo was looking as surprised. 'It sounded like the mountain, didn't it? Perhaps it was saying hello.' He smiled, though his joke sounded a little uneasy.

'Is the volcano active then?'

'It was a hundred years ago but not since, as far as I know.'

Nancy flopped down on the blanket again. 'Let's hope it stays that way.'

He lay down beside her and stroked her arm. 'Don't worry. We'll have a peaceful few weeks while we're here. And tomorrow—I forgot to tell you—we have an invitation to tour the Serafina, followed by afternoon tea. Isabella came into the office today and promised to pick us up on her way to the hotel. We're to be ready for three o'clock.'

Nancy had started to say that Virginie had mentioned

an invitation, but then bit her tongue. She wasn't supposed to have met the housekeeper. She wasn't supposed to have gone into town. This was why secrets could be so perilous. Instead, she murmured, 'It will be an interesting afternoon.'

'Yes. I'm looking forward to seeing the hotel. We met its owner a few days ago at Garcia's. Do you remember? I'm told Ambrose Martin has done a splendid job with the place.'

'When you met him the other evening, did you like him?'

Leo nestled up to her. 'He seemed nice enough. An easier character to deal with than Jackson, at least.'

She propped herself up on one elbow. 'Are you finding Mr Garcia difficult then?'

'Not exactly difficult. Demanding, I would say, and not very knowledgeable about art.'

'Which is why he's employing you.' Nancy gave him a little poke in the ribs.

'True, but his lack of knowledge means we spend a lot of time discussing things that frankly won't work. Like this morning. He simply wouldn't listen to Cy Devaux when the man told him that, at its present angle, the space he'd been allotted would mean too great a contrast in temperatures between morning and evening. It would cost the gallery a fortune to regulate it properly. Then there was an argument between Jackson and the construction chaps about how much it would cost to build in the necessary controls and how much higher that would push their estimate. Hours of discussion which ended with the shape of the building being slightly changed, as Cy had wanted from the start, and the estimate staying exactly the same.'

'A result then?'

'Eventually, yes, but it's wearying. Garcia appears used to getting his own way and that can be a problem.'

'He certainly seems to in the Assembly.' She sat up,

suddenly hot and irritated. An ugly thought had infiltrated the beautiful day.

Leo sat up, too. 'Is that still bothering you? I don't think it should. From what I can gather, Garcia isn't omnipotent. He's facing growing opposition to his plans. And that young man—Sekela—appears to have had some success in changing minds. He's continuing to cause difficulties for Jackson.'

'From his hospital bed? It seems unlikely.'

'He's out of hospital now and apparently charging full speed ahead, even though he can hardly walk. I heard Jackson swearing about him this morning.'

'That's not good news.' A deep frown creased Nancy's forehead. 'It could mean another attack on him.'

Leo rounded on her. 'What are you suggesting? I hope it's not what I think.'

'Why are you surprised? You've just said that Jackson is intent on getting what he wants, and what he wants is to rid himself of any opposition to grabbing land that's not his.'

'What I didn't say was that he would use intimidation.'

'I think he already has.'

'That's a shocking accusation, Nancy.'

'Perhaps, but how much do you actually know about him?' oHow muH

'You know more?' Leo's tone was cold, suppressed anger in every word. 'You have to stop this. Jackson is a perfectly decent man and I'm sure he had nothing to do with the attack we witnessed.'

The beauty of the day had been shattered, and she paused, wondering whether to continue the argument. But she knew she would have to. 'How can you be so certain? Someone paid those thugs to hurt Gabriel. And Jackson Garcia has a motive.'

'So, no doubt, have many others, and Jackson would never

risk his reputation as a trusted businessman to get involved in such a thing.'

It was a valid point, but it didn't convince Nancy. Bad things were happening on Malfuego and seemingly there were a number of people willing to risk more than their reputations. Leo had decided that Jackson Garcia was innocent, and she knew from past experience what that meant— her husband would not allow himself a change of mind.

Garcia had been a fêted visitor at the small London museum where Leo had first met him. He was known to be an extremely wealthy man, though the source of his wealth wasn't clear. But he'd donated large sums to the museum of which Leo himself was a trustee. Several meetings between the two men had followed, the upshot of which had been a lucrative contract for her husband here on Malfuego. It was no wonder Leo had decided that Jackson was innocent. It was in his interest to do so.

Nancy wondered if he'd be as willing to give others the benefit of the doubt and wanted to ask him what he knew of Scott Hastings, but to do so would reveal another visit she shouldn't have made. There was certainly something strange going on at *Le Citronnier*. A burglar who ignored valuable silverware, but broke into a locked desk. It could be, as Renzo suggested, that the man had been looking for cash, but she had a hunch after meeting his father—she hadn't warmed to Scott Hastings—and witnessing his argument with Bass, that it was more than that.

'Shall we eat?' Leo's light tone signalled a truce. He gave her a kiss on the tip of her nose. 'But first we should move. We're getting burnt here.'

It seemed that Zamira had overcome her distress sufficiently to pack them a delicious meal: chicken joints, fried plantains, sweet potato curry, grilled vegetables, and a large flask of very cold mango juice.

'My, that was good.' Leo finished his chicken and cast around for a napkin. 'We must remember this meal when we get back to London.'

Nancy began to pack away the empty food containers. 'I'm sure we will—when the days get shorter and the skies greyer.'

'Which reminds me. We don't have that much time and we need to plan. When we get home, we must talk about the nursery. I know which room I think it should be, but it's up to you to decide. You're the important one here.'

'I really don't mind, Leo. Whatever you think.'

'You must have a preference. I'd hoped you would have decided already. It's early days, I know, but there's a lot to prepare for a baby—or so my colleagues tell me.'

'There will be stuff to buy,' Nancy conceded, 'but we can do that in an afternoon and get the shop to deliver.' It was taking her time to get used to the idea of being a mother, and she wasn't ready yet to make preparations.

Leo looked taken aback. 'You'll want to take care in selecting the best equipment, surely? And you'll have plenty of time to shop now. Take a friend with you and choose exactly what you want. You can show it off to me later.'

'I won't have that much time,' she said tightly.

He was filling his glass with juice, but paused to look at her. 'Why not?'

'I have to be in the studio a certain number of hours each week,' she reminded him. 'The apprenticeship requires it.'

'But you won't be going back to the studio.'

It was uncompromising, a statement of fact. His fact, Nancy thought. 'Why won't I?'

'You're pregnant,' he protested. 'You're having a baby.'

'Having a baby isn't an illness, Leo. It doesn't stop me working.'

'I thought when we left for Malfuego, that was it. I believed you'd forgotten that nonsense.'

Nancy's lips were compressed, trying to keep back the hasty words that were bursting to get out. After a moment, she said as evenly as she could, 'It isn't nonsense. It's what I want to do with my life. I hoped you would understand.'

'Nancy, your life now is being a wife and a mother. Working for dirt poor wages in a difficult environment, where any kind of accident could happen at any time, is something you shouldn't even consider.'

He must have read the stubbornness in her face, because he dropped the hectoring tone and instead set about persuading her. 'There will be other opportunities, once the baby is older. And we might well have other children and that would make working impossible for you.'

'But not for you.' Those were words she couldn't keep back.

The idea that Leo might expect more children had startled her. She'd been stunned when she'd first found herself pregnant. It wasn't that she hadn't wanted a child, more that she'd been undecided, and then suddenly a baby was coming. But she'd known that Leo was desperate to be a father, and for his sake she'd tried to be glad. But, if now, she was to be allowed no other life…

He ignored her comment and said smoothly, 'I was thinking that when we're back in England and we've settled the nursery question and booked the obstetrician, I could take you down to Cornwall for a long stay. A few months, say, until nearer your time. It's a tranquil place, and all that fresh air is certain to be good for you—and for the baby.'

'No!' The word exploded out of her mouth. 'I mean,' she

said more mildly, 'it's thoughtful of you, but I think I'd be happier staying in London.'

Their visit to Cornwall last year—the first she'd made to Leo's family home—had not been an unqualified success. His brother, Perry, had been sweetly welcoming and tried hard to make her feel at home, though his bafflement was clear as to why his sibling had decided out of the blue to marry a girl so much younger than him and without any obvious attributes. The elder Mr Tremayne, however, had been a different prospect. From the moment Nancy had walked through the doors of Penleven, she had felt the air heavy with his disapproval, and had vowed to herself that she would stay away from Cornwall for as long as possible.

'Why wouldn't you want to spend time there?' Leo was looking genuinely bewildered. 'It's a beautiful spot. Penleven is beautiful. You couldn't have a better place to spend these few precious months.'

Or a place as far away as possible from the work I want to do, she nearly retorted. She was trying to think of an anodyne response, when a loud roar split the silence. There was a flurry in the trees above and a host of small birds took flight. Instinctively, she looked behind her at the trees and then out towards the sea. A powerful launch had come into view, a bent figure at the wheel and another just visible, hunched in the stern.

The boat rapidly drew nearer, then juddered to an abrupt halt a few yards from the shore. The man who had been steering grabbed the other by the arm and hauled him off the vessel and into the sea. Then proceeded to drag him through the shallow water up to the beach. The fierce undertow that Nancy had experienced earlier knocked them back several times, but still the man kept coming, the other figure seeming to be his captive.

Nancy gave a little gasp and then hoped that Leo hadn't heard. She had recognised the figure in the lead. The face beneath the fisherman's cap was that of Gibbon Bass—the man she'd seen arguing with Scott Hastings this morning—and if she weren't mistaken, his hand was locked around the wrist of Luke Rossiter, the man from the Serafina.

'That's Rossiter, isn't it?' Leo squinted into the sun. 'The chap from the hotel?'

'It looks like it.' She hoped she sounded uninterested.

'What on earth's going on? And who is the other man?'

She made no attempt to enlighten him and then, just as suddenly as he'd arrived, Bass turned and tried to push his unwilling companion back towards the boat. He must have seen us, Nancy decided. Tucked away in dark shade, they would have been invisible before, and it was evident the man wanted no observers.

But Rossiter wasn't playing his game. As Gibbon Bass turned to retrace his steps, he must have loosened his hold slightly, and Luke wrenched his arm free and began to sprint up the beach towards them.

'Hello, Professor, Mrs Tremayne,' he called out as he came within earshot, as though he had been invited to their picnic and was just a little late. Incongruously, he was wearing a dark grey suit, but his expression was at odds with the elegant attire, now decidedly bedraggled. He looked scared.

'How good to see you,' he said, as he reached them. 'Enjoying all our wonderful Caribbean can offer, I hope.'

'Yes,' Leo said uncertainly. 'We are, but I'm afraid you're out of luck if you're looking for lunch.' He gestured to the empty picnic basket.

'No problem, Professor. I won't be staying.' He sounded as nervous as he looked.

Gibbon Bass had by now regained his boat and was

staring hard at them. Then, as though giving up on whatever he'd intended, he reversed his craft and accelerated. The boat roared forward, leaving a deep white furrow in its wake.

'How extraordinary,' Leo said.

'Mr Bass was giving me a lift,' Rossiter offered in explanation.

Leo and Nancy looked at each other. His claim was so patently false that neither of them said a word.

'Well, I'll be off then. Leave you in peace,' their visitor said with a false cheeriness, the plum now firmly back in his mouth, and made for the path through the trees.

'How extraordinary,' Leo said again.

Chapter Nine

Nancy was relieved to see Roland bumping his way along the track towards them as they emerged from the wooded path. Despite the beauty of the place, she was more than ready to leave. The day had been wonderfully relaxing, except for the strange intrusion of Bass and Luke Rossiter, but in the last hour her back had begun to ache badly and, as Roland expertly steered the car to a halt, her stomach started cramping again. Too much sun, she thought.

As soon as they arrived back at the villa, she threw her bag on the bed and went to run a bath.

'Zamira should do that for you,' Leo remonstrated. 'It's what she's paid for—to look after us.'

There had been no sign of the maid when they'd arrived home, but she had evidently been busy. The house was sparkling clean and, knowing what she did, Nancy had no intention of making extra demands on the girl. She still hadn't mentioned Zamira's plight to Leo and wasn't sure why she hadn't. Possibly because she knew he would disapprove. He was a kind, generous man, in many ways liberal in his views, but at times she found him uncomfortably traditional.

'It's not important,' she said soothingly. 'The bath is running and I'm going for a long soak.'

The long soak did the trick. The back pain eased and the

cramps disappeared. She lay there until the water began to cool, thinking over their day together. Blissful, paradise, were a few of the words that came to mind, but also dubious— that was when she thought about Gibbon Bass's appearance on the beach and the scared look on Rossiter's face. Bass seemed a threatening figure. Earlier that day it had been Scott Hastings; this afternoon the young man from the hotel. What possible connection could there be between them? And did it have anything to do with Gabriel Sekela and the danger he faced?

It would have been good to have talked it over with Archie. He'd pretend he wasn't concerned, but after their adventure in Venice, she knew him better than to believe it. The fact that he'd bothered to visit the hospital and talk to Gabriel betrayed his interest. But she'd barely seen him today. She imagined he'd used any free time to visit the airfield, maybe even begin his flying lessons, though Leo had made no mention of them.

And tonight she wouldn't see him either: Archie would be drinking at some bar or other in town. That could be useful, she reflected, if he said little and listened more. In Venice, the gossip Archie had picked up from his drinking mates had helped her begin to fit together pieces of the jigsaw. Malfuego was another jigsaw and she felt herself intrigued by the puzzle. Leo would hate her becoming involved, but her promise to Renzo echoed loudly in her mind and it bothered her that so far she had done nothing towards helping him find Gabriel's attacker.

Their dinner of red snapper was delicious—Zamira cooked as well as she cleaned—but afterwards Nancy felt incredibly tired. When they wandered back to the sitting room, she had little energy to do more than flick through the magazines that had been left at the villa. She yawned heavily and Leo yawned with her.

'Too much sun,' he said wryly, unconsciously mirroring her earlier thought. 'Let's have an early night.'

She was glad to climb the stairs and even gladder to slide between cool sheets. Leo cuddled up beside her, his head sinking into the large feather pillow. 'How are you feeling?' he asked in a drowsy voice.

'Wonderful.' It was near to the truth.

'It was the best day, wasn't it? We must do it again.'

'I'd like that. Whenever Jackson lets you off the hook.'

'We'll make it soon.'

He put his arms around her and kissed her deeply. Then began tentatively to caress her breasts, but when she didn't respond, he kissed her on the cheek and turned over. His attempts at lovemaking had been half-hearted ever since she'd told him she was pregnant. It was slightly strange, but she wasn't repining. She loved Leo, loved his company, appreciated his expertise, but passion had always been missing—at least for her. And the pregnancy hadn't changed things. If anything, the idea of a child had lessened whatever physical attraction she'd felt. But Nancy was content enough. Passion was a danger she didn't want in her life—she was too aware of its power to disrupt.

She was soon asleep, drifting into a dreamless slumber. A few hours later, though, she woke with a start. Stretching out a hand for her watch lying close by on the bedside table, she peered at its dial in the strand of moonlight that had crept beneath the window blind. It was only two o'clock. What had woken her? A sudden pain ripping through her stomach told her clearly. She gasped at the onslaught and had to hold her breath to stop herself yelling out. Gradually, the pain subsided and she could breathe again, but she had barely turned over in bed searching for a cool spot, when a second pain, equally fierce, tore at her stomach. Then she felt a sticky wetness between her legs.

As quietly as she could, she slipped out of bed and padded along the corridor to the far bathroom, holding her stomach tight as though by doing so she could prevent the pain returning. Prevent what she dreaded, happening. But return it did, again and again, until just when she felt she could bear no more, a long drawn out scream, barely voiced, and which she had no sense of uttering, signalled the end of her ordeal. The end in so many ways.

When she found sufficient strength, she stumbled to the washbasin and turned on the taps, leaning heavily against the cold white porcelain. Slowly, she washed every inch of her body, finding comfort in the balm of warm water. Then delved into the linen chest—thank goodness it was handy— and found a clean nightdress. The stained garment she had been wearing was bundled into the back of a cupboard. She would have to wash it later herself. She wouldn't ask Zamira—it was far too personal a chore—but it was more than that.

Nancy wasn't sure she trusted the maid. She was an angry young woman. Those threats she'd made against Gabriel— she'd looked implacable at the time, and Nancy could believe she meant him real harm. And she was unpredictable, too. In her distress at being pregnant, Zamira might turn against a woman who had lost her baby and tell the professor, as she called him, what she'd found. And Leo mustn't know. Of course, he must know, but it was his wife who must find the right moment. When that would be, Nancy had no idea. Whenever it came, telling him there was no longer a child would be one of the most difficult things she'd ever had to do.

She slid back into bed, but Leo hardly stirred. Desperately needing comfort, she half turned to him, her hand hovering over his sleeping form. She wanted so much to wake him.

To pour out to him the dreadful thing that had happened and to have his arms hold her close. But she was scared. Leo wanted this child so very much—she knew the depth of his longing—and she dreaded his reaction. He would be baffled, angry. He would blame her perhaps. And he'd be right to. After all he'd done for her, she had let him down with the one thing she could have given him.

Her body felt sore and tender, but her heart? How did that feel? Right now, there was a worrying void. Was that because for days she'd suspected something like this might happen? Or because, deep down, she'd always known she wasn't meant to bear children?

Her mother had had multiple miscarriages before Nancy was born—it was the reason her parents were so much older than those of her schoolfellows. And when, at last, a child had arrived, she had been a disappointment—a girl, and not the son her parents had wanted. For all Nancy knew, her mother could have continued for years trying for that elusive boy, until reluctantly settling for the one child. Now it looked as though her daughter couldn't manage even that.

She felt an innate sadness that the small beginnings of life had been snuffed out but, if she were honest, this pregnancy had never seemed truly real to her, though she'd hoped it would as the months passed. But now that hope had gone—time would not be her friend. Nor Leo's. How was she to tell him his dream was shattered? How on earth would she help him cope with this tragedy? In the short time they'd been wed, Nancy had experienced many difficult moments in their marriage, but this was by far the worst.

And after the grief, the anger, the recriminations, she could foresee further storms. If she were no longer pregnant, Leo would have lost his argument against her returning to work. Once they were back in London, he would have to let her live the life she chose—but that was certain to make him even less forgiving. A hard tussle lay ahead.

*

That night she managed to sleep only a few hours, and in the morning felt so worn and weary she could barely stumble down the stairs to find Zamira. There was no need for the maid to cook for them that night, she told the girl—a light supper was all they'd require, as they were to eat a full tea at the hotel. The visit to the Serafina was weighing heavily on Nancy. This afternoon she must be smart and happy, interested in whatever she saw, when she would have liked nothing better than to sleep the day away. But short of telling Leo what had happened in the night, there was no escape. And she couldn't do that—not yet, not right now.

As it turned out, there was no chance of even an hour of rest. After breakfast she went back to her room, pushed the double doors wide and laid down on the bed, hoping to doze in the pool of sunshine that spread across the counterpane. But within minutes, Zamira appeared in the doorway.

'A man downstairs,' the maid said bluntly.

Nancy propped herself upright, pushing wayward curls behind her ears and trying hard to focus. 'Who? What man?'

The girl gave a peremptory shrug. 'American boy. He want to speak to you.'

With a sigh, Nancy swung her legs out of bed and shuffled her feet into raffia sandals. She followed the maid down to the hall where the girl promptly disappeared, escaping to the kitchen and leaving Nancy to greet her visitor. Renzo Hastings was standing awkwardly just inside the open front door.

'You wanted to see me, Renzo?' It was obvious he did, but Nancy felt dazed—from misery, from tiredness, from the surprise of unexpectedly seeing him here—and she was not making a great deal of sense.

'Yes. Sorry if you were asleep.'

'I had a bad night.' She must look even worse than she felt. 'I was just resting, that's all, but come and sit down. Can I get you a drink?'

'Nothing, thanks.' He followed her into the sitting room and sat down on the wicker rocking chair, bouncing backwards and forwards, seemingly hesitant to begin speaking. 'The thing is...'

'Yes,' she prompted.

'The thing is,' he tried again, 'I've done some thinking since I saw you last. About Riel.'

Nancy had known it would be Gabriel Sekela who had brought the boy here. Renzo appeared to think of little else.

Her head had begun to throb, but she tried to sound patient. 'And what conclusion did you reach?'

'It's not exactly a conclusion, more a hunch. All this time I've been certain the threats to Riel were because he's messing with politics.'

Nancy nodded and he went on, 'When he joined this new nationalist movement, I warned him it was dangerous. Especially as Riel was right up there organising the protests. But he was on a mission and wouldn't listen. Malfuego is really poor, but there's a small number of people—most of them white—who own all the island's assets and live in luxury. It's fairness Riel wants and a decent government.' Nancy nodded again, wondering when he was going to get to the point. 'But then I had another thought. Perhaps it's not politics after all. Perhaps it's drugs.'

That did make her start. 'Drugs?' Zamira had mentioned smuggling, but Nancy hadn't expected Renzo Hastings to be so aware. Although why not? His past wasn't exactly the purest. 'I suppose it's not surprising that it happens here,' she said, 'but is it a major problem?'

'It's becoming one, and Riel wants to stamp it out before it gets too much of a hold.'

'Your friend is ambitious. He must have upset a lot of people.' She'd already realised that the threats against Gabriel could come from any number of directions.

'So…' Renzo paused. 'Although I've always thought it was the political stuff that would make Riel a target, I'm not as sure now.'

'It certainly looked like the political stuff when we saw him attacked outside the Assembly building,' Nancy said. 'But now you've mentioned drugs—'

'Exactly.' Renzo leaned forward. 'That burglary at my house—it wasn't usual. I mean, we don't usually get burgled, but there was something about it that didn't seem right to me.'

It hadn't seemed right to Nancy either, but when she spoke she was cautious. 'What makes you think that?'

Renzo's expression had become uneasy and he looked down at his plimsolled feet. It seemed as though he was finally getting to the reason for his visit. 'The only thing that was touched was Dad's desk, and that was ransacked. I tackled him about it. At first, he tried to put me off, laughing at me, that kind of thing, but eventually I got him to admit there had been a document in the desk that could incriminate him.'

'Did your father say what the document was?' Now Nancy was leaning forward, too.

'Apparently he loaned money to Gibbon Bass. It was to buy a faster boat. Dad says he didn't know why the guy wanted another boat—but I don't believe him,' he finished bleakly.

'You're assuming it's being used to smuggle drugs?'

Renzo nodded miserably.

'And you think Gibbon Bass was your burglar?'

'I don't know, but I'm pretty certain it was someone who wanted to make sure they had a hold over Dad. Whatever bit of paper they were after must have stated somewhere that my father had loaned that dough.'

'But the loan could have been for anything,' Nancy objected. 'All it proves is that Mr Hastings is owed a large sum of money.'

'Dad has a stake in the boat, I'm sure. He'd have to— after all, why would you lend that much money without conditions? And the document must have detailed them. To buy a boat is okay, I guess. Dad wouldn't necessarily need to know what it was being used for, but if he's been taking a commission from any smuggling going on, then he's in it knee-deep. The loan agreement is a piece of evidence the police could use against him. He says it's in a safe now at the bank, but they could get a search warrant. Even if the paper doesn't spell out the agreement with Bass too precisely, the police will want to know why Dad would lend money without security to a man they know is a badass.'

'It might not be what you think. It's possible that Bass offered some security and the document lists it,' Nancy suggested, trying to come up with the most positive interpretation.

'Bass wouldn't have had anything to pledge. He's a bum making money out of whatever crime he can get away with. That row we saw when he was heckling Dad—he wants more cash. I got that out of my father. And I can guess why. He'll want to buy another boat, then he'll take on someone to sail it. Expand his business.'

'Your father told you that?'

'He said enough for me to join up the dots.'

'If Bass wants to borrow more money from Mr Hastings, he can't be the burglar,' Nancy reasoned. 'He'll want good relations with your father, and in any case, I can't see what possible benefit he'd gain from that document.'

'It implicates Dad, doesn't it? Bass could use it as blackmail.'

'He could, but how valuable would a rogue's black-mail be?'

'I guess that's true, but I can see Dad is in real trouble. He wouldn't say more, but I know he wants to get out of whatever this is and can't see a way. He's been hopping around like he's on hot coals ever since I got here, and I've known something wasn't right. Then Bass turning up the day after the burglary. It made me think.'

'All true, Renzo, but I can't see Bass as the kind of man who would blackmail. He doesn't need to. Look at him— he's bigger and stronger than most of the men he deals with, and I'm quite certain he's not afraid to use his strength to force people to do what he wants. If Bass had wanted that document, he would have stridden into your house, strong-armed your father, and taken it.'

They both fell silent until a sudden illumination had Nancy continue. 'I suppose it might explain why he was quarrelling with Mr Hastings the day I visited. Maybe it wasn't just about borrowing money. The document could be as dangerous to Bass as it is to your father, if it laid out details of how he was to repay the loan. If Gibbon Bass suspected the burglary threatened him, he's the kind of man I'm sure who'd be itching to find the person responsible. I've seen him in action. He made Luke Rossiter a prisoner on his boat and was dragging him up the beach to do—I don't know what. Luke was lucky that day. We were there, picnicking in the same bay, and I think that dissuaded Bass from whatever wickedness he'd planned.'

There was another silence while Renzo considered this. 'Do you think Rossiter might be involved in the smuggling, too? He's got a top job at the hotel and access to wealthy guests—he could easily be selling drugs to them.'

'If he is, then Bass has quarrelled with him as well, judging by that incident on the beach. But where does all this leave the threat to Gabriel?'

'I'm not sure,' the boy said gloomily. 'It's just that when I started to put things together, it made me feel sick. If the drugs are why Riel is being targeted, then my own father is responsible.'

'But not directly. You said yourself that he's desperate to get out of whatever trouble he's in. I doubt your father would ever be involved personally in threatening anyone.'

Renzo looked unconvinced and Nancy felt forced again to promise her help, though it was the last thing she needed at this moment. 'I'll try and find out more, Renzo. Maybe go to the hotel and talk to people about Luke Rossiter—when I feel better.'

He jumped up. 'I'm sorry, Mrs Tremayne. I shouldn't have come.'

'Nancy, and I'm glad you did. I'll let you know straightaway if I discover anything that might be useful.'

Chapter Ten

Renzo had been gone only a matter of minutes when the sound of the front door opening had Nancy wondering if he'd returned. But it was her husband and Archie arriving back, much earlier than she'd expected.

'Sorry to surprise you, darling,' Leo said, putting his head around the sitting room door. 'Isabella has carried Jackson off to talk to one of the ladies' groups she runs, and we thought we'd get some work done at home before we leave for the tea party. There's still stuff from London to sort out. But we'll be out of your hair—down in the office.'

Leo was as good as his word, only appearing to shower and change a short while before they were due to leave. In the interval, Nancy had tried to make herself look a little less ill, but the mirror told her she was haggard and much too pale. Her husband, though, seemed to find nothing amiss with her appearance. Archie wasn't so easily deceived. Meeting him in the hall, she tried to avoid his gaze, but his blue eyes were intent and she could see the questions spinning through his mind. She was grateful when he said nothing.

She had changed into a plain cotton dress in a muted shade of green, hoping she would blend into the background. And when, punctually at three o' clock, Isabella's car swept up the drive, she was glad of her dull choice. Jackson's wife, in her bright pink Cadillac and bright pink straw hat, would easily be the focus of attention. For a moment, Nancy wondered if the hat and car were deliberately ironic, but when their hostess jumped out and came to greet them, it was clear that irony was quite foreign to her.

'How are you, Nancy? Looking forward to our tea, I hope.' The way she dressed, the car she drove, fitted her perfectly. The woman was irrepressibly sunny.

Nancy greeted her with a warm smile. 'I am. I'm sure this afternoon will be splendid.' She had no real hope of matching Isabella's cheerfulness, but she tried to sound as enthusiastic as she could manage.

'Good, good, then let's be off. Mr Jago—Archie.' Isabella smiled sweetly at him. 'I wonder, would you take the front seat beside my dear Ernesto?' When he looked bemused, she added, 'My driver?'

'Right.' Archie climbed into the front of the car, while Nancy slid into the rear seat beside Isabella, and Leo took the space on the other side of their hostess.

The ride to the hotel was short, barely ten minutes, and much of it spent travelling up the Serafina's winding driveway. Glossy palm trees lined either side, and beyond them Nancy saw a sweep of trimmed lawns stretching into the distance, dotted here and there with large splashes of scarlet bougainvillea. The hotel itself was built in the style of a colonial plantation house. Had that been a sop to his parents by Ambrose Martin? A way, perhaps, of softening the anger they'd felt when he'd attacked tradition by tearing down a sugar mill that had been in the family for generations. To Nancy's mind, though, the architecture resonated uncomfortably with the region's terrible history.

Luke Rossiter was waiting on the front steps, standing between two massive white pillars with potted palms on either side, their leaves rustling in the slight breeze that had sprung up. He glided down the stairs to greet them as the car came to a halt. Nancy thought he looked sheepish and, after yesterday's fiasco, it would be no wonder. Not to mention the possibility of criminality that Renzo Hastings had raised only a few hours ago. But Luke's greeting was effusive and betrayed no awkwardness.

'Welcome to the Serafina,' he said grandly. 'It will be my pleasure to show you around our wonderful hotel.'

'And mine, too. I am Virginie Lascelles.'

The housekeeper had appeared from behind his shoulder and was smiling broadly. Nancy had a moment of panic, desperate that Virginie would not mention they had met before, but catching the older woman's eyes, she saw a definite wink and knew she was safe. Perhaps Virginie had realised that Leo was ignorant of his wife's foray into town.

'Yes. Quite.' Luke sounded annoyed, momentarily losing the strangled accent. 'Miss Lascelles is our housekeeper and will be happy to answer any questions you may have on that particular aspect of the hotel.'

His tone suggested it was highly unlikely they would, and it seemed he was intent on diminishing Virginie's status. Nancy had not particularly liked him before, but now she took him in positive dislike. And even more so, when he turned slightly and made a grab for the hand of the young girl who had followed him down the steps and been standing shyly to one side. Ambrose Martin's daughter, Anya, looked as beautiful today, Nancy thought, as she had the previous evening—long, dark hair, soft brown eyes, and wearing a dress of buttercup yellow that flattered her slender figure.

'And this is Anya Martin,' Rossiter continued. 'But, of course, you've already met each other at Mr Garcia's house.

Anya is learning the ropes, so to speak, and I'm enjoying teaching her.'

The sentiment should have been warm, unexceptional, but his smile was too slick and he held the girl's hand a little too long.

He ushered them up the steps and into a large circular space, the floor tiled a brilliant white and with walls hung, floor to ceiling, with landscapes of Malfuego. Nancy found the effect dizzying, as though she were being taken on a high-speed tour of the island.

'This is the atrium where our Reception staff are available twenty-four hours a day.' Rossiter waved his hand at the long, polished desk, curving its way around the circle. 'But let me walk you through the rest of the hotel and around our extensive gardens.'

A grand piano stood opposite the desk and a pianist was running through a selection of popular music, moving without pause from one piece to another. He wore a sequinned black jacket, a glittering totem amid the formally attired couples relaxing in cushioned chairs. The men were in suits despite the eighty-degree heat outside, and the women in flowered tea dresses. An elderly lady, leaning heavily on her stick, and with legs mutilated by mosquito bites, shuffled past them towards the lift. The hotel clearly attracted an older generation and one that looked extremely wealthy.

'We have a number of sporting facilities if you would care to see them,' Luke Rossiter said quickly, his eyes following Nancy's gaze. It seemed he was eager to dispel the notion that the young and active were no part of the Serafina's clientèle. 'There are indoor and outdoor swimming pools, tennis courts—we're building a squash court, too—and afterwards our guests can relax in a spa that is the most up-to-date in the Caribbean.'

He said these last words with a flourish, a satisfied smile filling his face. Nancy guessed that becoming a deputy manager at the hotel had meant a considerable promotion and he was intent on extracting as much glory from it as he could.

The strains of *Unchained Melody* were left behind as their small party, including Anya, dutifully followed in Rossiter's footsteps: in and out of lifts, up and down stairs, around corners, across lawns and past flower beds, until they ended their grand tour in one of the hotel's most expensive bedrooms.

At some point on their journey, they had lost Isabella—knowing the Serafina extremely well, she must have taken the opportunity to slip away. Nancy wished she could have joined her. Her body had begun to ache badly and she felt herself gradually falling into a mist of discomfort. Given last night's events, she supposed it was inevitable, but she could say nothing of her troubles—for now, at least. But when was she to tell Leo the dreadful news? She felt haunted, longing to share her pain, but fearful of the result.

By the time their small group crowded through the doorway of the spacious, sea-facing room, Leo, too, was looking fazed and Archie decidedly tetchy. His expression said plainly that they had come for tea and when were they going to get it?

Not yet it appeared. They had to stand nodding agreement while Rossiter pointed out the luxury of velour dressing gowns, the fine cotton bedsheets, the sumptuous bathroom and a brand-new innovation—a portable radio the guests could take with them wherever they wished. And look at that view! They did as they were told, following him onto the large balcony. The view *was* magnificent—the sea a deep, deep blue, and thickly frilled with white, as the waves pounded on the rocks below.

'The Serafina is built on a corner site,' he said. 'On this side of the hotel, it's the Atlantic. The coast here is wild and precipitous. When we get to the conservatory—that's where we'll be serving you tea—you'll see the contrast. In comparison, the Caribbean is amazingly placid.'

Caribbean wavelets against Atlantic breakers, a lullaby versus an overture. But it was the neighbouring terrace rather than the sea that caught Nancy's attention. The balcony was covered in tubs of flowers and, among the blooms, she saw a man looking out over the ocean. But the woman seated beside him was staring at her feet, her arms crossed, hugging herself fiercely. As Nancy watched, the man gave up his contemplation of nature and leaned towards his companion, speaking urgently.

The woman continued to ignore him, and after he'd tried several times unsuccessfully to garner her attention, she reached down into her handbag and drew out a packet of cigarettes. Very slowly she lit one, blowing a ring of smoke past the man and out towards the sea. Somehow the small vignette crystallised Nancy's feelings about the hotel. So much luxury. So much comfort. So much money. But at its heart, a lack of joy.

A large bird landed on the balcony and the husband rose to shoo it away. 'I saw a similar bird the other morning,' Nancy said. 'I wondered what it might be.' By now the creature had taken flight, circling in the clear air and landing on the rocks below, where it sat hunched against the spray.

'That's a tern,' Luke said with confidence.

'No.' Anya's tone was quiet. 'It's a skimmer. It's very like a tern but has a longer bill. It uses it to feed by flying low over the water and skimming the surface for small fish.' And when he leaned forward as if to challenge her, she said, 'I should know, Luke. I've lived my entire life here.'

'What was it like growing up in Malfuego?' Nancy asked, genuinely interested and glad to see that Anya had spirit.

'Wonderful. Sunshine, beaches, sea.'

It sounded an ideal childhood, though to Nancy it felt as though the girl was trying too hard to inject happiness into her voice.

'It must have been a paradise to grow up in,' she responded. 'But did you ever travel abroad?'

Anya gave a smile that lit her whole face. 'We used to holiday in America—on the East coast, and several times in California. Once we spent a whole month in Brazil, but that was before…'

She left the sentence open, and in her mind Nancy filled it for her. Before Jacinta Martin, before her mother, had taken off into the unknown, were the words that remained unsaid.

Chapter Eleven

At long last, Rossiter led them back to the ground floor and into the large conservatory that ran along one side of the hotel, its tall glass doors leading out to a terrace that fronted a very different sea. The sound of splashing water against rocks trickled through one of the doors that stood open. Tables covered in crisp white linen greeted them, alongside sturdy wicker chairs with blue striped cushions. A row of waiters stood to attention along one side of the room. One of their number came forward and escorted them to a long table, set for ten, that faced the sea. Isabella was already there, and Nancy sank gratefully down into the next chair, her body aching and her heart leaden.

Archie, she noticed, stood to one side, waiting for the rest of the party to catch up. She saw his expression visibly brighten when he noticed the waiting tiers of sandwiches, scones, and cakes.

But they were not yet to eat or rest—Nancy was forced to her feet once more when the older generation of Martins walked into the room and Anya came forward to introduce her grandparents. The elderly woman was dressed entirely in black, as though she had come from a funeral. Nancy thought the outfit badly out of place in a setting that was meant for pleasure, but when the woman opened her tightly-pursed mouth for the first time, the dress, the gloves, the bag, were a perfect fit. The voice was thin and sharp, as though honed by a whetstone.

'Eugénie Martin,' the woman announced. Her imperious expression made Nancy feel she should curtsy.

'And my grandfather.' Anya stood back for the silver-haired man to shake hands with Nancy.

'I am Lionel, Mrs Tremayne.'

At first sight, his weather-lined face and stubby silver thatch made him seem more congenial than his wife, but when Nancy looked directly into his eyes, she saw a watchfulness that was hardly inviting.

At that moment, the tall figure of Ambrose Martin, who had been invisible since their arrival at the hotel, appeared in the doorway, his badly creased white linen jacket suggesting the haste with which he'd arrived. He dashed over to the small party, waving to them to take their seats at the table.

'Do stop flapping your arms, Ambrose,' his mother said, and obediently he subsided.

When everyone was seated, Nancy was glad to find herself opposite Anya. This afternoon had made her curious as to how this family worked. Or didn't work, if Virginie were correct. And it seemed she was. Lionel and Eugénie Martin, together at the foot of the table, sat straight-backed and inexpressive, neither making any attempt at conversation.

When Lionel eventually spoke, it was to ask Isabella, 'Is Jackson coming?'

'I doubt it.' Eugénie answered for her. 'He'll be much too busy making money.' The voice was now razor-edged.

'He is coming, Lionel. He should be here soon,' Isabella answered peaceably. It would take more than Eugénie Martin to disturb her, Nancy thought.

There was a general flurry of activity as several stands

of finger sandwiches made their way to the table. The older Martins took nothing, but accepted a cup of tea each. Almost immediately, though, the elderly woman rejected it.

'There is a stain on this cup, Ambrose.' It seemed she was willing only to speak to her husband or her son.

'I'm sorry, Mama. I'll get it changed immediately.' He signalled to one of the waiters, but when he saw his mother's thunderous look, added, 'And I'll talk to housekeeping.'

'You can, but you won't get anywhere. And what do you expect?' She gave a dismissive little snort. 'With an African in charge.'

'Miss Lascelles is very good at her job, Grandmama.' Anya was showing spirit again. Behind those pansy-soft eyes, there was evidently a strong young woman.

'But not quite good enough,' her grandmother replied, giving Anya a terrifying stare.

They had progressed to jam and scones by the time Jackson Garcia arrived. He strode across the conservatory to them, a wide smile on his face, his turquoise and yellow shirt the gaudy flag he chose to fly. Mrs Martin glowered darkly.

'You're late,' she snapped, glaring at his shirt so fiercely it was a wonder it escaped incineration. 'This is supposed to be afternoon tea.'

'True. And I'm looking forward to it.'

Jackson was still smiling. He was not about to apologise for his tardiness or his choice of clothes. 'I'm late because I've just taken a call from Bombay.' He bent his head to peer down the table at Leo, who had been given the seat of honour at the top. 'Joshi isn't coming after all, my friend. His wife has been taken to hospital. We'll have to manage without him.'

'Who is Joshi?' Lionel Martin asked.

'My expert on Indian art.'

Lionel looked sceptical. 'An Indian? And Indian art?

Really? You must be beginning to regret your gallery.'

'Not a bit. There's bound to be a few setbacks, but we'll get there. It's what this island needs, Lionel—a push into the twentieth century. And about time, too. We're halfway through it already.'

Isabella sent him a look that Nancy interpreted as a warning. Jackson Garcia was tolerated, it seemed, but only just, and tolerated no doubt because of his immense wealth.

The silence, as they munched their way through the scones, was suddenly shattered by the raucous beat of a steel band, the noise floating towards them through the open glass doors. Nancy shifted to one side of her seat and, turning, could just make out a red-painted boat bobbing in the distance.

'It must be the *Jolly Roger!*' Jackson laughed aloud, and when he saw Nancy's puzzled expression, said, 'It's a pirate ship got up especially for the tourists. The rum punch will be flowing this afternoon.'

'Presumably that is the kind of twentieth century push you have in mind for Malfuego?' Mrs Martin's voice was ice.

'Not at all. And you know that, Eugénie. It's culture I'm after. Culture with a capital C.'

'We already have culture. Our own culture, though I fear it's one you don't recognise. This island has a long and glorious history. Why not celebrate that?'

'Long, certainly, but not that glorious. Tossed between European powers—Spain, France, Britain. A fairly spotted history, I think you'll agree. And one founded on privilege and race.'

'And your bright new world, what is that founded on but money?' She almost spat the words. 'How different is that?'

'In terms of money, not that different. It's how we make it—a good deal more pleasantly.' He kept his voice calm, though Nancy could sense the anger bubbling beneath. But then Jackson threw up his hands in surrender. 'Worlds die, Eugénie, and surely this is a happier one. If my plans succeed, the island will turn its back on poverty. People will have a better life. As long as we don't allow the firebrands to take over, that is. God knows what havoc they would create.'

'Another scone, perhaps?' Ambrose looked hopefully around the table and signalled to the waiter to bring more. If they were eating, he must reason, they couldn't be bickering. He was seconded in his attempts to save the tea party from disaster by his daughter.

'Cook has made some beautiful tarts,' she said. 'It's her own recipe for lemon curd.' Anya sounded a little desperate.

Curd tarts, scones, jam and cream, smoked salmon that had travelled thousands of miles. This afternoon had been a surreal experience, and when Nancy glanced across at Archie, he grimaced. He, too, must be wondering what on earth they were doing here.

Jackson had now joined Leo at the top of the table and the two of them were deep in conversation. Her husband, it seemed, found nothing odd about the afternoon. He looked completely happy, immersed in discussing Jackson's plans and oblivious to his surroundings. The thought that she was about to destroy his happiness had Nancy quail and look around for distraction.

Several of the smaller tables had gradually filled with guests, and she became aware that people's heads were turning towards the restaurant entrance. Glancing over her shoulder, she saw Gabriel Sekela standing in the doorway, and behind him a queue of people.

The Martins had seen Gabriel, too.

He cut a striking figure, tall and slim, and despite his injuries, radiating energy.

Lionel glared at his son. 'What is *he* doing here?'

Nervously, Ambrose got up from his chair. 'He's a tour guide, Papa. He has brought his group for tea.'

'He belongs in the kitchen, with the rest of his compatriots,' Eugénie Martin said. 'See to it.'

'There are twenty people in his party, Mama. Twenty teas. The hotel cannot afford to lose such business.'

'You prostitute yourself, and for what?'

'To make a living.' His voice was taut.

'You could have done that well enough without constructing this circus.'

Ambrose looked as though he were about to retaliate, but must have decided against it.

When Nancy turned back to the table, she stared. A moment of revelation.

Anya was looking towards the entrance, too, but not at the gaggle of visitors who were now being seated at tables to one side of the conservatory. She was looking at Gabriel and he was smiling back at her. His eyes told their own story. This was the girl that Zamira had spoken of! It was Anya Martin for whom she had been forsaken. It was Anya Martin with whom Gabriel had fallen in love.

Anya sat, her hands folded primly in her lap, but her face a picture of suppressed joy. No-one else noticed—at least Nancy thought not, but then she became conscious of Luke Rossiter's clenched fists and granite face. He had seen that look and understood.

Luke sprang up, scraping his chair noisily behind him. 'I'll get him out of here.'

'No.' Anya's voice was firm. 'Mr Sekela has as much right to be here as anyone else.'

She jumped up, too, and walked quickly across the restaurant to join Gabriel, lingering by the entrance. Her grandmother looked after her in astonishment as first Anya, then Gabriel, disappeared. 'You need to have a care for your daughter, Ambrose. She needs discipline. She is becoming insolent.'

With that, both the older Martins rose from their seats as though pulled by the same pair of strings and, without bothering to say goodbye to their fellow guests, stalked from the room.

The small charade left Nancy bewildered. She had to pinch herself to remember she was still living in the middle of the twentieth century—the scene she had just witnessed would have been at home a hundred years ago. She was depressed and sick at heart. In pain and tireder than ever. Her body had not yet recovered from last night's ordeal and all she wanted was to be home.

Jackson had broken off his conversation with Leo and was nodding towards the empty doorway. 'There goes one of the firebrands I mentioned. The chief of them. But not for much longer.'

Isabella looked hard at him.

'No more pamphlets, at least,' he said. 'No more posters either. Did you hear that Bellamys had their press smashed to pieces? Our young champion will find it difficult to get another printer to work for him.'

Isabella put out a hand. 'Jackson—'

'Not me, darling. But fortuitous, wouldn't you say?'

Nancy didn't believe him. If he wasn't behind the destruction of the printing press and the attacks on Gabriel, who was? She wondered what Leo had got himself into by agreeing to work with this man. What had Archie said in Venice? That Leo was a great judge of paintings, but not so much of people. And how true that had proved, so why not now on this island?

Archie pushed back his chair and surprised her by walking round to hers. 'Do you want to go?' he asked.

'We'll have to wait…' She gestured to her husband and Jackson, who had resumed their talk.

'I'll get the bloke on the desk to ring for a taxi.'

'But Leo?'

'He'll be discussing this benighted gallery for hours yet.'

As Archie was speaking, Leo pushed back his chair and walked over to her, dropping a kiss on the top of her head. 'Do you mind, Nancy? We've a few things to talk over—now that Joshi isn't coming. Archie will take you home.'

*

Without another word, Archie made for the reception desk, but he'd gone only a moment when there was a loud crash from the terrace outside. A table had gone flying and a chair was soon to join it.

Luke Rossiter was fighting Gabriel, while Anya, frozen to the spot, stood aghast. A loud crash reverberated through the conservatory. Rossiter had grabbed his opponent by the shoulders and banged his head violently against one of the glass doors, at the same time kneeing his opponent in the groin.

Nancy jumped to her feet, her heart thumping. Gabriel was an injured man, barely able to defend himself, and Rossiter's face wore a vicious smile. She glanced wildly around the table—someone must stop this fight.

The young man, handicapped by broken ribs, had staggered forward, almost toppling over the terrace to the sea below. Was that Rossiter's intention? Nancy felt her throat tighten and her hands turn clammy with fear. But as she watched, Gabriel, hardly able to breathe and doubled over in pain, somehow managed to haul himself straight. He pulled his arm back, his hand crunched into a fist. Nancy's eyes widened. In slow motion, it seemed, the blow arced in the air and, with a loud crack, connected with Rossiter's chin, flooring the man and leaving him gasping.

Anya gave a small clap of her hands and then, seeming to remember her father's assistant was her mentor, wiped her face clear of expression. But only until Gabriel put his arm around her and kissed her gently on the cheek.

Ambrose was standing close to Nancy and she saw the horrified look on his face. Was that a reaction to the violence or to his daughter being kissed? For Anya's sake, she hoped it was the former.

'Shall we go?' Archie had returned from the atrium and was beside her. 'The taxi's outside.'

Chapter Twelve

Archie took the rear seat beside her. It would have seemed too obvious if he'd chosen otherwise, though part of Nancy wished he had. She could feel the warmth of his body, smell the freshness of pine—soap, shampoo?—sense the solidity of him. Too close. Her hands were still trembling from the violence she'd witnessed, and she wanted to pour out her feelings to him. But Archie didn't speak, and she felt too shaken to begin.

It was only when they reached the front door of the villa that he began to talk. 'What's going on?' He stood squarely in her path and it was clear he expected an answer.

Nancy glanced around as though seeking inspiration. Dusk was close and the scent of tree sap and blossom was strong. A tiny whistling frog had begun its call and soon, she knew, the garden would be alive with the piping of these invisible creatures, their chorus only fading with the coming of the day.

'You mean about Gabriel Sekela?'

'No, I mean about you.'

'Nothing's going on.' She tried for a confidence she didn't feel. 'Why should it be?'

'I'll tell you why. Your face is chalk white, you've hardly spoken a word all afternoon, and it was obvious you were desperate to leave the hotel. So, what *is* going on, Nancy?'

It was his use of her name that broke down her defences and, without warning, the tears spilled down her cheeks.

'Here,' he said roughly, handing her a clean handkerchief, then took her arm and steered her through the door and into the long sitting room that fronted the ocean. He pushed her down onto the sofa and took a seat opposite, while she dabbed ineffectually at her cheeks. 'Something is wrong and you're going to tell me.'

Nancy didn't know how she was going to say the words, but Archie was looking his most menacing—and his most concerned. Somehow, she stuttered out, 'I've lost the baby.'

His eyes widened and he shifted in his chair, trying to take in the news. 'I'm sorry.' It was the conventional thing to say, but he said it as though he meant it, which surprised her. He'd not been exactly joyful when they'd announced a baby was on the way. 'When did it happen?'

She twisted his handkerchief into a knot. 'Last night,' she mumbled.

'Then you shouldn't have gone to the hotel. You should have rested today.'

'I couldn't. Not without—'

He looked hard at her. 'You haven't told Leo,' he said.

She shook her head wordlessly.

It was a while before he spoke again. 'Is there a reason for that?'

'I couldn't, Archie. I couldn't tell him. He'll be devastated.'

'He will, whenever you tell him. And he's going to realise pretty soon that things aren't right. Better now before, well, you know…'

'Before I should look pregnant, you mean? I know I have to tell him—it's finding the right time.'

'There is no right time. You must know that.' He leaned

across and took her hand and she felt some of his strength seep into her. 'Once Leo knows, you can talk about it together. Share with him how you feel.'

Nancy hung her head but said nothing.

'That's right, isn't it?' he pressed.

'I don't know how I feel.' The words seemed to be dragged out of her. 'My body feels as though it's been through a mincer. But losing the baby… it's how Leo will react that I'm dreading.'

Archie let go of her hand and got up to walk to the wall of windows that opened onto the veranda, standing there for several minutes and looking out as the last golden sliver of sun slipped behind the horizon and the shadows deepened over a blue-black sea.

'You're bound to be affected, and not just Leo,' he said, turning to face her. 'When you least expect it. I've seen it happen—to my brother's wife.'

Nancy got up and joined him at the window. 'You may be right. I'm not sure. I have this sense, deep down, that I was never meant to have a baby, but I've tried to be happy for Leo's sake. And now I've failed him, and he's been so good to me—keeping me safe, looking after me, loving me.' She felt the tears begin to well again.

'What you need is a glass of grappa,' Archie said prosaically. 'Or failing that, rum.'

She tried hard to swallow the tears. 'Is alcohol always the solution?'

'Pretty much. Let's raid the kitchen. If we can't find any, at least we can get some coffee. I'm afloat on tea.'

'But Zamira… I'd rather not see her right now.' Nancy hesitated, wondering whether to say anything of the maid's condition. But Archie seemed as close to her now as he had in Venice and she wanted to confide in him. 'Zamira is pregnant, too,' she said quietly.

'Yeah, I know.'

Nancy gaped. 'How do you know?'

'I've been in town the last two evenings and she's part of the local gossip.'

'Oh, poor girl. That's even more reason not to upset her. We'd better stay clear of the kitchen.'

'She won't be there, remember? She's got the night off — probably gone home to Ma.'

'You're right. I told her she could leave us a cold meal, though after the tea we've just had I doubt I'll manage even that.'

Following Archie downstairs to the kitchen, Nancy watched while he rooted through several cupboards.

'No rum. There should be a coffee pot, though.' He stood on tiptoe and began to search the tallest wall cupboard, pulling out a bundle of tea towels as he went. 'What are these doing here? Phew, they stink.'

Nancy went over and took the linen from him, holding the cloths to her nose and then rapidly pushing them away. 'Paraffin? It smells like paraffin.'

'I'd say so, but they're soaked in the stuff. How did that happen? And why hide them away?'

'Perhaps she means to wash them later.' The linen reminded Nancy of the nightdress, also awaiting a wash, and thrust into another cupboard. For the moment, that was her secret. She wondered what secrets Zamira might be keeping.

After the paraffin, the smell of fresh coffee was welcome. Archie pushed a mug towards her. 'This will do you good.'

She took a sip. 'It's strong.'

'It needs to be. Drink it—then you'll be fit enough to come flying with me next time.'

'What!'

'It's early days but I'm making progress. A few more lessons and I may even go solo. You'd like it. I saw your face when we circled the island the day we arrived. You were fascinated.'

She realised then how much Archie must see when she was unaware of his notice. 'It did look beautiful,' she agreed. 'But would your instructor mind? Is there even room for a third person?'

'There's a seat at the rear. And I'm a paying customer, so why would he mind? Maybe the day after tomorrow? You should be feeling better by then. But right now, drink your coffee.'

Obediently, she took another sip while he watched her. He seemed to be weighing in his mind what to say and eventually broke the silence. 'It was all for Leo then?'

Somehow, she no longer minded talking about it. At least, not to Archie. 'I suppose so. He wanted a child so much and when it happened, I tried to feel good about it.'

'But you didn't?'

When she didn't answer, he looked at her steadily. 'Having the baby may have been a mistake, but marrying the wrong man—that's the real mistake, isn't it?'

Nancy's reaction was immediate, jumping off her stool and slamming her mug down so hard that a large puddle of coffee spread across the countertop. 'I thought we'd agreed to forget that particular refrain,' she said angrily.

'You may have agreed, but I didn't. And I won't, because I'm right.'

She turned her back on him and rushed towards the kitchen door, but he followed and grabbed her by the hand.

'The truth always hurts, Nancy.' She could feel his breath on her cheeks, feel her hand in his.

They were standing inches from each other and for what

seemed an age, he held on to her. She had an insane desire to pummel her fists into his chest and an equally insane desire for his arms to wrap her round and pull her close. With an enormous effort, she wrenched herself free and made for the stairs.

Chapter Thirteen

Archie's words formed a tight coil in Nancy's mind, entangled and hurtful. That she had married the wrong man. That her confused reaction to losing her baby was the result of a bad decision. The suspicion that Archie might be right made it even more difficult to tell her husband the dreadful news.

For several days, though, she was spared the need since Leo was hardly at home. Now that Joshi was indefinitely delayed, her husband spent hours in the office with Cy Devaux, discussing and adjusting detailed plans of their particular sections of the gallery or making further visits together to the proposed site. Meetings between Jackson and the construction company were apparently going better now and, altogether, Leo seemed content.

Should she wait, Nancy wondered, until they returned to London before she broke the news? Being on home territory might soften the blow, make it less likely that Leo would react with anger. Here on this tropical island, emotions seemed heightened and less under control—she had only to think of the appalling fight at the Serafina. But was that simply an excuse, when in truth she was guilty of a hateful cowardice?

She had still not made up her mind what to do when, a few days after the tea party, Archie whistled his way into the sitting room several hours after Leo had left. Nancy was surprised to see his figure in the doorway, having assumed he'd gone with her husband to Jackson's office.

'I'm off to play with planes,' he said casually. 'My instructor can fit me in at twelve. Are you coming?'

They had hardly spoken since their argument in the kitchen and Nancy had pushed the idea of flying to the back of her mind, vowing to keep out of Archie's way as much as possible. His nonchalance today vexed her, and she had to bite back a tart retort.

'No, thank you. I have things to do here.' She spoke in her primmest voice.

'I can see you're busy.' A pile of magazines lay scattered at her feet. 'You don't want to come, fair enough, but be honest—with me, at least.'

She was stung by the veiled attack. 'I don't want to come with you. Is that honest enough?' She picked up a magazine and pretended to read, waiting for him to go.

Instead, he walked over to the sofa and sat down beside her. Then took the magazine and turned it round. 'It's usually easier to read this way up.'

Nancy flushed with annoyance. 'Hadn't you better get going?' She peered at the clock hanging on the opposite wall. It was shaped like a wooden barrel and difficult to read. 'It's eleven already.'

'So it is. Which is why I'm here asking you to come. You know you want to.'

She lowered the magazine and turned to him. His blue eyes looked guilelessly back, then he pulled a face mimicking her scowl, and despite a still sharp anger, she couldn't stop the beginnings of a smile.

'You see. I'm right. Come on, the cab's outside.'

'But I'm not dressed.'

'What do you mean, you're not dressed? You've got clothes on, haven't you? And I'll lend you the Biggles glasses, if you must have them.'

Nancy tried and failed to stop a laugh. Archie was impossible, but so was the feeling in her heart. She wanted to spend the day with him and knew she shouldn't want it quite so much.

*

It was good to be away from *Belvoir*. The days since her miscarriage had been long and fretful and, although her body was mending, there was little to distract her mind. She had read her way through most of the books she'd brought to the island and the magazines that had been left in the house were flimsy and uninteresting. As for keeping busy with housework, it failed to occupy even an hour—Zamira saw to that. But this morning was an unexpected bonus, though it meant swallowing her annoyance.

Once out of the villa gates, they turned away from the town, driving in the opposite direction, and very soon Nancy noticed that the landscape had become flatter and more scrubby. Less populated, too, with small wooden houses only occasionally appearing along the roadside.

Archie barely looked out of the window, but then he'd already done this journey a number of times. And maybe, she thought, he had to prepare himself for flying. He was the last person she'd expect to be nervous, but you never knew.

'What kind of plane is it?' she asked.

'A Cessna, if that means anything to you.'

'It doesn't, but I imagine it's a small aircraft.'

He nodded and closed his eyes.

'How many flights do you have to do before you go solo?'

Archie opened his eyes again. 'It depends. I'll be going

for my licence in England and it's likely to be more rigorous there. At least fifty hours' flying all told, I should think, and a good bit of that solo. But Malfuego has given me a useful start. I know my way around the instrument panel now—not that different to a car dashboard.'

'Will you actually be at the controls today?'

He grinned. 'I will, but don't panic—the instructor has his own set.'

They were now in sight of the sea again and, conscious of the Atlantic breakers in the distance, Nancy had a moment's doubt. The island had numerous sandy bays, but they lay between even more numerous rocky headlands. And it looked as though they were heading for just such a place. She prayed the instructor was good and his set of controls even better.

The taxi dropped them off at a small white-painted hut, and almost immediately a large man with a big smile came out to greet them.

'Archie! You choose a good day for flying. Tomorrow or the next, it rains. Not so great, eh?'

They had not seen a drop of rain since arriving, though Nancy had read that from May to October was the island's rainy season. A break from the overwhelming heat would be welcome.

'And you bring me a guest.'

'I hope that's all right,' she said, shooting an accusing glance at Archie, but the man smiled more broadly and held out his hand.

'Welcome. My name Marlon. Happy to entertain guests.'

'This is Mrs Tremayne,' Archie offered.

'Nancy,' she said, hoping that Marlon's idea of entertainment didn't involve any looping of loops.

He was a professional, she reminded herself, and a mature

114

man, but when they walked out to the plane, her nervousness returned. The airfield was on a promontory, and the one runway—a grass strip—seemed to peter out to nothingness, falling away into the sea with rocks on either side.

Marlon grinned at her, guessing her thoughts. 'It safe, Mrs Nancy. Here, I help you up.'

The instructor took the right-hand seat, and Archie the left, while Nancy scrambled to the rear of the aircraft. Before he started the engine, Marlon went through a checklist—rudder and brake pedals, throttle, flaps. There was someone talking to him on the radio and she craned her neck to see if she could spot the control tower, but all she could make out was the small hut from which Marlon had emerged. Checks complete, he started the engine and they were off, taxiing slowly from the parking area to the top of the runway.

'When does Archie fly the plane?' she asked.

'He get his chance.'

And then they were off, the instructor advancing the throttle and rapidly accelerating down the runway. 'Speed coming up,' he said. 'Temperature and pressure all good.'

The noise was deafening, but just as Nancy wondered how she would cope with an hour of this, the vibration faded as the wings started to develop lift and Marlon pulled back the control yoke. 'Rotate. And we flying!'

She watched as scrubland disappeared from her window and sea and sky took its place. Once they had left the airfield behind and were flying straight and level, Marlon handed the controls over to his pupil. 'Okay, Archie, ease in, try some turns.'

Archie took up the invitation and performed a few gentle turns left and right, then a climb and a descent. 'What do you think?' he asked.

She guessed he must be speaking to her. 'It's good.' She

looked down at the intense blue of the sea, then the narrow shoreline at the edge of her vision. On a distant hill, a coffee plantation with an estate house spread itself before her, the surrounding forest reaching down at this point to meet the water. Two small vessels were moored in the bay, evidently waiting for coffee to be loaded, and a muddy creek oozed out between the trees, spilling across the sand into the boisterous surf. And all around, lush vegetation.

'In fact, it's wonderful,' she said.

'*You* try next time, Mrs Nancy,' Marlon said.

'I'd love to,' she heard herself reply, not quite knowing why, except that it was a moment of pure exhilaration. A moment of freedom: from the villa, from its tensions, from the burden of gratitude she carried. Freedom to soar in the company of a friend. A friend, she repeated to herself severely.

They flew for over half an hour, Archie at the controls, until they were once more approaching the airfield. Nancy heard the flaps go down and then Marlon was talking over the radio again.

'This is the bit I haven't tried yet,' Archie said. 'It's pretty scary. You need to make just the right turn at just the right time and get the speed and rate of descent correct, too. And there are some nasty crosswinds on this island.'

'Next time, Archie,' Marlon said. 'You ready, I think.'

The instructor brought the nose of the aircraft up, putting it into the correct position, and closed the throttle. Gradually, its speed drained away and the little Cessna settled onto its main wheels. Straight as an arrow, it hit the centre of the runway and taxied to the parking area.

When Nancy climbed down from the aircraft, her cheeks were flushed and her eyes bright.

Archie laughed aloud. 'You need to fly, Mrs Tremayne. I

can see that.'

Marlon was agreeing when he turned and looked over his shoulder. 'Someone callin'.'

Nancy followed his glance. A small figure was running towards them, arms waving wildly.

'What the Dickens?' Archie peered into the distance. 'It's bloody Renzo Hastings. Trust him to ruin a glorious afternoon.'

Renzo had never been a favourite with Archie, and coming after the excitement of the flight, the boy was probably the last person he wanted to see. Or, for that matter, Nancy wanted to see. But Renzo was still calling and still running towards them. It seemed he was in a panic and, out of nowhere, Nancy was gripped with a terror she hadn't known since her days of being stalked. Something was badly wrong, but this time it had nothing to do with Philip March, her stalker.

'What the hell are you doing here?' Archie asked roughly, when the gasping boy finally drew abreast.

'I had to come.' Renzo was bent nearly double, struggling for breath. 'I had to tell you.' And when he looked up, Nancy saw he was crying.

'What on earth—?' she began.

'Riel. It's Riel.' The boy made a loud gulping sound. 'He's dead.'

Chapter Fourteen

For a moment, Nancy was shocked into silence. She stared vacantly at Renzo, who stared back, his face frozen but his eyes wild.

'Gabriel Sekela is dead?' she asked hoarsely. 'But how?'

When the boy didn't answer, Marlon stepped forward and took Renzo's arm in a firm grip as though to shake him out of the coma he'd fallen into. 'How?' he repeated.

The deeper voice seemed to waken Renzo and he stuttered, 'Fire. The house—it burnt down.'

'And you're saying that Gabriel was at home at the time?' Nancy was trying to make sense of what appeared senseless.

'Of course he was,' Renzo said bitterly. 'They waited until he was in the house and then set fire to it. They wanted him dead and now they've got their wish.' His voice broke, cracking with pain.

'But couldn't it have been an accident?' Nancy was willing it to be, though she had a sinking feeling that it was no more an accident than the death she'd investigated in Venice.

Marlon nodded. 'More than likely. Wooden houses burn. Happens all the time. A cooker catch fire, an oil lamp get pushed over.'

'It wasn't an accident.' Through his tears, Renzo's voice was harsh. 'It was deliberate.'

'How do you know that?' Archie was matter-of-fact, seemingly unaffected by the dreadful news. 'Best to go with the accident theory.'

'You might be happy to accept it,' the boy said angrily. 'But I won't rest till I find out who's killed the best friend I ever had. The best friend this island has ever had, if it only knew it.'

Renzo's furious denunciation had the small group fall silent again, until a deep rumble from afar pulled them from their thoughts. Nancy felt the ground quiver beneath her feet and her eyes went immediately to the horizon. Had Leo been right in thinking the volcano was no longer active? It seemed as though the mountain was speaking, passing judgement on Gabriel's death. And judgement on their inadequate response to such horror.

'I gotta be off,' Marlon said a trifle awkwardly. 'Someone waitin' for me.' He turned to Renzo, clasping him by the arm for a few seconds. 'Sorry for your friend, boy, but take advice, don't go accusin' people of murder. Plenty of accidents. If you live here as long as me, you know that.'

He gave Nancy a friendly handshake and clapped Archie on the back, then strode off towards the white-painted shed.

'I don't care what he says.' Renzo was obdurate. 'There are accidents. Of course I know that. But this fire was deliberate. You should see the site—there's not a thing left. They wanted to make sure of that before the fire brigade arrived. It had to be an enormous blaze. Come and see for yourself, if you don't believe me.'

Archie shrugged his shoulders. 'What good will viewing a burnt-out wreck do?'

Renzo looked as though he would burst into tears again, and Nancy said quickly, 'Naturally, we'll come with you.'

She glared at Archie, but his only response was another

shrug and a muttered, 'The cab should be here any minute. It can drop us off at Sekela's house if we really must drag ourselves there.'

We must, Nancy thought. I need to see it, if only to help me believe it was an accident. It didn't bear thinking of otherwise.

'How did you find us, Renzo?' she asked, hoping to distract herself as much as the boy.

'It wasn't easy,' he said with something of his old truculence. 'You weren't at the villa. No-one was. But then I hit on phoning Garcia's house and his wife said Archie wasn't working, he'd gone flying. I figured you'd be with him, Nancy.'

A look passed between herself and Archie but neither said a word.

*

The taxi dropped them at the corner of Gabriel's street, although track would have been a better description. A dusty, deeply pitted thoroughfare along which a straggling line of wooden houses ran to one side, and on the other an equally straggling line of trees. The houses sat atop wooden piles, and beneath was stored everything that couldn't be accommodated above—barrels, bicycles, the odd chair, even occasionally a run filled with chickens.

Nancy pointed to the wooden piles. 'Houses on stilts. Yet we're way above sea level and there's no river.'

'It's a legacy of slavery,' Archie offered. Nancy looked at him in surprise.

'I do read the occasional book,' he said tartly. 'The houses could be dismantled quickly —they're all wood and assembled without nails. They're designed to be moved from place to place as slaves changed owners. Though this lot don't look as if they've moved for a century or two.'

Nancy had to agree. The wooden piles had sunk deep into the ground, and the dirt and dust of years was now encasing a good portion of them. The houses themselves, perched precariously on their platforms, looked battered and heavily patched. Yet outside each small dwelling, scraps of earth had been cultivated and a blossoming of flowers greeted them as they made their way towards what Nancy could just glimpse—an ominous gap in the line of buildings.

Renzo had stayed silent during their walk and, from a brief glance, Nancy saw his face was rigid. He evidently believed wholeheartedly that the fire had been deliberate, and she thought he had reason. The other so-called accidents that had befallen Gabriel had seemed anything but.

They slowed their pace, almost instinctively, as they neared the yawning hole in what was a close-packed cluster of dwellings. Even from this distance the smell was pungent. Burnt timber, burnt fabric… burnt flesh.

Renzo had stopped and she looked back at him. 'Aren't you coming with us?'

He shook his head. 'I've brought you here, but I guess it won't do Gabriel any good—you don't believe me, though I know I'm right. But I can't go any further and I never want to see this place again.'

He turned then and stumbled his way back along the track. Archie raised his eyebrows. 'Well?'

'We'll look,' she said decidedly, though she would have dearly loved to follow Renzo.

In a few minutes, they arrived at the space that had once been Gabriel's house. There was absolutely nothing left, and if the young man had been inside—and it seemed he had— his body was now part of the water-soaked ashes lying in heaps on the ground. A desperate scene. At this close quarter, too, the sickly smell was overpowering, catching at the back of Nancy's throat until she felt she would choke.

She swayed on her feet but then Archie's hand was on her arm, steadying her. 'Come on. We've seen enough. If the poor bugger was in there, no-one could have saved him.'

'You lookin' for someone?'

It was a woman's voice coming from beyond the burnt wreck. She was walking down the steps from her front door and, when she came into full view, Nancy saw an impressive figure: plump and shining, dressed in bright yellow, with an orange headband tied around black curls.

'Mr Hastings asked us to look.' Nancy sounded apologetic. She felt uncomfortably like a voyeur, deriving pleasure from a fearful human tragedy.

'Oh, that one. The American?' The woman's smooth unlined face broke into a grimace. 'This morning he cryin' on my doorstep.'

'Mr Sekela was his friend.' Nancy felt upset for Renzo. The boy was genuinely grief-stricken, and this woman seemed happy to make light of it.

But then she surprised Nancy. 'Gabriel my friend, too,' the woman said. 'But his mother more. I Marissa King.'

'King? You're not…'

'Zamira's Ma? Yeah, that's me, for my sins. That no good girl.'

Nancy was about to protest when Archie said, 'We know Zamira. She works at the villa where we're staying.'

'Ah!' Mrs King nodded. 'And did that girl tell you what trouble she in?'

'Yes, she did. I'm very sorry for her,' Nancy said quickly

'Don't be. She one silly girl. And now Gabriel gone, what she goin' to do?'

Zamira must have told her mother that Gabriel was the

father of her child, Nancy realised. The girl was so distraught she had probably told the whole town.

'She go to Trinidad, to my sister,' Marissa continued. 'She don't like it, but too bad.'

With no wish to hear Zamira abused any further, Nancy pointed towards the distressing scene to one side of where they stood. 'Do you know what happened?'

'A lamp mebbe. A cooking pot. Easy enough. And that boy here one minute, then gone the next. One time the house beautiful, but it ain't cared for no longer—not since poor Mary passed.'

'Gabriel's mother? You knew her?'

'My best friend, sweetheart. Her death long and full of hurt, but her boy good, I'll say that. He look after her well and I help when I can. Zamira, too.'

'And her husband? Gabriel's father—is he on the island?'

Marissa laughed out loud. 'Mebbe. Mebbe not. He the invisible man. Mebbe Mary don' even know his name.'

If there had been no husband, Mary Sekela had done well to raise Gabriel unaided. For one thing, she had afforded a good-sized house. Even though it was no more than ashes now, Nancy could see it had occupied a much larger space than Marissa's or any of the other houses in the street.

But Marissa was speaking again, returning once more to her daughter's woes. 'And what now? A baby no-one want, and a dead father.'

Nancy steered her back to the fire. 'I imagine the blaze must have caught so quickly that the fire brigade had no chance of rescuing Gabriel.'

The woman smoothed down the sides of her yellow dress. 'It was dark. No light on the street, and the first thing I know is the smell and then I hear the crackin'. So, I go to the window and the building lit up. Like a fireball. Then the firemen come but no chance of puttin' the fire out. The water point two streets back, and by the time the hose is goin', no house. And no Gabriel.'

'You were lucky to escape. And lucky that you still have your house.'

'Sure thing, lucky,' Marissa agreed. 'But poor boy, huh? And poor Mary, for her son to end like that. He come back when she fell sick. He look after her. A clever boy, you know. Got a job as a tour guide—that ain't easy.'

'Was he always here at night?' Archie asked.

'Most nights. All day, in and out. Posting leaflets, talking talk. But most nights he come back. Why you askin'?'

'I was wondering if there was any chance that he wasn't in the house last night.'

'No chance. I saw him come home. I check chickens okay—them damned dogs are always around—and see him go in. He wave to me.'

It seemed such a poignant gesture that Nancy felt the tears gather. She swallowed them down and let Marissa continue to talk. There was a lot of grumbling about the dogs Marissa's neighbours kept but didn't control, and Nancy's mind began to wander. Then she stopped listening altogether. She was conscious there was something behind her. Someone? Someone watching them? She felt a bristling at the nape of her neck and quickly turned her head to look over her shoulder. Had there been a movement in those trees? She could see nothing, and neither Zamira's mother nor Archie seemed aware of any intruder.

She turned back to Marissa, trying to sound calm and reasoned. 'I imagine the police will investigate the fire,' she said. But before Marissa could respond, Nancy was nearly knocked off her feet by a ball travelling at speed and hitting her squarely in the legs.

'Jaden! What you doin'? You come here and apologise to the lady.' A boy of about nine shambled into view, his head hanging low.

Archie frowned at him. 'You need to be careful where you aim that ball. You've got quite a kick on you.'

The boy's head came up immediately. 'I'm good, mistah, eh?' He grinned at them.

'Maybe.' Archie bounced the ball. 'But you've got to have direction. Here.' He kicked the ball over to the boy. 'Go on. Show me. Hit that door over there.' He pointed to a small wooden hut that had been built to one side of Marissa's house.

Nancy was annoyed. Archie seemed to be trivialising what had been a terrible event, but short of dragging him away, she was forced to watch as Jaden made a short run up to the ball and then produced an almighty kick. The ball arrowed straight for the shed but, instead of hitting the door, it smashed through its small square window, shattering every pane of glass.

'Get in the house,' his mother screeched at him. 'You pay for this, boy.'

'It wasn't his fault.' Nancy started to protest but was interrupted by Archie striding towards the shed, saying over his shoulder, 'I'll fetch the ball.' Before she could stop him, he had disappeared inside.

'Please don't punish Jaden. It was my friend's fault entirely,' Nancy said.

Marissa folded her arms in a martial pose. 'We see about that. No cinema, not this week, not next.'

Archie was a long while emerging from the shed and, when he did, he wore an expression that Nancy was at a loss to interpret. 'Sorry,' he said. 'It took a while to find it. I reckon you've got another house in there.' He handed the ball over to Mrs King. 'And sorry about the broken window. That was my fault. I challenged your boy.' He put his hand in his pocket. 'Take this please. It will buy the glass at least.'

Marissa looked surprised but took the money and slipped it into her dress pocket. 'Thank you, Mister. And when you get back to that villa of yours, you tell that no good girl to get herself packed or I be callin'. I go put her on the boat myself.'

When she'd walked back into her house, Archie asked, 'What was all that stuff about Trinidad?'

'You know Zamira is pregnant? Her mother evidently believes Gabriel was the father, and that her daughter's been left on her own. I think Trinidad could be Marissa's choice of punishment.'

'Sekela refused to see her the afternoon I visited him in hospital, so I'm presuming he didn't fancy being a daddy.'

'He wasn't the father. According to Renzo, they weren't... they were simply friends,' she finished awkwardly. 'Zamira went a little crazy when Gabriel broke it off with her. Well, you've heard the stories yourself.'

Archie gave a low whistle. 'What an island, eh? And what a maid!'

They walked back along the track in silence and were almost at the main road when she asked, 'What were you doing in that shed? There was something there, wasn't there?'

'You have a suspicious mind, Nancy.'

'Only where you're concerned.'

'Not true. You suspect everyone and everything. It's unsettling.'

'Don't dodge my question. You were an age finding that ball. What were you doing?'

'Just having a scout around—I thought it might be interesting.'

'That's why you asked the boy to kick the ball there?'

'I didn't expect the young idiot to break the window. I thought he'd hit the door and I could walk over to the shed and collect the ball, but have a nose through the window at the same time. As it was, he gave me the chance to have more than a nose.'

'*Was* it interesting?'

'It depends on your viewpoint.'

She stopped walking and fixed him with a severe look. 'Don't tease, Archie.'

'I'm not teasing. I'm serious. Deadly serious—and that's literal. There were two empty paraffin cans in that shed. Marissa King said the house went up like a fireball. Paraffin is my bet.'

'So it *was* deliberate.' Nancy caught her breath. 'But the shed—Mrs King—surely not.'

'No, I don't believe so. But another King entirely? Remember the tea towels that smelt of paraffin?'

Without thinking, she reached out and clutched his hand. 'Oh my God! Zamira!'

'Well…' Archie gently disentangled her fingers from his, but she was too intent on following her train of thought to notice.

'Zamira said she would make Gabriel pay,' she said.

'Then the girl certainly carried out her threat. And I guess, if the fire was deliberate and it looks like it, Zamira is the most obvious culprit. She had a grudge.'

'Too obvious, I hope. She loved the man and it's his baby she's carrying—at least that's what she insists. What she believes.'

'If she believes that, then she's living in a world of delusion. In which case, chucking a couple of cans of paraffin and throwing a match might seem perfectly reasonable.'

They had reached the main road by now and paused

before crossing to allow a horse and cart to trot by. It was several minutes before Nancy spoke. 'How would Zamira do it, though? It would be really difficult. She would need to buy the stuff, store it in secret, then creep out of the villa, do the deed, and creep back without anyone being aware she'd gone.'

'She was staying at her mother's last night,' he pointed out. 'And it wouldn't be too difficult to buy the fuel in her time off and store it in her mother's shed. Marissa King looks a pretty busy lady—I doubt she'd have noticed anything amiss.'

'I suppose it's possible,' Nancy said unwillingly. 'And I did feel she meant that threat when she spoke to me, but I still can't believe she would do something so terrible.'

'She may have had only the haziest idea of what would happen. But there's only one way to find out. Come on, let's get moving.'

'You're going to ask her?'

'What else? She's either innocent or she'll confess.'

Nancy gave him a sideways glance. 'She could lie.'

'I reckon we'll know if she does.' Archie was unfazed. 'She's unlikely to make a convincing liar.'

'Then it's back to the villa to ask her.' Nancy quickened her pace. 'That's if she's not already packed and on her way to Trinidad.'

Chapter Fifteen

A s soon as they reached the house, Nancy hurried towards the stairs that led down to the kitchen, only for Archie to bar her way with an outstretched arm.

'Think, before you say anything. We can't accuse the girl of murder, point blank. We're making a supposition, and it's based on pretty flimsy evidence.'

The mention of 'we' gave her a glow, the feeling of being partners again, but she was determined to talk to Zamira. 'I won't do any accusing, I promise, but I must find out what she was doing last night and how that cloth came to reek of paraffin.'

When Nancy put a cautious head around the kitchen door, though, Zamira wasn't there and there was no sign she'd been there that morning. The breakfast dishes lay untouched in the sink and the floor remained unswept. Had the girl run away? Had she been consumed by guilt and done something stupid to herself? Perhaps she had meant merely to frighten Gabriel, but the blaze had spread too rapidly for the fire brigade to drag him to safety.

Nancy was about to climb back up the stairs when she heard the distinct sound of sobbing coming from the end of the passage. From Zamira's room. The girl hadn't escaped— she was still here and seemingly full of remorse for her dreadful deed. Tentatively, Nancy knocked on the maid's door. There was a muffled scraping sound of a chair being pushed back and then the door opened a few inches and a tearstained cheek appeared in the gap.

'Can I come in, Zamira?'

The door opened a few more inches. The girl's beautiful face appeared ravaged: her eyes red raw, her cheeks bloated, and her hair dull and lifeless. When she shuffled back from the door, Nancy took it as an invitation to enter.

The small room was rectangular in shape with a barred window overlooking the scrubland that lay on the far side of the villa. Zamira had tried to make it homely: a brightly woven rug on the floor, a posy of wildflowers on the wicker chest, and a single picture on the wall—a portrait of a young man who looked very much like Gabriel Sekela.

'I'd like to talk to you,' Nancy said, 'if you're willing.'

In response, Zamira waved her to the empty chair, then slumped onto the narrow bed which took up one whole side of the room.

'I met your mother this morning,' she began, and saw an expression of alarm cross the girl's face. 'She tells me you're going to Trinidad. Is that right?'

Zamira's eyes were downcast and she mumbled a 'yes'.

'And will you be living there alone?' Despite her suspicions, Nancy was genuinely concerned for the girl.

'My aunt. I go to my aunt until...'

'Until the baby is born. And then what?'

Zamira shook her head. 'I don't know. I don't care. Not now.' Nancy could see she was finding it difficult to hold back the tears.

'Because of Gabriel?' she asked gently. 'I saw what was left of the house this morning.' The maid gave a huge sob and the tears began coursing down her cheeks.

Nancy waited a while, unsure how to go on, but eventually Zamira stopped crying, then blew her nose and wiped away the tears. 'You saw the house?' she asked in a low voice.

'Yes.' There was a pause before Nancy said, 'Have you any idea how the fire might have started?'

Zamira shook her head. 'An accident,' she mumbled.

'I think it was too fierce a blaze to be an accident. Forgive me for dwelling on it, but the fire must have been intense — it burnt as though something had been used to spread it. Paraffin, for instance.'

At that, Zamira looked directly at Nancy, her eyes startled. She was visibly shocked, and though Nancy would like to have questioned her further, something told her she needed to leave the girl alone, at least for the moment. There had been a recognition in Zamira's eyes when Nancy had mentioned paraffin. That didn't necessarily signal guilt, but it was significant.

'When do you leave the island?' Nancy asked, deciding a change of subject might be best.

'When you go.'

'You don't wish to leave before? If you did, we could manage here, I'm sure. And if not, Mr Garcia could probably find someone to help out.'

Zamira shook her head. 'I stay. My aunt is fierce woman.' It was evident the girl was dreading her exile.

'Your aunt may be fierce, but she will look after you,' Nancy said, trying to comfort the girl.

Zamira blew her nose again, loudly. 'And you, who look after you? You are sick lady.'

Had the maid found the bloodstained nightdress she'd hidden? It seemed more than likely.

'I'm not sick,' Nancy said quickly, 'but things haven't worked out as I expected.' She paused a while before adding,

'The professor doesn't know yet.' There was guilt at confiding such an intensely personal secret, but Zamira merely nodded.

Nancy got up to go, but at the door, said, 'If you want to talk more, Zamira, I'll be upstairs.'

When she walked into the sitting room, she found Archie sprawled in an armchair reading the local paper. 'Well?' he asked, lowering the page.

'She's too upset at the moment to tell me anything, but I'm sure she knows more than she's said. I think she'll come to us when she's ready to talk.'

Archie looked sceptical. 'The murderer volunteers a confession? Hardly.'

'I don't think she is the murderer,' she retorted. 'Not any more. She knows something, but she was shocked when I mentioned that paraffin had most likely been used to start the fire.'

In the event, only half an hour passed before the maid appeared in the doorway. Archie had got up to go to his makeshift office—a parcel of forwarded post had arrived that morning—but when he saw Zamira, he sat back down again.

'Come in,' Nancy said warmly. 'Come and sit down.'

The girl shook her head but made no attempt to move. 'The paraffin mine,' she said in a voice that was barely audible. She looked as though she would burst into tears again.

Nancy was scrabbling in her pocket for a clean handkerchief to give to the maid, when Archie asked, 'Your paraffin—in the shed?'

Zamira nodded silently. Then blurted out, 'But I don' do it. I love him. I never hurt him.'

'But you bought the paraffin?' Archie pressed her.

The maid's head hung low. 'I want to burn motorbike,' she mumbled. 'Stop him travelling. Stop him see that girl.'

The mention of Anya had Nancy suddenly wonder if

Gabriel's sweetheart knew of his death. She was so young, and there would be no-one at the Serafina to comfort her. Her entire family were hostile to Gabriel.

'I store cans in our shed,' Zamira went on, 'but I never use them.'

'Someone did. The cans are empty—I saw that for myself.' Archie's tone was uncompromising.

The girl began crying, but between sobs gasped, 'It my fault. All my fault. I the one who buy it.'

Nancy was baffled at how best to proceed and looked across at Archie for help. But he was watching Zamira closely—waiting, it seemed. And then the girl suddenly burst out, 'I should go move it. After I see him.'

Nancy was immediately alert. 'Saw who, Zamira?' At last, it seemed they might be getting somewhere.

'I don' know,' the girl whispered. Then more strongly, 'I don' see his face. He had hood.'

'A man, though?'

'Yes, a man. His clothes black but the moon bright.'

'Which night was this?' Archie asked.

'Few days ago. I go home to tell Ma… we had bad quarrel… about baby. It go on for hours and it get late. And I too upset to come back. So I stay in my room there. But no sleep. Then the chickens clucking—it was two, three o'clock. Before sun rising. When I look out my window, I see a man. The man look like he want to break in.'

'And you didn't raise the alarm?' Archie sounded incredulous.

'You'd fallen out with your mother and you didn't want more trouble?' Nancy suggested quietly.

Zamira nodded. Her eyes sought Nancy's and she seemed grateful for the understanding. 'Any case, nothing in shed worth stealing,' she said simply.

'And last night—did you go back home again?' Nancy felt her heart tighten a little.

'I said so, but I don' go. I stay here. I don' want to speak to Ma again, not after she tell me I go to Trinidad.'

Nancy felt herself breathe more easily. The girl's words had rung with honesty, and it was unlikely Zamira could have done the deed.

When she and Archie were alone again, Nancy said, 'Nothing worth stealing maybe, but two large cans of paraffin ready to use. And if the police decide after all that the fire wasn't an accident and begin asking questions, it will be Zamira they'll suspect. It was Zamira who bought the paraffin and had a strong motive for revenge. The whole town will know that.'

'It's a clever move, but how could our mystery man know there'd be paraffin to hand?'

Nancy jumped up and walked to the window, looking out at the calm sea, its waters glinting beneath a hot sun.

'Perhaps,' she mused, 'he went there simply to check out the place. Maybe to see what harm he could do. Then when he'd had a look around Gabriel's house, he went next door and peered through the shed window and saw the paraffin cans. And that suggested a plan—he'd come back another night and do the deed.'

'The cans might have been empty,' Archie objected.

Nancy turned her back on the sea and sat down again. 'It's possible he went into the shed to check, but Zamira didn't see him—by then, she'd gone back to bed. It has to be this hooded man who started the fire. But who on earth is he?'

'We've quite a choice. Mr Sekela was good at making enemies.'

'Do you think it could be Jackson Garcia?'

Archie pursed his lips. 'It's possible, but it doesn't seem

his style. He's more of a veiled-threat merchant. That's what I've heard in the bars, at least. He employs a heavy mob who turn up on the doorstep and that's usually sufficient for Jackson to get his way. He makes sure he keeps his distance, of course.'

'Everyone must know who pays this gang—including the police.'

'I guess so, but Garcia's got away with it so far. Enough of the police are in his pocket, I suppose.'

It was exactly what Renzo had claimed. 'And to think,' she said, 'that this is the man Leo is working for.'

'Leo will be okay, but the sooner we get off the island, the better. As for the hooded man, we need to look further than Garcia. He wanted Sekela gone. Breaking up protest meetings, smashing a printing press to stop leaflets going out—I can believe Garcia was behind all those, but somehow I don't think he'd go as far as murder. And arson is a far more dangerous ploy. Fire spreads and he could easily have killed more than his man.'

'If we're exonerating Zamira—we *are* exonerating her?— and if it isn't Garcia, who started the fire?' she asked again.

'Evidently someone who has a grudge. Someone we don't know?'

'Or someone we do know,' she said thoughtfully. 'Luke Rossiter? Have you considered him? He hated Gabriel.'

'For taking his girl?' Archie stretched his legs full length and gave a long yawn. 'There you go again—love is the culprit.'

'It most often is,' she retorted. 'But Rossiter has more to lose than Anya's love. Even if she rejects him, he has a good job at the hotel and will probably take over when Ambrose Martin retires. It's important to Rossiter that the Serafina is a success, but if Gabriel had had his way, there would be no land grab, no extra development on the island, and no great influx of tourists. But plenty of trouble to deter guests from coming. The hotel depends on money from abroad—you could see that when we went there.'

'Still, setting fire to a house seems a bit extreme, don't you think?'

'I think this island breeds extremes, and Gabriel was fighting on all fronts. Renzo reckons there's a gang on Malfuego that Gabriel was trying to nail—they're running drugs from South America. Gibbon Bass is part of it, but Rossiter could be involved, too. It would give him another reason to want Gabriel gone.' She paused for a moment. 'Though I may be speculating too far.'

Archie grinned. 'Surely not.'

'I'll speak to Virginie,' Nancy said decidedly. 'She'll know more. She works with Rossiter every day.'

'And who else do you need to talk to?'

Nancy looked at him, trying to work out his meaning.

'Leo?' he prompted.

She flushed. 'I will when I'm ready.'

Archie got up from his chair and leant over her. 'There will never be a good time. Leo needs to know what's happened. He needs to look after you.'

Once more she felt the warmth of his body speaking to her and a deep yearning she couldn't lose. 'I'm perfectly fine,' she answered, with as much self-possession as she could manage.

Chapter Sixteen

Archie had left for his nightly trip to town before Leo arrived home.

'Sorry, I'm late, darling,' her husband called out. 'The legal chap turned up at Jackson's office just as I was leaving, and he was keen to go through the contract with me. I didn't actually sign anything before we left London.'

Nancy walked out into the hall to greet him, kissing him on the cheek. 'You'll have your own solicitor check it, though? Here, let me take those.' She took a pile of papers into her hands before going back to the sitting room.

He followed her, shrugging himself out of his linen jacket as he went. 'I don't think I'll worry about a solicitor. I'll ask Archie to go through the paperwork tomorrow. He's developed quite a legal brain these last few years—saved me pounds in fees. What's for dinner? I'm starving.'

'Zamira made chicken curry, but that was a while back. It's waiting for us on the terrace.'

He walked out of the French doors and lifted the lid of one of the tureens set out on the table. Nancy peered over his shoulder. The curry looked dry and unappetising.

'I think we might go out this evening, don't you?'

'What about the curry?' Nancy asked. 'I feel bad about leaving it.'

'We'll bin it and Zamira need never know. Let's go, Nancy. We haven't eaten out since we got here, except for the meal at Jackson's. And I've barely seen you these last two days. We'll make it an occasion.'

Nancy had little appetite and would have been happy to settle for Zamira's meal, but she could see her husband was set on what he hoped would be a romantic evening.

'And wear that beautiful red dress,' he said, as she made her way to the bathroom.

*

The taxi dropped them at the harbour and, hand-in-hand, they strolled along the wide promenade, its wooden boards warm beneath their thin sandals. Lights blazed from several of the larger moored vessels and were echoed by lamps strung along the waterside. In the distance, Nancy glimpsed the mountains, encircling and heavily wooded, glowing gold in the embers of a dying sun.

When they'd reached the end of the promenade and inspected every restaurant, Leo said, 'I think we'll go for fish, don't you? The restaurant we passed a little way back?'

Nancy was feeling queasy—her stomach seemed not to belong to her still—and the suggestion of fish made her feel worse. It was more than a physical unease, though: the loss of the baby had begun to haunt her thoughts. And after today's terrible tragedy, it felt even worse—the image of that ruined house was imprinted on Nancy's mind and the knowledge that a young man had perished in its ashes.

The last thing she wanted, though, was to spoil the evening, and she forced herself to sound happy with Leo's choice.

The restaurant he had chosen was an attractive place with one entire wall open to the ocean. Its furniture was painted blue and its walls decorated with sea motifs. Large, open shells held clusters of small flowers while the candle holders were blue ceramic sailboats. The head waiter came bustling towards them as soon as they stepped over the threshold. There were few other diners and she wondered if Leo had chosen poorly.

But the fish stew and potatoes were tasty and the carafe of water—all Nancy could manage—was cold and refreshing. Even so, she ate listlessly. There was too much on her mind, and in the end she couldn't stop herself asking, 'Did you hear about Gabriel Sekela?'

'I did, as I was leaving Jackson's. Isabella came in with the shocking news. Apparently the fire was intense and the house burned to the ground.'

Nancy was well aware of how intense that fire had been. She put down her fork and sat looking out at the bay.

A dilapidated craft not much bigger than a yawl, with tattered sails bleached with age and a hull that needed a coat of pitch, was anchored close to the restaurant. It creaked and ticked in the air currents passing over the harbour. Longing, Nancy imagined, to break free, and with a snap of the mainsail catch the wind and ride its way through the waves, out into the bay where the flying fish skimmed, their tails twitching and shining like polished metal.

'Eat up.' Leo dragged her from her reverie. 'Your risotto will get cold.'

'It's fine,' she said. And then suddenly, 'How did Jackson react to Isabella's news?'

Her husband looked at her askance. 'As you would expect. He was shocked.'

'He didn't like Gabriel.'

'He didn't like what he considered rabble rousing, but that doesn't mean he was happy to hear the poor man had met his death in such a terrible fashion.'

'Do you think the police will investigate?' Nancy shuffled her fork around the plate, still unable to eat.

'Why would they? It was an accident. These wooden houses are bonfires waiting to go up. Isabella heard that a lamp was involved—the fire brigade found its remains, apparently—but that could be hearsay.'

'Whatever the cause, it was a most dreadful thing to happen.' She put down her fork, giving up the unequal struggle.

'It was, but it's given us even more reason to crack on. The island needs bolstering and the gallery should do it. It will bring in visitors and, with them, money. Before the legal chap arrived, we did another site visit—to make some last-minute adjustments to the plans. What did you get up to?'

'Archie took me flying,' she said, without thinking.

'Flying? Why would he do that?'

'He thought I'd like it. And I did,' Nancy said defensively. 'He's already pretty good.'

'I'm glad to hear it, but I'm paying for Archie's lessons so that he can pilot a light aircraft and cut my travel time where possible. Not to take my wife joy riding.'

'We weren't joy riding, Leo. The instructor—Marlon—was very strict.'

'I don't want you to go up in that plane again. You have the baby to think of. I know you'll say it's perfectly safe, but I'd much rather you keep both your feet on the ground.'

This would be the moment to break the news, but the restaurant had filled up since they'd arrived and it felt too public a place—Leo would be badly shaken by what she had to tell him, perhaps angry. She hesitated, and in that instant her husband signalled to the waiter.

'Could we have coffee, please? That's if you've eaten all

you want, Nancy? You don't have to eat for two, but you do need to keep up your strength, my darling. You look tired, and I was hoping to pick your brains. I have to decide on some broad themes for my part of the gallery. They'll determine the paintings I buy. It's a limited space and though there's plenty of money, art is obviously costly, so I have to consider budget, too. At the moment, I'm thinking three main motifs for the European works. I shan't tell you what they are. I want your suggestions first.'

Nancy was flattered. It was rare for Leo to ask her opinion and she wished she could give it her full attention. But too much else was fighting for space. She must tell him tonight, she thought. Archie knew, and now Zamira. It was grossly unfair that her husband, the father of this child, was the only one to be unaware of its loss.

An hour later, when Leo walked out of the bathroom, she readied herself to confess. But he had other ideas than talking and, as soon as he'd slipped into bed beside her, he enfolded her in his arms and pulled her tightly into his body, his mouth seeking hers. His lips were on her neck, on her breasts, and he was tugging at her nightdress.

'I've had a lovely evening,' he murmured. 'It's reminded me of how good we are together. And how shamefully I've deserted you these last few days. I'm sorry.'

She could feel him hard against her, but she was sore and tired and gently wriggled free. 'I can't, Leo. I'm sorry, too. But there's something I need to say.'

'Forget it. I'm too tired.' He turned abruptly away from her, his shoulders hunched.

Not knowing what best to do, Nancy switched off the bedside lamp, then she reached out to him, trying to take his hand. But he shook himself free. She turned on her side, saddened. And still she hadn't spoken the words that could bring even greater division between them.

*

She breakfasted the next morning feeling no more cheerful. Leo's goodbye had been brusque and he'd followed Archie into the car without a backward glance. The day stretched endlessly before her. It seemed that everyone except her had a role to play on the island, and she felt a nagging anxiety that it would be no different when they were back in London. In her head, she was planning to return to her work in the studio, but in her heart she knew that Leo would do his best to frustrate it.

She had wandered several times out of the sitting room and onto the terrace, then back again, when the noise of a car reached her through the open window. She walked across the room and peered out. A bright pink Cadillac had arrived on the driveway and the dainty figure of Isabella was waving at her.

'I've surprised you,' her visitor exclaimed, as Nancy opened the front door.

'Well, yes, but it's good to see you, Isabella.'

'Leo didn't tell you? About the country club?'

She shook her head. 'Should he have done?'

Isabella put her hands on her hips. 'I knew I should have telephoned. You can't trust a man to take a message. He should have told you. In fact, he should have checked with you that you were happy to come with me this morning.'

Last night's feelings of guilt disappeared in a flurry of annoyance. It was high-handed of Leo to make an arrangement without consulting her.

'I'm sorry, Nancy.' Isabella was looking concerned. 'Of course, if you're not happy to come... but I was hoping you would.'

'It's a lovely idea,' she said swiftly, feeling bad for this generous woman. 'You've saved me from a friendless day.'

Isabella's face cleared and the sun returned to her smile. 'Go and get your handbag then—and a hat. It can get hot even under the umbrellas. Oh, and a swimsuit. The pool is divine.'

'I think I may give swimming a miss, if that's all right, but I'll certainly find a sunhat.'

She was gone only a few minutes and found Isabella waiting in the car, the faithful Ernesto at the wheel.

'It's not too far,' her hostess said. 'Just along the coast, in the other direction to the town.'

'Near the airfield?'

'We turn off before we get to the promontory. But the club has a wonderful beach—actual sand as well as rocks. You know about the airfield? I heard that Archie was having flying lessons—do you know how he's getting on?'

After Leo's chill last night, Nancy had no wish to return to the subject of flying. But Isabella seemed amused and continued to talk. 'Don't say you've been up with him? Such courage, my dear!' She gave a small laugh. 'After that, my country club will seem tame.'

Tame was a good word for it, Nancy reflected, as the Cadillac swept between white stone pillars and snaked its way up a drive that was bordered its entire length by an orderly line of palm trees. On either side were wide expanses of mowed lawn, dotted at regular intervals by bougainvillea in full flower. It seemed the natural world had been repressed in favour of a foreign ideal of harmony.

Harmony, too, in the bright white walls and the symmetrical windows and doors. Nancy was ushered into the main meeting room of the club—more white walls, a dark wood floor, and dark wood ceiling beams. Isabella flopped down into one of the wide wicker chairs.

'Let's have a drink first. Then I'll introduce you. I've already seen a few friends out on the terrace. You must meet as many people as you can while you're with us.'

Nancy could see her companion wanted her to feel welcome. She was an oddity in Isabella's society, she knew, having no part in planning for the gallery but no affinity with the leisurely lifestyle her friend enjoyed. Nancy was used to work. There had never been a time when she hadn't worked, either studying hard for her diploma or striving to make a success of the job at Abingers. Her career at the auction house had been cut short by the nightmare of Philip March's stalking, and for months afterwards she had struggled to find where she belonged, until the miraculous apprenticeship in art restoration had come her way.

'You're looking a little peaky, Nancy. Is that the right word?' her hostess asked, as two tall glasses of iced lemonade arrived at their table.

'I had a bad night.' That was true at least. 'But really I'm fine.'

'The early months of pregnancy are the worst, I believe.'

Nancy had wondered before why Isabella was childless— she seemed a woman made for motherhood. But the subject was troubling, and instead she asked, 'Were you born on the island?'

'I was. Jackson, too. We met at a party my father threw for his students who were leaving that year. He was a school teacher,' she explained.

'And Jackson was one of his students?'

'A clever student. A bit too clever, my Papa always said. He wasn't keen on my marrying him, nor was my mother. They had bigger ideas for me.'

'Bigger?' Nancy sounded surprised.

'My family were quite well off, by island standards. Papa was a professional. But when Jackson and I married, we were poor. Church mice, you know? But Jackson is bright, just like my father said, and he worked very hard and used his brain very hard, and here we are.'

'I have a feeling it was more of a struggle than that suggests.'

Isabella took a delicate sip of her lemonade. 'You're right. The island is owned by a very few people and none of them look like us. At first, they laughed at Jackson, then they sneered, but finally they had to give him respect.'

'And now they come begging, I imagine?'

'Oh, yes. But you know, Nancy, we are cute. We know we're only tolerated because of the money Jackson has made. We belong to this club, to the yacht club, to various societies, but if we became poor again, you would see us discarded in a second.'

'That is horrible.'

'It's the reality. How easy would it be for you to be friends with a black person, even in London?' Before Nancy could answer, Isabella said, 'Not easy, I know. And that's even truer in this region, and particularly so in Malfuego. The island has been very slow to adapt to the modern world.'

'Jackson must have built some friendships, though—with businessmen, at least.'

Isabella gave a small sigh. 'I suppose, but my husband is not popular. He's not always sensible and sometimes I don't like what he does. You understand?'

Nancy glanced at her hostess, wondering if this might be the chance to find out just what role Jackson Garcia had played in Gabriel's death, if any.

'I'm not sure I do,' she said, hoping it might prompt Isabella to talk more.

'I love the man. Love him dearly, but he can be impulsive. Orders people to do foolish things which he regrets afterwards. He has this vision for the island, you see. He wants the best for the people here—he *is* one of the people, and so am I. But his vision isn't everyone's and he gets impatient, sees them as stubborn and stupid, and then he gets out of hand. But really, he's a good man. He has his heart in the right place.'

Nancy wanted Isabella to keep talking, wanted to ask her whether Jackson had been the one to order the attack on Gabriel at that demonstration, but her courage failed. She couldn't do that to such a sweet-natured woman, and she was fairly certain in her own mind that he *had* been responsible. And maybe responsible for other incidents in which Gabriel had suffered. But not the fire. That was someone else.

Chapter Seventeen

Isabella began waving frantically at a woman who was about to leave the room. 'That's Winnie. I must speak to her about the Bring and Buy before she leaves. It's in two weeks, and as far as I know, nothing has been organised. And she's the one who should do it, but unless you remind her, she's hopeless. Will you excuse me, Nancy? I'll only be a minute. Then I'll take you on a tour of the club. It won't take long, it's not that big, but you'll love the beach.'

Isabella rushed over to the doorway and put a hand on Winnie's arm. She had been talking to her friend for only a few minutes when someone else slid into the seat she'd vacated.

'Mrs Tremayne, Nancy, it's good to see you here.' It was Scott Hastings, a glass of whisky in his hand. He gave her a broad smile that had her shrinking back. Those strong, white teeth were almost shark-like. But scolding herself for being foolish, she tried to look welcoming.

'It's good to see you for more than one reason,' he went on. 'I've been wanting to talk to you.'

'Really?'

He settled himself more firmly in the chair. 'I'm very concerned for Renzo. You were kind to the boy, went out of your way to help him when you knew nothing about him, and I thought that perhaps... perhaps you could talk some sense into him. I can't.'

'What kind of sense?' Nancy was cautious.

'I don't know if you're aware, but he made a great friend of this boy, Sekela. The poor chap is dead, but Renzo won't let go. He talks about nothing else.'

'You didn't like it that they were friends?' Renzo had told her as much the first time they'd met on the island.

'I tried to steer him away, it's true. For his own good.' Scott's smile vanished. 'Gabriel Sekela was a problem and I didn't want Renzo involved with him. There were plenty of others he could have made friends with, but he had to seek out the island's number one troublemaker. I thought when Sekela died, that would be it. But no, since the guy's death, Renzo is even more obsessed.'

'That seems natural enough. If Gabriel was such a good friend, Renzo must need to grieve, surely?'

'The grieving isn't the difficulty. Well, not all of it. What's really bad is that Renzo is spreading a false rumour that the guy's death wasn't accidental, and that's seriously upset some folks. My son is out of his depth, Nancy. He's never fitted in here. From the time he arrived, I've tried to tell him how to go on, but he doesn't listen. Or if he does, he ignores my advice. That's why I thought he might listen to you rather than his old dad.'

The 'old dad' jarred with her. This was the man who had happily abandoned Renzo in Venice, and never once bothered to discover how his son was faring, whether in fact he still had a home. She and Archie had found the boy desperately ill, half mad from the effects of bad alcohol. It was only their intervention that had saved his life.

'I'm not sure how I can help.' She was determined to keep her distance. 'You say it's a false rumour, but surely the jury

148

is out as to whether the fire was an accident or not.'

Scott Hastings looked stunned. It was evidently not the response he'd expected. 'The fire brigade is quite confident it was an accident,' he blustered. 'A lamp that fell over.'

Nancy nodded. 'There's room for doubt, though, isn't there? And if Renzo feels so strongly on the matter, I don't see how you can stop him talking about it.'

'Accident or not, the boy shouldn't get himself involved.' His voice had a harsh edge that Nancy hadn't heard before. 'And if I might take the liberty of saying this, you should be wary, too. You're as much a stranger on the island as Renzo.' He leaned forward and his bulk blocked the pool of sunlight Nancy had been enjoying. 'You need to be careful not to suggest that Sekela's death was anything other than accidental.'

She stared at him. 'And why is that?'

Cold eyes fixed her with an answering stare. Hastings leaned further forward still, his face now only inches away. 'There are forces on this beautiful island that you know nothing of. Harm could come to you, and I would hate a visitor to be hurt in any way.'

They were soft words to disguise a hard threat. But Nancy would not be deterred; she could attack, too. 'Have the police found your burglar yet?'

For the first time in the encounter Scott looked uncomfortable and she delighted in having turned the tables on him. 'Not yet.'

'Or perhaps they don't even know about the burglary? Perhaps you didn't tell them? And that would be as curious as Renzo's conviction that the fire wasn't an accident. Why didn't you report the break-in at your house?'

'There was no point.' He was blustering again. 'I didn't lose anything.'

'And that doesn't strike you as odd? A beautiful house with a number of valuable artifacts, yet nothing was taken. Though I believe there was an attempt at theft.' She was allowing herself to play with him a little, and enjoying it. 'Renzo tells me that someone tried to break into your desk— apparently it was the burglar's only interest. You must have kept something very valuable there.'

Scott Hastings stood up abruptly. 'It's been pleasant chatting to you, Nancy, but I have to go. Work calls.' And with a brief nod to her, he walked away, passing Isabella and her companion still talking in the doorway, without a word.

Nancy was undaunted by his threats; rather, she was buoyed by the conversation. She was sure now that Hastings was a villain, if a milky one, and that whatever had once been hidden in his desk was incriminating, just as Renzo suspected. It was equally clear that he knew something about Gabriel Sekela's death, or suspected something. He may not have been the man to throw the paraffin, but if he was involved in drugs and Gabriel had uncovered evidence, Scott Hastings would gain from the young man's death. He was certainly trying his utmost to stop Renzo digging any deeper. What would he do, she wondered, to ensure his son left the Sekela business alone? What would he do to *her* if she didn't leave it alone?

'Sorry about that, Nancy.' Isabella plumped herself back into her chair. 'Winnie is a dear but has no head for arrangements. I don't know why the committee asked her. Probably because she's the only one who would say yes, and now I've been landed with the job of finding someone special to open the sale. I suppose you wouldn't do it?'

'Me? I couldn't, Isabella, I'm sorry. And I'm definitely not special enough.'

She said it jokingly, but in two weeks she hoped not to

be at a Malfuego Bring and Buy sale but back in Cavendish Street. It was a jolt to realise how near their departure must be. She'd promised Renzo she would do all she could to help him find the man he considered a murderer, but so far it amounted to very little, and she worried the boy would become impatient and take on the search himself, perhaps recklessly.

'I'll have to pull some strings to find someone who's willing,' her companion said, 'but I can think about it later. Right now, let me walk you around this magnificent property and afterwards we'll have a light lunch and a big ice cream. How does that suit?'

'Just fine,' Nancy said, and her smile was warm.

Chapter Eighteen

When Leo arrived home that evening, he seemed to have forgotten his earlier coldness and Nancy breathed more easily. It was important for this evening to go well and, though she made a brief mention of the visit to the country club, she said nothing of her surprise at Isabella's appearance on the doorstep. They ate a leisurely dinner together on the terrace, watching the light gradually dim and a glorious sunset take its place. When Leo rose to pour coffee for them both, Nancy took a deep breath.

'Leo, there's something I have to talk to you about.'

He drank down his coffee but made no attempt to sit down again. 'I'd love to stay and talk,' he said breezily, 'but I've important decisions to make and they can't wait.'

She looked confused.

'I've come to the conclusion I've requested too many Italian paintings,' he explained, 'and I need to think it through again before I see Jackson. Establish a better balance. Include more of the Northern Renaissance.'

'But we need to talk, Leo. It's about us.'

'Sorry, darling.' He bent down to pat her hand. 'We'll talk later, I promise. But right now, I have to get this done.'

She could have blurted out the truth, she thought, but at the last moment, she'd held back. Apart from his mother's early death, life for Leo had run smoothly. In many ways, it had been a golden life. It seemed he'd been given all he'd ever asked for, had rarely encountered a barrier to his happiness. This miscarriage would turn his world upside down and she had to tell him gently. Allow him time to absorb the news, time for them to talk things over together.

But lying in bed a few hours later, she realised that it wouldn't be tonight. He'd been right when he'd said his final list would take some time. Nancy must have slept for several hours before she felt him slip into bed beside her. The morning, she thought sleepily, it will have to be the morning.

*

But when morning came, she found that both Leo and Archie had left for Jackson's earlier than usual, and she walked down to the sitting room thinking of the long day that lay ahead. She needed to do something purposeful. The visit to the club had been interesting, convincing her that Scott Hastings was deep in trouble, but at the moment she couldn't see a way of probing further into his affairs. His partner in crime, Rossiter—if indeed he were a partner—was a different matter. Unlike Hastings, he had work colleagues who might be induced to talk. Unlike Hastings, too, he appeared to be thoroughly scared. Gibbon Bass had argued with Scott but nothing more. Yet he'd clearly intended real harm to Luke Rossiter on that beach, suggesting to Nancy that the man had greater involvement in whatever criminality was going on.

As usual, Zamira had set breakfast on the terrace and disappeared, and when the maid reappeared with coffee, she hardly spoke. The flood of tears Nancy had witnessed seemed no more than a dream; the girl had once more become a servant—formal, taciturn, refusing to display the slightest hint that she had suffered a wrenching bereavement.

Before starting on the light meal, Nancy rang for a taxi to take her to the Serafina—she was eager to get to the hotel and speak to Virginie. She guessed the housekeeper would have more time to talk the earlier in the morning she managed to find her. The cab was at the door by nine o'clock, before she had finished her coffee.

Once at the Serafina, she asked the driver to drop her at the rear of the hotel; Nancy had no wish to meet any of the Martin family, and certainly not Luke Rossiter. A large consignment of clean laundry was being delivered, and she asked the two men unloading it where she was likely to find Miss Lascelles.

'Her office, I guess,' one of them sang out from the interior of the van. 'See the door behind you? Go left at the end of the corridor. Her room on the right.'

Nancy thanked him and hurried into the building. If Virginie weren't in her office, this visit could prove tricky. She had no wish to wander the hotel, broadcasting the fact that she was looking for the housekeeper. But she was in luck.

'Nancy! Come in. This is a surprise, but a nice one.' Virginie jumped up from her chair and held out her arms, kissing Nancy on both cheeks.

Her office was small and looked out onto a quadrangle of grass. But from the amount of paper that covered the desk and the stack of files in one corner, it seemed Virginie had little time to take in the view.

'I'm sorry to barge in like this when you're working,' Nancy said, 'but I needed to talk to you.'

'But, of course, talk away! First, though, can I get you a drink?'

She shook her head. 'No thanks. I've only just had breakfast.'

When the housekeeper raised an eyebrow, Nancy said, 'I

know. Incredibly lazy, but when I finally get to sleep, I can't seem to stop.'

'You're well, though? The baby is well?'

She said nothing. It was impossible to tell yet another person before she spoke to Leo. Her hesitation, though, had been noticed.

'Not well? Really not well?' Nancy looked down at her feet. 'I'm so sorry, honey. But it happens sometimes. As long as you're okay. Maybe see a doctor to check all is good?'

Nancy shook her head again. 'I'm fine. I came to see you about Gabriel Sekela,' she said, determined to change the subject.

'Oh, my! So sad. And Anya—she is devastated. But the poor darling daren't show it. She wasn't supposed to know the guy well. At least, that was the fiction the Martins told themselves.'

'Is she at work then?'

'Trying,' Virginie said laconically. 'But how did you hear about Gabriel?'

'Renzo Hastings told me. He's the American boy. He was a great friend of Gabriel's and he's pretty cut up.' Nancy paused for a moment. 'Renzo thinks it wasn't an accident.'

Virginie frowned and Nancy went on, 'He thinks that someone started the fire deliberately and,' she finished in a rush, 'I do, too.'

Her companion blew out her lips. 'But that's awful. Mad. Why would you think that?'

'Empty paraffin cans were found nearby,' Nancy said vaguely. She would keep quiet on Zamira's role in the drama. It could mean more trouble for the girl.

'That's a big jump to make. Fires are frequent here—houses made of wood, you know.'

'I realise that, but the blaze was too intense and spread too quickly. There had to have been an accelerant.'

'I know the boy made a lot of enemies, but you're saying it was murder? Who would do such a thing?'

'An enemy, like you say. A rival. Someone here in the hotel?' She looked hopefully at her companion.

'Luke Rossiter?' Virginie hadn't needed long to work it out. 'He had a motive, I guess—Anya.'

'And not just Anya,' Nancy was quick to say. 'Gabriel's political activities were a threat to this hotel, to Rossiter's job.'

'And a threat to mine, for that matter! But Rossiter is certainly ruthless enough,' the housekeeper mused, 'and I'm pretty certain he's involved in something illegal. He's not always where he's supposed to be, and I've seen him speaking to some odd-looking characters. But murder?'

'Do you know where he was the night before last?'

'Here, I imagine.'

'But you didn't see him?'

'I was in town. It was Clara's birthday and we celebrated. Boy, how we celebrated!' Virginie's laugh rang out and her eyes sparkled at the thought.

'Then he might not have been here? There's no check on staff coming and going?'

'Not in their free time. And Rossiter works office hours, so what he does in the evening...'

Nancy sat for a while staring out at the grass square beyond the window. At length, she said in a quiet voice, 'Would it be possible... could I see his room?'

'Whoa! You want to break into his room?'

'Not break in exactly.'

'You want me to use my pass key?'

'Yes.' Nancy was blunt. There was no other avenue she could think to explore. 'I'll only be in the room a few minutes. There might be something that ties him to Gabriel's death.

And if there is, Anya deserves to know, doesn't she?'

She could see Virginie was wavering, and employed her last scrap of ammunition. 'If I found something incriminating, it could mean the end of Rossiter working here. That would be good news for you. I've heard the way he deliberately undermines you. Surely, you'd like to see the back of him?'

Her friend gave a slow smile. 'He's engaged with a party of tour reps this morning, so—'

'His room will be empty?'

Virginie jumped up as if she'd made a sudden decision. 'Come with me. But we'll need to be quick.'

*

The hotel's live-in staff were accommodated on the lower floor of the hotel, several corridors away from the housekeeper's office, and it was a matter of minutes before they were standing outside Luke Rossiter's room. On their way, they'd been fortunate in meeting only a gaggle of housemaids making ready to clean the guest bedrooms; they'd bobbed their heads to Virginie but had seemed incurious about her visitor.

At Rossiter's door, Virginie peered up and down the corridor and, satisfied they were alone, turned the key to reveal a long, narrow bedroom, beige-painted and anonymous, lacking the slightest hint that anyone had made this room their home.

'When you've finished, pull the door shut behind you,' Virginie said quietly. 'It will lock automatically.'

Nancy took her hand and pressed it warmly. 'Thank you. I promise not to get you into trouble.'

'You better not!' The housekeeper grinned. 'But be quick. The reps will break for coffee very soon and I've no idea whether Luke will stay with them or not.'

The curtains—more beige—were half drawn, and Nancy left them as they were. The less she touched, the better. In any case, the room looked out onto scrubland; it was unlikely anyone would pass by the window and look in. Furniture was sparse and her search wouldn't take long. She started with the two shelves that were fixed to the wall at one side of a long mirror. A few books were all they held. There was nothing behind the books and, as she shook each volume, nothing in them, either. What had she expected to find? Would Rossiter have written down his plans? Hardly. But there might perhaps have been a note from an accomplice. She had always in her mind that strange scene played out between him and Gibbon Bass. The sailor had to come into it somewhere.

On to the chest of drawers that revealed little except neat underwear and a pile of clean handkerchiefs. And a diary. Excitedly, she scrabbled through the pages, but it proved another disappointment. It contained nothing in the least incriminating—Rossiter's work rota was clearly noted, the address of a shoe shop in Malfuego town, the telephone number of an expensive London hotel. This man seemed to have no existence apart from the job he did.

She crossed the room to the wardrobe but this, too, proved a frustration: a number of suits, still with their dry-cleaning labels attached, several pairs of polished shoes, and a collection of freshly ironed shirts. Luke was clean and tidy to an extreme.

Very carefully Nancy replaced everything she had touched, and turned despairingly to look around the room. The bed. Perhaps there was something about the bed worth looking at. But the covers were crisp and tight, tucked in hospital fashion, and when she got down on the floor and looked *under* the bed, her reward was an empty suitcase with no hidden pockets. She felt stupid. She resembled, she told herself, nothing more than one of those schoolgirl detectives she'd loved to read about as a child.

Defeated, she started back to the door, but then stopped at the bathroom. It was probably worth a quick look, but it would have to be quick. She had already spent too long and Virginie would be getting anxious. A swift scrutiny of the room took in toothbrush and paste, a razor, a manicure set, and a bottle of aftershave. In the one cabinet, some pills— simple headache pills. Nancy replaced them with a sigh.

But as she did, she felt something taped to the underside of the shelf, and with a little scratching, managed to release the tape and brought out a very small packet. A packet filled with something white. Her pulse began to thrum. She had little knowledge of drugs, but she was almost sure this must be cocaine. She had seen it once in the cinema—an old Hollywood film in which cocaine addiction had been the plot line. Rossiter was taking drugs! She put her hand into the cabinet again and felt along the shelf. There were more packets, all carefully taped to be invisible. The drug was unlikely to be for Rossiter's use alone. He could be selling it, could have hidden larger stashes elsewhere.

She had to think. Gibbon Bass and his boat sailed to Venezuela and back frequently, and they were not innocent voyages. Renzo was worried that his father was involved. Rossiter almost certainly was. The struggle with Bass that she and Leo had witnessed on the beach could have been accomplices falling out.

She must go to the police. Renzo had said he knew trustworthy men in the force and she would ask him to help. But dare she take one of these packets as evidence? It would be enough for the police to raid the hotel. On the other hand, Rossiter must know precisely how many packets there were—they were worth money—and if he missed one, he'd know he'd been found out and would likely flee.

Nancy burrowed into her skirt pocket and found a clean handkerchief, then with the utmost care opened the packet she'd taken from the cabinet and sprinkled a little of the powder onto the linen. Folding the handkerchief into a small square, she thrust it back into her pocket.

She was just re-taping the packet beneath the shelf, hoping that Rossiter wouldn't miss the small amount she'd taken, when she heard a key turn. She held her breath—Virginie come to tell her to leave immediately? Footsteps on the polished wood floor. No, not Virginie. She slid behind the half-opened door and tried not to breathe, but her heart was banging so hard, it hurt. All her old fears returned in that instant: hiding from a man, hiding from her stalker. But this wasn't London, she told herself. She might be in danger, but it wasn't from Philip March.

Nancy breathed out again as silently as she could. The sound of a drawer opening and closing came to her. Then a stifled curse as something heavy fell on the floor. She tried to look through the crack in the door. Luke Rossiter was picking up a book—the diary she'd seen earlier—and putting it in his pocket. Then taking it out again and flicking through the pages. Nancy closed her eyes and died a thousand deaths. If only he would go.

If he were to need the bathroom, she'd be discovered. Rossiter would be desperate to silence her. To kill her. And he could easily escape justice. Dump her body in the wildness of the jungle. Or throw her off a cliff into the sea. She felt beads of sweat forming on her face and trickling down her neck. Only Virginie knew she was here. The housekeeper might confess she had let Nancy into the room, but then what? Anything could have happened once Virginie had left.

And even if she survived unharmed, Rossiter would know his activities had been discovered and could flee. Perhaps even try to brazen it out, citing an intruder into his room. Then Virginie would lose her job, and Leo would become involved, and a marriage that had never been secure would become a whole lot shakier. Nancy squeezed her eyes more tightly, as though in some fantastic fashion that would make the man disappear.

And he did, shutting the door firmly behind him. She let out a long breath but could feel herself trembling from head to toe. Forcing herself to remain where she was for several minutes in case Rossiter was waiting outside, she slipped out of the bathroom and opened the door to the corridor one small inch. Then another inch. And another. No-one was around. She slid free of the room and walked boldly towards the lift, the crumpled handkerchief burning a hole in her skirt pocket.

Chapter Nineteen

As soon as the lift doors closed, Nancy felt misgiving. She should have found her way back to Virginie and the rear entrance—it wouldn't have been too difficult. And her misgiving was fulfilled when the lift bumped to a halt, its doors rolling back to reveal the hotel's large atrium and a group of people—all of whom she knew. Anya Martin, her face raw from tears, stopped whatever she had been saying to her grandparents, and all three pairs of eyes fixed on Nancy with varying degrees of surprise.

'Good morning,' she said, trying to sound as though arriving unexpectedly in the Serafina's lift was the most natural thing in the world. 'I was out walking and thought I'd call in for a drink.' She knew she sounded vacuous. How likely was it that she'd choose to walk in a temperature of over eighty degrees, let alone emerge from the hotel's lower floor?

'Mrs Tremayne.' Lionel Martin stepped forward and shook her hand. 'How nice of you to visit us again.'

'Have you brought your husband with you?' his wife asked, in a sweetly cutting voice. Mrs Martin, dressed once more in severe black, wore an expression to match.

'No. Leo is working. I've ventured out alone.'

'You're very welcome, Mrs Tremayne,' Anya managed

to say. 'I'd love to stop and talk, but I'm afraid I can't—I've a whole list of things to do before lunch. My grandparents, though, will be happy to look after you.'

The girl gave a weak smile and was gone. Over Eugénie Martin's shoulder, Nancy glimpsed Scott Hastings and his son, and her heart sank further. After yesterday's encounter at the country club, she had hoped to avoid Scott, but it seemed that this tight little bunch of people, a group who appeared to rule the island, had chosen this morning to gather here. Nancy's mind began its usual busy speculation, but not before she'd noticed that Anya had stopped to speak to Renzo. The two young people appeared close—Gabriel's death would mean they had much to share.

Lionel Martin gestured to an empty circle of chairs. 'Please, Mrs Tremayne, do take a seat.' He clicked his fingers at a passing waiter. 'What will you have?'

'A lemonade would be fine, thank you.' Having said she'd called at the hotel for a drink, there was little she could do but accept the offer.

'No alcohol? But you are thinking of the baby perhaps? I did read somewhere or other that strong drink might be a problem in pregnancy.' Eugénie's eyes bored into her, as though she could discern the lie Nancy was living.

'And how are you enjoying your stay in Malfuego?' Mr Martin asked, making himself comfortable in the chair opposite.

Nancy dissembled. 'I'm enjoying it very much. I've made some new friends and discovered an old acquaintance—the younger Mr Hastings.' She inclined her head towards the trio still talking by the lift. 'I met Renzo in Venice, and he introduced me to his father a few days ago.' She felt confident that she could mention the city without causing Renzo difficulty. No-one on the island was likely to be aware of his criminal past.

'Scott Hastings? Oh, yes. He's here to see Miss Lascelles, I believe.' Mrs Martin's voice announced her extreme boredom, though her grim expression never varied. 'Some business about a consignment of tablecloths that have gone astray. Mr Hastings functions as our freight manager.'

A legitimate reason to be here, Nancy thought, but one that gave him the opportunity to see Luke Rossiter for whatever nefarious business the two of them shared. She took hold of the handbag she had dropped on the floor and tucked it tightly between her ankles.

'I believe Renzo worked here for a while,' she remarked, taking a sip of the lemonade that had arrived at the table.

'He's helped out once or twice,' Eugénie said dismissively. 'In the winter season when the tourists arrive. At the moment, my son has no need of extra staff.'

But perhaps Anya had need. The thought came to Nancy as she glanced across at the girl and Renzo. Scott Hastings had gone to the reception desk, no doubt to summon Virginie, but his son had his arm around Anya's shoulder, his face close to hers, and was clearly trying to comfort her.

'That boy needs to work instead of lazing around at his father's home or throwing paint at canvases that no-one will buy,' Mrs Martin said. 'Work is a great preventer of mischief. But people these days—even Americans, whom we're told are the hardest workers in the world—seem not to know the meaning of it. The young prefer to trivialise life.' The glare she directed at her granddaughter was one of barely concealed anger.

'That is harsh judgement,' Nancy couldn't prevent herself saying.

'Is it? It's certainly true. Our forefathers were different. They shaped the modern world. The sugar industry shaped the modern world. Have you ever thought of that, Mrs Tremayne?'

Nancy blinked. She couldn't truly say she had. But Eugénie, in any case, was indifferent to her guest's views. She had launched herself on what was evidently a favourite topic.

'For one thing, it revolutionised the food people eat. But far more than that. The profits from sugar built amazing cities back in Europe, and that didn't just happen. The Martins worked their hearts out to establish the most successful business in this part of the Caribbean. The Saussures, too— my family—worked day and night to make their fortunes. And now look what we have come to.' She gestured to their opulent surroundings.

There was a parallel story that Eugénie Martin chose not to mention: the brutal lives and early deaths of millions of enslaved Africans. But it was one, Nancy realised, that meant nothing to this woman.

'I believe there are sugar mills still working,' she said, thinking it best to feign interest.

'One or two,' Lionel put in, 'but the industry is a shadow of what it once was. Sugar used to be the most important commodity in the world.'

'How did your families come to settle here?' It was an innocuous question, Nancy thought, and might encourage her companions away from their grievance. She was mistaken.

'Do you know the history of the island, Mrs Tremayne?' Eugénie asked imperiously.

'I'm afraid I don't.'

'It has a mixed inheritance. Columbus was the first to discover the island, and for a hundred years Malfuego was a colony of Spain. There are still a few families here of Spanish descent. My one-time daughter-in-law was from such a family. The Spanish, when they arrived, made slaves of the Arawaks. Not the best idea. The natives died in spectacular numbers—European diseases, you know—so they started importing slaves from Africa. The Africans did better, but Spain was too focussed on South America to make a success of the place, and eventually Frenchmen were brought in to establish new plantations. Malfuego became a magnet for those with ambition, those willing to work for their wealth. A member of my own family, Claude Saussure, was one of those Frenchmen.'

'But your husband is English?'

'Through and through,' Lionel said. 'My family settled here after the British conquered Malfuego. The very first Ambrose sailed from England early last century and established mills throughout the island.'

'And they're still working?'

'Some are, but sadly sales have dwindled badly. The family tried cocoa instead, and for a while it worked. But even those days have gone now.'

'And this is what we're left with.' Eugénie once more gestured to the showy atrium, her despair evident.

'The waiter who served us?' Nancy cast desperately around for a new topic. 'He was Indian, wasn't he?'

'Was he?' Mrs Martin's voice had regained its *ennui*.

'I'm interested, because my husband tells me that a large area of Mr Garcia's new gallery will house Indian art. And yet I've still to meet an Indian.'

'You don't need to,' her hostess said. 'They are all the same. Tradesmen, money-grabbers.'

Nancy could have pointed out that much the same could be said of the Martins, but she held her tongue. 'The island does have a large Indian population, though?'

'Too large.' Eugénie Martin sniffed. 'But we've only

ourselves to blame. Or the English have. They brought them over from India when they couldn't use slaves. Indentured workers, they were supposed to be, but they're far from that. Now they own too much of Malfuego.'

The woman's arrogance, her casual dismissal of whole swathes of the island's population, finally proved too much for Nancy. There was something deeply unwholesome about the older Martins, as though they walked with death, bringing with them the sour taste and smell of a long-buried century.

She finished her lemonade and pinned on a smile. 'Thank you both for your hospitality, but I mustn't keep you any longer.'

'You are always welcome here, Mrs Tremayne,' Lionel Martin said almost jovially, 'and next time bring your husband. He will be just as welcome—even though he is working for Garcia.' *Even though he is working for a former slave family*, the man could have said. It would have caught precisely the way Jackson Garcia was viewed by these people.

Nancy merely smiled again, collected her handbag, and walked to the reception desk to order a taxi home.

Chapter Twenty

On the drive back to the villa, she wondered how many other families were like the Martins: families, who were what Virginie called former slavers, people who had never lost the brutality, the disdain and casual superiority of their predecessors. English families, French families, too, she supposed. A tight-knit, closed little group. It was why the State Assembly functioned as it did, why the ordinary folk of the island remained poor and had little say in their future.

Ironically, there were a few black Malfuegans like Jackson, who seemed to have taken on the system and made it theirs, though at the expense of their fellows. It was no longer skin colour alone that dominated decision-making in Malfuego, but money, too. Garcia's fortune had given him huge sway on the island, no doubt an ability to pull strings, to encourage the Governor to make appointments that were useful to him. In a true democracy, he would lose that power. No wonder he was so opposed to reform.

Nancy was suspicious of Jackson, and fairly certain that he had been the one behind Gabriel's so-called accidents, but there was a part of her that couldn't help applaud the way he had usurped the system from within. That was what conversing with the older Martins did, she thought wryly.

When she reached the gates to *Belvoir*, the taxi had to pull to one side to allow a sleek, black saloon to pass. Roland was at the wheel and he waved to Nancy as he drove through. Leo must have returned home early, she realised, and the first thing he'd want to know was where she'd been. She cast around for an excuse, but realised almost immediately that the truth would have to do. At least a partial truth.

Her husband was in the sitting room, and even before he spoke, she could see he was ruffled. 'Where have you been?' It was a demand as much as a question.

'To the Serafina, that's all,' she answered quietly. 'I had a drink there.'

'But why?' The demanding note had become more evident.

'I wanted to call on Virginie. When we were at the hotel last, she offered to show me around the parts we didn't get to see.' When he looked baffled, she added, 'The housekeeping.'

'Since when have you had an interest in bedlinen?'

Nancy collapsed into an armchair, realising for the first time how tense she had been. And seeing Leo so unexpectedly wasn't helping either. She took a while before she answered. 'Virginie's job isn't only about bedlinen. I really liked her when I met her before—I thought I'd like to talk to her. It can get rather lonely here, Leo.'

'You wouldn't have been lonely if you'd stayed in the villa. I've been waiting for you.' He frowned as he said this.

'I saw Roland leave as I came through the gates. You couldn't have been home long.'

He frowned again. 'I've been waiting over an hour. I asked Roland to stay and drive us. I wanted to take you to the bay we went to the other day, but when you didn't come back, I had to let him go. We could have had a late lunch and gone swimming, but you preferred to look at sheets.'

He seemed unable to free his mind of linen, which should

have been comical but somehow wasn't. Nancy felt herself bristling. 'I didn't know you were coming home early. How could I? Did you bring Archie back with you?'

'He's gone to the airport for another flying lesson. Why do you want to know?'

She badly wanted to see Archie, wanted to tell him what she thought she'd found. She clasped her handbag a little more tightly, but said as casually as she could, 'I wondered if you'd brought work back with you, that's all.'

'I told you, I cleared the decks, especially. And now I've wasted the entire afternoon.'

'Then I'm sorry.' She got up to go. She had had enough of being reprimanded like a small child.

'I was wondering when I might hear an apology.'

That made her sit down again. 'You're being unreasonable, Leo.'

'Am I? Am I really? I deliberately postpone an important discussion to be here, and when I get back, there's no Zamira—where she's gone, I've no idea—no Archie, and no you. I've been hanging around like a spare part for over an hour.'

Inwardly, Nancy gave a sigh. It was evidently up to her to mend bridges. 'We could still go to the beach. Collect some sandwiches on the way. Why don't we ring for a taxi to take us?' She wasn't hungry and had no real wish to go anywhere, but was hoping to placate him. She'd rarely seen her husband so irritated. Maybe something else was going on, something at Jackson Garcia's that she wasn't privy to.

'It's far too late for that,' he said in a sulky voice.

He was behaving like a small child himself, she thought, and her patience had come to an end. She wanted to be away from him. 'Then if you don't want to go, I think I'll take a rest upstairs.'

'It's what you should have been doing all along, instead of gallivanting around the island. Yesterday the flying, today the hotel. You know what I feel about your pregnancy. I accept you're not ill, I know that thousands of women have babies every week, but you're not strong, Nancy. You need looking after. I'm trying to do just that, but you don't make it easy.'

How did he get this strange impression of her? Not strong? Because she had been brutally targeted by a fiancé who couldn't accept dismissal? Because she had married for protection? She supposed she had only herself to blame if Leo saw her as weak. She had not been honest with him. He had no idea she had fought for her life in Venice, so much worse than Philip March had ever thrown at her. How, with Archie's help, she had survived almost certain drowning. Her husband didn't know her, and that was partly her fault. It was time to be honest… about one thing at least. She'd tried before. This time she had to succeed.

'Leo, do you remember I had something I must tell you.'

At this, his head came up quickly and he stared at her. 'Yes?'

She swallowed hard. 'There is no baby,' she said baldly. 'Not any more.'

A look of complete incomprehension filled his face. 'What do you mean?'

'I've been having pains on and off for quite a while. I didn't want to worry you and I hoped they would disappear. I'd read that mild pain can be common in the first few months and then everything goes well. But that's not going to happen for me. The pain got worse, not better, and… I lost the baby.'

'What do you mean "lost the baby"?' Still the incomprehension. It was as though Leo could only understand one version of their future, unable to contemplate anything different.

'I mean that I've had a miscarriage.'

'But how? When?' He sounded even more bewildered.

'Several days ago—in the night, while you were sleeping.'

He staggered to his feet then and, white-faced, loomed over her. 'And you didn't think to tell me?'

She felt a crushing guilt. She had delayed and delayed, fearing his reaction but hoping for a time when she might defray his anger and offer comfort. Leo had known loss before, the terrible loss of his mother when he was still no more than a child. But since then his path had been smooth, his life securely under his control. Now, that certainty had been blown away.

'I couldn't bring myself to say the words,' Nancy stammered. 'I was waiting for the right moment, but it never came. I know what dreadful news it is for you.'

'But not for you, it seems.' His bitterness cut through the air.

'Of course, for me, too. But I've had a little more time to get used to the idea.'

'And I will, too. Is that it? Given time, losing my child will become just one of those things?' He bent close to her and, for the first time in their relationship, she felt threatened. 'This is your fault, Nancy. You've been the one to refuse to rest. You've deliberately gone against my wishes, done precisely what I asked you not to. If you hadn't chosen to rush around the island, you would have given your body the best chance. The pain you experienced might have subsided. But no. You brought on this miscarriage.'

'That is grossly unfair.' She jumped up from her chair and pushed him away. Her face had flushed red and she felt the heat rising in her body. 'I'd been on the island only a few days when it happened. My rushing around, as you call it, had

172

nothing to do with it.'

'Maybe, maybe not. But this loss, this terrible loss, appears to mean little to you. Except as a chance to continue doing exactly what you want.'

'And that's unfair, too. I couldn't prevent the miscarriage happening and I've had to deal with it.'

'And I must, too? Is that it? Do you ever actually think of me, Nancy? How I feel, as a person, I mean? Not just someone who rescued you from a crazy man, who protected you to his utmost, married you because he thought he might persuade you one day to love him as much as he loved you?'

'Of course I think of you, Leo. I care for you deeply.' She tried to take his hands but he evaded her grasp. 'But I didn't deliberately lose the baby.'

'Are you sure? You never wanted a child. I remember your attitude when we talked about it in Venice. You were lukewarm. On reflection, not even that.'

'We were on our honeymoon. Talking of having a baby seemed premature—it wasn't how I saw my life at that moment.'

'And it still isn't, is it? The job you've found is far more important to you than any child.'

'The job has nothing to do with it. It's possible I could have fitted both into my life.' She paused for an instant and looked directly into his face. There were tears in his eyes and she desperately wanted to comfort him. But he was in no mood for comfort.

'I'm sad about the baby,' she said, her voice cracking slightly. 'I'm grieving, too.' And it was true. The sadness was hitting her over and over again, punching home in a way she hadn't expected. 'But it's wrong of you to blame me for what's happened.'

He shrugged his shoulders in an angry gesture, and she

was goaded into saying, 'You might as well blame yourself. You brought me here. It was you who insisted I come, even though you knew I preferred to stay in London. And if I *had* stayed, it's possible I might never have miscarried.'

It was an unkind suggestion, but he'd hurt her deeply and she was hitting back in the only way she could. She turned away from him and walked to the door.

Chapter Twenty-One

The quarrel with Leo had left Nancy craving space and air. And desperate to break away—from the island, from Leo, from her life? She ran down the stairs to the lower floor; there was no sign of Zamira. Since the girl's outburst, the maid had taken to spending every hour of her free time locked in her room. Whether it was guilt at having bought the paraffin that killed Gabriel or dread at what lay ahead of her, she had become a recluse, only appearing at meal times or glimpsed on the stairs with a brush or duster in her hand. *Belvoir* was a sad house these days and Zamira's plight made it sadder.

Nancy let herself out of the rear door and into the garden, walking back and forth along paths and between flowerbeds, trying to still the ache in her heart. Trying, too, to slough off the anger she couldn't subdue. But it was useless, and by the time she neared the door again, she knew she had to escape the villa entirely. Break free and walk until she was too tired to walk any more. Into Malfuego town perhaps? But its raucous bars and noisy restaurants held little attraction. Or… maybe… she could return to Gabriel's street.

Not to his house or what was left of it, but to the house next door. Marissa King's. Now the shock of the young man's dreadful death had faded a little, Nancy had begun to think she should talk to Marissa again. Neither she nor Archie had been thinking clearly the day they'd met her—hardly surprising after the news they had just heard—and there were questions they'd neglected to ask.

If Zamira hadn't used the paraffin, someone else had. A someone who remained a mystery. The girl had seen a hooded figure several nights before the fire, but couldn't identify the man. Was it possible her mother had seen something, too? Someone idling in the street, someone watching the house, even perhaps someone in the shed? Filled with a new sense of purpose, Nancy whisked herself back into the house and up the stairs to the hall. An uncomfortable stillness filled the air, and there was relief in quietly closing the front door behind her.

She crunched her way along the gravel drive, the air now pleasantly warm. It was good walking weather. Good thinking weather. She mentally arraigned her list of suspects as she walked. Garcia was almost certainly guilty of threats to Gabriel, but his goal seemed to be to stifle unrest, albeit violently, rather than murder. So, who was left? Bass, Rossiter, maybe Scott Hastings? Perhaps even someone she had no name for yet. And out of those she knew, who had the most to gain? If they were all involved in smuggling, they would all benefit: Gabriel's death had brought his investigation to a halt. But it was Luke Rossiter, she thought, and his infatuation with Anya, who would gain the most.

Marissa's house was in a street halfway to town, and within a quarter of an hour Nancy was walking along the dusty track that she and Archie had taken only two days ago. Even in the distance, and with the line of trees blocking her vision, she was aware of the void at the end of the road, the empty space that had once been Gabriel's home, impressing itself on her mind far more than the living buildings she passed.

The sun was already dipping towards the horizon and the chatter of birds had noticeably diminished, though a pigeon trilled somewhere above her and a lone dove cooed. Drawing near to Marissa's house, she could see no lights, but perhaps it was too early to fire up the lamps. Mrs King had a young son and would surely be home at what must be the boy's teatime.

Nancy took a deep breath and opened the garden gate, walking boldly up to the front door. This interview would not be easy. Somehow she had to secure whatever useful information Marissa held, without revealing Zamira's role in the drama. The girl was already in deep trouble with her mother and Nancy had no wish to make life more difficult for her.

She climbed the wooden steps to knock at the shabby door, and waited. There was no answer, and after a minute she knocked again, this time more loudly. Still no answer. Emboldened, she stepped across the wooden deck to one of the front windows, cradling her head between her hands and peering into the room. Toys were spread untidily across the coconut rug, spilling out across bare floorboards, and on the dark wood table there were signs of a meal having been eaten. It looked very much as though Marissa and her son had finished tea and gone out for the evening.

Nancy felt deep disappointment. She had been counting on getting the woman's story, hoping it would provide a clue, a hint even, to the identity of the hooded man. That hope was now extinguished—and how long would it be before she could make this journey again?

Heavy-hearted, she turned to retrace her steps. As she did, out of the corner of her eye, she caught a glimpse of the shed Jaden's ball had damaged. A last resort, but it might be worth a look. Archie could well have missed something— he'd had little time to investigate. But again, she met with disappointment. The window had been mended and when Nancy tried the door, it was locked. She had to accept that this evening she had run out luck. It was as she rattled the shed's door handle for the last time that she sensed there *was* someone here—not in the house or the shed, but behind her. She turned quickly. The front garden was empty, the gate she had opened remained ajar.

Uneasy, she walked quickly back up the garden path. A house further down the lane showed a light, but she felt solitude pressing down on her. She had been uncomfortable the last time she was here, had sensed someone watching from the shadows, but then Marissa King and Archie had been with her and noticed nothing. And it had been daylight.

She closed the garden gate behind her, vowing that if she came again—and she must—it *would* be in daylight. The trees that lined the far side of the track seemed to have grown taller and thicker since she'd walked this way minutes ago. Ridiculous, she thought, and gave herself a mental shake, but nevertheless increased her pace.

She was passing a particularly dense clump of trees when she felt something or somebody close behind her. Suddenly a hazy shadow was there in front of her, spreading across the ground, elongated in the dim light flooding the lane. A hand grabbed her arms from behind and pinned them roughly together.

'What are you doing here?' The voice was harsh but low, its very quietness threatening. She recognised the voice instantly, though the smooth tones of hotel management were no more. Luke Rossiter! Had he somehow discovered that she'd searched his room this morning? Did he realise that she knew about the drugs? Nancy's heartbeat sounded loud in her ears and she forced herself to quell her panic.

Steeling herself, she tried to twist around to face her attacker, but he had her clamped in an iron hold. 'Let go of me—immediately,' she commanded, knowing how foolish she must sound.

'I don't think so. Not until I know what you're up to. And maybe not even then.'

It angered Nancy that she must justify her presence to this man, but if she were to have any chance of freeing herself, she would need to. Rescue would come from nowhere else. 'I'm not up to anything, Mr Rossiter,' she said.

He was silent. I've surprised him, she thought. He hadn't expected to be recognised. Was that good for her, or did it make her predicament worse?

'What precisely are you doing here?' His grip tightened and she felt sure her wrist bones must soon crack.

'Is it forbidden to walk here?' It was a puny attempt to turn the tables on him.

'I find it a strange choice, Mrs Tremayne. A dirt track, poor houses, a good way from your luxury villa.' The luxury evidently grated on him. 'Perhaps you should remember you're a tourist here. A guest on the island.'

'You have an odd way of treating guests.'

He ignored her comment. 'You still haven't answered my question. Why are you here?'

'Exercise, Mr Rossiter. Our villa is quite close. A few minutes' stroll. And even tourists need to walk.' Despite the throb in her arms, she felt her strength returning. She would defeat this man in whatever way she could. 'But what about you? You *are* a long way from home.'

His hold relaxed slightly. He seemed to be judging his best course of action and, sensing his hesitation, Nancy took her chance. Painfully, she wrenched her arms from out of his grip. He lunged forward in an attempt to recapture her, but she spun around and faced him directly.

'So much better to see who you're talking to, don't you agree?' She should make a run for it, she knew, but she was too angry, too ready to do battle. 'Ambrose Martin might be interested to learn he employs a man who thinks nothing of assaulting a lone woman on her evening stroll.'

'But you weren't, were you? Simply taking an evening stroll.'

He took a step towards her, his hands impatient. Ready, she thought, to grab her again.

'You were spying,' he said in a voice that chilled her. 'Otherwise, why come to a lane that no tourist ever visits? What were you hoping to do? Sift through the remains of Sekela's house?'

Was that what he was afraid of? That she would find something in the ruins? Something incriminating.

'I didn't come to gawp,' she said contemptuously. 'I was passing close by and thought it would be a friendly gesture to call on Mrs King. Her daughter is our maid.'

She tried to instil as much indignation into her voice as possible, but she could feel her limbs beginning to shake. She was convinced now that this was the man who had lit the match and begun the terrible conflagration. Gabriel Sekela had been too much of a threat for Rossiter to allow him to live.

He had moved even closer now, towering over her in the fading light, a mere breath away. 'But you didn't find her,' he said softly. 'And you would have been much better never to have come. A great deal better, Mrs Tremayne. I would hate anything bad to happen to you.' His eyes were cold and unforgiving.

The moon was already in the sky, the dusk coming early as always here, and his face in its unsparing light was haunted. The creases in his skin were tightly drawn, carved almost into his face, and he looked worn and far older than his years.

'This is a dangerous neighbourhood,' he went on. 'You can see what happened to poor Mr Sekela. It would be a shame—'

Suddenly his hands were around her throat. Utterly shocked, she froze. He will slowly squeeze the life out of me, she thought. But before he could begin, she jerked herself awake and, with as much strength as she could muster, landed a sharp blow to his groin. He let out a howl of pain and his hands dropped.

This time she did run, pulse thudding heavily, expecting that at any moment Rossiter would overtake her. She sped along the lane, a woman possessed, and only when she reached the main road did she dare to pause for an instant and look back. There was no sign of her attacker, but still she kept running, her breath coming in painful gasps. She crossed the main road, then half walked, half ran up the hill towards the villa and safety.

To one side, she could see the distant ocean, the light from a myriad of stars glimmering across its surface, while nearer to hand, the silvery blue light had turned the roadside bushes into gleaming beacons. Every so often a tall tree displaced the bushes and loomed over her as she ran. A malefactor could perch in those branches, she thought, darting anxious glances at them as she passed, but she knew that it was her fear talking.

There had been cold fury in Rossiter's eyes, and she knew he'd wanted to kill her—she was a threat to be neutralised. How easy it would have been for him, too. No-one knew where she was; no-one even knew she had left the villa. And there had been no witnesses in that solitary lane. He could have murdered her in seconds, leaving her body for an unwary passer-by to find. The police would suppose her the victim of a random mugging. And why not? There was no connection between herself and Rossiter, no earthly reason why they would question him.

She was almost spent by the time she reached the house. The front door was still unlocked and, breathless, she crept up the stairs to her bedroom. From the kitchen below, she could hear Zamira banging saucepans into the sink and pulling crockery from the cupboard.

Nancy was dishevelled and her nerves still on edge, but her absence appeared to have gone unnoticed. She would wait to be called for dinner, and pretend that for the last few hours she had been resting in her room.

Chapter Twenty-Two

The evening meal was eaten in silence, and as soon as Zamira had cleared the table, Leo disappeared to his makeshift office. What he was doing there, Nancy had no idea. All she knew was that he didn't want to be near her.

She had been in bed for almost an hour before her husband joined her, but once more he said nothing, though he must have known she was awake. And awake she stayed as the night hours passed. The two of them had to find a way through this, she told herself; it was a sadness they should be sharing. But Leo, it seemed, had turned away, dismissing her feelings as unimportant, false even, and directing his own sense of impotence towards hurting her.

It was nearly dawn before she slept, and Leo had already left the villa when she finally tumbled out of bed. She dressed hurriedly and made her way to the kitchen, wondering if Zamira had given up expecting her and cleared breakfast. The maid wasn't there, but Archie was. Nancy looked at him in surprise.

'You haven't gone with Leo?'

'As you see.'

'Why not? And where is Zamira?'

'In reverse order, Zamira has gone to the market to shop and I wasn't wanted at Garcia's. Leo is doing a tour of the island along with Cy Devaux, courtesy of our benevolent host.'

'But you're not?'

'As you see again. Remember—'

'I know,' she interrupted. 'You're the hired help.' The fruit this morning seemed sparse, and she reached out for a slice of bread to toast.

'—and we all know that the hired help doesn't go on pleasure trips.' There was satisfaction in Archie's voice.

'You don't seem too upset about it.'

'Why should I be? I get to go flying again. How about you—want to come?'

She turned a stricken face to him. 'I can't. Leo wants me here. Or, at least, not flying.'

'What's happened now?' He sounded weary.

'Nothing,' she said quickly. 'He just doesn't want me going up in a small plane.'

Archie began to stack his empty crockery. 'Come for a walk—when you've finished the toast.'

'I've finished already.' Talking of Leo, remembering their dreadful quarrel, had made her feel she couldn't eat another mouthful. 'But aren't you going to the airfield?'

'Plenty of time for that. I've got all day and you look like death. You need fresh air, and it's still reasonably cool out there.'

'The garden won't give us much of a walk,' she objected. 'It's quite small.'

He tapped his nose with his forefinger. 'Ah, that's where you could be wrong. The villa's grounds lead on to a cliff path. I discovered it yesterday. There's a small hedge you have to squeeze through, but then you're on a track that winds its way around the cliff and down towards the harbour.'

He led the way through the rear door of the villa, but

instead of turning towards the garden where Nancy had walked the previous day, he took a narrow path that had been cut between newly planted saplings. At its end was a tall, bedraggled hedge, at first sight appearing impenetrable, but when Archie walked up to it and pulled back a chunk of greenery, a small gap was revealed and, beyond that, a rough track.

'I reckon the servants once used this path as a quick way into town. When the place was lived in regularly. See, the track bends around the headland but all the time it's moving downhill. Watch your step, though. The surface is uneven.'

She followed him through the gap and onto a track that was wide enough for them to walk side by side. Vegetation sprouted from the cliff face like a green waterfall, disguising the vertical drop to a sprawl of rocks and sea. Quickly, Nancy stepped back from the edge.

'Wise move,' Archie said. 'But it's worth a little danger, don't you think?'

She had to agree: the view was spectacular. The sea stretched blue-black into the distance, but in the shallows close to the cliff base it was pure green. There was a swell this morning, the troughs and peaks mesmerising in their movement, the occasional foamy mist toppling from a breaking wave. Above it all, a luminous sky, pearly at the horizon, but burning to gold as the sun tracked ever higher. A gathering of swifts, perched on a spike of rock just below them, suddenly took flight, their long swept-back wings forming the shape of a crescent.

'Like boomerangs,' she said, pointing to the black cloud flying overhead. Archie gave a nod but stayed silent. It was a few minutes before he spoke. 'You've told Leo?'

'How did you know?'

'I'm not a genius, but it didn't take too much figuring

out. You look unwell and Leo stomped off to Garcia's this morning without a word.'

'He blames me for losing the baby.'

'He's angry. He's got to blame someone. He'll get over it, given time.'

'But it's so unjust.'

'Life is unjust. You should know that.'

Archie had moved several paces ahead, but stopped now and looked back at her. When he saw her face, he retraced his steps. Tears had started to trickle down her cheeks and, without warning, he put his arms around her and held her close.

Nancy felt the deepest sense of peace. She wanted him to hold her like this for ever, but in a moment he'd released his grip and handed her a clean handkerchief from his pocket. She felt shaken by the sheer need to cling to him. For comfort, yes. But so much more. Yet Archie never crossed the invisible line they had drawn between them. Never. He had taken her hand several times, had held her in his arms when he'd saved her life, but nothing more.

Years of working for Leo as his assistant—dealing with auction houses, with wealthy patrons of art, with galleries around the world—had meant he could turn on the charm, the courtesy, when it was needed. But Archie was still essentially the soldier he'd been for six years. Rough and curt at times, but honest, and always, always loyal. Loyal to Leo, as she should be. She must fight thoughts that should never have crossed her mind. And banish them for good.

She blew her nose while her companion stood, hands in his pockets, looking out to sea. 'Did you get to the hotel yesterday?' he asked. 'Did you see Miss Lascelles?' It was clear he was trying to distract her.

Nancy gave a loud sniff and tried to concentrate. 'I did,

and there's something important I wanted to ask you.' She delved into the pocket of her floral skirt and took out a small square of linen, carefully smoothing its crumpled folds.

Archie's gaze was intent, his eyebrows rising astronomically. 'Talcum powder? I don't think so. Is it—' He dipped his finger into the powder and gave it a swift lick. ' — cocaine? Yep. It is. Where the hell did you get that?'

'From Luke Rossiter's bathroom.'

'What! What were you doing there?'

'Virginie used her pass key to let me in. I was hoping to discover something that would tie the man to Gabriel. I'd just found this,' she pointed to her hand, 'when Rossiter came back to the room.'

'Presumably he didn't see you?' Archie was looking worried.

'I hid behind the bathroom door. He'd only come back to collect something from his desk—his work rota, I think. He had it marked in his diary.'

Archie blew through his lips. 'You had a lucky escape. So… Rossiter is taking drugs?'

'Dealing drugs, I think. There were packets of the stuff taped to the underside of a shelf in his bathroom cabinet.'

'The packets you saw—couldn't they have been just for Rossiter's use?'

Nancy shook her head. 'I don't think so. I believe he's selling it to guests at the hotel. And there's a network, I'm sure. Gibbon Bass is someone he's working with.'

'Gibbon who? Is that a real person?'

'Oh, he's real. Extraordinarily handsome and very powerfully built. With a mean streak, too. I think he meant to harm Rossiter the afternoon Leo and I went to that bay. Maybe teach him some kind of lesson. Rossiter seemed to be a prisoner on his boat, and Bass was dragging him up the beach when he saw us and changed his mind. Then he sailed away and left Luke to limp home. It was all very strange.'

'Let's walk to where the path curves inland. If we go too far, it will be an almighty pull uphill. A chap with a boat figures,' Archie said thoughtfully. 'The cocaine must come from Columbia, then into Venezuela, where I imagine this character, Bass, collects the stuff. Then he distributes it around the islands. Rossiter could be one of his agents.'

'I think so, but there's something I haven't told you.'

Archie stopped walking. 'I'm not going to like this, am I? I can tell by your voice.'

'I went back to Gabriel's street last night,' she confessed. 'And Rossiter was there. He threatened me, grabbed hold of me. I thought he might kill me. I'm convinced now that he's our hooded man.'

Archie ignored this to ask angrily, 'Why the hell did you go there? And on your own?'

'I wanted to speak to Marissa King again.'

'And did you?'

'Marissa wasn't in,' Nancy said forlornly.

'You risked being hurt by that clod—or worse—for nothing? Why didn't you ask me to go with you?'

'You weren't around. You never are. And I did get hurt.' She suddenly felt very sorry for herself.

'Let me look.' He took hold of her hands and turned them palm upwards. Ugly blue bruises stretched across both her wrists and he shook his head at the sight. 'You're crazy, Nancy. Why do you do this?'

'You know why. Because I have to find the truth. And they're only bruises.'

He dropped her hands abruptly and strode ahead. It seemed that Leo wasn't the only one she'd alienated.

'Rossiter was scouting the remains of Gabriel's house,'

she said to Archie's back. 'I think he was looking for anything that had survived the fire. Anything that might incriminate him. Gabriel was onto the drug ring, we know, and that's got to be a strong motive for Rossiter to get rid of him.'

'So you say.' Archie grunted. 'Let's stop here.' He held out an arm to shield her from the cliff edge and turned back to walk towards the sun.

'There's also Scott Hastings,' she said hopefully.

'Who?'

'You haven't met him, but I'm sure he plays a part in this. He's Renzo's father, and he's quarrelled with Bass as well. If I'm not mistaken, Renzo is very uneasy about the company his father keeps.'

'He should be, if the boy's the reformed character he says he is.'

'I remember now how surprised I was when I saw the Hastings house. It was very luxurious. A mansion, in fact.'

Archie sighed. 'Okay. A drug ring. Bass, Rossiter, Hastings. Maybe even our friend, Garcia. He didn't make all that money simply shipping crates from one island to another, I bet.'

'Scott Hastings runs a freight business, too.' She was puffing a little as they began the uphill trek.

'Evidently a lucrative line.' He gestured to the pathway. 'Watch out for those ruts. They're particularly deep around here.'

Nancy thanked him for the warning, keeping her eyes on the ground until they were in sight of the villa's straggling hedge.

'If Rossiter is the killer, was he tasked by the drug ring to be the hit man?' Archie asked. 'Or was setting that fire a bit of private enterprise?'

Nancy thought about it for a while. 'Out of all those men,

Rossiter has most to gain. He could have acted alone. He's infatuated with Anya Martin and now he's rid himself of his rival.'

Archie grabbed a piece of the hedge and held it back for her to step through. 'That's what the fight was about—at the tea party?' he asked, once they were at the other side.

'Almost certainly. Anya really loved Gabriel. Yesterday at the hotel, she was trying to keep working, but she looked terrible. I felt so sorry for her. She has no mother, her grandparents are gargoyles, and now she's lost her sweetheart. She seems very much alone, except for Ambrose. Even the aunt she loved is dead. That was Ambrose's sister.'

'What happened to her?'

'She drowned when she went swimming. But there was something odd about the death. The woman was a very good swimmer and shouldn't have drowned. Virginie hinted that it was suicide. Something very bad happened in the Martin family. Something pretty awful between brother and sister, though Virginie didn't want to spell it out.' Nancy surprised herself that she could speak so calmly of the unspeakable.

Archie was unfazed. 'It fits with what I've picked up in town. This group the Martins belong to—French families, English, maybe one or two Spanish—they're descended from the original settlers. Slavers, all of them. And they have the same attitudes still. They keep to their own. And you're asking for trouble when that happens.'

'You should hear Anya's grandparents talk,' Nancy said warmly. 'Or rather you shouldn't. It would make you feel ill.'

'I've heard plenty of it elsewhere. Apparently, this cosy little group own most of the island and syphon off most of its wealth. No wonder there's huge resentment here. And anger. These people live behind high fences and marry their own kind. If you marry out, it's on pain of death. Most of their offspring must be barking.'

'Think how they'd react to Anya marrying an ordinary Malfuegan.'

'An ordinary black Malfuegan,' Archie said grimly. 'Our Mr Sekela certainly led a dangerous life.'

Their conversation made Nancy more determined than ever to find the young man's killer; tomorrow's lunch at the island's yacht club could prove helpful. 'We've been invited to the yacht club for Sunday lunch,' she said. 'I imagine Scott Hastings will be there, as well as Garcia and the Martins. It seems to be a gathering of the island's elite, and it could be that I can find out more.'

They had walked around to the front of the villa, and Archie stopped at the door. 'You need to be careful,' he warned. 'Watch what you say. You've no proof as yet that anyone has done anything wrong. I can keep my eyes open, too.'

'You're going to the lunch?'

'Surprised?'

'A little. Not so much the hired help then.'

'I think Isabella Garcia felt sorry for me. Her husband made it brutally clear I wasn't welcome on their jaunt today.'

'I'm sure that upset you,' she said wryly. 'But you better get moving if you want to grab Marlon for an hour.'

'Changed your mind about coming?'

'I better not,' she said wistfully. 'Leo didn't like it when I went with you last time.'

'Fair enough. But when he gets back from his guided tour, cut him some slack. It's going to take time for him to accept the situation. The baby meant a lot to him.'

'Meaning it didn't to me?'

'Not so much. At least, not at first. Did it, Nancy?' He looked directly into her eyes and she couldn't lie to him. 'I'm off then,' he said cheerfully. 'Just got to collect my pilot's gear!'

'What about this?' she called to him, when he was halfway up the stairs. She pointed to the crumpled handkerchief she still held in her hand. 'Should I take this powder to the police?'

'And tell them where you found it?'

She shook her head. 'I can't, of course. I'd get Virginie into trouble.' She followed him up the stairs to the landing, but then a thought struck and she said excitedly, 'Virginie has access to all the rooms. It's quite legitimate—she's the housekeeper. She could say she found the stuff when she was checking the staff accommodation.'

'You could try to persuade her, though she might be unwilling to stick her neck out. Rossiter probably has clout with the management.'

'I think I could persuade her, but I daren't go back to the hotel.' Nancy felt frustration build. 'It would make Leo even more angry. He thinks I should be at home, not buzzing around the island. And the Martins would think it very odd if I appeared there again.'

'Don't look at me. I'm going nowhere near the Serafina.'

'Perhaps Virginie will be at the club lunch tomorrow.'

'Perhaps she will,' Archie said, disappearing along the corridor to his bedroom.

Chapter Twenty-Three

Knowing that Archie had been invited to the yacht club lunch made Nancy feel a good deal happier about going. It was stupid, since they were unlikely to have the chance to talk, but it was the sense of his being there, the feeling of strength, of certainty, that she had when he was around, that stayed with her.

As the hours ticked by, though, she felt her cheerfulness seep away. By late afternoon, Archie still hadn't returned, and she guessed he must have gone into town to eat at the harbour. Very soon Leo would be home, and she was crushed by the thought of hours more of resentful silence. But until her husband was willing to talk, there was nothing she could do to make things better. Collecting a plate of fruit from the kitchen, she returned to the sitting room and chose an armchair beside the open French windows. She would read, she decided—*A Caribbean Journey*, borrowed from the Marylebone Library what seemed an aeon ago. In reality, she absorbed little of the book, but there was comfort in listening to the whisper of the sea and in feeling the warmth of the sun as it flooded the room.

A sharp click of the front door had her spring alert, the haze she'd fallen into disappearing instantly. In a few seconds, Leo stood in the doorway. Several long strides brought him to her side.

He reached out and stroked her tangle of dark hair. 'I'm sorry, Nancy. So sorry.' Kneeling down beside her, Leo took her hands in his, raising them to his lips and kissing them repeatedly. 'I was shocked. I didn't know what I was saying. How could I say it was your fault! You must have suffered dreadful pain and suffered it alone.'

She disentangled her hands and laced them around his neck, pulling him close to her. 'It was horrible, but it's over now,' she murmured.

He didn't seem reassured, his face anguished. 'Why didn't you wake me that night? Am I such a monster?'

She put her lips to his and kissed him tenderly. 'You're no monster, Leo. But I knew how wretched it would be for you. I wanted to find a time when I could break the news gently. Then I realised there would never be such a time.'

His arms tightened around her and he snuggled his face into her hair. 'I love you, Nancy. I want you beside me always. We have to live through this sadness together. And maybe we'll be given another chance.'

'Yes,' she found herself saying eagerly. 'We may be luckier next time.' Deep instinct told her that it would never be, but she couldn't bear to hurt this dear man any further.

'Yes. Next time,' he said, and his arms clung more tightly.

For some minutes they remained locked in each other's embrace, until Leo got to his feet and said with a weak smile, 'Go and put on a nice dress and we'll get Roland to drive us into town. We'll have a drink on the waterfront. There's no need to eat if you don't want to. I've noticed your appetite is quite poor these days.'

She looked surprised at the mention of his driver. 'Is Roland still outside?'

'He is. I asked him to wait. I was hoping you'd forgive me

and let me take you out for the evening.'

'There's nothing to forgive and I'd love to come. I'll go and change straightaway. But ask Roland to come in for a drink. Zamira isn't around and the kitchen is free.'

'Is Zamira okay? She's never been exactly friendly, but I've had the impression lately that she really doesn't want to be here.'

'I'll tell you about it when we get to town.'

*

They said goodbye to Roland once he'd dropped them in town, and within a short time had settled themselves in a bar just off the waterfront, its candy-coloured façade having attracted Nancy's attention as they'd walked around the harbour. The slatted wood tables and chairs were simple but clean and the rum punches tasted good.

'At least, now you can enjoy the local tipple,' Leo said.

'The fruit punch was fine.' Nancy pulled a small face. 'This is even better, though!'

'Now... tell me about Zamira.'

'She's pregnant,' she said baldly.

Leo immediately reached out for her hand and squeezed it. 'That can't be easy for you.'

'It's not easy for her either,' Nancy said sadly. 'There's no father. At least, not one she knows.'

'No wonder the poor girl looks so unhappy. But the father—she must have some idea.'

'Apparently not.' Nancy was deliberately vague. She had no intention of mentioning Gabriel. Renzo had been adamant his friend wasn't involved and she'd no wish to blacken the dead man's name. Garcia and his cronies must have done that already.

'What will happen after we leave?' Leo asked. 'Does she

have a family to support her?'

'She has a mother and at least one sibling, but she's being sent to an aunt in Trinidad until the baby is born. After that, I don't know. Maybe adoption. Maybe her mother will relent and help her look after the child.'

Nancy took a sip of the punch and thought it wise to change the subject. 'How did your tour of the island go?'

'It was interesting. Malfuego town is by far the biggest settlement, as you'd expect, but there are villages dotted around the whole coast and some of them are quite big. Certainly large enough to become tourist destinations. There's a historic dockyard, too, just out of the town, and a slave museum on the other side of the island—desperately sad, but I think it would attract tourists if it could be developed. Then there's Ambrose Martin's luxury hotel and Jackson's planned gallery. Most of the island is very poor, but it has potential. I can see why Jackson is keen to get things going.'

'Except that he'll be the one to benefit if he succeeds in making the island popular. Not the poor.'

'I suppose it's true that Jackson and his comrades will become richer, but surely it should help everyone if there's a vibrant tourist trade: the shopkeepers, the boatmen, the farmers, for that matter. More hotels will need more produce.'

'You agree with him then?'

'I don't like the way he's going about things—forcefully buying up land from people who don't want to sell. But I do see Malfuego needs something to combat the poverty. And other problems.'

Nancy sat up straight, her curiosity sharpened. 'Like what?'

'Drugs.' Leo said the word very quietly. 'There's an illicit trade going on here, Nancy, though you'd never know it.'

Now wasn't the time to confess what she did know, but

she was keen to learn what Leo had heard. 'Did Jackson tell you about it?'

'He's got his ear to the ground where the island is concerned and he's worried. Ambrose Martin, too, I think. It seems the problem has got worse lately—there have been dealers hanging around town trying to sell their wares. If that kind of thing gets widely known, people will stop coming here. At least, the people Jackson is hoping to attract. The island could become something of a drug haven and that would certainly put paid to his dreams.'

Garcia would seem not to be involved in the drug running, Nancy thought. Nor Ambrose Martin. She should have realised they would both fight against anything that might jeopardise the island's reputation. Jackson and Ambrose innocent of that particular charge—she ticked them off in her mind. But Scott Hastings? Not so clear. And Rossiter? He was almost certainly guilty.

The evening had been a success and they sauntered back to the villa hand-in-hand. It was an uphill walk, in parts steep enough to render them breathless, but tonight it didn't matter. The air was warm and a thousand scattered stars spilled themselves profligately across a violet sky, like an upturned bag of diamond dust, bathing everything in the world silver. The moon had temporarily disappeared, but the night was so clear that Nancy could see her own shadow.

For a moment, an even brighter light flared out. A shooting star blazing a path across the dark heavens. They stopped for a moment, still holding hands, and watched as its brilliant embers died away over the vastness of the sea. Only in the far distance was there a bank of cloud and the curling chaos of white water. But as they watched, the clouds began to lower and gather speed, powering across the sky and fixing themselves above Monte Muerte. Muted thunder drifted towards them, just audible above the sounds of the night: the creak of bamboo at the wayside, the call of a nightjar, the trill of a pigeon in its nest.

'We better get moving,' Leo said. 'We're not dressed for rain. And when it rains here…'

Nancy took hold of his hand again and they walked on, still in harmony. They reached the front door of the villa just as the first fat drops of rain fell, and tumbled into the hall, laughing at their escape.

'All's quiet,' Leo said, glancing up the stairs. 'Archie can't be back yet. How about an early night?'

Nancy felt panicked. Their lovemaking had never been easy, and right now she was unready to begin again. Leo must have guessed something of her thoughts. 'Just a cuddle,' he said. 'It's too soon for anything else, I guess.'

She was grateful. She wanted to be close to him, wanted to feel she was at least trying to be the wife he wanted and deserved, so she tucked her arm in his, and side by side they climbed the stairs to their room.

Chapter Twenty-Four

Nancy woke in the night to the sound of heavy rain hissing off the tiled balcony. The wind was blowing fiercely, the window shutters jangling on their hooks. Through the open doors, a wash of cold air tumbled into the room, leaving her cool and refreshed. Her body felt stronger, felt her own, for the first time in weeks. And with this new strength came resolve. In the next few days, she must find proof that Rossiter had killed Gabriel Sekela.

She'd done it in Venice, discovered who'd killed Marta Moretto and seen a kind of justice done. She'd enjoyed the working out, the putting together of pieces of a puzzle, and if she were honest, had relished the unexpected, even the sense of danger. It had made her feel alive. It was the same feeling she'd woken with now.

She turned over, careful not to disturb Leo, and thought about the day ahead. The men she'd cast as villains would all be at the club—it was the best chance she would have to make the discovery she needed. But the rain was relentless, drumming loudly in her ears, and if it continued, lunch at the yacht club would be a disaster.

But it didn't continue. When Nancy woke early the next morning, the sun was already breaking through a grey mist and, as it rose above the horizon, turning the sky the palest lemon. It was going to be another hot day. She flipped through her scanty wardrobe and chose the splashy sundress she'd worn to Malfuego town the first time she'd met Virginie. It might bring her good fortune in finding the housekeeper among the guests. She needed to show Virginie the handkerchief and its contents, and persuade her to conduct a lightning inspection of the staff quarters, including Rossiter's bathroom. With luck, it would lead to his arrest and charges for drug dealing. And once the police began to dig into Rossiter's affairs, a murder investigation might follow. In the meantime, she must do her best to prove him guilty.

But when they arrived at the yacht club, smoothly chauffeured by Roland, Nancy saw no sign of Virginie, though the place was awash with people. Her eyes swiftly scanned the crowd for the face she hoped to see, but was met with disappointment. It seemed that, after all, she would have to risk another trip to the hotel.

She felt Archie watching her, his lips pulled down as though to say, bad luck. Unusually, he seemed to have caught the mood of the event, wearing a brightly coloured shirt he must have bought on the island. It was her husband who looked out of place in trim grey slacks and white shirt and tie. It made Nancy smile: Leo would be far more at ease in a London gallery, she knew, and his clothes proclaimed it.

The two of them were shown to a table where the Garcias and Cy Devaux were already seated, while Archie was funnelled to a place at the other side of the large terrace. Her eyes widened as she followed his progress—Luke Rossiter was sitting there. Her heart jumped a beat as she noticed Archie check for a moment. She'd told him of the man's murderous intent, but she needed him to pretend ignorance. It might be possible then to prise out of her attacker why he'd been in Gabriel's street that night. Why he was so desperate to keep others away that he was willing to kill.

Rossiter was staring across at her now and Nancy felt her stomach give a painful twist. Baleful, that was his expression. Her hands went involuntarily to her throat, feeling again the crushing pressure of his fingers. As long as she was with friends or at home, she was safe, she told herself.

'Hallo there, Nancy' Jackson called to her, as they approached. 'It's good to see you again.' He beamed expansively. 'Isabella was saying only yesterday that apart from your trip with her to the country club, we haven't seen enough of you. Too much of your husband, though.' He laughed at his own joke and everyone laughed politely along with him.

'And how are you today?' Isabella asked her.

It was the kind of question everyone asked a pregnant woman all the time, and Nancy wasn't sure she could keep up the pretence much longer. But neither did she want to explain what had happened. She felt Leo's eyes on her and saw the sympathy in them.

'I'm well, thank you, Isabella,' she replied, as casually as she could. 'And you?'

Once initial greetings were over, the three men were soon deep in conversation, while Isabella seemed content to smoke a cigarette and smile vaguely into the distance. It gave Nancy a chance to look around her. To reach the club entrance, they had driven through a green expanse dotted with palm trees—an almost complete replica of the country club's surroundings—but the beautifully maintained grounds were invisible from here. It was the sea that took all the attention.

The club building itself was simple, red-roofed, with white walls and dark casements. But the obligatory colonial architecture was present, too, in the classical columns that adorned several of the doorways. And though the chairs and tables were made of local wicker, their white linen tablecloths, stiff and starched, suggested a desire for formality.

Just below the terrace, she caught a glimpse of a long boardwalk where blue-covered sun loungers had been spread in a neat line. The boardwalk appeared to act as a jetty as well, for further along she could see a number of boats bobbing at anchor in the gentle swell.

'Do you like sailing, Nancy?' Isabella leant towards her, breaking into her thoughts. 'I saw you watching the boats.'

'I think maybe watching boats is the nearest I'll get to sailing,' she replied lightly. She had almost drowned in Venice, and ever since boats had lost much of their attraction for her.

'Perhaps we should stay safely on land then? I would love to take you around the island. We have some wonderful landscapes and unusual buildings, too.'

'I'm sure I'd find them interesting,' Nancy murmured politely.

'There's a church that's certainly worth a visit. It's hugely old, built in the sixteenth century by the very first settlers. And it has the most beautiful interior—but there's a bit of a climb to reach it. Do you think you could manage?' Isabella looked anxious.

'I'm feeling a lot fitter now,' Nancy responded, hoping this would end any further speculation on her health. Out of the corner of her eye, she caught a glimpse of the Martins arriving: Ambrose, his parents, and his daughter. She studied Anya's face. The girl still looked woebegone and, within a few minutes of taking a seat at one of the largest tables on the terrace, she had jumped up and walked over to the temporary bar set up beneath a bright red canopy.

'Would you excuse me for a moment?' Nancy asked the table at large, interrupting the men's conversation. 'I think I'll find myself a juice.'

'The waiter—' Leo began, but she was already halfway to the bar.

She slipped onto the stool next to Anya, smiling a greeting at the girl. 'Does your family have lunch here most Sundays?' she asked.

'Once a month—usually.' The young woman had a little more colour today, though her face looked thin and drawn. But she was still devastatingly lovely in a sundress of pale pink seersucker with a sweetheart neckline and flaring skirt.

'I suppose it's a chance to dress up,' Nancy suggested. 'I love your frock.'

'I was admiring yours,' Anya responded. 'Did you buy it in London? You must have done. You're lucky to have such smart fashion on your doorstep.'

'I'm afraid it was only from a market stall, but you must come to London one day and see for yourself.'

The girl looked down at the counter, her fingers twisting the long-stemmed glass she held. 'Gabriel...' she began wistfully.

'Gabriel?' Nancy prompted.

'He wanted to visit England. We'd made plans, you know.' Her voice cracked and her eyes began to fill with tears.

'I'm so sorry, Anya. It was a terrible thing to happen. But you'll go to London one day, I'm sure, and meanwhile your dress is just as beautiful as anything you could buy there.' The remark was frivolous, but she hoped it would give the girl a chance to regain her composure.

'I have a very good dressmaker,' Anya said at length. 'She was my mother's, really. I've kind of inherited her. My mother was very elegant...' The girl looked hopelessly into the distance.

Nancy was in two minds whether to pursue her original

aim. The conversation had so far been painful, and if she went ahead, she might trigger more tears. On the other hand, she was unlikely to have another chance to talk to Anya in private. 'Can I speak to you about Gabriel?' she asked. 'If it's too upsetting, you can tell me to go away.'

The girl looked doubtful but waved a hand as though bidding Nancy to continue. 'I wanted to ask you... what happened to Gabriel was terrible, but have you any idea how the fire started?' Nancy was clear that *she* knew the answer, but she hoped she might encourage Anya to talk. The girl worked with Luke Rossiter, and just maybe he'd let something fall.

Anya made a visible effort to steady herself before she said, 'The police say it was an accident. They've gone through the... the ashes,' she stumbled. 'And they're sure it was an overturned lamp.'

Nancy said nothing for a moment, but then Anya burst out, 'If it was, I don't see how Riel didn't get out. If the lamp caught fire like they say, the house wouldn't have burned immediately. There would have been time for him to escape.'

'Unless he was asleep and overcome by smoke.' Nancy didn't believe that for a moment, but she hoped this sad young girl might find some peace of mind in the thought.

'But if he was asleep, why was the lamp still lit?'

It was unanswerable, but Nancy tried. 'Perhaps he left it on by mistake. We'll never know.' The small hope that Anya might help fill the gaps in the story, had disappeared.

'No, we'll never know,' Anya repeated. 'Like so many things on this island.'

'Such as?'

'Why my mother up and went. Why she abandoned me. Why one day she was here, the next gone, and never a word from her since.' The words tumbled out. 'And why my aunt died. She was a friend to my mother, a friend to me, but she drowned. Did you know?'

'I heard there was a tragedy.'

Nancy held her breath, wondering if at least one of the island's mysteries was about to be solved. But Anya had no ready answer. 'We're a family of tragedy,' she said in a forlorn voice. 'But why that should be?'

Why should her mother have been driven away? Why her aunt presumably killed herself? Nancy hardly knew what to say, but this girl was riven by despair and her heart went out to her. Gabriel Sekela must have been a breath of fresh air after the darkness of the Martins' history. And now Anya had lost him.

'I can see—' she began, when the sound of a scuffle stopped her mid-sentence. Two waiters, breathing hard and with sweat on their brows, were trying to restrain a struggling figure. A woman. But she had broken free and was hurtling towards them. For a moment, Nancy felt herself freeze. It was Zamira.

The maid had reached them now and her frighteningly rigid form towered over Anya, her finger pointing histrionically at the girl's heart. 'You stole my man! You stole my Riel! And now he dead—your fault, your fault. You kill him.'

Anya slid from her stool, at first cowering from the onslaught, but then facing the angry woman directly and defending herself with energy. 'I stole no-one. I loved Gabriel and he loved me. If that's who you speak of.'

'You know who I mean. You know you a man stealer. A killer, too. See this—' and she pushed out her stomach, now visibly swollen, towards Anya. 'You murder his father. How that make you feel?'

'You're having a baby?' Anya was wide-eyed. 'I'm sorry

for you then. But you are wrong about Gabriel.'

'You think I don't know my own lover?'

The exchange had been short and sharp, while Nancy had unsuccessfully tried to take Zamira by the arm and lead her away. By now the waiters were upon them, followed by Jackson Garcia and Renzo, of all people. Of course, the Hastings would be here, though Nancy hadn't noticed them. At the same time, Ambrose Martin appeared from the opposite direction. The scene would have been farcical, if it had not been so distressing.

'I'll take charge of this,' Garcia announced, dismissing the two waiters. Obviously enraged, he turned on Zamira. 'What the hell are you doing in this place? You've no right to be here. You should be at the villa. That's what I pay you for.'

The maid was about to rail against him—just as angrily, Nancy was sure—when Renzo unexpectedly intervened.

'Go with your father, Anya,' he said, 'and I'll take Zamira home.'

The young girl allowed Ambrose to put his arm around her and lead her back to the Martins' table. Her grandparents had remained seated throughout, bolt upright, with expressions of incredulity on their faces.

'Come,' Jackson ordered. 'I'll see you off the premises. And tomorrow, King, I want you gone.'

The maid looked ready to fight on, until Renzo said quietly to her, 'Let it go, Zamira. I'll get my father's driver to take us back into town and we can talk on the way.'

For all his assumption of authority, Jackson looked pleased that the immediate problem had been taken out of his hands. He resumed his smile and shepherded Nancy back to their own table. From there they watched, along with the entire restaurant, as Renzo led Zamira from the terrace and into the club drawing room on their way to the exit.

'How unfortunate,' Isabella said with rare understatement, once the pair had vanished.

'Unfortunate, but not the end of the world.' Cy Devaux seemed keen to make light of the incident.

It was clear, though, that Jackson did not. 'King was not a good choice.' He glared at his wife. 'Whatever made you employ her?'

'I'm sorry Zamira has turned out badly,' Isabella said peaceably. 'I can see she'll have to go. But I'll find another maid for the villa very soon, I promise.'

'There's really no need,' Nancy put in quickly. 'We'll be leaving the island in a few days and I'm quite able to do what's needed in the house until we go.'

She looked over at her husband for confirmation and he gave a brief smile and an imperceptible nod. Nancy wondered if the smile suggested Leo was glad to be leaving. Garcia couldn't be the easiest person to work with, and perhaps new difficulties had emerged.

'Isabella will find you another maid,' Jackson said firmly. 'One who won't embarrass us.' He glared at his wife again, but Isabella wasn't looking at him. She was smiling at the waiter who was handing her lunch.

Chapter Twenty-Five

It was a mediocre meal: a tough joint of meat with half-roasted potatoes, beans, and okra that had become slimy in the cooking. Nancy did her best, but when the waiters came to clear, there was an embarrassing amount still on her plate. She was thankful that fruit was a choice for dessert: the sponge pudding would have sunk her. Why was it that 'English' establishments abroad had this need to replicate a cooking they considered the national cuisine?

With coffee, came a general shifting of chairs—families splitting up, people moving to be with friends. Isabella was becoming restless. 'Can I introduce you to anyone, Nancy?' she asked. 'These men, 'she gestured around the table, 'will be talking business for ever.'

It was a kind offer, but Nancy refused it. 'I'm happy to stay here,' she said, 'but don't let me stop you from meeting your friends.'

'Well, if you're sure…' Isabella jumped up and waited only seconds before disappearing across the terrace to a corner table. Loud greetings followed, then gales of female laughter.

Nancy tried to concentrate on the conversation at her own table. For some time Cy Devaux had been discussing his choice of artists for the new gallery and Jackson had been interrogating him closely, primarily on the cost of such acquisitions. Leo, she saw, was listening hard. Presumably whatever Cy bought would have an effect on his own purchasing power.

She lay back in her chair, closing her eyes to the sun and feeling its warmth soak through her. The voices around the table began to meld into one, and she was almost asleep when she felt someone slide into Isabella's empty chair. Forcing herself awake, she saw Lionel Martin's faded blue eyes watching her. She sat up straight when he offered her his hand.

'Did I startle you, Mrs Tremayne? I'm sorry to interrupt your siesta. I am of an age when resting after lunch is almost *de rigeur*, but I understand from my wife that babies can be tiring creatures even before they are born.' He looked at her hard, as though he knew the truth of her situation. He couldn't do, she reasoned. None of them could. It was her own sense of being an imposter that was hard at work.

'I took the liberty of joining you as I thought you might welcome a conversation that wasn't to do with money.' He glanced meaningfully towards Jackson. It seemed neither of the older Martins could resist a barb at Garcia's expense.

Nancy picked up her coffee, now almost cold. 'It's a beautiful club,' she said, determined not to become embroiled in his prejudices. She waved her hand vaguely in the air. 'You must enjoy meeting here.'

'We used to. Life is very different now.'

Again, he looked pointedly at Jackson, who was busy scribbling figures on a paper napkin. Then he half turned, his gaze taking in Scott Hastings and Renzo. The boy had reappeared only a few minutes ago. Rescuing Zamira had meant he'd missed his lunch, Nancy realised, but perhaps he wasn't too bothered. It had hardly been appetising, and Renzo had come a long way from the festering slices of salami that had been his mainstay in Venice. But it was clear from the expression on Lionel Martin's face that the Hastings family, despite their skin colour, were as much intruders as Jackson Garcia. For him, they would never be part of the small clique that rightfully owned the island.

'That was a regrettable incident earlier,' he said. 'It upset my granddaughter a great deal. Quite unnecessarily. What on earth was that woman doing here?' Nancy wondered if she was being taken to task for not minding her maid more thoroughly. 'But I hope you were able to enjoy your lunch despite the disturbance,' he went on. 'The cooking at the Serafina is far better, but eating at the club can be pleasurable on occasions. And how often can one say that these days?'

She gave him a smile which she hoped would excuse her from comment, then let her glance drift across the terrace to the Martins' table.

Eugénie Martin, dressed as usual in her austere black and wearing a bored expression, was listening to her son explaining something in which she evidently had little interest. Anya was looking across at Renzo, sitting close by. She must want to be with another young person, Nancy thought, and as she watched, the girl managed to slide away from her family and change tables. The look on Renzo's face when she sat down beside him told its own story. Another doomed passion, it seemed. The boy was a drifter, but he had a good heart, and Nancy had warmed to him since they'd met again in Malfuego.

'We have Renzo to thank for the day staying pleasurable,' she said. 'He acted very quickly, don't you think? And has given us a peaceful afternoon.'

Lionel sniffed, but made no attempt to respond. In the silence that followed, Nancy looked across at the young couple again. They were talking animatedly now but not, it seemed, for long. Luke Rossiter had walked over to them and dragged a chair up to their table. Renzo's shoulders, Nancy saw, literally drooped.

Lionel was following her gaze. 'That young man is too full of himself,' he declared. 'That assistant of Ambrose, or whatever he calls himself.'

Nancy wanted to agree, but felt it prudent to keep her true thoughts to herself. 'It's understandable that he's eager. Your granddaughter is very beautiful.'

Lionel sniffed again. 'There are different kinds of beauty, you know, Mrs Tremayne. Anya's tends to be skin deep.'

'I'm sure that's not true.' She was shocked that this man could speak so disparagingly of his granddaughter.

'She is far too much like her mother. Eugénie and I both agree.'

'What was she like? Anya's mother?' Nancy asked suddenly.

Lionel at first looked startled, then angry. 'Beautiful,' he snapped. 'Too beautiful for that poor son of ours.'

'They weren't happy, then? That's sad.'

'*She* wasn't. Jacinta. Always agitating to get off the island, travel places, do things. Ambrose had mills to run—I depended on him—but she would never accept that. Well, she got off the island in the end.'

'Let's hope she found happiness,' Nancy said lightly. 'It must have been such a difficult time for her daughter. And her husband. And sad for you to lose her at the same time as your own daughter.' If she were to be pestered by a man she disliked intensely, she might as well drag as much information from him as she could.

Lionel twisted in his chair to face her. His eyes, though dulled with age, had become alert and watchful. 'What do you know about that?'

'Very little. I thought it a tragic story when I was told of your loss.'

He looked slightly mollified. 'We have suffered loss, it's true. The Martins are an old family, after all, but we've survived. Do you know, our ancestor, Ambrose, came to this island without a penny? Back in Hampshire, he'd been shown the door. His father decided he must become a churchman and, when the boy refused, he was pushed out of his family home with only the clothes on his back. He had nothing, but by God he didn't stay with nothing. He travelled here on a tramp steamer. Borrowed money for the ticket and found a job on Malfuego under one of the sugar barons. Worked himself into the ground, fought slave rebellions, battled with disease—dengue fever and the rest—while other whites were succumbing. And saved enough to buy a small place of his own and a few slaves to work it. Then set about modernising the whole sugar process. That's how he made money. Enough to build four other mills and a grand mansion his descendants enjoy to this day. What do you think of that story, Mrs Tremayne?'

She was saved from answering by a low rumble that became louder by the second, until it seemed to fill the air they breathed. Conversation on the terrace had stopped, heads bobbed, eyes were on the watch.

'Is that the mountain again?' she asked. 'We've heard it before.'

'It's an old volcano. It does that every so often. This year it's been particularly tetchy, but there's nothing to worry about. See, it's stopped already. The last time it erupted was a good century ago. It's had its uses, though.'

'How do you mean?'

'It provoked fear. If ever a slave ran away, the volcano

made sure they were caught. Slaves couldn't use the port or the beaches to get off Malfuego—too many eyes, too many guards. So, where did they go? Run into the interior and up the mountain? I don't think so. Monte Muerte was angry, a lot angrier than it is today. Some rebels braved it, but most were too fearful. They were trapped. They couldn't get off the island, and they couldn't hide on it.' Lionel looked delighted with his story, but it left Nancy feeling sick and desperate to flee. His next words fell like honey on her ears.

'I'm afraid I must go, dear lady. Eugénie will be wanting to take a rest at home. A word of warning before I leave.' He looked over at Jackson, who had tucked the napkin in his pocket but was still deep in conversation with his colleagues. 'Don't get too close to the Garcias. Mongrels, the pair of them.'

Still feeling queasy from the conversation she'd endured, Nancy pushed back her chair with a murmured excuse to the others, and walked to the low wall that separated the terrace from the boardwalk. Fresh air, she needed fresh air.

'What was that all about?' It was Archie, drink in hand.

'You don't want to know. Lionel Martin is a truly horrible man.'

'Try the punch.' He held out the glass to her. 'It softens the blow. What a Godawful place this club is.'

'Isn't it? But I did glean something from him at least.'

'Like what?'

'That I'm right to think there was something decidedly odd about the sister who died— Charlotte Martin—and the way Anya's mother disappeared at exactly the same time. Lionel Martin pounced on me when I mentioned it. He didn't want to speak about it. Or only if he could throw mud at his daughter-in-law.'

'You were talking to him a fair time. Did Sekela come up

in the conversation?'

'Gabriel's murder will mean nothing to a man like Lionel Martin. But Anya is suspicious. She doesn't believe that a lamp caused the fire. If it had, she said, Gabriel would have had time to escape. It's what I've always thought. And if drugs are the reason he had to die, Rossiter must be number one suspect. Unless there's someone else in the background we've no idea about.'

Archie ignored the suggestion and looked over her shoulder at the Garcias' table. 'And Jackson—I presume he's no longer in the frame?'

Nancy shook her head. 'He's so taken up with this project, I don't think he'd have any part in whatever racket is going on. For the last few hours I've heard him talk about little else but the gallery. He wouldn't dabble in anything that would destroy his dream. And drugs certainly would, if the police got involved. It would create a scandal that would scare away the very visitors Jackson wants to attract.'

'Not guilty after all?'

'Guilty of the accidents, I think. Or some of them. Staged to dissuade Gabriel from interfering in the island's politics.'

'But you're not much further forward, are you? You've a murder that's not being treated as a murder, and no evidence to support the claim that it should be. None of it's too promising. And neither was enduring a meal opposite Rossiter. I'd liked to have thumped him on the nose after his attack on you. Instead, I had to listen to him banging on about what a great fellow he is and what a future he has in store. Until he got bored with trying to impress the two elderly ladies who were unlucky enough to share our table. The food wasn't much cop either.'

'No, but how ghastly to have to do this every month. Anya told me they do, more or less.'

'No wonder her mother did a runner.'

Nancy leaned on the parapet, watching a canoeist far out cut a path through the water's calm surface. 'Rossiter gave nothing away while he was boasting?'

Archie grinned. 'I kept hoping he would offer the Misses Trimble a snort, but no luck.'

'Seriously, Archie.'

She wanted to scold him but found it difficult. He was irrepressible. There was a time when his jokes, his casual jibes and spiteful asides, had hurt her. But she'd come to realise they were his response to Leo's sudden marriage. Archie had harboured grave suspicions about his employer's young wife and the reason she'd married a man much older than herself—a man she hardly knew. Nancy hoped those suspicions were dead now, abandoned in the dangers they'd shared in Venice.

'I did manage to drop Gibbon Bass into the conversation,' he said casually.

'How?'

'I pretended I was interested in going deep sea fishing.'

'You—fishing? In a small boat?' She spluttered.

His expression was one of hurt innocence. 'How is it my fault I'm seasick? He didn't need to know that. I said I'd heard that Bass owned a yacht that might be up for hire.'

'And…'

'He was guarded. When I asked if he could introduce us, he said he didn't know Bass very well.'

'Which is a plain lie. And stupid. You work for Leo. He knows that, and he must know there's a chance that Leo would have told you about the incident on the beach.'

'You'd think so, but under all that bombast, I reckon the man is a simpleton. And what the hell is that?'

A shattering roar cut through the loud chatter. Coffee

cups hung suspended, glasses were lowered, eyes became fixed on the sea. Peering into the distance, Nancy saw a white-painted launch sweep into view, a churn of froth in its wake. The engine was cut abruptly as it neared the landing stage, narrowly missing the iron stanchions that secured the jetty. A magnificent figure threw a rope over a mooring post and leapt from the boat.

'Is that Superman?' Archie asked.

'It is. This should be interesting.'

Whether Luke Rossiter found it interesting was a moot point, Nancy was to think later. Ambrose Martin's personal assistant, as he styled himself, was halfway through a sentence, leaning ever closer to Anya, when Gibbon Bass strode along the jetty, jumped the dividing wall between boardwalk and terrace, and barged his way towards his victim. Tables, plates, and cutlery were sent flying. Broken glass was ground into the paved floor by a large pair of sea boots.

With one huge hand, Bass yanked Rossiter upright by his collar. Anya had been watching open-mouthed, but now leapt from her seat in alarm. She need not have worried. Gibbon Bass had his quarry—the only one that interested him. He appeared almost to tuck the man beneath his shoulder, then dragged him down the flight of stairs he'd ignored on his way onto the terrace, and along the boardwalk. Was he taking him back to the bay, intending to finish what he'd started? Nancy wondered. But why now, after all these days? Perhaps Rossiter had been playing hard to find and Bass, tired of waiting to get the man alone, was prepared to wreak his vengeance in full view of Malfuego's elite.

He steadied the young man at the edge of the jetty, then took hold of both Rossiter's shoulders and, with a kick at his legs that crumpled from the blow, sent him toppling into the water. She looked at Archie, who had a wide smile on his face. It might do Luke Rossiter good to have a ducking, she agreed. And he'd been made to look foolish in front of Anya. That might mean he would leave her alone.

But then Anya was rushing down the steps to the boardwalk and racing towards the end of the jetty. She was shouting and her hands were waving wildly.

'What's up with her? What is she saying?' Nancy asked.

Archie's expression had changed. 'He can't swim,' he said quickly. 'That's what she's saying. She needs to throw him a lifebelt. Where the hell is it?'

Urgently, they scanned the jetty together, and then the terrace and the wall of the club building, but there was no sign of a lifebelt.

'Sod me,' Archie said, and leapt the low wall onto the jetty, tearing off his shoes as he ran. Galvanised, Nancy ran after him. Rossiter was thrashing the water in a frantic struggle to stay afloat as Archie plunged in. He reached the drowning man just as he was about to go under again, dragging him to the surface and turning his limp body to face the sky, his hand beneath Rossiter's chin.

'Lie still and float,' Nancy heard him shout. 'I'll get you ashore.' But Luke had fainted—presumably from fear—and he was a dead weight for Archie to manoeuvre to the iron ladder at the end of the jetty.

All this time, Bass had not been idle. He'd cast off the rope and restarted the engine. Nancy looked hopelessly around. Bass was making a getaway after trying to drown a man. Were they going to let him? Nobody had moved. It was as though every member of the club had become an involuntary audience for a matinee performance.

'Someone telephone the police,' Nancy yelled. 'He's getting away.'

That seemed to spur at least a few. Leo had jumped up and was making for the interior, looking for a telephone, she hoped. Ambrose Martin was at his heels. But Gibbon Bass wasn't finished yet. He revved the engine until its roar was unbearable, but instead of heading out to sea, he turned the launch parallel to the jetty and put his foot down on the accelerator.

Nancy held up her hands in horror. Bass was deliberately aiming for Archie and the man he was trying to save.

'Archie, look out!' she cried uselessly.

'Oh, my God.' Leo was back and right beside her. 'Save yourself, Archie,' he yelled. 'Let him go.'

But Archie wouldn't let go. Doggedly, he kept swimming to the jetty steps, his hand clasping the unconscious man's head, holding it clear of the water. The boat was on top of him now. Nancy turned her back, unable to watch. Not Archie. Please, not Archie, her whole being cried out.

It seemed an age before she felt Leo's arm around her. 'It's okay, Nancy. He's all right. But not Rossiter, I'm afraid.'

Chapter Twenty-Six

Archie clambered up the iron steps of the ladder, clearly exhausted, but helped by two of the waiting staff who had sprung suddenly to life. Of Rossiter there was no sign. Leaving the shelter of Leo's arms, Nancy ran towards the dripping man.

'I couldn't hang onto him,' were his first words, water cascading from his sodden clothes. 'That bastard got him.'

Nancy clasped his arm, not caring how wet she became. 'You tried. And you're safe.'

'But *he's* dead.' Archie shook his head from side to side, drops of water flying across the jetty.

'We need to get you to the hospital.' Jackson had bustled up them, now all action. When Archie started to protest, Jackson held up his hand. 'You need to be checked. An x-ray on the arm. See, it's badly swollen already. And a tetanus jab. You're bleeding.'

Archie looked down at his ankle. A wide gash had opened, and blood was pouring out. Horrified, Nancy stared at the wound, not knowing what to do. It was Leo who stepped in and said quickly, 'I'll go with Archie. Roland can take us. If you could get Nancy home?'

'Sure thing. Isabella can drive her. I should stay and see the police. I want them to be clear what happened. The last thing we need is idle gossip being spread.'

That sounded very much like a cover-up to Nancy. But, worried for Archie and appalled by what she'd just witnessed, she lacked the energy to mount any kind of challenge, and as soon as Leo had helped his assistant through the door into the club lounge, she went back to their table and collected her handbag and scarf. The older Martins hadn't moved from their seats, she noticed. They'd sat watching events unfold, stiff and expressionless.

Her glance travelled across to Renzo. His face wore a bewildered expression, but Scott Hastings, sitting next to his son, looked terrified. Beneath his tan, the man's face had taken on a grey hue. Nancy wondered why. Had there been a threat to him? When Gibbon Bass strode ashore, leapt the dividing wall and crunched his way onto the terrace, had Scott thought it was he who'd been chosen for extinction? It was becoming clearer by the day that Renzo's father was as deeply involved as the other two men. A police investigation was bound to follow Rossiter's death, though it might not lead to Scott's door. He appeared to have powerful friends. Jackson, for instance, with whom he'd done 'business' and who was even now preparing to bludgeon the police into accepting his version of today's events.

Nancy followed her hostess through the club and immediately spotted the pink Cadillac. A quick look around the car park confirmed that Roland and the saloon were gone. Archie was on his way to hospital.

'Don't worry.' Isabella beamed at her. 'Your friend is a strong chap and the doctors will patch him up beautifully.'

Nancy gave her a swift look. Had Isabella somehow divined feelings she dared not acknowledge? But that was foolish. To the outside world, Archie would seem as much a friend as an employee—to both Leo and herself.

'I'll drop you off and run, if that's all right,' her companion said. 'I should get back to Jackson as soon as I can.' It seemed Isabella was as concerned about the police as her husband.

At the villa, she watched Nancy walk to the front door, then had Ernesto swiftly turn the car. 'I'll call tomorrow to check on the invalid,' she called out.

*

It was several hours before the invalid returned. Nancy heard the two men stumbling along the hall, Leo evidently helping his assistant to manage the walk to the sitting room, one step at a time. When Archie appeared in the doorway, she was shocked. His complexion was wax-like, his arm was in a sling, and a thick bandage cushioned his ankle.

'Walking wounded,' he said, managing a faint smile.

She jumped up and walked over to them. 'What did the doctors say?'

'No breaks,' Leo answered. 'But a badly bruised arm, and an ankle that needed half a dozen stitches.'

'Come in and sit down. I've made a salad, if you fancy a light meal. I'm afraid there wasn't much else in the kitchen. Zamira has vanished. I looked into her room and all her possessions have gone. It's been completely stripped.'

'Thanks for the offer,' Archie said. 'But if it's okay with you chaps, I think I'll take myself to bed. I feel done in for the moment.'

He declined Leo's help of assistance up the stairs, but above her head Nancy could hear his progress along the landing and it was painfully slow. When his bedroom door closed, she looked at Leo.

'That was a dreadful thing.'

'Inexplicable. Though Jackson told me quietly that he's had his suspicions something like this was brewing, and was fairly certain that someone at the hotel was involved. Drugs are at the bottom of it. Bass, apparently, is already well known for his criminal activities, and drugs would be a lucrative sideline. Dangerous, though.'

'I doubt Bass is the kind of man to be discouraged by danger.'

She was certain Jackson knew a great deal more than he was telling Leo. He must, for instance, have a strong suspicion that his business pal, Hastings, was involved, too. And he would probably know of others. The three men she was aware of could be the tip of an army of carriers and dealers, most of whom would stay in the shadows. But her guesswork appeared to have been vindicated: Gabriel had met his death because he'd dared to interfere with what was a successful drug ring. Why then did a small niggle remain?

'As you've gone to the trouble of making dinner, shall we eat?' Leo asked.

'It's not exactly a feast, but I scoured the fridge and the cupboards and did my best. I'll have to shop tomorrow.'

'It's a chore you shouldn't have to do. What do you think has happened to Zamira?'

'She might have gone home to her mother, though she could be halfway to Trinidad by now. It's what Marissa King threatened.'

They wandered down to the kitchen together and Nancy took two full plates out of the refrigerator, putting them down side-by-side on the counter. 'Shall we eat here?'

'We might as well.' Leo pulled out a kitchen stool and sat down. 'Are you sure you won't take up Isabella's offer to find a new maid?'

'I'm sure. Let's keep it peaceful. It won't hurt me to cook for a few days. And who knows, when Archie is feeling better, he might turn out to be a dab hand in the kitchen!'

'When he's feeling better, I want him on a ship to England.'

Nancy put down her fork with a bang and stared at him. 'You, too,' he continued. 'I've been thinking about it for a couple of days, and this afternoon's drama has decided me.'

'I don't understand. Are you saying that you're staying, but I'm to go?'

'I don't want to, Nancy, believe me. But Jackson has floored me rather. Floored Cy, too. We were both expecting to pack up, but Joshi is arriving from India in two days' time—unless his wife has a relapse—and Jackson wants to finalise plans with all three of us here. It means I have to stay longer than I expected.'

'Then I'll stay. And Archie, too. We'll both stay until you're finished.'

Leo shook his head. 'Archie is more use to me now in London, and I want you off this island. I have a bad feeling about the place. I have ever since we arrived,' he confessed. 'The sooner you're back in Cavendish Street, the better. And you won't be travelling alone. You'll have Archie to escort you.'

She picked up her fork again and tried to concentrate on eating. A long journey with Archie. Two weeks on a ship together. She couldn't do it—but neither could she tell Leo why.

'Don't I get a say?' she asked lightly. 'Because if I do, I'd much rather sit it out with you.'

'I'll be fine, darling. I'll take up Isabella's offer and whoever she sends can rustle me up an evening meal and change the bed. That's all I need.'

'But I've got to quite like it here,' she said desperately.

'Really?'

'Yes,' she lied. 'It's taken a while, but now I've made a few friends. I'd be happy to stay.'

Leo gave her a steady look and she tried to make her face happy. 'If you do stay—' he began.

'Yes.' She held her breath. She had created a doubt in his mind, but would it be sufficient?

'If you do stay, you must promise to keep clear of any of future unpleasantness. Stay away from the town, stay away from the hotel, let Isabella take you out and about. And I'll try to wrap things up as soon as I can. I know Cy doesn't want to stay a minute longer than he needs to.'

'That's settled then. And Archie?'

'He might as well stay. No point in just one of us leaving, and I suppose it will take a while before he's fully fit.'

The meal was over and the washing up despatched in record time. 'Bed?' Leo asked on the stairs. 'It's only nine o' clock, but I'm exhausted.'

Nancy smiled her agreement, her heart feeling a great deal lighter. She waited until her husband was in the bathroom and then walked quietly along the corridor and gave a soft knock on Archie's door. There was no answer and she opened it a few inches. He was sprawled across the bed, shoes kicked off, but otherwise fully dressed. He'd slept where he'd fallen.

She slipped into the room and grabbed the patchwork eiderdown that had been bundled into the easy chair, then covered the sleeping man, taking care not to disturb him. He would need some warmth as the night wore on: his windows were wide open and the air was already noticeably cooler.

She made it back to the bedroom just as Leo emerged from his wash, towel in hand. 'Who would have thought life on a quiet island could be so disturbing?' he said. 'And there was me thinking that bringing you to Malfuego was the right thing. I honestly believed sunshine and rest would put you back on your feet after those weeks of sickness. But look what happened. And now all this. What a joke!'

'You weren't to know.'

'No,' he said thoughtfully, the lines on his forehead deepening. 'If I had known…'

He left the sentence trailing and she knew he was thinking of their lost baby. If they'd stayed in London, would she have miscarried? She wanted to tell him that she'd never felt secure in the pregnancy, that it could have happened anywhere, but that was hardly reassuring.

'If you'd known, you wouldn't have accepted the job,' she finished for him.

'I'm beginning to regret it. But Jackson is still wildly enthusiastic and I can't let him down. Let's hope a good sleep makes the world look a little brighter.'

*

It seemed to have done when, the next morning, Nancy looked into the kitchen to find her husband finishing his breakfast.

'You're early.' She gave a yawn.

'A meeting,' Leo said between mouthfuls, 'with the town worthies, as Jackson calls them. I don't really have to attend, but I think he'll need some support in selling his project.'

'Do they have the power to stop it?' She sat down on the stool next to him.

'Not exactly. It's his land and he can build what he wants, but if they give it the thumbs down and don't back him, I'm sure they'll find a hundred and one ways of being awkward. This morning is given over to diplomacy. Explaining what the gallery will look like, what it will contain, what the hopes are for its future. That kind of thing.'

'Was Archie supposed to go with you? He's still asleep, I think.'

'Let him sleep. It's not necessary he's at the meeting and

there's nothing for him to do at Jackson's today. In fact, he needn't come to the office again. I'll want him to write a few letters, make some phone calls, but he can do that from here. And otherwise take it easy. I think he needs to. Definitely no flying.'

'He'll be disappointed.'

'Maybe, but then he shouldn't go being a hero.'

She wasn't sure if it was lightly said or whether she detected a hint of waspishness in Leo's voice. 'Anyway, must go.' He took his plates to the sink. 'Roland is due at eight, and the man is punctual to the minute.'

After her husband had left, she dropped bread into the toaster and looked hopefully around the cupboards for a jar of marmalade, settling in the end for something labelled guava jam that turned out to taste delicious. But she would have to go shopping, buy bread and fruit and vegetables at least. The freezer—Jackson had supplied the villa with all the latest conveniences—still contained several packets of meat and one or two whole fish. That would feed them for several days, and hopefully it wouldn't be too much longer before they were on their way home.

She was clearing the crockery when Archie appeared in the doorway, heavy-eyed and very pale.

'Go back to bed. You look awful,' she told him.

'Thanks for the vote of confidence. Where's Leo?'

'He left for Jackson's a good half hour ago. He says you're to stay home today. There's a meeting with the town's bigwigs and there's no need for you to be there.'

'Not being a bigwig myself.'

'Exactly. Do you want some breakfast before you go back to bed?'

He yawned loudly, then reached up with his one free arm and stretched to the ceiling. 'I'm not going back to bed. As far as I can, I'll shower, shave, and find some clean clothes. You won't recognise me.'

Nancy realised then that she needed clothes herself. She was still in her nightdress and it was flimsy. She felt herself redden, but tried hard to pretend there was nothing amiss.

'And breakfast?' she asked.

'What is there?'

'Not much. Well, not anything really, just toast.'

'Then toast it is—and coffee, if we have any.'

'There's a little, but I need to go shopping. If you had two arms, you could help.'

'As a beast of burden, I presume.'

'Yes, but you're lucky, you're excused. You can't carry.' Pouring a cup of coffee for him, she pointed to his left arm still in a sling.

'I have another arm, or haven't you noticed?' He made a show of taking the cup in his right hand and drinking.

She noticed every single thing about Archie, just as she was sure he did about her. 'If we could be ready by nine thirty, we could catch the bus down the hill.' She remembered what Zamira had told her of the timetable.

'I'll see you at the front door then.' He picked up a spare piece of toast. 'Don't keep me waiting.'

Chapter Twenty-Seven

They were in good time for the bus which dropped them halfway down the hill to Malfuego town, where the local market was situated in a side street. The market was a sunny place. The weather, of course, made it so, the sun hardly ever refusing to shine, but it was sunny in mood as well. It helped Nancy forget for a while yesterday's tragedy. She hoped it helped Archie, too. She'd noticed that his earlier chirpiness had disappeared, and his face was now unusually serious.

'It looks like you were right,' he said, as they did a second tour of the fruit and vegetable stalls before deciding which one to patronise.

She looked enquiringly at him. 'About the drugs. Rossiter was almost certainly in cahoots with Bass. Young Luke must have done something to displease him.'

'Hastings, too,' Nancy said. 'You wouldn't have noticed, but he looked positively green. He must have been thinking that it could have been him rather than Rossiter.'

'If it had, I wouldn't have been able to save him either,' Archie said gloomily.

She came to a halt, balancing a basket on her arm. 'You have to stop thinking like that. You did all you humanly could. Gibbon Bass was mowing the pair of you down. He wanted to kill you as well as Rossiter. Or at least, he didn't care whether you lived or died. And don't forget—not one other soul went to Rossiter's aid. It was left to you.'

'He was just a kid.' Archie was morose. 'Vain, boastful, a complete moron, but just a kid. He shouldn't have died.'

'No, he shouldn't. But neither should he have got involved in something as dangerous as drug running. What was he thinking? He had a career and a good future in front of him.'

'Greed? It does strange things to people. Maybe he thought more money would win fair lady.'

Nancy picked up a sweet potato. 'Some of these? And courgettes and carrots. What do you think?'

'Fine.'

'I'll get some red onions, too. No aubergines, though, I promise.'

He smiled at that and she was glad to see it. He'd complained in Venice that Italian food was never without aubergines. It wasn't true, but Archie hated them with a vigour that could sniff them out anywhere. He took one of the baskets, now filled to the brim, in his right hand and together they walked over to the fruit stall that looked most promising. Here, she was spoilt for choice: bananas, naturally, but jackfruit, naseberries, Spanish limes, all piled high. She knew the names but wasn't sure just how these exotic fruits would taste, and instead went for guavas and safety.

'I suppose I can ask Virginie to search Rossiter's room now and she won't need an excuse,' Nancy said, handing over a fist of notes to the stallholder. 'If she passes those packets to the police, it will help them build their case.'

'Ever thought of becoming a private eye?' he asked, as they sauntered to the end of the market.

She laughed. 'I might when I've got art restoration under my belt.'

'I'm serious. You're made for it. You're nosy—'

'Curious,' she amended.

'Nosy and determined, and you've got a brain.'

'Which you've just discovered?'

He shook his head. 'I realised that early on. It's why—'

'Why you thought I'd engineered the trouble I was in with Philip March. That I was duping Leo into believing I was in danger when I was simply a gold-digger.'

'Let me have the other basket,' he said roughly. 'I can manage two in the same hand.'

'Don't be silly.'

'I'm not. I don't think you should be carrying anything too heavy yet. It's what Ma always said, though she'd no reason to—four sons and no problem.' When he saw her face, he said, 'Sorry, that was stupid of me.'

'It doesn't matter. And I'm fine. Look an ice cream stall. What do you think?'

'Why not?'

They chose large cones packed with creamy swirls of vanilla ice, and found a seat in the shade to eat their booty before it melted.

'You've grown a moustache.' He took a handkerchief from his pocket and rubbed it across her upper lip.

'And you're sporting a beard. How did you get it on your chin?' She reached over and removed the offending line with a swish of her fingers.

There was something intimate and very much too tempting in those small gestures. She jumped up sharply and looked at her watch. 'Come on, or we'll miss the bus back, and it's uphill all the way.'

*

'The villa has been a comfortable home,' she said, as they walked through the gates, 'but I won't be sorry to leave. I don't think Leo will either. He's beginning to wonder what kind of commission he's taken on.'

'I could have told him months ago it was likely to be dodgy.'

'The soothsayer,' she teased. 'But he'll have to come back, I imagine. To supervise—when the pictures he buys are hung.'

'Not necessarily. He could get a scale drawing made of the gallery space. That would enable him to direct someone else as to where he wants each work to go.'

'He'll need to return for the gallery opening, though.'

'True, but that's a long way off. And maybe never, if much more goes wrong.'

Nancy looked ahead and saw a splash of pink motor car through the palms. 'Isabella is here. She said she'd call.'

Archie gave a groan. 'More Garcias.'

'Stop it. She's a lovely woman.'

'Nancy! And Archie! How are you?' Isabella's voice was so warm that Archie had the grace to look slightly ashamed.

'I'm okay, thanks. Just a bit battered.'

'Of course, you are. Such a brave thing you did. But you shouldn't be carrying that heavy bag. And nor should you, Nancy.' She fussed around them both, helping them to the front steps, and seeming upset they had been forced to go shopping. 'I'm very sorry about Zamira. I thought she was a trustworthy girl, or I would never have employed her.'

'I'm sure she was,' Nancy soothed. 'She had troubles of her own, that was the problem.'

'Now apparently she's disappeared to Trinidad. But won't you let me find you another girl? You can't go heaving great bags around every day.'

Nancy shook her head.

'Well, if you won't have another maid, at least telephone me and I'll get Ernesto to pick up what you need.'

'I wasn't sure what we needed, and the market was fun.'

'Really?' The idea of a market being fun was evidently a new concept for a woman whom Nancy guessed hadn't shopped for food for years. 'But in any case, I've bought you a treat. Cook has made you a chicken curry. I think it's chicken, though it could be goat.' She turned to her driver who was leaning against the Cadillac's bonnet. 'Ernesto, be a dear and carry the casserole into the kitchen.'

'Won't you stay for a cup of tea?' Nancy asked, praying that Zamira had left a spare packet in the cupboard, but relieved when Isabella refused the invitation.

'I must be getting back, my dear. We're knee-deep in State Assembly members, and the police are waiting to interview us. They've already taken statements from many of the people who were at the club. I rather think you'll be next.'

'And Luke Rossiter?'

'The police divers recovered his body this morning. There will be a post-mortem, of course, but it's fairly clear what the conclusion will be. Oh, and more news, we heard just before I left home that the Trinidad police have arrested Gibbon Bass, so he hasn't escaped after all. He'll be charged for your injuries, Archie, as well as Luke's murder. It's all very upsetting. It does the island's reputation no good at all. Hopefully, Jackson will be able to bring pressure where it's needed, and the police can wrap up the case without too much noise.'

Nancy exchanged a look with Archie. It was clear they were thinking alike, but Isabella didn't notice. She was already planning ahead.

'Now, how about a little trip tomorrow? I think you'd like the church I mentioned, Nancy. And you, too, Archie. You won't be going back to work just yet, and though the church is on a hill, we can drive most of the way up. And afterwards, lunch? Ernesto can take us on to Loredo. There's a wonderful restaurant in the main square. What do you both say?'

*

Leo returned from his meeting with the town's worthies extremely tired. They had not been an easy group to convince: one man had been particularly difficult, asking endless questions, most of them irrelevant, while another had spent the entire meeting sneezing into a none-too-clean handkerchief.

'Jackson was brilliant,' Leo said, spreading himself across the sofa, a glass of rum in one hand. 'He's a natural salesman. I tried to back him up where I could, but Cy was worse than useless, saying nothing for most of the meeting and only agreeing with Jackson when really forced to. I can't say I blame him. The right to view great art shouldn't need that kind of justification.' He gave a sigh and stretched himself lengthwise, dangling his toes over the edge of the sofa. 'Thank the Lord I'm excused duty tomorrow.'

'Then you can come with us,' Nancy said immediately. 'Isabella was here today to ask how Archie was doing. Oh, by the way, she left a curry for tonight—I'm hoping it's chicken not goat—and invited us out for the day tomorrow. She wants to show us the oldest church on the island and then take us on to a small town she knows for a brilliant lunch. I've a feeling the food is the main attraction as far as she's concerned.'

'As far as I'm concerned, too, if the curry really is goat.'

'I'll cook some rice to go with it and we won't notice the difference.'

'How about Archie, then? Is he home? Is he feeling any better?'

'A lot better, I think. He's still wearing the sling, but he helped me with the shopping this morning and he went into town an hour ago. He's coming with us on the trip tomorrow.'

Chapter Twenty-Eight

But Leo himself wasn't coming. He was still sleeping the next morning after Nancy had washed and dressed and was ready for breakfast. Yesterday's meeting must have been more fatiguing than she'd realised, and she left him to sleep on. But when he appeared in the kitchen half an hour later, he looked decidedly ill.

'I—' He sneezed loudly. 'I think I've caught that dreadful man's cold. My head feels like a bowl of porridge and my legs are cotton wool.'

Nancy pushed aside a dish of sliced fruit and jumped up from her stool. 'You must go back to bed,' she said, crossing the room to him. 'I'll bring you a hot drink. Then I'd better telephone Isabella—unless Archie will still want to go. I haven't seen him this morning.'

'No,' Leo said thickly, 'you're to go. Both of you. I'll be perfectly okay here. I'll probably sleep for most of the day.'

'But there's no-one to bring you a drink or get you food, if you fancy something.'

'I won't, I assure you. And as for a drink, there must be a thermos somewhere in the kitchen. You could leave me that.'

'There is. There's one at the top of the corner cupboard. I saw it the other day.'

'Good. Problem solved. I think I'll drag myself back to bed

now and hope you don't get this. It's a corker.'

*

Archie missed breakfast, but was waiting for Nancy in the garden when the pink Cadillac drew up at the front door.

'Poor Leo,' Isabella exclaimed, when she heard of his illness. 'I know the wretch who's given him the cold. That man was coughing and spluttering the whole day. He's probably infected my entire household, but I hope we three can still go.' She sounded anxious. 'It would be a shame to miss lunch.'

'Leo insists that we go, and I'm keen to see the church,' Nancy said brightly.

Archie didn't look that keen, but the alternative was a tedious day spent at *Belvoir* with only an invalid for company, and she wasn't surprised to see him slide into the front of the car beside Ernesto.

From what Nancy had seen on the few journeys she'd made, the island was a mass of vegetation and, as they travelled along the straight road that ran parallel to the coast, it was lushly emerald fields they passed, stalks of sugar cane unmoving in the windless air. They turned inland onto a road that wound its way up the mountainside but the cane fields continued, spreading themselves across the lower slopes of Monte Muerte. High above, a wreath of cloud crowned the mouth of the volcano.

'The cane is almost tall enough to cut,' Isabella remarked. 'But it's late this year.'

'I've been told that sugar is a dying industry,' Nancy said. 'How much does the island actually produce?'

'The crop is certainly nowhere near as lucrative as it was. And not as lucrative as in some other islands. But cane means sugar and sugar is money, and until the money dries up there will be cane fields in Malfuego. And the harvest is a big moment, you know. There'll be a week-long festival to celebrate and an opening ceremony where they crown the King and Queen of the harvest—they're the season's best cutters.'

Isabella laid back in her seat and closed her eyes against the brilliant light pouring into the car, but Nancy was too interested in the passing landscape to doze. They'd journeyed a little way up this mountain before, she realised, but on a different road. The evening they'd arrived on the island and gone to dinner at the Garcia's. This time, though, they were travelling a good deal higher.

She watched as the fields gradually dwindled in number. Twisting in her seat, she looked back the way they'd climbed and could glimpse in the far distance a ribbon of sea, shading to an intense blue-black beneath the golden disc of the sun.

Bend followed bend, Ernesto steering them expertly up the helter-skelter of a road, until finally they were rounding the last curve, and the church was in front of them, its square stone turret weather-beaten and pitted.

'1608,' Isabella said proudly, coming awake. 'That's when it was built—for the first settlers. Almost as old as the churches in England! And the graveyard is enormous.'

The church in Riversley, Nancy's home village in Hampshire, had been built at least two centuries earlier. But it would be unkind to mention it, she thought, and followed Isabella out of the car and into the graveyard. Archie trailed after them. Throughout the journey, she'd been aware of his silence, and wondered if he was still in pain. He'd dispensed with his sling today and perhaps that hadn't been a good idea.

When he interrupted their conversation to say, 'Why don't I wait inside the church?' Nancy was happy to agree.

'Before you do, could you go back to the car and tell Ernesto we'll be leaving in about half an hour?' Isabella asked him.

Archie signalled agreement, and the two women resumed their walk around the cemetery. Whole families had been buried here together, Nancy noticed, but without any mention of why they had died. It was the word 'Providence' that appeared frequently. She wondered how many of these people had been sent out from England never to return, and how many had managed to retire and die in places like Cheltenham.

A tabby cat was twining its way around the tombstones and she bent to stroke him. 'There's a whole colony of cats here,' her hostess said. 'But look, Nancy, look at how ancient these monuments are.' Nancy looked.

The gravestones might be old, but their inhabitants had not been: Daniel McKinnon, aged 40; William Kerr, aged 17; Mary Ann Hosier, 28; Millicent Taylor, 13. There were a distressingly large number of infants, too, their small graves mere bumps in the greensward.

'I'm glad I didn't bring Anya,' Isabella said. 'I'd forgotten how many premature deaths this place holds. Far too many for her to deal with at the moment.'

'Was she coming then?' Nancy was surprised.

'I thought a day out—somewhere away from town— might help her forget a little, she's been badly cast down. But when I rang the hotel and spoke to Ambrose, he said she was busy dealing with a trade delegation and couldn't come. They'd arrived unexpectedly. It's just as well, really. Dealing with a clutch of new customers will be a far better distraction for her.'

They turned and wandered back the way they had come, towards the church entrance, the turf soft beneath their feet.

'I'm beginning to understand a very little why the older Martins hold the attitudes they do,' Nancy said thoughtfully. 'Malfuego must have been a literal graveyard for Europeans, and those that stuck it out had to be resilient. Brave, too.'

'And cruel, don't forget.'

'No, I can't forget that. But so many children,' Nancy said, glancing around.

'It's the climate, my dear. It can be hostile to the young and the vulnerable. Then there are insects that bring disease with them. But you shouldn't be looking at those—they are too sad. Particularly not in your condition. It's very thoughtless of me to walk you here.'

Her companion looked so crestfallen that Nancy was forced into the truth. 'I'm not pregnant any more, Isabella,' she said very quietly. 'I lost the baby days ago.'

Isabella clasped hold of her arm and pulled her into a close embrace. 'I am dreadfully sorry. You poor thing. Even more of a reason why we shouldn't be spending time with these,' and she waved her hand at the lichen-covered headstones. 'But are you well? In your body, I mean.'

'Yes. I feel fine. In a way, I was fortunate that it happened early on.' Her body had healed well, her heart less so. She carried with her still a sense of emptiness, a sharp sadness, that she hadn't expected. Archie had been right when he'd said that feeling bereft might come later.

Isabella nodded wisely. 'I lost a child, you know. But I was much further along than you and it left me in a bit of a mess. In fact, it meant we couldn't have children after that.'

Nancy felt dreadful. She had kept her secret hidden, refused to share it, as though she were in some way special. Yet Isabella had suffered far more. She gave her friend an answering hug. 'And *I'm* sorry. This place can't be any better for you.'

'It was way back in the past, and Jackson and I accepted a

long time ago that we'd be on our own. It's worked well, and we're happy enough.'

'But still—'

'These things happen, Nancy, and we have to deal with them as best we can. I was lucky—I had a lot of support. Jackson has always been the most amazingly positive person. He has his faults, I know'—Isabella looked as if she might say more—'but at bottom, he is a good man, just sometimes too intent on getting what he wants. And after we lost the baby, he seemed more intent than ever. Seemed to need to fling himself into business and make sure it always went the way he wanted.'

That summed up Jackson well, Nancy thought. If he had set those hoodlums on Gabriel—and she was convinced he had—it wasn't from personal animosity, but simply that the boy stood in the way of what Jackson wanted.

They'd reached the church porch and Isabella paused for a moment. 'And I didn't just have Jackson to help me,' she said. 'I had a wonderful nurse. Mary Sekela. Poor Gabriel's mother.'

Nancy was suddenly on the alert. 'Mary Sekela?'

'Yes. Dead now, of course, but she was an amazing woman. I was desperately sad about what happened to Gabriel. Mary would have been devastated. Even Jackson was shocked. He knew how good Mary had been to me, and Gabriel was her son.'

'Mrs Sekela was a nurse?'

'She cared for me for months—and I needed it.'

Mary had been employed then, but would a nurse have earned the kind of money that enabled Gabriel to pursue his education for as long as he had?

'Did she become a matron eventually, or perhaps an administrator at the hospital?' Nancy was hazarding a guess, but when she looked at Isabella, her friend's expression was blank.

'Bless you, Mary wasn't that kind of nurse. She was a wise woman.'

It was Nancy's turn to look blank and Isabella said, 'Wise women are very important. They can often heal a sick person better than a fancy doctor. And Mary Sekela was an expert. She knew herbs, spices, and what afflictions they could remedy. It's lore handed down from mother to daughter, though the dear woman never had a daughter.'

'And no other job—apart from being a wise woman?'

Isabella shook her head, clearly puzzled by Nancy's interest. 'She had Gabriel to look after. He was the light of her life. She needed no other job.'

How had Mary managed to run a good-sized house and keep her son in education for years, when on the surface she had so little money? It had been a question at the back of Nancy's mind for days. A small anomaly, but for some reason it had felt important—and still did. And that was often the case. A tiny hiccup, something that chimed oddly, could unravel a much greater mystery.

'It's a sad end for them both,' she said softly, keeping her thoughts to herself.

Isabella gestured to the sturdy oak door, standing open in welcome. 'Archie must be getting bored waiting for us. Shall we go in?'

Archie was slumped onto one of the rear pews, but got up when he heard them approaching. 'Had enough of death for the moment?' he greeted them.

'It's an interesting graveyard,' Nancy remonstrated. 'There might even be Cornishmen buried there. You should have taken a stroll.'

'I did—to Ernesto. And his bottle of rum was better company.' She was glad that Isabella hadn't heard. Her friend had gone ahead and was leading the way up the aisle.

'How wonderful!' Nancy exclaimed, when they joined her at the altar. 'And amazing for such a small island.' They stood a while, taking in the elaborate carving, the brilliant stained glass and several feet of gold leaf.

'Someone must have had money to spare.' Archie's expression was cynical. It was a look with which Nancy was familiar.

Unaware of Archie's prejudices, their hostess was eager to tell them more. 'This used to be the main church of the island, and a lot of money was spent on it. The sugar barons liked to be seen as philanthropic, and they funded the upkeep of the church and provided money for this altar. And for the stained glass and several of the gold statues.'

'Is the church used these days?' Nancy asked.

Isabella shook her head. 'Not for twenty years or so. Malfuego town has grown enormously in that time, while the mountain villages have shrunk. Most of the young people leave home to find work in the port or they travel on to one of the bigger islands. The population of the countryside is very small now and certainly not sufficient to fill this church.'

'It's a big space,' Nancy agreed. 'But did the barons actually drive here from the coast every Sunday?'

'Every Sunday, I believe. It was a kind of ritual, a parade of wealth almost. Who had the best carriage? What was Mrs So-and-so wearing? You know the kind of thing. They were French and Spanish families, of course. It was a Catholic church.'

Nancy knew the kind of thing very well. It wasn't too far from her childhood in Riversley, only there the Nicholsons had stuck rigidly to the Methodist chapel, her parents scornful of worshippers of any other denomination, whom they'd stigmatised as vain and idolatrous.

Isabella turned to walk back along the aisle, but Nancy hung back and tugged at Archie's shirt, signalling him to stay. 'I've heard something interesting—from Isabella.'

'What now?'

'There's someone we haven't considered. It's been worrying me ever since we saw what was left of Gabriel's house. It's been in the background but drowned out, I suppose, by all the drama.'

Archie looked bewildered.

'The person who bought Mary Sekela her house,' Nancy went on. 'The person who kept it going and funded Gabriel's years at university.'

'Mary herself, perhaps?' Archie's expression was glum. 'Or is that too simple for you?'

'Mary never earned enough. When I asked Zamira what job Mrs Sekela had done, she didn't seem to know, and now Isabella tells me that Gabriel's mother was never employed. Mary must have had a benefactor. But who was he?'

'I have the feeling you're going to tell me.' Archie sounded weary.

But the chance to talk was gone; Isabella was waving to them from the top of the aisle. 'Have you seen enough, you two?' she asked as they came up to her.

Archie was beginning to say a heartfelt *yes*, when Nancy smiled at her hostess and said, 'One minute, perhaps, Isabella? I saw a staircase as we came in. A flight of spiral steps to the right of the entrance.'

'Ah, yes. They lead to the crypt. And it might interest you. There are a couple of very important Englishmen buried there. And a plaque to Admiral... Admiral... I've forgotten his name, but he was very important.'

'I can see that,' Archie remarked laconically, and settled himself back into a pew.

'Aren't you coming down?' Nancy asked him.

'Count me out. I'll keep Isabella company,' he said.

Chapter Twenty-Nine

The flight of spiral stairs plunging into semi-darkness gave Nancy pause, but her instinct was always to explore, and she made her way carefully down the stone steps into a cavernous underground space. It was as dusty as she'd expected and very dim—she looked for a light switch without success. It was fortunate that several small oblong windows had been cut high up in the walls, giving her just enough light to walk safely across the flagstones to the tombs that were lined against the right-hand wall. A little further along was the plaque Isabella had mentioned. Nancy scanned both as best she could, but neither tombs nor plaque proved particularly interesting. Admiral Lister was the man her hostess had been trying to remember, but since he had spent most of his life in Portsmouth, only succumbing to disease when he visited Malfuego, it was hard to rouse enthusiasm for his story.

Nancy had turned to go when she realised that the end wall of the crypt hosted a row of shelving, hardly recognisable in its thick coat of dust. It seemed an odd place to have a bookcase but, as she drew near, she saw it was more a continuous run of shelves stretching the entire length of the wall and full, not of books, but of what appeared to be old ledgers. Large, leather-bound ledgers. She stood and looked at them for a moment. They might be as interesting as the gravestones outside, and it was a pity that she hadn't the time to browse. Her companions were waiting for their promised lunch, and no doubt counting the minutes.

But on impulse she leant forward and chose one at random, brushing away the dust of years to read the date on the spine. 1856. Scanning through several of its pages, she realised the ledger was a record of all the marriages that had taken place in the church that year. A considerable number, as it turned out.

She replaced the file and ran her fingers along the row of embossed spines. The next ledger recorded deaths from the same year, and the one on the other side, the births. It was meticulously organised: births, marriages, and deaths for each year the church had been used.

A thought leapt into her mind, a starburst of inspiration. If the church had been functioning until twenty years ago, one of these ledgers might contain details of Gabriel Sekela's birth—and possibly provide a clue to the mystery benefactor. Rapidly, she did a mental calculation and reckoned he must have been born in 1932. Hadn't Renzo said his friend was twenty-four? And that seemed right, if the young man had attended university for three years and been back in Malfuego for some time.

The lettering had been almost invisible on the older volumes, but crouching down to study the lowest shelf, she found that on these more recent ones, the gold leaf was still bright. 1932 was there: births, marriages, and deaths.

Nancy carried the ledger nearer to the light. There was just sufficient to make out the writing if she held the volume beneath one of the small windows high in the wall. She turned the pages, January, February... until... at July, she struck lucky. There was the name: Sekela. And there was the record of his mother, Mary Sekela. But his father? She made out the faintest of pen marks. There had been a name once, she thought excitedly, she was sure of it. But whatever name there had been, had been scratched out. She bent over the page, bringing it close to her eyes in an attempt to decipher at least some of the degraded letters, tracing the scored name with her finger —

The blow was sudden and forceful. Nancy jolted forwards, striking her head on a piece of jutting masonry as she fell, her lifeless form sprawled across the cold flagstones.

*

Voices from a distance. A name, over and over. Her name. She sensed someone kneeling by her side, a body warm and comforting.

'Did you get any?' Archie's voice. Then a woman's answering, 'Only this, but it might help.'

A splash of water and she choked awake. Archie's face close to her. Isabella's just behind.

'It's done the trick,' he said, then put his arms around her, scooping her limp form from the floor in one movement and carrying her across the crypt to the spiral staircase. Now they were in the church once more and Archie was laying her full length on a pew. She felt him tweaking her dress, trying to pull it back into place.

'Let me do that,' Isabella said reprovingly, smoothing the wide skirt to cover Nancy's knees.

Her eyes had begun to focus. The roof's gnarled wooden beams seemed to be pressing down on her and she attempted to sit up, but her head no longer belonged to her body. Dazed, she saw the walls of the church moving in unison, as though following some strange rhythm.

'Lie down again,' Archie commanded.

Isabella's face appeared over his shoulder. 'My dear, whatever happened? Did you faint?'

Nancy tried to shake her head, but it hurt too much. Her hand went to her scalp. There was pain, but something else — something wet and sticky — and her fingers came away red.

Isabella gasped. 'She's bleeding. She's been hurt on the back of her head. But how? It's her forehead that's damaged — that's where she hit the floor.'

'She's been hit from behind and sent flying,' Archie said harshly. Then in a gentler voice, 'You're going to have a magnificent swelling, Nancy. Take your time, but when you can, tell us what you remember.'

'I was reading,' she said, grappling with memory. 'I took down one of the ledgers and was reading. And then I felt something hard and heavy at the back of my head. I remember pitching forward, but then... nothing.'

'Someone hit you? But how could that be?' Isabella sounded incredulous. 'There's no one here except ourselves. And why would they, anyway?'

Nancy's mind had begun to work again. She had been attacked because of the ledger. It was the only possible reason. The entry in the book, the scrubbed-out name of Gabriel's father. She'd been uneasy about this unknown man for some time, and it seemed she'd had cause. But Isabella was right. She had seen no-one, heard nothing, and neither had her friends. Whoever had attacked her, had come and gone like a spirit.

'Perhaps it was one of the long departed.' She tried to joke. 'Annoyed that we've disturbed their rest.'

'Is everything okay now, Mrs Garcia?' It was Ernesto, framed in the church doorway. 'Need any more water?'

'No, but thank you for finding some,' his mistress said. 'Ernesto, we need to get this young lady into the car. Can you carry her?'

'I can walk,' Nancy protested, 'but I'm afraid I won't manage lunch.' She had begun to feel nauseous, her stomach churning in a worrying fashion.

'Lunch is out of the question,' Archie said. 'You look ready to faint. Home is where you OmHomneed to be.'

'But—'

'No, my dear, Archie is right. We'll do lunch another day.'

'A day when you don't get floored,' he said drily.

Isabella bustled ahead, gesturing to Ernesto to help the invalid into the car. Nancy had just sufficient time to say quietly to Archie, 'Go back to the crypt and look for the ledger. I dropped it when I fell. It's the one for 1932, and Gabriel Sekela's birth was in July of that year. See if you can decipher his father's name.'

By the time Nancy had been shuffled into the rear of the car and, at Isabella's insistence, a rug grabbed from the boot and draped lovingly over her legs, Archie had rejoined them. Isabella had chosen to sit by her driver, and Archie slid into the vacant seat next to Nancy. But when she looked questioningly at him, he shook his head.

'Couldn't you find it?' she whispered, under cover of the engine's noise and Isabella's chatter with her chauffeur.

'I found it,' he said in a low voice. 'At least, I found the ledger you spoke of, but there was no mention of a Sekela.'

She stared at him. 'Of course, there was. His mother was named—Mary Sekela—and there had been a father's name there once, but an attempt had been made to scrub it out.'

He shook his head again. 'The page was missing.'

'What do you mean? How could it be?' Her whisper was getting louder.

'It had been torn out. The ragged edges were clear. And so was the gap in dates. It jumped from June to August.

Apparently, no child was registered in July.'

'My attacker—he must have taken it.'

'Evidently he wants to remain invisible,' Archie said lightly.

'And why is that? Because he has something to hide, and I'm certain it's connected to Gabriel's death.' She could feel her pulse strengthen. She was finally getting to the truth. 'So, what do we do next?'

'Next! There isn't going to be a next for either of us. You've just been attacked. That should give you a clue as to how dangerous this whole business is. Leave it. Bass and Rossiter are accounted for. There's nothing more we can do.'

She grabbed Archie's arm. 'But neither of them is the killer. There's someone else involved. I've been concentrating on the wrong thing. It wasn't drugs that got Gabriel killed, it was his birth.'

'Whatever wonderful new theory you've come up with, you've got to leave it.' Archie's tone was uncompromising.

'Leave what?' Isabella asked from the front seat, her conversation with Ernesto at an end.

'Nancy was thinking of going dancing tonight,' Archie joked, deflecting the dangerous moment.

The journey seemed much shorter on the way home and, within the hour, the Cadillac was pulling up at the villa's front door. Ernesto helped her out of the car, but Nancy insisted on walking into the house unsupported. She was surprised to find Leo in the wide hallway. He was still pale and tired, but seemed to have stopped sneezing.

'You're back early,' he said. 'I was just going down to the kitchen to get a sandwich.'

'You don't look as if you could butter a slice of bread,' Isabella said. 'Go and sit down. I'll make you one.'

And with that, she bustled down the stairs to the basement,

leaving Leo slightly dazed. 'Why are you back so soon?' he asked of no-one in particular.

'Nancy had a bit of a tumble.' As always, Archie was economic with his words. But for the first time, Leo seemed to realise that Nancy looked as pale as himself.

'Good Lord,' he said. 'You've got the most enormous bruise on your forehead. Look in the mirror there.'

'I'd rather not. But can we go into the sitting room? I'm still feeling a bit woozy.'

'My poor darling,' Leo said, putting his arm around her shoulder and guiding her gently towards the door.

'If there's nothing you want, Leo, I'll get off to town,' Archie called after them.

Nancy glared back at him. He wasn't going to stay around to help explain her predicament, and when she looked down the stairwell and saw Isabella emerge from the kitchen, tray in hand, she knew Archie would take the chance to slide away.

'Leo, I've made a sandwich for you,' Isabella said, puffing up the stairs, 'but only tea for Nancy. If you think you can eat, though, I'm happy to rustle something up.'

'No,' she said hurriedly, nausea not far away. 'Tea is perfect. And I forgot to say this morning, but thank you for the casserole you brought. It was delicious.'

'Delicious,' Leo seconded. 'I'd no idea goat could be as tasty.'

'Chicken,' Isabella said sternly, following them into the sitting room and arranging the tray on the three-legged coffee table.

'Yes, of course, chicken.' He sounded abashed. 'But why didn't you make tea for yourself?'

'I must be getting back, my dears. Ernesto is waiting, and the two of you need to be quiet. I can see that Nancy is still very shocked. Look after her, Leo.'

Before they heard the front door click, Leo had begun to make inroads into his sandwich which he pronounced surprisingly good. But after a few mouthfuls, he put his plate to one side, and asked suddenly, 'What were you doing to have a fall?'

The explanation Nancy had dreaded was here. 'I was looking at some old books in the church crypt and the volume I was holding was very heavy. It slipped out of my hand. Unbalanced me, I suppose, and I fell to the floor after it.'

Leo looked a little blank but seemed to accept this version of events, until she leaned forward to pick up her teacup and he caught sight of the patch of red in her hair.

'What's that? What's happened to the back of your head?'

'I fell,' she said. 'As I mentioned.' Inwardly, she cursed herself for not having gone straight to the bathroom and sponged the mess away.

'You fell on the back of your head? So how come, you have the most enormous bruise on your forehead?'

What could she say that would sound anything like plausible? She had to be honest. Hadn't she sworn to herself after Venice that she wouldn't deceive Leo again? 'Someone hit me,' she managed to say.

'Hit you?' He sounded as incredulous as Isabella had in the church, and sat bolt upright, sweeping the plate to one side and toppling his sandwich onto the crochet rag rug. 'But who would do a thing like that?'

'I've no idea.'

'Where were you when it happened? Where were the others?'

'Like I said, I'd gone down to the crypt and Isabella and Archie were waiting in the church.'

'And you saw no-one?'

Gingerly, she shook her head.

'Was it theft? What did they steal?'

'Nothing. They stole nothing.'

She hoped that might be the end of his questioning, but it wasn't. 'None of this makes sense, Nancy. You must have been attacked for some reason. What on earth were you doing?'

'I told you. Reading one of the ledgers that are kept in the crypt.'

Leo was silent for a long time, evidently mystified, though she sensed a growing anger in him. Then out of the blue, his anger was confirmed. 'You've been poking around again, haven't you?' he burst out. 'Getting involved in things that don't concern you. Getting yourself into bad situations.'

He jumped up from the sofa, but swayed a little on his feet. Nancy felt contrite. He wasn't at all well and she'd brought trouble home with her.

'I don't know what went on in Venice,' he continued, his voice taut. 'Except that you were dabbling in things that had nothing to do with you. I told you then you had to stop.'

Her contrition faded. 'It's a good job I didn't. Otherwise a poor woman'—she couldn't say an innocent woman—'wouldn't have had justice. And the man you thought so much of wouldn't now be in jail.'

'I was wrong, I've already admitted it. But that doesn't mean you have to keep getting involved in stuff that has nothing to do with you and is clearly dangerous.'

He paced up and down the room, then out onto the terrace and back again. 'Is this about March?' he asked eventually.

She looked at him blankly. 'Philip?'

'Yes, Philip, your one-time fiancé and stalker-in-chief.'

'How could it be about him?' She was bewildered.

'Don't look so shocked. It makes perfect sense to me. He

251

terrified you and it's affected you badly. Is still affecting you, would be my guess. Maybe you feel stronger if you're the one doing the stalking.'

'That's ridiculous. And I don't stalk.'

'Then whatever you do—poke around, "investigate", if you want to dress it up. But Malfuego isn't a place you can afford to do that. This island has problems. It's a paradise if you're a visitor, but not if you go digging into island affairs. Think what I told you about the drugs. It's obvious there's dangerous business afoot here and you've been utterly foolish if you've got involved in it.'

'The attack on me had nothing to do with drugs. How could a church ledger be of any importance? Gibbon Bass and Luke Rossiter are the ones involved in the drug ring, and since they're either dead or in custody, neither of them could have hit me over the head. And I'm sure it wasn't Renzo's father, either. I imagine that by now Scott Hastings will have cut any links he has to the business.'

Leo stared at his wife as though he hardly recognised her. 'How do you know all this?' He collapsed onto the sofa beside her, as though she had driven the air from his body.

She lowered her voice. 'I talk to people. And keep my eyes open and my ears listening.'

'In other words, you mind other people's business. That's why you get into trouble. Why you have a purple lump on your forehead and a gash in your scalp. You have to stop this. Do you hear?'

'I hear you, Leo.'

'And…'

'I'll try.'

'You'll do more than try.'

'Now you sound like a bully.'

His grievance was justified, she admitted, but there was a

streak in Leo that had to command: people, events, even his wife. Apart from the loss of the mother he'd adored, life had gone smoothly for him, and he was used to being in control. Perhaps it was that early loss that made controlling his world so essential to him. Nancy understood his need, and understood, too, that it sprang from the best of motives, but she couldn't accept it. Her life had followed a very different pattern to Leo's. She'd had to struggle hard for what she'd achieved, fought every inch of the way to be her own person, and her husband's refusal to acknowledge that she was a grown woman with a mind of her own angered her. She was not an extra in his life's journey, but someone with a journey of her own.

She sat stiffly beside him as he tried to take her hand. 'I'm not a bully, Nancy. I'm simply trying to protect you.'

'I don't need protecting.'

'Plainly, you do.' He waved his hand towards her wound. There was a minute's tense silence and then he said in a voice that had grown suddenly cold, 'I said I was wrong in blaming you for losing the baby. But I wasn't. This is the reason it happened.'

She looked at him, open-mouthed. 'What are you suggesting? Of course it wasn't. The miscarriage happened days ago, before I became involved in any kind of investigation.'

Leo shook his head. 'It's too much of a coincidence. You've been fractious ever since we got here, and now I know why. You spotted something you could put right. At least, you're vain enough to think you could. I remember that dinner party at Garcia's, the first night we were here—what you said then about the protest we'd seen. It's clear now that from that moment you intended to get involved in whatever skulduggery was going on. In other words, you've put your own selfish whims first and lost the baby as a result. How could you do that?'

She quailed under his attack and tried to fight back. 'That's complete nonsense. I had pains from the moment we arrived in Malfuego. The pregnancy was never secure. It was never going to work.'

'So you say,' he said bitterly. 'But forgive me if I don't believe you.' He jumped up again, this time seeming a good deal stronger. 'I'm calling Roland. I'm going out.'

'But you're unwell. You have a bad cold.'

'Anything is better than staying here. I can't speak to you, Nancy. To do such a thing!'

'You are very mistaken,' was all she could say.

He strode to the door. Then turning, delivered a last blow. 'It suited you to marry me. It gave you a husband and a way to protect yourself. But it was never anything more for you. You thought you could marry and continue your life exactly as you wished, without taking the slightest notice of what *I* wanted. It's *you* that's mistaken. If we are to stay together, Nancy, you need to start behaving like a wife.'

Chapter Thirty

Nancy walked to the gates of the villa several times that evening, hoping she would see Roland and his magnificent saloon turn into the driveway. But there was no sign of the car or of Leo. The low rumbling from Monte Muerte sounded louder tonight. An omen, she thought disconsolately, wandering through the garden, the perfume of night-scented flowers hanging heavy in the air. She had never felt more lonely.

It wasn't a new feeling: loneliness had been with her for as long as she could remember. Her parents had fed and sheltered her, but she'd been an alien child, the proverbial cuckoo. Not just the wrong kind of sex but the wrong kind of girl. One who didn't conform, didn't want what she should. She'd hoped work would be different, but at Abingers' she'd been just as much an oddity, trying to carve out a place for herself in the male bastion that was fine art.

Since her marriage, though, that ever-present sense of solitude had faded a little. Leo had been her friend as well as her husband. There were difficulties between them, it was true, but he'd given her a new life, one where she was loved and cared for in a way she had never been before. Yet now, it seemed, he had gone, if not in body then in heart. Lost, along with the baby. It hurt. There had been moments when she'd imagined them as a family, herself at the centre, and wondered how it would feel. Now she would never know.

Dusk had fallen and the bats were already skimming the sky on their nightly patrol. The high-pitched sound of tree frogs, a chorus that would last until morning, filled her ears. She took several turns up and down the paved paths before deciding it was futile to wait. She would give up and go to bed.

But even here, the waiting continued. She lay watching the hands of the bedside clock slowly turning, desperate to hear Leo's footsteps. It was nearly midnight before he returned, and she watched beneath half-closed eyes as he silently undressed and got into bed beside her, making sure his body never once touched hers. Where he had been and what he'd been doing she had no idea. No idea, either, how this awful gulf that had opened between them could be bridged.

Leo knew that she was hiding secrets. He'd suspected as much ever since they'd left Venice. They had been in the city for their honeymoon and it was there she had met Marta Moretto, the very day the woman had plunged to her death. She had liked her instantly, had felt her sadness and her wish to make a better future. In Marta, she had discerned a fellow spirit. It was why she'd pursued justice for the dead woman with such verve.

But Gabriel Sekela—why was she intent on finding his killer? She had seen him at the demonstration and witnessed the brutal attack, had heard from Renzo of the great plans the young man had for the island, then seen the very real love between him and Anya that afternoon at the Serafina. But she had never properly met him. Had never spoken to him. Why was she so invested in discovering the truth of his death?

Could Leo be right that somehow she was trying to prove she was no longer the fearful girl she had been in London? That somehow by winning now she could put aside the defeat she'd suffered at Philip March's hands and banish for ever the terror he'd instilled? But it wasn't fear that motivated her, was it? It was excitement. The thrill of finding out. On reflection, it was not dissimilar to the restoration of an artwork, in which you unpeeled layer after layer of concealment to discover finally the painting's shining truth.

Perhaps, though, it was more simple. Seeing evil go unpunished made her desperate to redress the wickedness; her own small attempt to make the world right. That sounded pompous, but it was what she felt. Renzo's affection for Gabriel, the young man's ideals for a better Malfuego, the love of Anya—snuffed out by a malefactor who would never receive justice. Justice. That was the key.

*

It seemed as though she'd hardly slept before she heard the sound of water cascading from the shower in the adjoining bathroom. Leo was already up and evidently planning to leave early. She slipped on her dressing gown—the negligée that Leo had bought her for their honeymoon—and went down to the kitchen, glad to find that she was alone. In a short time she had assembled a breakfast she hoped would tempt her husband. She badly wanted him to share it with her and then maybe they could begin to speak again. But when he appeared through the door, it was to give her a brusque nod, gulp a few mouthfuls of pineapple juice, and take a single slice of toast from the array on the counter.

'Won't you stay and eat a proper meal?' she asked.

'I've not the time,' he said curtly. 'I've asked Roland to collect me early this morning. I've a busy day ahead.' And with that, he turned and made for the stairs up to the front door. Several minutes later, she heard him call to someone— presumably his driver—then the noise of an engine, and the crush of gravel beneath tyres.

She sank down onto a kitchen stool, its red plastic uncomfortable beneath the flimsy negligée. Her heart ached that this was what her marriage had come to. She had tried hard to make it work—at least, as hard as she was able—but it was clear it had not been enough. She could feel the tears very close and tried to brush them away.

Archie sauntered into the kitchen, whistling his favourite tune. But when he saw her face, he stopped abruptly. 'What's going on?'

'Nothing.' She tried smoothing her cheeks dry with the back of her hand.

'You look like a ghost—and all this—' He waved a hand at the breakfast spread across the kitchen counter.

'It's Leo,' she said, her voice cracking. Then the tears did come.

Archie walked quickly towards her, and somehow she was off the stool and in his arms. He held her for long minutes until her sobbing quietened. She felt his lips on her hair and on her cheek, and her arms tightened around him.

Eventually, he released his hold and held her at arm's length. 'Stop crying and tell me what's happened,' he said.

She felt bereft—his warmth gone, the comfort, the sheer sense of belonging, all gone. Why was it she could feel this way about a man she shouldn't? 'We quarrelled,' she said miserably.

'Yes?' His tone suggested that it was hardly unexpected.

'I thought we'd made peace, but Leo is still blaming me for losing the baby. He says it happened because I won't stop poking my nose in where it's not wanted.'

It sounded almost comical, but Archie didn't laugh. 'At least he's right about the poking nose.'

'But not about the baby. That was cruel.'

Archie pushed her down onto the stool and took the

one beside her. 'It's unfair. But he's hurting and he needs someone to blame. Your little adventure yesterday gives him something to rail against.'

'But it wasn't an adventure. All I did was wander into a crypt.'

'Come on, Nancy. It was more than that. Most visitors, if they ventured there at all, would have done a quick shuffle around the place, glanced at the tombs, read the plaque perhaps, but that would have been it. They'd have scurried up the stairs back to the church thinking there wasn't much to see below ground. Only you didn't. You started checking the church records.'

'It didn't warrant a blow on the head.'

'Ordinarily, no. But this place isn't ordinary, is it?' Archie prodded at the plate of sliced guava, but instead took a piece of toast.

'Someone wants to make sure the name of Gabriel's father stays hidden,' she said, her voice steady. 'The fact that when you went back to the crypt, the record of Gabriel's birth had disappeared, is proof of it. Whoever his father is, he's still on Malfuego. I think he's been here all the time. He has to be the one who bought Mary her house and paid for Gabriel's education. He's Marissa's invisible man.'

'And what if he is? Why is it so important?'

'He may have played a part in what happened.'

'Played a part, as in burnt his son to death?'

Nancy was rendered silent for a moment. 'I didn't say that. But why hasn't he shown up? If it was your son who'd been killed and you were living close by, wouldn't you have done something?'

'Like what? If he's kept himself secret all these years, why would he burst into the limelight now?'

'Because his son has been murdered! He'd surely want to see justice done.'

'It will be. Rossiter is dead and Bass is in prison.'

Archie's hand hovered over the eggs she had prepared earlier, but then began methodically to peel a peach.

'But that's not justice,' she objected. 'They won't be accused of Gabriel's murder. The fire will still be treated as accidental. If this unknown man has cared enough for Gabriel to support him all these years, why hasn't he come out of the woodwork and tried to help?'

'I can think of several reasons—and so can you, if you use your head.' Archie's face wore a pugnacious expression. 'Because there's bugger all he can do to help? Because the money he paid was hush money and he didn't in fact give a sod about the boy? Because he doesn't even know Gabriel is dead? Because he doesn't even live on the island?'

'He does,' she said with certainty.

'You can't know that.'

'I feel it.'

'Feel it,' he mocked. 'Stop feeling and think.'

'I am thinking. I've been thinking all night. About a host of things. This man, whoever he is, is frantic to conceal his identity. My injury proves that. Did Gabriel suspect who he was, I wonder? Maybe tried to make contact with him after his mother died? And, for some reason, that spelt danger. The man saw it as a threat that required desperate action.'

Archie held up his hands in protest. 'Desperate action that requires Daddy to kill his son?'

'I know it sounds mad, but Gabriel posed a threat to someone and that's why he was killed.'

'He posed a threat to Bass and Rossiter. You're building a case that doesn't exist. It was Rossiter who poured that petrol, and he did it because Gabriel was endangering his lucrative sideline or because he didn't want the bloke to nab his girl. Possibly both.'

Nancy slipped off her stool and began stacking plates to one side of the sink. 'I thought it was Rossiter,' she conceded, 'at first. But now it doesn't make sense. If Rossiter was responsible for the fire, why would Bass kill him? He did Gibbon Bass a favour in getting rid of Gabriel, someone who could have destroyed their whole operation.'

'Perhaps Bass didn't want to share the proceeds any longer. Perhaps Rossiter tried a spot of blackmail on him.'

'Yes,' she said, considering the idea. 'I've wondered about blackmail. It's something Rossiter would be good at. I think he was hoping to blackmail Scott Hastings. That's why he broke into *Le Citronnier*. If he'd found the papers he was looking for, he could have used them—against both Scott Hastings and Bass.'

'There you are then. Bass decided to get rid of Rossiter's threat in the way he knew best. And he did a good job,' Archie finished grimly.

'Gibbon Bass must have been telling Scott what he was planning when I saw them together,' she said thoughtfully. 'Scott Hastings would have argued against the killing— he's a softly, softly man—and that's why they quarrelled.'

'And we're back to Rossiter again. Not your mystery man. You know how to spin a story, Nancy, but go for the simplest explanation. They could all be in it together, blackmailing each other. Or they simply fell out over dividing the spoils. Plenty of opportunity for that.'

'But Gabriel's father—'

'Forget him. It's done. The police have Bass. He'll pay for Rossiter's murder at least, and the smuggling ring will most likely be finished.'

She would have continued the argument, but a loud bang on the front door had her drop the cloth she was wielding and climb the stairs.

Chapter Thirty-One

A pink Cadillac was parked on the driveway and Isabella stood on the threshold, a wide smile on her face. It was kind of her friend to call, Nancy thought, although she could happily have foregone the social chit-chat. Defending her case against Archie's cynicism had made her head throb.

'Isabella, how nice of you to come.'

'I had to see how you were doing. That foolish husband of yours has taken himself to work and he looks quite dreadful.' Isabella stepped into the hall.

'I know. I tried to persuade him to stay home.' Nancy felt guilty. She was becoming a fluent liar. And she was conscious that Archie had followed her up the stairs and was listening to every word.

'At least *you've* had the sense to stay home.'

'I have, and I'm feeling a great deal better today.'

Her friend put a hand on Nancy's arm. 'You don't think you should go to the hospital? I thought about it last night after I got back and nearly telephoned you.'

'My head hurts a little, but not seriously enough. Can I get you a drink?'

'No, my dear. I'm on the way to a meeting, but I thought I'd ask Ernesto to pull in here for a moment so I could check on you. And on you, too, Archie.' She looked at him over

Nancy's shoulder. 'How are you feeling now?'

'Okay, thanks. I'm okay.'

'Well, if I can't help either of you with anything?' Isabella walked back to door and stood irresolutely on the threshold. 'Oh, I nearly forgot. I do have something to tell you both. I heard it just before I left this morning and thought it would brighten your day, Nancy. I know how upset you've been about the Sekela boy.'

'Yes?'

'Jackson had it from the Police Commissioner—he's a good friend of ours—and perhaps I shouldn't be telling you, but it will soon be common knowledge. It's early days for the investigation, but the police have decided to look into Gabriel's death. They're not satisfied it was an accident. Not after they arrested Gibbon Bass and heard what he had to say.'

'What has Bass to do with it?' Nancy asked innocently, though certain he had a good deal to do with it.

Isabella lowered her voice. 'Bass was running drugs! And the police are fairly sure that Luke Rossiter was involved as well. Isn't that shocking? It was what that dreadful business at the yacht club was about. Presumably a thieves' falling out.'

'But Gabriel? How does it involve him?' Nancy tried to keep the impatience from her voice.

'Apparently when the fire brigade searched the ruins of the Sekela place, they came across a locked tin box and handed it into the police. It must have been hidden in the house—beneath the floorboards maybe. Anyway, somehow it survived the fire. Just a little charred. And inside were papers, notes, all kinds of evidence really that Gabriel must have collected against Gibbon Bass and his activities. Jackson was very surprised. He assumed that all Sekela was interested in was wrecking the State Assembly.'

So she'd been right. It was as Nancy had thought. It was why Rossiter had been in Gabriel's street that night and why he'd been desperate to frighten her away. He'd been looking for anything incriminating that might have survived the fire, and worried that in some way she might come across it. He hadn't realised he was already too late.

'That is good news,' she managed to say.

'I thought it would make you happy. Bass has already been charged with murder, but now he could be charged twice over.'

And I can step back, Nancy thought, and let the police do their job, knowing that Gabriel will get justice. And yet—it wasn't justice, was it?

Isabella turned to go and was about to climb into the car, when Nancy ran after her. 'Isabella…'she began. 'I wonder… do you have any idea who Gabriel's father might be?'

Her friend seemed taken aback at the question, and Nancy struggled to find an excuse. 'When I've thought about Gabriel recently, I've realised how very much on his own he must have been.'

'Since his mother died? That's true. Gabriel *was* alone, poor boy. He must have felt Mary's death very badly. But he was a good son to come back from Florida. His father, though? Mary never spoke a word about him. I always imagined he'd disappeared the moment Gabriel was conceived. There were rumours, but—'

'What kind of rumours?'

Isabella took her time to reply. It was evident Nancy's persistence was making her uncomfortable. 'Mary's own family was very poor, you know,' she said after a while. 'Her parents and siblings died from dengue fever and she was on her own from an early age. She worked in one of the Martins' mills as a young girl, the Gladstone Mill—it's the Serafina now—and then left suddenly. If I remember rightly, that was when the rumour started. About one of the supervisors.'

'A white man?'

Isabella's eyebrows knitted. 'Who knows? At the time, supervisors were both black and white. But Gabriel was certainly much lighter skinned than his mother.'

'Perhaps he wasn't quite alone then. His father might not have abandoned him entirely,' Nancy suggested. 'He might have supported Mary and paid for Gabriel's education.'

'To be honest, I've never thought about it. Mary lived very modestly, and I thought she survived on what people gave her for her remedies. But it's true, it would never have paid for an American education. Still, all that's history now. Both of them are dead, unfortunately, and it's always best not to trust rumour.'

Maybe not, Nancy reflected, but a supervisor earning a white man's wages answered the problem of how Mary Sekela had managed to survive in reasonable comfort. It also offered a clue why he might not want to be known.

*

Archie was waiting for her in the sitting room. 'What was that all about?' He jerked his head towards the driveway and the pink Cadillac making its way to the gates.

'That is going to help me find Gabriel's father,' she said jubilantly.

'You're still banging on about him?'

'Whoever the man is, he's involved in some way in Gabriel's death. I'm convinced of it. And Isabella has put me on the right track.'

'And what is the right track?'

'She mentioned a supervisor at one of the Martins' mills.

Gladstone Mill, that was the name. There was a story that Mary Sekela's baby was down to him.'

Archie's expression was sceptical. 'A story? How useful is that? And why a mill worker?'

'Gabriel's mother worked at the mill when she was a very young woman, but then left suddenly. I'm assuming because Gabriel was on the way. And stories are useful. They're often accurate.'

'And often inaccurate. If this chap was a supervisor, it was a long time ago. He could be dead by now, and the people he worked with as well. No-one is going to know anything about him.'

'If he was around the same age as Mary, he could easily be alive still.'

Archie pursed his lips. 'A supervisor would be much older than her. That's how you get to be one.'

'You just want to throw obstacles in my way, but I know exactly what I'm going to do. Brave the hotel again and find Virginie.' She felt a new zeal emerging.

'For information? What is Virginie Lascelles going to know? She's far too young.'

'She's lived on the island all her life and among people who could have talked about the mill and what had gone on there,' Nancy said defiantly, 'She might have heard a name mentioned, even if she's never met the person. I should have asked her before, but it didn't seem important then.'

'You'd be much better to stay here. It's unlikely you'll find anything out and you'll be pissing Leo off even more.'

'I love your turn of phrase, Archie. But I don't think Leo will care. He won't even know—he's not back till later this afternoon. Unless you tell him.'

'I'm going to do that, aren't I?' He scowled at some inner thought. 'I should have been with you. In that crypt.'

'But why?'

'Then you wouldn't have been attacked. And if you hadn't been attacked, you wouldn't have suddenly got this crazy idea in your head. You're suggesting that Sekela's father is his murderer. Come on, Nancy! It's completely bonkers, even for you.'

'I'm not suggesting anything at the moment. I don't know what happened, but I'm going to find out. And it isn't a sudden idea. Marissa called him the invisible man and that's been niggling me for a long time.'

'A niggle that means more danger. You might not be so lucky next time.'

'Then I must be more careful.'

Archie shook his head. 'That's it, is it? That's your solution. Being more careful. You know, you're like a dog we once had. He was a mongrel but he had a lot of terrier in him. A Jack Russell. He wouldn't let go of anything once he'd got a hold — a sock, a lamb chop, even your leg, if it took his fancy. He hated rabbits and, if you took him out, you lost him for hours while he went digging in rabbit holes. He went missing on one walk and not just for hours but several days. It turned out he'd dug himself into a rabbit hole too deeply and got stuck.'

'I'm getting the analogy, but did he escape?'

Archie had a wry smile on his face. 'He escaped all right. I rescued him.'

'Then I've nothing to worry about, have I?' she asked saucily, her spirits a little recovered.

Chapter Thirty-Two

As soon as Archie went downstairs to his office, she rang for a taxi and within ten minutes was on her way to the hotel, asking the cabbie to drive her to the goods entrance. From here she could find her way to Virginie's office unaided, hopefully without attracting attention. Head held high, she walked unchallenged through the double doors she'd used previously and along the corridor to the housekeeper's office. It was amazing how an appearance of confidence protected one from unwanted enquiries. Virginie's cheerful voice answered her knock immediately but, once inside the room, Nancy saw that the housekeeper had company. Another member of staff—her deputy according to the name badge— was standing by her desk, a sheaf of papers in her hand. Nancy apologised and began to back out into the corridor.

'Nonsense,' Virginie said, flashing a sunny smile at her friend. 'Come in, honey, and take a seat. Florence was just going. We've been tussling with accounts.' She gestured to the swirling mass of paper strewn across her desktop. 'Florence, can you organise some coffee?' she asked, as her deputy went to leave.

'Not for me, thanks,' Nancy said quickly.

'So?' Virginie questioned as the door closed. 'What brings you here? Not another room search, I hope.'

'Nothing like that,' Nancy assured her friend.

'That's good. We've had enough excitement for now. After that lunch at the yacht club, the police were here the next day and ransacked Luke's room. They took away a basketful of nasty little white packets. They found them in his bathroom. Did you know about them?'

'I was going to tell you, but before I could, Luke got himself killed.'

'The police will use the stuff as evidence against Gibbon Bass, I guess, when he stands trial. Did you know he's already back on the island?'

Nancy shook her head, but there was concern on her face. 'No need to worry,' Virginie went on. 'He's in gaol. And he'll be there for a long time to come.'

'How did the hotel cope with the police swooping in like that?'

'Pretty well. The officers didn't make too much of a song and dance. Battering rams were not used! Ambrose was grateful. I doubt if any of the guests noticed anything amiss, and his parents have been kept well and truly in the dark.'

'And Anya? Does she know?'

'It's been another shock, but she's bearing up, I think. Only just, though. She was still coming to terms with Gabriel's death, and now Luke. Not that she liked him particularly, but she saw him die in the most horrible way. Come to think of it, I haven't seen her this morning. She's extremely busy, now we're short staffed. Luke Rossiter was a moron, but he did his share of the work. Ambrose is recruiting in his place, though it's likely to take some time. Personally, I think he should promote his daughter. She's well capable of taking over the job.'

'And you, Virginie?'

'Very busy, but happier now that snide little so-and-so has

gone. I'm sad for Anya, though. We miss the girl she was. It sounds trite, but she was a flash of sunshine until she lost Gabriel. She really loved the boy.'

'He's why I'm here.' Nancy seized the chance to turn the conversation. 'Or rather, his father is.'

Virginie looked surprised. 'Gabriel's father? He must have had one, but I don't know who he was. I don't think anyone does.'

'Isabella seemed to think he might have been a supervisor at one of the sugar mills. Gabriel's mother worked there as a very young woman.'

The housekeeper gave a low whistle. 'That would make sense. I've heard plenty of stories of the way women were treated by the men in charge. They behaved the same as the old slavers. Any woman was theirs for the picking.'

'Did any of the stories mention a name? Who that supervisor might be?'

Her companion gave a slow shake of her head. 'Sorry, honey, I can't help. I've heard a load of rumours in my time but not that particular one. My mother, God rest her, never said a word, though she worked at one of the mills. Gladstone. This hotel was built on its grave.'

'Gladstone was where Mary Sekela worked.'

'Well, if we're talking about a white supervisor, and most were white then, the workers wouldn't have blabbed. They'd have kept their suspicions to themselves. It wouldn't have been good for their prospects if they'd talked out of turn.'

For a moment, Nancy was deflated and sat staring blankly at a wall of typewritten lists and carefully drawn charts.

'Are you sure you won't have that coffee?' Virginie asked.

'Yes, sure, thank you. I wonder... did any of the Martins ever work at Gladstone?'

'Ambrose would have. It was their biggest mill. He'd have

been the manager—I've often thought that working here must be like old times for him.'

'Then he'd have known all the supervisors personally. He would have been aware if one of them had decided to pounce on Mary and make her his mistress. Aware, even if it was a single rape. As the boss, he might have chosen to look away, but he would have known.'

Nancy leaned across the desk, fixing her companion with such a determined look that Virginie inched backwards. 'Could I talk to Ambrose, do you think?'

'You are a girl,' her friend said admiringly. 'I guess you can, as long as he's no appointments on the horizon. But you'll try to be—'

'Diplomatic?' Nancy finished for her. 'Of course. What else?'

'I can imagine you do diplomatic—up to a point. But if you think you've got hold of something, Ambrose won't stand a chance.'

Nancy had jumped up and was already at the door. 'Now would be okay?'

'Sure thing. I'll walk you along to his office.' Virginie joined her at the door, a conspiratorial smile on her face.

*

Ambrose Martin enjoyed a large office on the ground floor, a few steps from the glossy reception area that had become familiar to Nancy. But once out of the lift, Virginie turned to the left, away from the luxurious seating and the restaurant, and into a corridor that faced inland. Taking another left turn, they came to a line of offices with identical mahogany doors, most of them firmly shut. The furthest door was open, however, and Virginie nodded in its direction. But as they drew close, a burst of angry voices spilled out, startling them and bringing them to an abrupt halt. Nancy peered through the half-open door—two figures were facing each other across the desk.

'How could you tell her?' Ambrose was shouting. 'My little girl. How could you tell her?'

His mother adjusted the black shawl around her shoulders, pulling it tight. Her mouth was a hard, narrow line. 'It was time she knew.'

'No, it wasn't. It was never time. We've lived with it. *I've* lived with the guilt, but Anya—she should have stayed protected.'

'Too protected. You are a fool where that girl is concerned, Ambrose. All this mooning over a boy she should never have met. An African at that. She needs to face reality.'

'Gabriel Sekela wasn't African. He was a Malfuegan, and the infatuation would have died.'

'It should have died when he did. But it hasn't. History repeating itself, wouldn't you say? Someone had to tell her the truth.'

Ambrose reached forward and gripped both of Eugénie's arms. 'You have destroyed her and destroyed me. To tell her about her mother!'

'Jacinta couldn't face reality, which is why she left her child motherless and pursued her own selfish ends. Life is hard, there are knocks aplenty, and you have to learn to deal with them. It's time Anya learnt to do it, too. And well over time to know exactly why her mother left this island.'

Ambrose let go of his mother and sank into his chair, holding his head in his hands and staring at the wooden surface of the desk as though he wished it would swallow him. 'My little girl,' he repeated in a whisper.

'And what about my little girl? My Charlotte? You didn't think of her, did you, when you bedded her? When you set her on a path to death?'

Nancy's breath almost stopped. She hardly dared look at Virginie, but when she did, she saw her own shock mirrored in the housekeeper's face. For a moment, both women stood motionless, as though glued to the floor, then Virginie grabbed her friend by the arm and pulled her back along the corridor. Nancy was unaware of being shuffled into the lift, unaware of the doors closing and opening. It was only when they reached the lower floor that she spoke, and her voice was shaking.

'You said... you hinted.'

Virginie pushed the thick waves of her hair back beneath the bandeau holding them in place, desperate it seemed to restore some kind of order. 'I thought it was just a rumour. At least, I hoped it was,' she amended.

'What they said—it was truly dreadful,' Nancy whispered.

'They are a thoroughly rotten family.' Virginie's voice sounded loud in the empty corridor. Angry, too. Nancy saw her companion's body tremble and realised just what this meant to her. Virginie respected her employer, she liked Ambrose, and though she'd heard rumours, it seemed she'd been able to shrug them off. Now she was faced with the ugly reality and must be wondering how she could continue to work for him.

'We need a drink,' her friend said, practical as ever. 'I've a half bottle of rum in the bottom drawer of my desk. That will do.'

Nancy was no fan of rum, but the severe shock they'd both received needed something to deaden it. Any solace they might have found in alcohol, though, was not to be theirs. As they turned the corner to Virginie's office, the figure of a frantic Renzo confronted them. The boy was hammering on the housekeeper's door and, when he heard them approach, he spun round in an almost complete circle. An enormous look of relief flooded his face as he realised who was walking towards him.

He wasted no time in greeting them. 'Have you seen Anya?' were his first words.

'Not this morning,' Virginie answered calmly. 'But the hotel is very busy, and Anya has had to take on extra work. She'll be somewhere around.'

Renzo shook his head, his face pale and set. He fished from his pocket a thin slip of paper and handed it to the housekeeper.

She glanced down at it. 'You better come into the office while I read this,' she said, unlocking the door and waiting for them both to find a seat before fixing her eyes on the paper Renzo had handed her.

As Virginie read, the lines on her face seemed to deepen. It was evidently bad news, and coming so quickly after the devastating argument she'd overheard, Nancy felt the throb in her head more intense than ever.

'You better read this, too, Nancy.' The housekeeper handed her the letter and she read it with increasing fear.

Dear Renzo

Please forgive me for running away but I can do nothing else. I can't face what I was told last night, you must believe me. I've tried but I can't. I don't know what I'll do—I need to think, and have gone to the mountain. I'll be alone there, and maybe in time the terrible voices in my head will stop. You have been a good friend to me and my darling Gabriel. I don't write that to hurt you. I don't want to hurt you in any way, and you mustn't worry about me. I am sorry if you do. You must forget me and make a success of your own life. I am bad through and through.

Anya

'What does she mean when she says she can't face what she's been told?' Renzo was bewildered.

The two women looked at each other and a silent message passed between them. It was for Anya to tell him when and if she wanted. 'There has been trouble in the family,' Virginie said smoothly, 'and it's obviously upset Anya badly.'

'But to run away…' he protested. 'And where has she gone? She says to the mountain. Which mountain?' The boy's voice was getting more strained with every sentence.

'She means Monte Muerte. To Malfuegans, that is the mountain,' Virginie said.

'But I thought you couldn't climb it. It's dense jungle.'

'There's a pathway, though I don't know how passable it is now. It was the old path the slaves used if they managed to escape. If they made it to the top, the mountain was a place they could be safe from capture.'

'Safe because no-one was foolish enough to follow them, you mean?' Renzo's eyes were wide and staring. Virginie could do nothing but nod.

'How dangerous is it?' he demanded.

'Dangerous enough,' she conceded. 'Snakes, ravines, rock falls. Even some poisonous vegetation, I think.'

'And that's where Anya has gone? We have to rescue her.'

'Do you have a spare machete?' Virginie asked dryly. 'Because that's what you'll need. You won't find the path easily.'

'But if it's overgrown,' Nancy interposed, 'Anya can't have got that far.'

'She might have got further than you think. Renzo doesn't know the track, but Anya will. As a child, she'll have been taken at least halfway up the mountain. Every child on the island used to go on that particular pilgrimage, even white kids.'

Renzo leapt on this. 'Then *you'll* know the way, Virginie. We can follow you.'

'I have work to do, Renzo. I can't leave the hotel and walk off goodness knows where. Anya says in her letter that she left last night. She'll have travelled a fair distance by now.'

The mention of a night-time journey seemed to tip Renzo over the edge. 'But she's in danger,' he almost screamed.

'Ambrose Martin knows his daughter is missing,' Virginie said carefully. 'He will have informed the police and they will find her.'

'Do you think he has?' Nancy asked. 'In the circumstances,' she added vaguely.

'If he hasn't, he will go himself. I really don't think there's anything we can do.'

'Well I do,' Renzo burst out. 'If you won't help, I'll go myself. I'll do my best to reach her.' The look on his companions' faces must have told him what they thought of the idea.

'If we could fly,' he said wildly. 'If we could land on the mountain, then we'd cut out most of the difficult journey.'

Nancy was about to say that it was even more of an impossible idea than hacking his way through the undergrowth or trying to find a path of which he'd no knowledge, when Virginie spoke. 'There is a place to land. It's near to the top of the mountain—for some reason, the jungle is sparser there. And the space is kept open, the vegetation cut back every so often, for the scientists to check the volcano. The helicopter lands them there and then it's only a short climb to the volcano's mouth.'

'There you are,' Renzo said excitedly. 'We can fly.' He thought for a moment. 'Archie Jago. He flies, doesn't he? We'll get Archie to fly us. If Anya has followed the path you mention, we should be able to find her.' His eagerness had him bound to the office door and then back again. 'What do you say, Nancy?'

'I say that Archie has never flown without an instructor. We'd have to ask Marlon. And this landing place won't be like a normal airstrip, I'm sure. It will be small and hemmed-in. Landing will be a difficult manoeuvre even for a helicopter and certainly for a light aircraft.'

'Light aircraft have been used in the past, but not often,' Virginie mused. 'You're right about the difficulty. I doubt you'd persuade Marlon to try. Honestly, Renzo, you'd be much better to leave it to Ambrose to figure out.'

'I have my suspicions about that guy.' Renzo's chin jutted aggressively. 'I think he's the reason Anya has gone. He's done something, said something, that's upset her badly. And why does she say *she's* bad? She's the loveliest girl I've ever met.'

Nancy exchanged another glance with the housekeeper. It was evident Renzo's interest went far beyond that of a friend. But he'd suspected rightly that Ambrose had played a role in his daughter's disappearance. And if her father was the one to find her on the mountain, how would she react? *If* he found her. The girl might know the path to take, but the dangers Virginie had described were very real.

'What are we waiting for?' Renzo tugged at Nancy's arm. 'Let's go and ask Archie. He'll persuade Marlon for us. He's paying him for lessons.'

'I don't think that fact is likely to weigh with Marlon if he thinks the flight too dangerous to make.'

'We've got to try.' Renzo's cry was anguished.

'You're right,' Nancy agreed. 'We've got to try.'

Chapter Thirty-Three

Nancy left Renzo waiting in the taxi while she rushed inside the villa and down the stairs to the office. She was praying Archie had not decided to forget work for a while and take a trip into town, but as she started along the ground floor passage, the clack of typewriter keys was clear. The office, as Leo had named it, was really not much more than a cupboard and next to the room Zamira had inhabited during her short stay with them. The door was open and the windows, too, allowing whatever breeze there was to keep the room a reasonable temperature.

She had to knock twice before Archie looked up from the document he was working on. He waved a hand at her to come in. 'This machine must have been around since the First World War,' he said. 'It's an absolute pig. German-made—must be their revenge.'

He turned in his chair to face her and she came straight to the point. 'Archie, I need your help.'

'So, what's new?' His expression was sardonic. 'Virginie not come up with the goods?'

'Seriously. I really need help. *We* need it. Anya Martin has gone missing.' Nancy stood stiffly beside him, her hands clasped and her face tense with anxiety.

Archie continued to stare up at her for some while before

he said, 'Anya Martin has gone missing and that's our responsibility—how?'

'Strictly, it's not. But she's in danger. Renzo is in the taxi outside and he's desperate to find her.'

'Ah, the dreaded Mr Hastings.'

'Archie, please! She's run away. Up Monte Muerte. The mountain is perilous, and she's been there all night.'

'Then shouldn't the hotel be sending out a search party?'

'I'm sure they will. Or, at least, Ambrose Martin will go. But he's only just learned his daughter is missing and it will be some time before he can get to her. Renzo wants to fly up to a landing strip that's near the top of the mountain. It's kept open for the scientists when they check the volcano.'

Archie had begun to look suspicious. 'And just how does that involve me?'

'You have flying lessons with Marlon. You could persuade him to take us there—it would help enormously. We'd be landing near where Anya must be hiding. Even if Ambrose Martin has already started out, it will take him hours to reach his daughter taking the path, and he may not get to her before nightfall. We could be there very quickly.'

Archie got up from his chair and looked hard at her. There was wonderment in his face. 'I thought I'd heard it all, but if that isn't the wildest idea.'

She edged towards him, her face close to his. 'It could be done,' she pleaded.

'I'm sure it could, but not with Marlon. I imagine it's helicopters that use the landing strip and, if you remember, Marlon flies a light aircraft. Added to which, why would he agree? Anya Martin is nothing to him and the flight would be very dangerous.'

'Solidarity?'

'What?'

'It's a small island. He'll know Anya and she's a young girl in danger.'

'So he has to put *himself* in danger. And me, too, by the look of it.' Archie took his seat again and began adjusting the document he'd been typing.

'*I'll* go,' she said desperately. 'And Renzo as well. You can stay, but if you could do the persuading first... You must know him quite well by now.'

For a while, Archie said nothing. Then he ripped the paper from the machine. 'I don't have your faith in Marlon, but if anyone goes up this benighted mountain, it won't be Hastings. He'll be like a demented ant. And not you either. You're in enough trouble already.'

'Will you do it then?' She clasped his arm and pulled him up from the chair. 'I've a taxi outside,' she repeated. 'Come with me. Please.'

He looked down into her eyes, then gave a small shrug. 'I'll try to persuade the fella, but I don't think you'll be lucky.'

The minute they closed the front door, Renzo appeared from behind the taxi, almost dancing with impatience. 'Hurry up. We've got to go. We can't waste a minute.'

'See what I mean?' Archie said. 'Demented.'

*

Renzo was to become even more unhinged when the cab rolled through the open gates of the airfield and up to the white wooden building. The place appeared eerily quiet, and when Archie went into the hut, closely followed by his companions, it was empty.

'Where is he?' the boy demanded.

Archie glared at him. 'I'm to be a clairvoyant now, am I? How do I know where he is? No paying customers at the moment and he's gone off for a snack perhaps? Which, by the way, is long overdue.' He looked at his watch. 'No wonder I'm starving. We should be eating lunch by the waterside, not searching for a missing pilot.'

'Eating lunch!' Renzo exploded. 'While Anya is facing snakes and poisonous plants and goodness knows what else!'

'It's a mountain. It's not going to be that dangerous.'

'It is,' Nancy confirmed. 'We have Virginie's word for it. And aren't they the keys to Marlon's plane?' She pointed to a single set hanging from a small hook over the cluttered desk.

'You could fly the plane,' Renzo said excitedly. 'You've had lessons.'

'Look lad, I've gone solo once, that's all, and it was a gentle trip around the bay, not halfway up a mountain.'

'But you could do it, couldn't you?' Nancy joined in, her voice urgent.

'You're suggesting that a novice flyer steals Marlon's plane and attempts to land it on a mountainside with no real certainty of bringing it back in one piece? Or bringing me back,' he said feelingly.

While they had been arguing, the hut had grown considerably darker and with one accord their eyes went to the window. The sky was low and threatening, and the rumbling Nancy had been conscious of since they'd arrived was growing steadily louder.

They stood and looked at each other, no-one willing to make the first move. The mountain's grumble had become continuous and Nancy could feel the floorboards vibrate beneath her feet.

'There's something wrong.' Renzo's eyes were wide and staring. 'There's something wrong with the mountain.'

Archie stiffened beside her. 'This is bloody mad,' he said, and snatched the keys from their hook.

The aircraft was parked in the same bay Nancy

remembered from her earlier visit, and it took only a few minutes' brisk walk to reach it. She kept hoping that Marlon would make a sudden appearance and take over, but he remained obstinately absent and it was Archie who opened the cockpit door.

'You stay here,' he said to her. 'He can come with me.' He gestured to Renzo, whose face was now alight with eagerness. 'He might be able to help, though God knows how.'

'I'm coming, too,' she said firmly. 'If we manage to find Anya, she'll want a woman around.'

'How do you make that out?'

Nancy was not going to stop to argue. 'I'm coming.'

'Renzo get in the back,' Archie ordered. 'And you,' he said, turning to Nancy, 'if you insist on coming, you'll have to act as co-pilot.'

'What do I have to do?' she asked nervously.

'Keep quiet and look. I need you to spot the place where we're supposed to land.'

'Virginie said it was near to the top, near the crater. There's a path that's been cut through the jungle and the airstrip is to one side of it.'

'So we follow this path. Easy. Except—where is the path? Any ideas?' Archie's face was glum.

'She said that if you follow the spire of the cathedral, it's directly in line with that.'

He brightened a little. 'Ah, now we're getting somewhere.'

Once they were safely strapped in, Archie began to run down the checklist Nancy remembered from her previous flight: rudder, brake pedals, throttle, flaps. Then he started the engine and taxied slowly to the parking area at the top of the short runway. She felt her stomach give a strong lurch. Pure fear, she knew. This time there was no comforting voice from the control tower, and no experienced pilot keeping her safe. It was up to Archie alone to guide the plane securely into the air, and—even more terrifyingly—to land somewhere on the mountain that loomed ahead of them.

'Final checks. When we're airborne, Nancy, see if you can spot the cathedral. Okay, the controls are working as they should, and the doors are secure. Off we go.'

Archie advanced the throttle and accelerated down the runway. 'Speed coming up,' he said. 'Temperature and pressure all well.' The wings lifted and he pulled back the control yoke. 'Rotate.'

And they were in the air, and Nancy was craning her head on the lookout for the church spire Virginie had mentioned. That was crucial or they could be searching entirely the wrong slope of the mountain. A few minutes into the flight, they had levelled off and she saw it. 'There. Archie, on your right.'

'You mean three o' clock,' he teased.

'Don't joke. This is serious.'

'You think I don't I know that?'

'And there's the path!' Renzo had craned his head forward, lodging himself tightly behind Nancy's shoulder. He was pointing down at a slight opening in the vegetation.

Archie brought the plane down several feet—he was flying smoothly, Nancy thought, perhaps this will end well after all—and then all three of them could see the track clearly. It was at least two feet wide, climbing the mountain in an almost vertically straight line. In response, Archie lifted the nose of the aircraft. It felt to Nancy as though they were literally flying up the mountainside, like some elongated insect crawling its way to the summit.

'This is where I need both your pairs of eyes, as well as mine,' Archie said.

The grey clouds that had felt oppressive on land appeared

even greyer and thicker at this altitude, and it was clear he'd have to bring the plane down to a dangerous level in order to make out the landing place. He flew low, wings skimming the treetops, while Nancy held her breath. Once, twice, the plane made a wide circle, and she pressed her forehead hard against the cockpit window, almost shattering the glass in her attempt to see.

Then at last, a shout from Renzo. 'There, there!' At the same time, Nancy's hand moved convulsively, as her shaking fingers pointed to the landing strip she'd spotted.

'Jesus!' Archie said beneath his breath.

Nancy heard and understood. The small open space was a rectangle of reasonable size for a helicopter, but for a fixed wing aircraft? That needed length and, at the end of the scoured strip, was jungle, unmistakeable jungle, a tangle of wild vegetation and thickly crowding trees. If Archie were unable to get the plane down swiftly enough, that was where they were headed. If so, there was no way the aircraft would survive in one piece. Nor any of them walk from it whole.

One more circuit and the plane was now so low it was actually clipping the trees. 'Brace yourselves,' Archie said. 'This is it.' She glanced across at him and saw the sweat dotting his forehead.

He raised the nose of the plane slightly and their descent slowed. But then it seemed as though the aircraft almost fell from the sky, plummeting down with enormous speed. Archie pushed the throttle in and the control yoke forward — she saw the sinews in his arm standing proud — and for tense seconds, they seemed to hang in the air, yards above the earth. Then, with a huge thud, they landed, only to bounce up and crash back onto land again, speeding towards the green fortress just yards ahead. Nancy half closed her eyes, hearing the brakes grind in a painful attempt to stop, and shaken almost out of her seat as the plane hurtled forward over the bumpy terrain. With a foot to spare, the aircraft came to a halt.

Archie slumped back in his seat, his face ashen. She took hold of his arm and clutched it tightly. 'You did it! You actually did it.'

He looked across at her and laid his hand on hers. There was a dazed expression in his eyes, and she could see he was finding it difficult to believe they were safe.

'We need to go,' Renzo said from behind. 'Anya is out there. We need to find her.'

Nancy pulled a face. 'Demented,' she said in agreement.

Chapter Thirty-Four

An unpleasant smell had crept into the cockpit as they'd flown closer to the mountain top but now, clambering down from the aircraft, Nancy grabbed a handkerchief from her pocket and thrust it against her nose. A foul reek of sulphur filled the air.

Archie glanced at the handkerchief. 'It could get worse. And dangerous, if the gas signals a likely eruption.'

'Thank you for that.'

'It's as well you know. And you, too,' he said, turning to Renzo. 'Landing the plane could be child's play with what we might face. Can you feel the ground changing? Almost moving?'

She could. The vibrations she'd experienced earlier at the airfield were much worse now. At this altitude, the air was cool, yet the earth felt hot and seemed to be swelling beneath her feet. Magna pushing to escape.

Renzo hardly registered the threat. He was looking around, a hopeless expression on his face. 'Where has the track gone? It was so clear from the air. This way, perhaps?' He began to walk back to the plane and then past it, and would have continued on if Archie had not called after him.

'Not that direction. I'm pretty sure it's through here.' He indicated the dense wall of vegetation in front of them.

Nancy's heart sank at the thought of finding a way through, but she knew Archie must be right. His soldier's sense of direction rarely let him down.

They started off in single file, Archie in the lead, attempting to push back the tangled undergrowth to make the semblance of a path for her to follow. Wild grass was everywhere, chin-high in some places, and the ground was thick with debris: dead leaves, shards of bark, and rotting orchid. The underbrush caught at her legs, scratching them mercilessly, while above, every tree was bound to its neighbour by giant creepers. Like a boat's rigging, she thought, strung from mast to mast, their leaves trailing across her face as she pushed a way through. She wondered what poisons must lurk there and, even worse, what this thick vegetation was concealing.

They had been stumbling forwards for several minutes when a rumble deeper than ever spread through the trees and the ground began to shake. Archie held up his hand for them to stop and she came to a halt immediately behind him. She stood silent, listening hard and feeling fear. Out of the corner of her eye, she caught the flick of a snake's tail as it slithered across their path, looking for cover.

'Can we move?' Renzo demanded.

He had been lost in his world of worry, but now pushed into Nancy and set them walking again along the treacherous green tunnel. There was an eerie silence. The birds no longer sang, and though Nancy heard the odd rustle in the depths of the undergrowth, there was nothing more. It was as though life on the mountain had been suspended. She had read that animals knew danger before human senses could detect it. It was how countrymen knew a storm was approaching — when animals and insects began to behave oddly. The knowledge didn't make her feel any better.

It seemed an age that they clambered across knotted roots,

pushed aside broken branches, and peered through thick curtains of tangled vines. But at last, battered and breathless, they tumbled out into open space once more. They had found the pathway.

Archie dragged a hand through his hair, frowning heavily. 'We have a choice here. Do we search up the path or down?'

Three pairs of eyes tracked up the mountainside and fixed their gaze on the summit, not that far above them now. In the harsh afternoon sun, the rim of the volcano appeared almost translucent: red, fiery, and terrifying.

'We have to go down,' Nancy said. 'If Anya saw that,' she pointed at the smouldering crater, 'she would surely have gone no further.'

Renzo nodded agreement and, wasting no time, he began to lope downhill on a path whose surface was far from easy to negotiate.

'Go carefully,' Archie called after him. 'There are fissures everywhere, and where there aren't, there's caked earth. Clumps of it. A broken ankle is all we need.'

But Renzo was deaf to the warning, striding ahead at a fierce pace, calling out Anya's name as loudly as he could. Nancy, though, kept her eyes glued to the ground. Cracks and crevices dotted the pathway; she had already tripped badly and only just saved herself from falling. Archie was slightly ahead of her and she saw how awkwardly he was holding his arm. Since Bass's attack, his injury had seemed much improved, but his fight to bring the plane down safely had had its effect and he was clearly in pain.

The heat of the sun, here on the bare mountainside, proved unbearable. The cool air had deserted them, and it was as though they were walking through an open furnace, their faces dotted with sweat and their limbs clammy. They walked on, Nancy feeling increasingly weary. How much further would they need to go? Was Anya, in fact, even on this forsaken mountain?

'Anya,' Renzo called once again, his voice much quieter now. The walk was taking its toll on all of them.

But then, some distance away, through a thick screen of vines that bordered one side of the path, a small figure appeared. 'Renzo?' The question came faintly, but it was Anya's voice and Renzo began running, taking no heed of the uneven terrain.

He had reached her now and, as Nancy watched, his arms went round the girl, hugging her as though he would squeeze the life from her. 'Thank God,' she could hear him saying, over and over.

'What are you doing here?' Anya sounded dazed. 'And Mrs Tremayne and Mr Jago?'

'We might ask you the same question,' Archie responded, as they reached the young couple. 'Why the mountain?'

Anya looked down at her feet. 'I had to escape. It was the only place I could think of.'

'A dangerous place to choose.'

'I realise that now, but at the time all I wanted was to run.'

Renzo took her hand with the utmost gentleness. 'You're safe now. You're with us. But it must have been scary. You were here all night.'

'It was frightening,' she admitted. 'Though I managed to find shelter. I hid in there.' She pointed towards the hanging vines that flanked the pathway, then walked over to pull the leaves apart and reveal a deep dip, seemingly hollowed from the mountain and forming a roofless cave.

'But the volcano,' Nancy said. 'It's been grumbling for hours. Surely you heard it?'

'Of course I did. And it seems to be getting worse. I was scared, but I had to stay. I didn't know where else to go. I couldn't go back to the hotel and I didn't want to be found.'

Nancy put a hand on the girl's arm and spoke quietly. 'Can you tell us why not, Anya? Tell us what happened?' The conversation between Ambrose and his mother had made events fairly clear, but Nancy wanted to know for sure. And Renzo deserved to hear the truth.

Anya lowered her glance, unable to meet their eyes. 'My father—' she began, but couldn't continue.

'Your grandmother told you something that distressed you badly,' Nancy suggested. Anya stared at her. 'I was at the hotel this morning,' Nancy went on. 'I couldn't help overhearing an argument Mr Martin was having with his mother.'

'Grandma Eugénie said I had to know. But ever since, I've wanted to kill myself.' Anya's voice shook with passion.

'What did you have to know?' Renzo had released his hold and was looking worried again. There was a pale sheen on his face.

'I can't say.'

Nancy was conflicted. The girl was distraught, but if she spoke now and said aloud what was eating her within, it might in the end be better for her.

'It was about your mother, wasn't it?' she asked gently. 'Your mother and your aunt.'

Anya gave a low sob. 'It's too dreadful to say… my mother… my mother went away—because of how my father behaved with Aunt Charlotte,' she finished in a burst.

'Behaved?' Renzo asked. 'Like—'

'Yes,' Anya said, cutting him off.

'With his sister?' Renzo was aghast. He was finding it difficult to absorb something so appalling.

Nancy stroked the girl's arm and felt it trembling. 'You've been brave to tell us, Anya. But now you must put it as far out of your mind as possible. What your father did, what your aunt did, has nothing to do with you. It robbed you of your mother, and that's dreadfully sad. But you can't let it ruin your life. It's ruined your father's, I think, but you must be strong and walk away.'

'But how can I ever face him again, knowing what I do? And face my grandparents? They *knew*. They knew all the time and kept silent.'

'You can and you will.' Nancy was firm. 'You're young and healthy, and you have your whole future in front of you.'

Renzo reached out for the girl's hand, gripping it tightly. 'Nancy is right,' he said. 'You can get over this. It's not your mess. You must come back to town with us. If you want, you can stay with me.'

'One thing's for sure, you can't stay here.' Archie, as always, was pragmatic. 'This mountain feels like it's going to blow at any moment. The sooner we get down, the better. C'mon, let's go.'

'But what about Marlon's plane?' Nancy reminded him.

'You flew here?' Anya was open-mouthed.

'We had to,' Renzo told her. 'You were in danger and it was the quickest way to reach you.' He gave her a little hug. 'I've been terrified, thinking what might have happened, particularly in the night.'

'It was creepy,' she admitted. 'There were all kinds of noises. I had to put my hands over my ears.'

'And you must be starving. What did you eat?' he asked.

'I didn't. I haven't eaten since yesterday breakfast.'

Renzo produced a dented sandwich from his pocket. 'Here, this will help. I was going to have it for lunch,' he said in explanation. 'It's ham with a mustard dressing—my favourite.'

Anya gave a small smile. 'You are very sweet, Renzo, but

keep it for yourself. I can eat very soon. If we're flying, we should be off the mountain in minutes.'

'We are not flying,' Archie said severely. 'And if either of you,' he fixed Nancy and Renzo with a militant glare, 'think I'm going to attempt a take-off from that airstrip, you're crazier than I'd ever believe. Marlon will have to fly up by helicopter. Hopefully his plane will still be in one piece for him to collect. *He'll* have the skill to get it off the ground. I don't.'

'Then we'll walk down the mountain,' Renzo said. 'We'll walk all the way to *Le Citronnier*. You'll like it there, Anya.'

Archie took the lead. The rest of their small party had fallen in behind him, when what sounded like a loud belch came from above. Frightened, they looked up. The crater was still glowing but now a head of steam was pouring forth.

'We're going to have to speed.' Archie's stride turned into something approaching a gallop.

But the small party had gone only a short way when a voice sounded from below and, as they breasted a raised section of the pathway, a man came into view. It was Ambrose Martin. He'd made far better time than Nancy could have imagined.

Anya stopped dead. 'I can't meet him.'

'It's okay.' Renzo was soothing. 'We'll tell him you're fine and you're coming with us. He can turn around and go home.'

But it was clear that Ambrose Martin had no intention of going home. He was climbing the mountain path towards them as though he had wings on his back, his eyes fixed on the ground, but all the time calling, calling. When he finally looked up and saw the small group, he wiped his forehead with the back of his hand and called out a final, 'Anya!' Then, 'Thank God, you're safe.'

Anya made no reply, but he came on towards them, his

pace only increasing and the sweat streaming down his shirt front.

When he was a few feet away, he spoke again, panting with each breath. 'I'm sorry, my darling. So terribly sorry, for this dreadful hurt. I never wanted you to know. I've kept the secret for so long, even though it's torn me in two.'

When his daughter made no response, he burst out bitterly, 'My mother is a termagant. She is filled with evil or she would never have said to you what she did.'

'Grandma Eugénie told me the truth, which you never have. You let me believe my mother left because we weren't enough for her. Because *I* wasn't enough.' Anya's voice shook.

'No! I never said that.'

Anya let go of Renzo's hand and faced her father directly, her eyes sparking with anger. 'No, you never said it, but it's what you made me feel—that my mother didn't love me—when all the time she left Malfuego because she was sickened by what she'd found out about you. As I am,' she finished.

Ambrose pushed back the damp hair from his brow. His face was stricken. 'I wronged your mother, I know. Wronged Charlotte, too. But my sister and I were close. She was the only one who understood. She knew what it was like to be brought up in that house, to be made a prisoner in our own home. Whereas Jacinta… Your mother and I…'

He hesitated, seeming unsure how to continue. 'Your mother and I were pushed into a marriage neither of us wanted. It was our families who insisted on it, and we obeyed. I obeyed, just as I always had. Jacinta was from the right background, the right class, the right race, but she didn't love me and I didn't love her. How could I when I loved another woman so dearly?'

'You loved someone else? Why didn't you marry *her*?'

Anya's imperious young voice sliced through the stifling air. It was becoming hotter by the minute, and Nancy was finding it difficult to breathe normally.

'I couldn't.' Ambrose Martin hung his head. 'It was forbidden.'

The word 'forbidden' rang loud and clear in Nancy's head. Suddenly she understood. Of course, that was it, but then—

'Because the woman you loved was black?' she asked.

He nodded, and his face was lined with pain. 'She was beautiful, so full of love, so full of life. I wanted to be with her always. Wanted us to go out into the world together. I hated my parents' spiteful ignorance. Hated that my father had chained me to the mill and to a certain kind of life. But I had to choose. Stay in that life or abandon my parents, and if I'd dared to marry out, maybe even kill them. I couldn't do it. But I've never loved another woman since.'

'It was Mary, wasn't it?' Nancy asked. 'Mary Sekela.'

Ambrose stared at her. 'How did you know?'

'There were rumours about a white supervisor who was Mary's lover. But it wasn't a supervisor, was it? It was the boss. And she had a child.'

Anya gave an enormous gasp as though every breath had been knocked out of her. 'Gabriel? Gabriel was your son?'

Chapter Thirty-Five

Ambrose's whole body seemed to writhe at the name, sinking into itself as though he would vanish from the world. For minutes, there was silence. Then Ambrose spoke, his voice a rough croak. 'He was born the week before I married Jacinta. He was your brother, Anya. I couldn't let you get fond of him.'

'I wasn't fond of him,' his daughter almost spat. 'He was the man I loved. But you—what did you do to him?'

Ambrose made a move towards his daughter, but she backed away. 'I tried to protect you,' he protested. 'That's all I've ever wanted to do. I tried so hard, but nothing worked.'

'You were the one!' Renzo's voice was hoarse. The furrows on his brow had gradually deepened as he'd attempted to follow the conversation. But this was something he'd understood immediately. '*You* caused those accidents.' His face had lost its pallor and turned bright red. 'You slashed the tyres on Gabriel's motorbike. It was you who arranged for some lowlife to mug him. And those thugs at the demonstration, it was you who paid them.'

Ambrose shook his head. 'Not me, not me,' he said frantically. 'I know nothing of those men.'

'But the fire?' Nancy asked quietly.

It was as though she had detonated an explosive: her

companions were stilled instantly, their bodies paralysed, their faces rigid as though carved from stone.

Ambrose Martin was the first to recover. 'It wasn't meant to happen,' he pleaded. 'I'd tried to get the boy to leave the island, but no matter what I did, he stayed. I was desperate, and when I came across the paraffin—I saw it in a neighbour's shed when I was checking out the house—it gave me the idea. I thought I'd set fire to the place, make it uninhabitable, and if Gabriel didn't have a home, he'd finally leave. I saw him go out that evening. I was sure the house was empty. But he must have gone back in there… I don't know why, but he must have done, and… somehow I didn't see him.'

Ambrose clutched at his head with both hands and rocked himself backwards and forwards. The small group stood looking at him, aghast at what they'd heard. Eventually, he seemed to become aware of their silence and let his hands fall. He fixed his daughter with a stare that was agonised. 'You've got to believe me, Anya. I didn't mean for it to happen.'

'You killed him! You killed him!'

Released from her paralysis, Anya jumped forward and threw herself at her father, her fists clenched and beating at his chest, his arms, then reaching for his face. Ambrose tried unsuccessfully to defend himself against the blows but, after a stunned moment, Renzo leapt after the girl and pulled her back.

'I didn't mean to,' Ambrose kept repeating. 'I would never have planned such a terrible thing. I've lived in hell ever since it happened.'

When he was met with silence once more, he burst out, 'I did everything I could for him. For Mary. Gave her the house, paid her bills, sent Gabriel to university. I wanted him to take a job in America, but then he came back when Mary was ill, and never went away. I was desperate when I knew he'd met

Anya, so I tried to persuade him to go.'

'By burning him alive,' Archie said laconically. 'That's certainly some persuasion.'

'I didn't know,' was all the broken man could say.

Was all he had time to say before the rumbling in the background became a sudden roar. The steam that had been pouring from the crater hissed so loudly now that it filled their ears, and stones began to tumble vertically down the mountainside. The earth beneath their feet cracked, and a huge gap—a virtual ravine—opened up at Renzo's feet. Frantically, he pulled Anya back to safety. But Ambrose was now on the other side of the gulf and holding out his arms to his daughter in despair.

More stones were tumbling, some large enough to wound badly, then a huge crashing noise from above and it was boulders, not stones hurtling towards them.

'Quick, into my cave,' Anya said.

'She's right,' Archie yelled. 'It's our only chance.'

In an instant, they'd pushed their way through the curtain of vines and flung themselves bodily into the hollow. Nancy felt her limbs jar as she hit the ground. Then Archie was on top of her, his arms flung wide, protecting her as best he could. Renzo and Anya had landed to one side of her, curled into a single ball and burrowing into the green surface of their refuge.

The chaos wrought by crashing boulders grew more and more deafening, until it seemed their shelter must be entombed beneath the cascade thundering from above. Only very gradually—and it seemed a lifetime to Nancy—did the noise abate. But finally, there was silence. For seconds, she lay prone, unable to move or speak. Then, shaking and tearful, she whispered to Archie, 'Is it over?'

He rolled to one side and lay beside her. 'I think so.'

Propping himself up on his elbow, he turned to face her. His finger traced the trickle of tears on her cheek. 'It seems okay. For now.'

They had come close to death, Nancy realised, and she put her hand on his and pulled him close. She felt his hard, warm body against her, his face touching hers. Instinctively, their lips met. And she was lost. The kiss of this cynical man, often rough, sometimes hurtful, who could rouse her equally to anger and laughter, was so tender, so moving, that she felt her breath catch. And then the well of desire broke free and she was kissing him back in the way she had dreamt of. It felt as sweet as she'd known it would. At some deep level, she'd recognised her fate from the very first moment she had met Archie—that he was home for her.

How long they would have clung together, she had no idea. But then she felt Archie reluctantly break away, and became aware that Anya and Renzo, now on their feet, were staring in amazement at their entwined bodies.

In a rush, Archie scrambled up. 'We need to get off this mountain before the volcano stages an encore.' He was trying to sound in control, she thought, trying to pretend that nothing out of the ordinary had happened.

The two young people exchanged a meaningful look but said nothing, and followed Archie through the creepers and back onto the pathway. It was now a sad version of itself, Nancy saw, as she followed them out, the enormous crevice gaping wide, and what was left of the path split and cracked open in a dozen places. It was evident their journey back to Malfuego town had become even more difficult.

Nancy looked across the yawning gap, her eyes searching. Where was Ambrose Martin? What shelter had he found to protect himself from the onslaught? It appeared he hadn't. He was nowhere to be seen.

'Papa?' Anya said in a voice that quavered slightly. 'Are you there?'

There was no answer, only a deep rumble from within Monte Muerte. It had earned its name today, Nancy thought, and probably many times in the past. Truly the mountain of death.

Archie looked up at the summit. 'The hissing has stopped, but there's still plenty of grumbling. It could come to nothing—or there could be a full-scale eruption. We'll need to make haste.'

'But Papa?'

'He may have gone ahead and joined the path further down,' Renzo suggested gently.

Archie looked at him and gave a hardly perceptible shake of his head.

*

The journey to the foot of the mountain proved tense. Watchfulness was key, for fear of a stumble or worse and, though the roar within the mountain had ceased, a loud rumbling accompanied their entire descent. There was tension, too, in the consciousness that Ambrose Martin was missing. Anya may have vowed never to set eyes on her father again, but the ties of childhood, the love she had for him, remained strong. And her set face, as they descended yard by yard without a sign of the man, was difficult to see.

As they approached the foot of Monte Muerte, the path they had been following became smoother underfoot, but overhead more thickly tangled. The last few yards were a fight to escape interlocking branches and the network of creepers that looped themselves through every available space. At last, they broke free and out into unencumbered space. But not empty space, as Nancy had expected. A small knot of people had gathered to greet them—Leo and Virginie among them.

She saw Leo before he saw her. Her husband looked pale and haggard, but the moment he caught sight of his wife alive and seemingly unhurt, he was transformed, the deep furrows banished, and a smile wider than Nancy had ever known.

He rushed towards her, charging past Renzo and Archie, to grab her around the waist. 'Nancy! Thank God! I've been beside myself. When I saw those rocks tumbling down the mountainside...'

He wrapped her more firmly in his arms, crushing her to his chest and smothering her attempt to speak. Nancy felt overwhelmed. The last time she had seen her husband, he had been furious and condemnatory. Now, in the relief of finding her again, he had lost whatever anger he'd felt.

'How did you know where we were?' she managed to say, emerging at last from a suffocating hug.

'It was Virginie. She telephoned to say that Anya was missing, that the girl had gone to the mountain and you'd gone to find her. In a plane. To be honest, I thought she must have been drinking, but when she asked me to take her to the airfield, I knew she was serious. I was at home when she phoned. I'd just got back from Jackson's, but Roland was still outside and I asked him to drive us. When we got to the airfield, I found this chap—Marlon, I think he said his name was—pacing up and down in the most amazing tantrum because someone had stolen his aircraft.'

'We should have left him a note,' Nancy murmured. 'But we were so intent on getting to Anya that everything else went out of our minds.'

'You really did use his plane?' Leo sounded incredulous. 'But how?'

'Archie flew it.'

'My God! But he's only just learning.'

'Well, he's learnt well. He was very good.'

'He would have to be. He crashed it?' he asked falteringly.

'No. It's still in one piece. Near to the summit. But it was a difficult landing and he didn't feel skilled enough to get it off the mountain.'

'Thank heaven for very small mercies.' Leo pulled her back into his arms, this time kissing her passionately on the mouth.

When she freed herself from his embrace, she became aware of Archie close by. He'd seen the kiss and turned away.

'Archie,' Leo called after his assistant. When Archie stopped, he went over to him, pumping his hand and giving him several thumps on the back. 'Thank you for looking after my wife, old chap,' he said.

'Always a pleasure,' Archie responded. But she saw the slight curl of his mouth.

'I'm afraid you're not yet finished for the day.' Leo drew his mouth down. 'The police want to see you about Rossiter's death. I've given them a statement—they came to Jackson's to talk to us both—but I could only tell them the bare facts. You were in the thick of it and they're keen to have your story. We can give you a ride to the police station.' Leo gestured to the black saloon and Roland in the driving seat.

'That's fine, boss,' Archie said. 'I can make my own way there.'

Leo looked surprised. 'If you'd rather. But don't be late back. We're off tomorrow.'

It was Nancy's turn to be surprised, but before she could ask for an explanation, Leo had hailed Virginie, who was busily clucking over Anya, and offered them a lift back to the Serafina.

Renzo answered for them both. 'It's okay,' he said. 'We'll

get a taxi and drop Miss Lascelles on the way. I'm taking Anya home with me.'

Leo was about to begin a question when Nancy gave his hand a sharp pinch. 'Anya isn't returning to the hotel just yet,' she said quietly. 'I'll explain when we get back to the villa.'

Chapter Thirty-Six

An hour later, after a shower and change of clothes, Nancy did just that. They were sitting on the veranda with cups of tea and slices of the fruit cake Isabella's cook had baked for them. Once launched on her tale, Nancy told him everything.

'Incest!' Leo said in a horrified voice. 'With his sister?' For a while he seemed too stunned to ask more, and they sat in silence, a soft breeze drifting across from the ocean and ruffling the skirts of Nancy's sundress.

'And this liaison with Mary Sekela—does that make Gabriel his son?'

She nodded and crumbled a piece of fruit cake between her fingers. 'That was the problem. The boy met Anya and fell in love with her. I guess Ambrose Martin saw history repeating itself and tried to frighten Gabriel away before the relationship became too serious. Slashing motorcycle tyres, arranging a false mugging.'

'It sounds as though he was too late. His daughter was already involved.'

'I don't think anything would have worked to separate them. But Ambrose was desperate.'

'And you say the man is a killer? Of his own son?' Leo was having enormous difficulty in absorbing the fact. 'I can't believe it.'

'He was an accidental killer, but it's still murder.'

'Did you know that he was the one to set the fire?'

'Not until today. To be honest, I suspected at first that Jackson Garcia was behind the threats to Gabriel. I think he was behind one at least—the attack we saw the day we arrived. And I think he had the printing press smashed, too. But it was Gabriel's politics he wanted to destroy, not the young man himself. Then I wondered if it was Luke Rossiter or Gibbon Bass. They certainly had a motive, with Gabriel waging war on the drugs trade here. I met him, you know— Luke—at the scene of the fire. I thought he might have come back to gloat, but in fact he was searching for anything that could be used against him. Anything that might have survived.'

'He sounds like a dangerous character to me.'

'He threatened me,' she admitted. 'But I got away. And the next thing I knew he was being mowed down at the yacht club.'

'Which should have told you to stop.' Leo's tone was sharp. 'But you didn't, did you?'

'Stopped poking my nose in? No, I didn't,' she confessed. 'Rossiter was killed because of a disagreement over drugs, I was sure. And though he had other reasons to want Gabriel gone—he wanted Anya for himself—it made me wonder if there was someone else involved in the young man's death. When I was hit on the head in the church—'

'That was why you were attacked? That was Ambrose Martin?' Her husband sat forward in his chair, but Nancy took a slow sip of tea before she answered.

'Isabella had told him we were making a trip to the church that day and he must have followed us. When Ambrose saw me reading the ledger, he panicked. I don't think he meant to hurt me as badly as he did. I would just have been stunned if

I hadn't hit a stone ridge on the way down. After that, I knew I was right about another person being involved. Bass was in prison and Rossiter dead, so neither of them could have been in the church. It was someone who didn't want the name of Gabriel's father known. I found the entry for his birth. His mother, Mary Sekela, was there and his father's name had been written in, but then scrubbed out. And when Archie went back to check the ledger, the page had disappeared.'

'What's Archie's role in all this?' her husband asked suspiciously.

'I asked him to look, that's all.' Leo need not know how far his assistant had been involved, either here or in Venice.

A flight of swallows passed overhead, and they sat and watched as the arrow-shaped formation disappeared into the distance.

'But why write in a name and then scrub it out?' Leo asked.

'I've no idea. All I can think is that Mary registered her son's birth, and subsequently Ambrose discovered she'd named him as the father and somehow managed to eradicate the entry. Almost eradicate. A handwriting expert could still have worked the name out, I think.'

'I'm wondering what we do now.' Leo leant back in his chair, his eyes fixed on the sea below. 'Should we go to the police, do you think, and tell them what we know? Or leave them to work out what happened on the mountain today?'

'Virginie will have to tell the older Martins what she knows about Anya's rescue. I think we can assume they'll put pressure on the police to accept their version of events: that their son went to look for his daughter on Monte Muerte and the mountain killed him. They'll say that's all they know and then do their damndest to keep anything else quiet. Perhaps it's for the best. It would only hurt Anya if the truth were widely known. Gabriel is dead, and now Ambrose. There are probably searchers out there now looking for his body.'

'You're certain he is dead?'

'You saw the rocks that fell. Some of the boulders were huge, and one must have hit him.'

Leo jumped up and came over to her chair, kneeling down beside her. 'I am the most fortunate man in the entire world. You escaped. You came back to me, my darling.'

She stroked his bent head, her eyes filling with tears. Lately, she seemed to have done a lot of crying. 'I'm sorry about the baby, Leo,' she said softly. 'I know how much it must hurt.'

'It's hurt us both, sweetheart. But we must put it behind us and look to the future. That's what's most important and it nearly didn't happen.'

'No, it didn't, but we were incredibly lucky. There was a kind of cave on the mountainside and it sheltered us.'

Nancy had to force herself to push the image from her mind. She hadn't meant to think of it. The grassy hollow, Archie's embrace, his kisses, must be blotted from memory for ever. 'We must organise a helicopter so that Marlon can retrieve his plane,' she said lightly.

Leo rocked back on his heels. 'We'll have to leave that to Jackson to sort out. Thank the Lord we're going home tomorrow. I shall be glad to see the back of Malfuego, beautiful though it is.'

'We're leaving? I thought that's what you said earlier, but I could have got it wrong.'

Leo got up and stretched his legs. 'You didn't. Cy Devaux has already gone. He had an enormous bust-up with Jackson this morning and walked out. They've never really hit it off, and I think Cy wanted to get out of the project from the very first day. So Jackson is without his experts. I'm the only one left.'

'Joshi, though?'

Leo shook his head. 'He's cancelled again. His wife has taken a turn for the worst. There's also the bad publicity. News of Gibbon Bass's arrest and the racket he was running has spread to America, and it's visitors from that country in particular that Jackson wants to attract. A volcano spilling steam and rocks isn't much of a tourist attraction either.'

'Will he abandon the project now, do you think?'

Leo gathered up cups and plates onto a tray. 'He might have to rethink. His ideas were always a little too grandiose. But knowing Jackson's determination, I'm sure he'll carry on in some form or another. It's not going to happen any time soon, though, and to be honest if he contacts me in the future, I might just be very busy.'

'When do we leave exactly?'

'Early tomorrow morning. I've booked boat tickets to the mainland. Just as well, after your flying experience today, although I'm not sure how Archie will fare on the water. The vessel isn't that big. And I contacted Cunard to check on our berths to Southampton. It's why I came back to the villa—to find Archie to do the bookings—but he'd disappeared, and I got on with them myself. Then Virginie Lascelles rang, and you know the rest. I only hope I've thought of everything.'

'What about saying goodbye to the Garcias? Isabella has been very kind.'

'I said goodbye for you. I hope that's okay. We'll be off too early to do it properly.'

Nancy got slowly up from her chair. The terror of the afternoon had been suppressed this last hour or so, but it was still with her. She could feel it in a pulse that beat a little faster, in limbs that felt as though they weren't quite hers.

They were leaving and she felt an enormous sense of relief. The island was truly beautiful, but it had been a testing few weeks.

'I better find my suitcase,' she said. 'I think Zamira stored it at the top of the wardrobe.'

'Can I help? You must be utterly exhausted.'

'It's been a difficult day,' she said with understatement, 'but packing shouldn't take me long.'

'I'll sort out the drinks for later while you're away. And how about supper?'

'Nothing much for me. Bread and some cheese would be fine, if that's okay with you.'

She left Leo clinking bottles and went up to their bedroom. The long windows were open and the breeze had picked up a little. She strolled out on to the balcony, watching the curling foam and the golden disc of sun as it slipped slowly to the horizon. She would miss this view, but not the sadness she'd too often felt here.

She scooped her clothes out of the wardrobe and emptied the four drawers of the wicker chest, piling the garments on one side of the bed. Methodically, she's begun to fold her dresses when Leo made a surprise appearance. He'd brought up the wrap she'd left on the sofa, but after she'd once more turned down his help, he left her to fill the suitcase. She was folding the last item when she sensed he was back, but turning, she saw it was Archie in the doorway.

'You're back soon,' she said quickly. Her voice sounded unnatural to her and her stomach was jumping uncomfortably. Would they speak of those kisses?

'The police were efficient, and I heard Leo say we're leaving tomorrow. I need to pack, too.'

His eyes looked directly into hers. 'Archie—' she began, but he held up his hand to silence her.

'But—'

He walked towards her until he was inches away, then cupped her cheek with one hand and bent his mouth to hers in a kiss filled with gentleness. Then he turned, and she heard him walk along the corridor to his own room.

The kiss had been tender but final. It had said I want this, you do, too, but it can't happen. And she knew he was right.

Chapter Thirty-Seven

Roland and his gleaming saloon were at the front door early the next morning. It took the chauffeur very little time to load their luggage in the boot, and even less to find a shady spot in which to wait for his passengers while they made a last check through the villa. As Nancy scoured the sitting room for anything she'd forgotten, voices from the basement signalled that Leo and his assistant were engaged on the same task.

When she emerged from the house a few minutes later, she was surprised to see Renzo and Anya walking up the drive towards her. After yesterday's dreadful events, she'd fully expected they would stay close to home.

'We heard you were going today,' Renzo said. 'We wanted to come and say thank you.'

Anya's face was paler than ever, Nancy noticed, but when she spoke her voice was strong. 'Thank you, Mrs Tremayne, for rescuing me.'

'It was a small thing, Anya. And I'm just happy that we found you safe.'

'Not so small. I'd survived the night, but if you hadn't come looking for me, I might have been swept away by those rocks like, like…'

She faltered to a stop and Nancy reached for her hand.

'I can't imagine how hard this must be for you, but you're a brave girl and I know you'll come through.'

'Of course she will,' Renzo said stoutly. 'She's got me.'

'And her grandparents,' Nancy reminded him. 'When things have settled a little.'

'No!' Anya was suddenly invigorated. 'I'm never going back to the Serafina. I don't want to see the hotel ever again. Nor my grandparents. Papa did bad things, terrible things, but I truly believe he was pushed into wickedness. His parents forced him to be something he wasn't, and in the end he couldn't stand the pressure. He burst apart and innocent people suffered.'

There was an awkward silence until Renzo said, 'We're going to the States in a week or so. Dad has promised us the fares and he knows someone we can stay with for a while. We'll get jobs there. Make a new life.'

'Maybe even find my mother,' Anya said wistfully.

'Is your father happy that you're going, Renzo?' Nancy wondered how Scott would feel to be abandoned by a son he'd more or less nursed back to health.

'He's okay about it. Really, he's better off without me. And I reckon I'm better away from him. He's no innocent, you know. I've heard stuff about what he got up to in Chicago and it looks like he's not changed much, cosying up to some dodgy guys, not asking questions.'

'He was definitely in business with Gibbon Bass?'

'He admitted it—finally. At first, he said he'd just loaned the guy money for the boat, but then he confessed he'd pocketed commission from whatever Bass was selling.' Renzo looked moodily into the distance. 'Not all of the deals he's done have been flaky, mind, but a lot have been way out of line.'

Nancy found it quietly amusing to hear the boy, who had

been a prolific forger in Venice, sound so disapproving of his father's criminal activities.

'He's promised me that from now on he'll forget the bad stuff and go straight,' Renzo went on. 'He's scared, so maybe he will. Rossiter tried to blackmail him—I was right about that burglary. And then Bass got involved and... well, you know the rest.'

'His promise of a new leaf hasn't persuaded you to stay on?' Nancy asked.

Renzo shook his head. 'There's nothing to stay for. Dad's done what he can for me, but he doesn't truly care. I guess I came into his life too late. In any case, I feel kinda cramped here.'

'And Anya?'

'Anya can't live here either,' he answered for her. 'Not with the Martins. Her life with them is over.'

'We must go, Nancy.' Leo had joined them, with Archie just behind, and nodded a greeting to the two young people.

Anya reached forward and kissed Nancy on the cheek. 'We mustn't make you late for your sailing. But thank you again.'

'Bye, Nancy,' Renzo said, giving her a quick hug. 'I hope we meet again, though I'm guessing you don't. You've rescued me twice—three times would be too much for anyone!'

She was in need of rescue herself, Nancy thought. From this tumult of feelings. With a great effort, she forced her mind back to the moment. 'If ever you come to London, you must stay with us,' she managed to say.

'Yeah, London would be great. A couple of weeks and you'll be back there. Think of that.' The boy made a thumbs-up sign.

'And back to what she loves doing—picture restoring,' Leo quipped. Was that a peace offering, a hint that her husband no longer disapproved of her new career?

'Restoration sounds good,' Renzo said. 'I might think of taking it up myself. You know, instead of the forging,' he added cheekily.

For a moment Leo fixed him with a frown, but then smiled. He's decided the boy is joking, Nancy thought.

'Are we going, by any chance?' Archie's voice broke through their conversation. He was leaning against the car bonnet, arms folded. 'We'll be lucky to catch the boat at this rate.'

'And we must catch it!' Leo exclaimed. 'Leave the excitement of Malfuego behind and get back to the old schedule. Same city, same office, same life, eh, Archie?'

Archie's face was expressionless, giving nothing away, but deep within Nancy knew there was no way back to the old life. Those kisses had changed it for both of them and for ever.

If you've enjoyed this novel, do please leave a review—a few lines is all it takes. It's helpful to readers and makes authors very happy! I'll be sure to read every review!
https://bookgoodies.com/a/B08K4MDGRW

And make sure you follow Nancy when she visits Leo's family home in Cornwall and finds even more trouble waiting for her.

Other Books by Merryn Allingham

Printed in Great Britain
by Amazon